Praise for Collision:

'When I visited CERN a couple years ago I couldn't actually believe it was real. Even standing in it, right next to the giant colossal Collider machine thing, it seemed like something straight out of a Marvel comic. I left there wanting to go home and make giant, complicated, beautiful, cosmic machines. It's like when you go to the Louvre in Paris, you just wanna go home and paint. That's what these writers have done, inspired by one great creation, they've gone home and created more!'
– *Wayne Coyne, The Flaming Lips*

'A rare journey into the inner world of the physicist's imagination; mind-blowing fiction inspired by research being done at CERN right now.'
– *Kenneth Lonergan*

'As scientist Carole Weydert writes, "every grey concrete wall holds the promise of undiscovered truths just below the surface". *Collision* lets laypeople glimpse, and share, some of them.' – *Boyd Tonkin in the New Scientist*

*In loving memory of our partner, dear friend
and colleague Chris Thomas*

COLLISION

Stories from the Science of CERN

EDITED BY ROB APPLEBY
& CONNIE POTTER

First published in Great Britain in 2023 by Comma Press.
www.commapress.co.uk

A CIP catalogue record of this book is available from the British Library.

ISBN: 1912697688
ISBN-13: 978-1-91269-768-7

This collaboration has been supported by the Science and Technology Facilities Council (STFC) and UKRI through the UK science project, HL-LHC-UK.

The publisher gratefully acknowledges the assistance of the STFC and Arts Council England.

Contents

CONTENTS

Introduction

THE SCIENCE AND ENGINEERING of CERN have captured the imagination of generations of people from all over the globe. The range of research being performed at the European laboratory is now vast, covering everything from antimatter and the Standard Model, to particle acceleration and even new ways of doing computing. The fundamental questions being asked at this laboratory, just a few miles northwest of Geneva, inspire (and indeed demand) new levels of ingenuity from countless other communities of scientists, engineers, data analysts and technicians, many of whom are based off-site, at universities and research facilities around the world. But if CERN is such a nexus of cooperation, such a global epicentre of intellectual collaboration, why should that collaboration stop with the sciences? Why shouldn't CERN's discoveries also disperse seeds of ideas, provoke thought and inspire new work in other, non-scientific disciplines?

Why shouldn't it inspire new fiction, for example?

CERN has collaboration written through it, like the word 'Blackpool' is found all the way through Blackpool rock. Founded in the aftermath of the Second World War with a mission to unite and strengthen Europe's physics research, and to bring it back in line with US research (which had recently raced ahead), it quickly became the centrepiece of European physics, performing a broad range of experiments, and hosting a number of accelerators that, over the decades, have grown progressively larger and more powerful, culminating in the Large Hadron Collider (housing four separate experiments along its circumference) which, in 2012, famously discovered the much sought-after, mass-giving Higgs boson. Twenty-three different countries now contribute to the project, as fully-fledged 'Member States', contributing researchers, students and resources, with an additional 60 plus other countries collaborating as non-member partners.

So where are the fiction writers?

Science and fiction, of course, have a long and rich history of cohabiting the same imaginative space; science has inspired fictional stories for centuries, and frequently fiction has inspired scientific and technological breakthroughs in return. Everything from the submarine to the helicopter, the Taser to the mobile phone, the rocket to the ebook owe inspiration, according to their own inventors, to ideas first elaborated in science fiction stories.[1] Knowing this, tech corporations have even begun actively commissioning fiction writers to predict how future societies might use advanced technologies that they themselves will soon create. In 2010, Brian David Johnson, a futurist at the Intel corporation, coined the phrase 'science fiction prototyping' to describe this process, and used short stories to forecast future market needs for Intel's next generation of integrated circuits (each new generation of chip takes 7–10 years to produce).

But the idea of creative writers and scientists/engineers *working together* still strikes many as anathema. The two fields have some common ground, for sure. Science and fiction both tell stories; a scientific explanation is ultimately a narrative, a series of causally linked events that tell us how a result, an effect, or a symptom came about. Cosmology and particle physics strive to tell perhaps the most fundamental of all stories – the 'creation myth' or 'origin story' of the whole universe. And there are similarities to how they both tell their stories: scientific experiments and fictional stories both tell us how systems go from one stable state, with the addition of some kind of destabilising 'encouragement' (in story terms this would be called an 'inciting incident'), through a series of elevated and unstable states, to another, ultimately stable state. But there are perhaps more dissimilarities than there are similarities. The ultimate arbiter of whether a fictional story rings true or not is us, the readers (including the reading author); while the only arbiter of whether an experimental conclusion is true or not is the world: i.e. repeated iterations of the same experiment *in* the world. One is internal, the other external.

There are also cultural differences between the practices of scientists and fiction writers. Fiction writers generally work in solitude; and although scientists are sometimes depicted (in fiction and fictionalised versions of history) as working in isolation, as 'mavericks' holed up their laboratories, 'fighting the scientific establishment', in reality, they work in continual cooperation with others. Contemporary research, especially the kind of research being done at CERN, is profoundly, almost mind-bogglingly collaborative. The first paper to come out of the LHC's discovery in 2012, for instance, boasted a total of 5,154 named co-authors: 24 of its 33 pages were needed just to list their names and institutions.[2]

So there is a conflict of working practices here, between the solitary author and the collaborative scientist. And any attempt to bridge this gap – for instance, by formally inviting a *delegation* of writers to collaborate with a corresponding delegation of scientists at CERN – would inevitably raise eyebrows, particularly on the literary side of the divide. The mere thought of something so calculated and collective challenges (perhaps even offends) our deeply held, romantic ideas of creative inspiration.

But invite a delegation we did.

As it happens, this kind of interdisciplinary bridge-building has been tried before by Comma Press. The first attempt was an anthology called *When It Changed* (edited by Geoff Ryman, 2009), which is when I first came into the orbit of Comma

Press. Other books in this series included *Litmus* (2011), about the history of scientific breakthroughs (picked as an *Observer* book of the year), and *Thought-X* (2017), which explored the use of thought experiments in science. But what this book attempts has never been tried before – to bring a delegation of leading authors, both intellectually and physically, into the world of CERN, and to let the work being done here ignite sparks for a whole book's worth of stories about what is, by general consent, the most famous laboratory in the world.

The collaborative process began with the scientists. First, we put a general call out to the community of scientists and engineers who work at CERN, or who work *with* CERN via partner institutions, asking for themes and aspects of their research that they felt could act as seeds for new pieces of fiction. This meant opening the doors to a huge range of research areas and types of contributors, leading to a book that truly came from the CERN community itself. Once we had gathered this list of scientific ideas, we let our authors loose on the list to pick whichever topics inspired them and then paired them with the scientists who'd suggested their topic so that they could meet and talk. A key part of the process was then inviting our authors to CERN to see for themselves the extraordinary scale of the work being done here, and to let them get up close and personal with real particle accelerators.

Then, once the stories were written, each scientist was asked to write a short afterword to the piece they consulted on, reconnecting the fiction with the original science for the reader. The result is what you hold in your hands. Hopefully these stories will offset some of the misrepresentations of CERN that have entered the popular consciousness, elsewhere, as well as bring other wild and unexpected (but still scientifically plausible) speculations to the fore. What emerges, in the pages that follow, is a series of unexpected collisions: collisions between different ways of seeing the world, between the personal and professional lives of its characters, between the past and present, and between scientific theory and the realities of scientific practice. And much like the LHC collides protons together (and CERN brings different institutions together), this book brings very different imaginative worlds together, smashing them into each other very deliberately, to imbue the stories that follow with an energy and vibrancy that the new particles being created carry.

It's an experiment, so we can't always be certain of the results. A big thank you is owed to both CERN and the STFC (who funded the project through the UK science project HL-LHC-UK) for allowing us to conduct the experiment. Hopefully you'll find the results as brilliantly illuminating as we did.

Prof Rob Appleby & Connie Potter,
University of Manchester, September 2022

Notes

1. Submarine innovator, Simon Lake, and helicopter pioneer, Igor Sikorsky credited Jules Verne's *Twenty Thousand Leagues Under the Sea* and *Clipper of the Clouds respectively for their inventions.* Robert H. Goddard, inventor of the first liquid-fuelled rocket, credited HG Wells' *War of the Worlds* for his inspiration; Martin Cooper, the father of the 'handheld phone', credited *Star Trek*'s communicators for his inventions at Motorola; while Jack Cover named his 'Taser' after a fictional character created by Edward Stratemeyer: 'Thomas A. Swift's Electric Rifle.'

2. Aad, G. et al. (ATLAS Collaboration, CMS Collaboration) *Physical Review Letters.* 114, 191803 (2015).

Going Dark

Steven Moffat

By the time you read this, I will have ceased to exist.

I'm being precise. I'm not talking about dying. I don't mean someone will have pushed me off a building or under a train or squashed my head with a well-chosen rock or any of the kind of things that might naturally happen to a person in my line of work. I mean that as you read these words, there will be no trace of me in the world. I won't have just stopped living, I will never have started living in the first place. I won't just stop existing, I will never have existed at all. These words, if they still cling to this page – as I hope somehow they can – will have been written by someone else.

If you mention my name to the people who used to be my parents, they won't know who you're talking about. If you visit the woman who divorced me four years ago, she will look blank when you ask about me. If you decide to be thorough and go to my old school, there will be no record of my attendance. No one there will have any recollection of me. The place where I carved my name under a low bench in the first floor Boys cloakroom will be unmarked. Or perhaps another name will be there. Maybe the name of the child my parents had instead of me.

This is not a trick. This isn't some sinister conspiracy to erase the facts of my existence. This is the actual erasure of every moment of my life from the physical world. I know how this

1

sounds, but take me seriously. By the time you finish reading this, you might never have existed either.

I could tell you a little of my background, but it seems pointless now none of it really happened. So let's just say I'm someone in a line of work you would barely understand, and would certainly not meet with your approval. When people ask me what I do, I'm used to shrugging and saying I'm a sort of troubleshooter. I have perfected a brief smile and a glance at my feet that reliably ends the conversation. Now and then, people persist. Once a slightly drunk woman called Evie asked if troubleshooting involved any actual shooting. For some reason, perhaps boredom, I told her the truth: 'Yes.' She was excited when she asked the question, but something in my tone when I answered it made her frown. I glanced at my feet to end the conversation and when I looked up again she was gone. Not gone in the sense I am gone – just walking away, a little unsteadily and a little too rapidly. From the set of her shoulders, she was clearly still frowning.

I mention Evie, because it was in that moment, as I watched her weaving among the other party guests, that I first laid eyes on the chimp woman.

I am going to be as exact as I can now. You have a particular responsibility when you write about people who no longer exist, and events that never happened, because your words are all that is left of them: the only trace remaining anywhere in the real world. This is the testimony of the never were.

★★★

She was tall, perhaps a shade too thin. Her dress was a poison green and strikingly asymmetrical: the right sleeve extended all the way down her arm, looping around her thumb, while her left arm was bare. Her hair was dark, elaborately styled and tumbled around the face of a grinning chimpanzee. I stared at her, trying to make sense of what I was seeing. Her cartoon eyes stared back at me, comically wide, and her teeth were bared in a banana-shaped grin. Even through the mask, I could tell she was looking directly at me.

She was standing near a partly open door at the other end of the restaurant, motionless and composed, her hands clasped in front of her. She stood so still it was as if she had always been there. I looked around to see if anyone else had noticed her: the party was petering out by then, with only twenty or so people still loitering. One or two of them glanced at the chimp woman, but preferred to look away again; whoever she was, it was late and she wasn't their problem.

She wasn't my problem either, I decided, and turned away. I fetched my coat from the cloakroom, and briefly considered saying goodnight to my host. I could see him a few feet away, laughing and joking with his wife and a few friends. I pictured how his face would fall if I joined them for a moment to say goodnight; I imagined the questions that would inevitably follow when I stepped away. In truth, Jonathan had invited me out of a sense of obligation that he would rather not admit to: I had done some work for him, and it is in the nature of the services I provide that people would rather not talk about requiring them. I liked him though, and appreciated his kindness in letting me be there among his fellow scientists. I decided to be equally thoughtful and made my way to the exit. With one foot on the pavement outside, I found myself glancing back at the chimp woman. She was gone and the door she had been standing next to was now clicking shut.

I hesitated. I could have hailed a taxi and gone home. If I had, you would not now be reading these words and I would still exist. But the truth is, I was bored and curious. So I walked back across the restaurant, stepped through the door and began my long fall out of this world.

I was standing in a narrow, cluttered corridor. There were stacked boxes and crates, and another opened door led to the clatter of a kitchen. Beyond it, at the end of the corridor, a wooden staircase rose up to a narrow landing lit by a single bare lightbulb; as it flickered, a green dress passed below it and a moment later I heard high heels climbing the next set of stairs.

I should have stopped then. Forgive me – if I hadn't followed her, you would not be in the danger you are now in. Perhaps, if curiosity hadn't got the better of me, the universe would have left me alone.

At the top of the stairs, there was another corridor and a row of doors, only one of them open. Beyond the door, there was an almost empty room: bare floorboards, a burst sofa under a grimy window, and a rough wooden table, with two chairs. She was sitting in the chair facing me, as calm and still as before. I stood in the doorway and looked at her. She didn't speak so eventually I did.

'Hello,' I said.

Her voice was ordinary enough, a little muffled by the mask. There was a trace of an accent I couldn't identify. 'Please step inside and close the door.'

'Why would I do that?'

'There is absolutely no reason why you should, and many reasons why you shouldn't.'

'Such as?'

'Possibly you value your life. Though given its superficial nature, probably not very much.'

I thought about that. It was possible she knew about me. It was equally possible she was insane. I thought about my journey home and how long it would take. I thought about my flat and my cat who would need feeding. I had no reason I could think of to be standing there talking to a woman who, it seemed likely, was out of her mind. I could just walk back downstairs and leave.

Instead, I stepped into the room and closed the door. 'There's a key in the lock,' she prompted. I locked the door, slipped the key in my pocket. 'I'm keeping the key,' I said.

'I suppose that's a sensible precaution.'

'I'm glad you think so.'

'It won't do you any good though. Would you like to sit down?'

'Not especially.'

'It won't make any difference, but suit yourself.'

'I intend to.'

'You haven't so far.'

'What makes you say that?'

'What made you follow me up here? What reason could you possibly have had?'

'Curiosity.'

'Curiosity is not a reason – it's an impulse.'

'Impulse then.'

'Impulse, yes. The literal opposite of self-control.' I still couldn't place her accent. The plastic chimp face leered at me. 'Step a little closer, please, and place your left hand, palm down, on the centre of the table.'

'Why would I do that?'

'Because you're right-handed.'

'Why would I do anything you tell me?'

'Because nothing else will happen till you do.'

From below there was a burst of laughter, like someone had opened a door to the party. The door closed again. The chimp face stared at me, waiting.

'I could just leave,' I said.

'You could. And you should.'

I could walk away. I could be home in less than an hour. 'Are you going to take that mask off?' I asked her.

'I would like to.'

'Go ahead then.'

'Place your left hand on the centre of the table.'

'Who are you?'

'No questions will be answered, literally nothing will happen, till you place your hand where I tell you.'

She was clearly intelligent, obviously educated; there was a well-controlled tremor in her voice so she was both sensible enough to be afraid, and strong enough to conceal it. I could feel events starting to slip out of my control and, as always, it was thrilling. I knew I should leave. I also knew my cat would survive a night without me.

I crossed to the window, looked out. There was no one in the street who drew my attention but the building opposite was in darkness, and anyone could have been watching from one of the windows. I found the cord for the blind and lowered it.

'Are you telling yourself you're being cautious?' she asked.

'Fortunately, I never believe a word I say.'

'I believe you. Place your hand.'

I placed my left hand in the centre of the table, palm down and looked at her. 'Is something going to happen now?'

'Yes.'

'I'm waiting.'

I didn't have to wait long; I was barely aware of the knife in her hand before it was in mine. For a moment, there was no pain. I looked down at my hand. The blade had slammed straight through it into the wood of the table and the point must have burst through the other side.

'Sorry,' she said, 'it's a necessity.'

'What the fuck are you doing??' I managed to say.

'Carving your neurons.'

'You're carving my fucking hand!'

'Collateral damage, my apologies. I have to reinforce the wave function. Now look at my face.'

The mask was gone. 'Look at it. Study my face.'

The pain and shock were jumping in my vision now, my breath was roaring in my ears – but I found myself looking at her face. She was gaunt, mid-forties, pale enough to look ill. Her eyes were bright, fierce, liquid. 'Memorise my face. It will be harder than you think.'

'I'm kind of focused on my hand right now.'

'You are experiencing an adrenaline shock, it will change the way you store your memories.'

'What the fuck are you talking about?'

'As I explained – I'm carving your neurons. Now study my face. Memorise me.'

'You think I'm going to forget you?'

'It's almost impossible that you won't. I'm about to list three

6

names. Memorise them too.'

Blood was flowing round the blade and pooling round my hand. I fought to control the panic. 'You ever heard of maybe writing things down?'

'Arthur Pendle. Say it back to me.'

'Jesus, I can remember a name.'

Her hand was still on the knife: now she twisted it. Pain burst through me like fireworks. 'Say it back to me.'

'Arthur Pendle.'

'Madeline Preston, Tariq Baddaur.'

'Madeline Preston, Tariq Baddaur, what the fuck is this??'

'Find them.'

'How?'

'I know you will be able to because I know who you are – find them.' She removed her hand from the knife and stood. 'May I have the key please.'

'I just give it to you, do I?'

'The sooner you give it to me, the sooner I leave. Then you can do something about getting help, you're bleeding rather a lot.'

I handed her the key. She looked down at the blood spreading across the table as if she found it mildly troubling. 'You have a phone, I presume?'

'Of course I bloody do.'

'Then I suggest you phone someone.' She went to the door, unlocked it. As she stepped through it, she turned back to me. Her smile seemed almost sad. 'Tell them you need a hand.'

I never saw her again. In fact, as it turned out, I'd never seen her at all.

★★★

Sometimes dreams are so vivid, it takes a moment or two to figure out if they really happened. When I woke up, I even checked my hand to see if there was a wound. There wasn't, of course.

I was still piecing it together over my morning coffee. There had been a party, yes, and rather against my better judgement I had gone. Drunk Evie had asked about my troubleshooting and I'd alarmed her with my answer. But there had been no chimp woman, no journey up the stairs, no knife through the back of my hand. I had simply left the restaurant without saying goodbye to Jonathan, hailed a cab, and gone home to feed my cat.

I couldn't shake the feeling that it had been real though: it was still impossibly vivid. Her bright, liquid eyes, the slight tremor in her voice, the shattering pain of the knife. I found myself checking my hand again. No wound, not a trace, nothing. I tried to remember how the dream had ended. One moment, I'd been trapped there, my hand pinioned to the table, the next... I was in a cab home. But the cab journey had been real; the chimp woman, and the knife and the strange, empty room – none of that had really happened. So how could it feel so real? The words 'carving your neurons' floated into my head. Her urgent stare, her sad smile as she left. 'You are experiencing an adrenaline shock,' she'd told me, 'it will change the way you store your memories.'

By midday, I'd managed to stop thinking about it – but that was when my phone rang. I didn't recognise the number, so I let it go to voicemail.

When I played the message back, this is what I heard. A man's voice, quite young by the sound of it; breathy, tense. 'Hello, sorry. Sorry to leave this message, but I need to talk to you urgently. I promise this is not a trick or a scam, I just... I just need to talk to you, and it's really, really important. I'm on this number, please phone. My name is Arthur Pendle.'

***

'You know about the Higgs, right?' Arthur Pendle had just turned 29, but he dressed and acted like he was seventeen. He sat on the edge of his single bed, rocking compulsively, wrapped in a hoodie that looked four sizes too big. His arms were tightly folded, like he was trying to twist inside himself, and bleached hair sprouted from under the hood over his thin, bone-white face. His blue eyes were so pale they barely seemed to have any colour at all. Downstairs, I could hear his mother in the kitchen and the clink of crockery. She'd looked startled when she opened the door to me, and then astonished when I said I was looking for Arthur Pendle. 'Are you a friend of his?' she'd asked.

'I need to speak to him. He phoned me to come round.'

She looked at me, so curious. 'He doesn't have a lot of visitors.'

'Well there's one of me, so I guess that's still true.'

'So you're a friend then?' she asked again. It wasn't just curiosity, I realised. It was hope.

'Shall I bring you up some tea?' she'd asked, as she'd showed me to the stairs.

'No, I'm good, thank you.'

'It's no trouble. I'll make you some tea. You can take tea together, it will be nice.'

The clink of crockery from downstairs had stopped. I wondered if the tea things had been loaded onto a tray, ready to come up. Her son was still rocking on the bed, waiting for an answer. 'The Higgs,' he repeated. 'The Higgs boson. You know about that?'

'No. Higgs Boson, who's that?'

'Jesus, you don't know about the Higgs??'

'I don't know about Higgs boson, I guess you could tell me though.'

'Are you even a scientist?'

'No, I'm not a scientist. I'm also not a grown adult who lives with his parents.'

He frowned at me, but not angrily. Like he was used to insults and in the habit of ignoring them. His frown was just puzzlement. 'What are you then? What do you do – for a living?'

'It doesn't matter.'

'Everything matters.'

'Ever had a girlfriend, Arthur?'

He stopped rocking for a moment, which was something. 'None of your business!'

'You see how this works?'

He considered that. Started rocking again. 'The Higgs boson is not a person, it's a particle.'

'Okay.'

'Do you know what that means?'

'It means it's not a person, it's a particle.'

'I don't have time to explain why it's important.'

'I'll contain my disappointment.'

A brief halt in the rocking again. 'You're kind of rude.'

'I'm sure we'll get along famously.'

A little flash of a smile, then more rocking. 'Okay, I'll give you the idiot's version.'

'From what I've seen of you so far, that shouldn't be a stretch.'

'There was... a theory, okay? You know what a theory is?'

'Is it like a palm tree?'

'A palm tree??'

'I know what a theory is, Arthur. I was experimenting with sarcasm to see if you understood it.'

'I know what sarcasm is.'

'You see? Famously!'

'I'll start at the beginning.'

'Popular choice.'

'There was a theory about... well, basically, the way the universe was formed. The way it's built.'

'You weren't kidding about starting at the beginning.'

Another flash of resentment on that bony face, like he wasn't used to being interrupted. But then, he probably wasn't used to anyone else being in the conversation. He set his jaw, or what there was of it. 'She didn't mention any of this then?'

'Who didn't?'

He waited a moment, like he knew he was about to land

one on me. 'The chimp woman.'

I said nothing. It wasn't difficult as nothing was exactly what came to mind.

'You saw the chimp woman, right? The one you thought was a dream.'

I checked my hand again. No wound, nothing. 'It was a dream,' I said. When I looked back at him he was checking his hand too. We stared at each other for a moment.

'Carving your neurons, right?' he said. 'Guess it worked.'

'She was a dream.'

'Which we both had.'

'I know it didn't happen.'

'So do I. But if the pain of a knife through the hand is what preserved the memory – how does that work if there never was a knife?'

I showed him my hand. 'There's no wound.'

'She gave me your number. I'm guessing she gave you my name. How can a dream do that?'

I tried to think about it. It jangled in my head. 'I don't know.'

'Then maybe I talk, and you listen, yeah?'

I wanted to tell him to go to hell, but it was just anger – and the anger was just confusion. I didn't trust myself to speak so I nodded.

'Higgs boson is the name of a particle that nobody could find.'

'Okay.'

He shook his head, irritated. 'No! No, no! Don't say okay, don't say that. Say "How can a particle have a name if no one even knows it's there?"'

'Can we just imagine I said that?'

There was a timid knock at the door. I could hear the tremor of best china on a tray momentarily balanced on one hand. 'Jesus!' said Arthur, rolling his eyes.

'Who knows, but more likely it's your Mum.' I stood and opened the door. I noticed she had changed her cardigan.

'Arthur, I brought some tea for you and your friend.'

'Tea's shit,' said Arthur, 'I want coffee.'

★★★

The cafe was deserted except for me and Arthur and the server leaning at the counter, glowering at us for intruding on his solitude.

'The Higgs was a theory,' Arthur was explaining. He paused, frowned, examined my face like he was trying to figure out just how simple he would have to make this. 'Okay. Okay. The universe is made of particles, right? Lots of particles doing stuff – we good so far?'

'Like atoms.'

'Smaller than atoms. Atoms are made of particles. Lots of little particles buzzing about, doing shit.'

'Okay.'

'Up to speed?'

'Clinging on.'

'Just fix it in your head. The universe is made of lots of tiny, little particles whizzing about. You, me, this coffee, these chairs, the past, the future, the moon, the stars, the space between the stars, Emilia Clarke's arse, the snot in your nose – all of it, everything, is just particles doing shit. Got it?'

'Still clinging on.'

'I mean, they're small. They're awesomely tiny. Some of them are so small the only properties they have are mathematical. Forget that last sentence – it's beyond your brain.'

'My brain says thanks.'

'Your brain is welcome.'

'My brain made of particles apparently.'

'Not just your brain. Your thoughts too. Your thoughts are made of particles because everything is made of particles, you need to get that.'

'I got it all the way to my particles.'

'So these particles, all these different kinds – we've basically found them.'

'Yeah, well they're everywhere, right? Whizzing.'

'We've studied them, we've got a handle on them. We've named them.'

'Always a mistake, you only get attached.'

'When I say we, I don't mean me. I mean we as in scientists. I mean the scientific community of which I am a part. I was a kid when a lot of this was going on.'

'You were probably still living with your mum.'

'But there was a particular particle – one very important particle that had to be there – that we couldn't find.'

'Higgs boson.'

'Correct. It was a theory. Just a theory. Okay. Need real focus now. ' He leaned forward, took my coffee cup away and placed it out of my reach on the windowsill behind him, like even that could split my focus now. 'We needed the Higgs boson to solve the problem of electroweak symmetry breaking.'

'Yeah, well, who doesn't?'

'You don't understand, right?'

'No, but I'm beginning to understand your girlfriend problem.'

He pressed his finger to his temples. 'Okay. I'm going to keep it super, super simple. I'll give you kind of the journalistic version, yeah? It's not strictly accurate. But it's not strictly inaccurate.'

'That does sound like journalism.'

'So. We had a theory about how the universe started – but if our theory was right, we needed one more particle. Which only existed, for a tiny moment, right after the universe began. We knew this particle only by its effect, by what it did – but there was no way to find one because none of them were still around. You with me?'

'Like finding a footprint. You know there's been a man passing by recently but he's gone now.'

'Yes. Well, no. Well, yes but worse than that. Like finding a footprint but you've never seen a man, or even know what a man looks like, and now you have to reconstruct what a man is from a partial print of the shape of his shoe, yeah?'

'Okay.'

'We called this particle the Higgs boson.'

'Do you have someone in charge of snappy names? Because I have notes.'

'So this was our idea. If we couldn't find a Higgs particle, maybe we could make one. Have you heard of the Large Hadron Collider?'

'Yes.'

He looked surprised. 'Okay, that's good. That's something. What do you know?'

'Well, mainly that there's a picture of it on your t-shirt just below the words "Large Hadron Collider".'

He sighed. 'Okay, okay. Basically it's a big machine and… it collides stuff. Particles. Kind of you shoot particles at other particles and see what trouble they cause.'

'Troubleshooting.'

'Kind of. I think that's what my boss used to call it. Really all you've got to understand is there was a plan to make a Higgs boson. To use the Collider to create the exact circumstances which – in theory – would generate a Higgs particle. 27 kilometres of underground tunnel in a big ring, full of superconducting magnets, so we could recreate the big bang that kick-started the universe!'

'Really?'

'No, not really – but you got to put something in the press release when you've got that amount of funding. More accurately – more boringly – they made a machine that could make a Higgs particle. That was the plan. And the moment there was a plan, that's when everything went weird.'

'Weird how?'

Arthur didn't reply. He was staring over my shoulder now, like he'd just seen something that scared the hell out of him. I glanced round but there was nothing to see. 'You okay?' I asked him. He blinked, seemed to turn even paler, and then his eyes found mine. 'I just realised something.'

'Realised what?'

'You're about to realise it too. And it might freak you out.'

'What might freak me out?'

'This cafe. This cafe we're sitting in.'

I looked round the cafe; the bored guy at the counter, the flaking paintwork, the faded mural of some old Italian town, 'What about it?'

'How did we get here?'

'Excuse me?'

'How did we get here?' There was a new, hoarse note in his voice; suddenly he was afraid. I studied his panicking face. His question was stupid, of course. Why was he even asking it? 'How did it happen?' he insisted. 'Actually think about it. What happened, how did we get here? What was the sequence of events?'

'We went looking for a cafe, we found this one, what the hell does it matter?'

'My Mum came in, remember? She said she'd brought us tea.'

'Yeah.'

'I said 'Tea's shit, I want coffee' and…?'

I thought about it. I thought some more. It was like walking into a room and for a moment forgetting why you were there. Except it was worse, because there was nothing. I reached for a memory and there was absolutely nothing there.

'Think about it, really think. I said 'I want coffee' then what happened?'

I concentrated; I knew I'd remember in a second. It was on the tip of my tongue. But still I found nothing. Nothing.

'I'll tell you what happened. Nothing happened. I said coffee, and suddenly we were sitting here. Boom! We cut like a movie. We just cut here – new scene. Like when you're reading a book and there's a gap and asterisks.'

'No,' I said. 'We left the house, you said there was a cafe nearby –…'

'Stop it! Stop it now. That's just your memory filling in the gap, there's nothing really there.'

'But we must have walked here, there's no other way −...'

'Where is this cafe?' asked Arthur. 'How long did it take us to walk here? The guy at the counter, did we talk to him? What was his accent? Was he nice? Have we paid for the coffees yet, or are we paying after?'

I kept reaching for the memories. I kept finding nothing.

'Okay, so don't panic. Just keep sitting here, keep concentrating, don't let your mind wander.'

'What the fuck is happening?'

He sat there for a moment, like he was trying to control his breathing. Finally he gripped the table, steeled himself, and said: 'Wave function collapse.'

'Excuse me?'

'Reverse causality.'

'What the hell is that?"

'It's what happened when they went looking for the Higgs particle.'

'What happened?'

His eyes were twitching round the room, like he was checking it was all still there. 'You know when you send an email, and then you recall it? Because, like, you made a mistake, or something?'

'Sure.'

'Okay, I know how this sounds. But what if it wasn't just emails that could be recalled... what if you could recall actual physical events?'

'Well, I've only got a Mac.'

He considered a moment, and then he was on his feet. 'We should keep moving.'

'What difference will that make?'

'Fuck knows, but I feel safer when we're moving. We can't let it happen again!'

'Let what happen again?'

★★★

The streetlamps were flickering on and I had no clear idea where we were headed. Arthur just kept striding along, talking faster and faster and turning corners seemingly at random.

'Holger Bech Nielsen of the Niels Bohr Institute in Copenhagen. Masao Ninomiya of the Yukawa Institute for Theoretical Physics in Kyoto. These are serious guys, okay? Proper scientists.'

'Okay!'

'Keep a hold of that thought. Cos what they said, it doesn't sound serious. They said the hunt for the Higgs particle wouldn't work out, because the universe didn't want it to.'

'The universe?'

'They said the universe didn't like Higgs particles.'

'Didn't like them??'

'Nielsen said this – exact words: "It must be our prediction that all Higgs producing machines shall have bad luck."'

'Which is nuts, yeah?'

'Totally nuts. Except...'

'Except?'

'Except they did have bad luck. They totally did.' He was walking faster now, like he was trying to get away from something. 'First attempt at recreating the Higgs, the United States Superconducting Supercollider, got cancelled after billions – literally billions – were already spent. That was an event so improbable it was called an anti-miracle. The European one, the Large Hadron Collider, the one on my t-shirt – the moment they switched it on, the connection between two magnets vapourised and closed the collider for a whole year. A particle physicist, working on the one of the Collider experiments, was arrested by the French police on suspicion of conspiracy with the North African wing of Al Qaeda. I could go on. You know how bad it got? How freaked they all got? They had a plan to draw cards to figure out if they should keep going.'

'Excuse me?'

We had reached a crossroads. Arthur looked both ways, hesitated, then gave me a wild look.

'Choose!' he demanded.

'Choose what?'

'A direction. Choose which direction, don't think about it, just choose!'

I pointed left. Arthur nodded, wheeled around, and headed right. He was walking faster and faster and I took a moment to catch up. 'What are you talking about, they drew cards?'

Faster and faster. 'They designed a game of chance – basically a card drawing game run on a computer, to make their decisions for them. If the outcome was sufficiently unlikely – like you draw one heart in a deck with a million spades – the machine would either not be run at all, or run at too low an energy to create a Higgs particle. Like, they deliberately invited bad luck in, to see if it would show up. They were going to give the universe a chance to stop them. They seriously talked about that, they did. They had meetings about a card game to choose what they did with one of the most expensive scientific projects in human history.'

'That's crazy.'

'They all thought it was crazy too. But they're scientists – they also thought it was just crazy enough to be true.'

'But they went ahead, yeah?'

'With the card game?'

'With the experiment, with the Higgs boson thing.'

'Sure they went ahead.'

'So they calmed down, stopped being crazy, and found the Higgs boson, yes?'

'They did, yeah. In 2012.'

'So the universe wasn't plotting against you. Like anyone sane or sober could've told you. What is the point of this story exactly?'

'Who says the universe wasn't plotting against us? Maybe we just beat the universe. Or maybe the universe just delayed us till the right time, till it was ready. Whatever. The thing is, that was just round one. That's before it got really nasty.'

'Nasty? What do you mean, nasty, what are you talking about?'

'My house.' For a moment I thought he was answering my question, then I realised he was pointing. We were now standing right across the street from the very house neither of us could remember leaving. It was a very ordinary, detached house but it somehow seemed crouched and quiet in the gathering dusk. 'My house,' he repeated.

'I assumed that's where we were going.'

'That's where I was trying not to go.'

'Why?'

'Doesn't matter.' He sighed, looked around. There was a bus shelter a few feet along from us. 'Doesn't matter an arsing shit,' he continued. He walked to the bus shelter, and sat on the little plastic bench inside. His shoulders were hunched, his hands rammed in the pockets of his hoodie. He looked desolated, defeated. I wasn't sure what to do, so I went and sat next to him. 'I don't understand,' I said.

He gave a bitter little laugh. 'You don't understand how much you don't understand.'

'Tell me then.'

'What time did you come round to see me?'

'About one o'clock?'

'How long have we been talking?'

'An hour, maybe a bit more. Maybe two.'

'Then how come it's dark?'

I looked around. A moment ago it had been twilight; now the sky was dark. I tried to keep my voice calm. 'Doesn't time fly when you're having fun.'

'Doesn't time fly when you're being unwritten.'

'What the hell are you talking about?'

He was rocking again. 'Okay. Try this. What's your name?'

'I told you my name.'

'I don't think you did, in fact. But tell me now.'

I told him.

He was silent a moment, then looked at me, impatiently. 'I said, tell me your name.'

'I did, I just told you.'

'Tell me again.'

I told him again. This time he laughed. 'You think you're speaking, don't you. You think you're telling me your name. You're not. You're sitting there in silence.'

'I told you my name.'

'Okay, let's try something else. Think your name. Don't say it out loud, just think it.'

I thought of my name – or at least I tried to. I reached for my name and there was nothing there. I tried again. Nothing. Nothing. Suddenly the night was very cold. 'What's happening? Explain this!'

'What do you do for a living? I asked you before, you said it was none of my business. So don't tell me – just think it. Just think about what your job is.'

I focused, I concentrated – nothing. What was I, what did I do all day? Who paid me, what did I do in return? I reached for the memory; there was nothing there, beyond vague and violent fantasies – a lot of adolescent nonsense about being some kind of hero. A troubleshooter. Even now I can't quite rid myself of the notion; but the fantasy is masking a truth I can no longer locate. As you may soon discover yourself, when your past is disappearing, you start filling in the space with anything at all.

Arthur was speaking again, in a low terrified voice. 'It's like we're being winnowed away. Piece by piece, dissolving. Like the universe is healing around us. It's hard to see it when it's happening to you. I mean, suddenly your head is full of blind spots – but blind spots are exactly the things you can't see.'

'What does that mean? What does any of that mean, just explain.'

'The chimp woman knew. She noticed it, she knew it was happening. She knew she was being... written out, erased. That's why she wore the mask, that weird dress. It's why she stabbed our hands. To be memorable.' He frowned. 'Why a chimp mask? Do you think that's important? Or was it just a strong visual image? To be hard to forget, to burn herself into our memories.'

'Carving our neurons.'

'That's what she said, right?'

'But she was a dream.'

'She became a dream. Because just possibly that's what dreams are. Dreams are the things that used to be real. And that's why they fade.'

I thought about it. It was insane. But I still couldn't remember my name or who I was or what I did.

'Dark matter,' he said.

'Dark what?'

'Dark matter. The biggest, best secret in the universe. The Higgs is peanuts next to dark matter. If reality wants to keep a secret that would be the one.' He was rocking faster and faster now. 'Okay. Okay. So dark matter is composed of particles that do not absorb, reflect, or emit light. So there is no way, none whatsoever, of us ever seeing it or observing it directly. We only know it's there because we can see its gravitational effect. We've found the footprint, but we can't see the man. If the universe is hiding something, that's it, that's the big one.'

'How can the universe be hiding something?'

'Why shouldn't it? Why not? You can hide things, I can hide things – we're much simpler entities than the whole universe. Suppose the universe has... like an immune system. Yeah, all of reality – all of history and the future, has something like an immune system. Maybe it's important that some things are never known, never witnessed, never observed. Maybe the act of some things being observed can be like... like a cancer. Like a cancer on reality. What if the universe has... I don't know, the equivalent of antibodies. And if a bunch of scientists gets too close to finding dark matter, they get... rewritten. Unwritten. Unpicked from the fabric of reality. Recalled like an email. The antibodies attack, and whole lives just get... burned away. Dissolved piece by piece in the time stream.'

'It's ridiculous.'

'Science lesson one: just because something's ridiculous doesn't mean it isn't true.' He stopped rocking, pressed his fingers tightly against his temples. 'I have this idea. The chimp woman, I think her name was Madeline Preston.'

'You recognised her?'

'No. Yes. I don't know − how do you recognise someone when your memory keeps changing? I think she was a scientist and I used to work with her. There was me, her, some guy called...' he tailed off, shook his head. 'No, it keeps fading, I keep losing it.'

I remembered the names from the dream. 'Tariq Baddaur?' I suggested.

'Tariq, yeah. Tariq Baddaur. There was another guy. Peter. Peter something, I can't remember. But I think we were close. Really close on dark matter. And... and then...'

'And then?'

'Where are we? Where are we all now? What happened to us?'

'Whatever happened to you, why would it be happening to me too?'

He was on his feet now, pacing. 'I'm not even a scientist any more, not a real one. You know what I do? I'm an assistant lab technician in a secondary school. I help high school kids do lab experiments. How did that happen??' He was staring at his house now. 'I didn't used to live with my Mum. That's not how it was! I was married! Why am I not married anymore?? Why am I living with my mum? It doesn't make any sense. It's like I'm... eroding. Disappearing, bit by bit!'

I tried to sound calm. 'Or it's something else. Something simpler. Maybe we're both... I don't know...' I tailed off − I had nothing. It was cold and dark and I didn't understand a single thing about what was happening to me.

Arthur was staring wildly at his house. 'Mum,' he said; then, louder. 'Mum!' He was striding across the road, heading towards his front door. I started after him. 'Mum!!' he bellowed like a terrified child. He was fumbling his key in the lock, now starting to push his way through the door.

I raced up the garden path, in time for the door to slam in my face.

Silence! I waited to hear any shouting from inside, but there was nothing; just the faint sound of laughter from a television. I didn't know why, but the silence chilled me. Why wasn't he shouting now? Why didn't he call for his mum again? My hand was shaking as I rang the doorbell.

It took almost a minute. There was the shuffle of feet, then the rattle of a door chain being put in place. The door eased slightly open. Arthur's Mum was peering at me through the crack. She'd changed her cardigan again. 'What do you want?' she asked.

'Sorry. I was with Arthur. He just came in, he was shouting.'

She looked mystified. 'No one came in.'

There was a cold wave through my stomach. 'No, Arthur did. Arthur came in, he was shouting at you. I'm Arthur's friend, remember me?'

I knew what she was going to say before she said it. 'Who's Arthur?'

★★★

Finding Tariq Baddaur's phone number was easy enough once I got online, although when you read this it will have become impossible: neither the number nor Tariq Baddaur will still exist. By the time I got back to my flat and logged on, my meeting Arthur had already become a dream: as with the Chimp Woman, a new memory track had overwritten it. In the new version, I had gone to Arthur's house, and his Mum had answered the door. But she had no knowledge of anyone called Arthur.

'Your son,' I insisted.

'I don't have a son. I've never had a son.'

As I turned to leave, she grabbed my arm and there was something wild and haunted in her face. 'How did you know?'

she asked almost in a whisper.

'Know what?'

She hesitated – then: 'If I'd had a son I'd have called him Arthur. I was always going to call my son Arthur.'

Underneath this new memory, the dream still rippled – hazy, fragmented and fading fast. Writing it all down has helped me fix it in my mind, but still none of it feels quite real. I know better, of course – because I know what dreams really are; the scar tissue of the surgery the universe does on itself; fossils of the once real. As I write this, I wonder if that's what fiction is too. Perhaps all the stories in the world once really happened before the universe rewound their forbidden knowledge and overwrote them. 'Wave function collapse,' as a man who had never existed had once never said to me. I have an idea that these words I'm writing might somehow reach you, but I wonder in what form. Perhaps something you read online, or in a magazine: perhaps a story in a book. Your past, even now, is being re-written. In a previous reality you were a scientist: by now you could be a lawyer or a doctor or a high school teacher. Please understand, everything I have written here is true – or it once was – and as the last survivor of the Dark Matter team your very existence is in danger. It is, of course, too late for me; but I only understood that when I tracked down Tariq Baddaur.

I could only find one physicist by that name online; he was listed as having done some groundbreaking work at CERN with someone called Peter Dong (you, of course). It seemed they were in pursuit of something called Chronometrically Interacting Massive Particles – or ChIMP for short. There was a brief mention of four people being on the research team, but for some reason only two names were listed. Perhaps it was a mistake. Or perhaps two of them had ceased to exist. Perhaps. My hand was shaking as I reached for my phone. In every possible sense, time was running out.

I tried Baddaur's cellphone first, but it was engaged. I then tried his landline. It was in that moment that the last piece fell into place, and I understood that I was leaving this world.

Because when I called Tariq Baddaur's landline, the phone on my own desk started to ring.

Afterword: The Unwritten Me

Dr Peter Dong
Illinois Mathematics and Science Academy

IT'S ALWAYS A BIT creepy to see your name in print, especially in a story that's already a bit creepy, but of course this story is not a letter or e-mail I received from an untraceable or mysterious source, but rather an e-mail from a writer who wanted me to check the physics of his story. I'd say he did a remarkable job on the physics, which I would categorise as implausible but not impossible, and as Arthur said (or rather, didn't say), just because something's ridiculous doesn't mean it isn't true.

Nielsen and Ninomiya are indeed real physicists, mildly famous ones – they even have their own theorem in lattice field theory. But they gained a certain amount of notoriety in 2006 with a series of papers that argued that the Higgs boson doesn't want to be found. Many physicists treated their suggestions as a crackpot hypothesis but it's hard to say that it's outright impossible. I'll try to summarise their ideas here.

Let's start with an interesting way of looking at the universe, due to the eighteenth-century physicist Joseph-Louis Lagrange. Suppose you want to know which of several candidates to hire for a job. You probably consider several factors – education, work experience, references, personality – and, in principle, you could assign a score to each candidate and choose the best score. Lagrange made the remarkable argument that the universe basically works the same way. If it wants to decide how a ball

26

will roll when placed in a given position, it considers all possible paths that the ball could take. It evaluates each path by calculating a quantity called the action. Then it chooses whichever path has the smallest action, and the ball goes that way. Remarkably, Lagrange showed that this approach gives identical results to Newton's laws of motion.

When we deal with subatomic particles, we use the same approach, but things are more complicated because quantum mechanics, which governs these particles, follows different laws. For one, it is governed by probability, rather than certainty. Instead of just choosing an action, quantum mechanics chooses the result at random. In our job-hiring example above, you would just choose a person at random, but the scores you assigned the candidates could determine how likely they were to have been chosen. Not necessarily the best way of hiring for a job, but it's how quantum mechanics works.

So in quantum mechanics, instead of just choosing the outcome with the smallest action, the universe calculates the action for each outcome, and then chooses at random, with some outcomes being more likely than others, based on the action. Quantum mechanics allows for what we would call impossible events – running at a brick wall and coming out on the other side unharmed, for example – but in most cases the probability is so incredibly small that we may as well call it impossible.

Nielsen and Ninomiya then make an interesting conjecture about imaginary numbers. The imaginary number, some of you may remember from maths class, is the square root of negative one, which of course does not exist. You might think that would make imaginary numbers pretty useless, but physicists actually use them all the time for a variety of important reasons – we just require that the final, measurable answer be a real (non-imaginary) number.

Now in normal quantum mechanics, we always assume the action is a real number. What happens if it is imaginary? You might reasonably ask if there is any reason why this would be the case. But, they reply, why not? It's not directly measurable, so there's no reason it couldn't be imaginary. They calculate the effect and find it very straightforward: any action that is imaginary will result in a very small probability. (For the mathematically minded, it just involves the difference between a complex exponential and a real exponential.) So anything that involves an imaginary action basically won't happen, or will at least be very unlikely. That also means that any attempt to cause such an event would have to fail because the final result is so unlikely. Since this means that present events would change to avoid a future action, this is sometimes called reverse causality.

Now, they speculate, what if observing a Higgs boson results in an imaginary number in the action? They give several technical reasons why this is not completely unreasonable, though it is far from proven. That would mean that any timeline in which the Higgs boson gets created automatically becomes extremely unlikely. And that means that any time anyone makes a credible attempt to create a Higgs, other timelines that end with not observing the Higgs, even if they are themselves unlikely, become more probable by comparison. Thus, increasingly improbable events will happen to prevent the ultimately improbable event from happening. This, they argued, led to the sudden shutdown of the Superconducting Supercollider in the US in 1993 and the magnet explosion at the Large Hadron Collider (LHC) in 2008. More improbable, potentially life-threatening events would continue to occur if people continued to search for the Higgs.

Nielsen and Ninomiya argued that this was an easily testable proposition. If the universe were given an easy way out to stop the Higgs from being found, they reasoned, it would take it. They proposed that the LHC staff create a machine that draws one card at random out of, say, a million cards. Exactly one card in the stack would have the phrase 'Shut down the LHC' on it. Management would promise that, if they drew the card, they would shut down the LHC. The universe then had an easy way out: an unlikely event that would make sure the Higgs would never be created, allowing the universe to avoid more drastic means. Nielsen and Ninomiya even calculated how many cards would be needed to do this reliably.

No, they didn't actually do this experiment, at least not that anyone admitted, because it sounds ridiculous, and it would be a pretty tough sell to the governments that had shelled out five billion dollars to build the machine. There was also no good reason to believe that producing a Higgs boson would have an imaginary action, even if it's not impossible. The Higgs was discovered in 2012, and thousands have been produced since then, so everything now seems fine. But it's still not impossible that the universe was working to avoid something else. Due to the magnet accident, the LHC has never run at its design energy of 14 TeV. At present, it's stuck at 13 TeV. And other things happened around the same time: for example, in October 2004 a freak electrical accident at the BaBar experiment at the Stanford Linear Accelerator Center prevented that experiment from finishing its planned data collection run. And so forth.

Hence the connection to dark matter. All we know about dark matter is that it must be there, because we can see it in astronomical measurements, confirmed many times over. And yet, all attempts to find it in colliders or sensitive underground detectors have come up empty. We have managed to get much clearer about what it is not, but have very little knowledge of what it is.

So the idea of this story is that dark matter, not the Higgs, is the particle whose observation causes an imaginary action. There are ways to make this work theoretically. The natural consequence is that any timeline which led to the observation of dark matter would be avoided by the universe – which would explain why our local searches have always turned up negative. Perhaps there is a dark matter particle that could be created if the LHC reached its design energy, or that might have been detected at BaBar.

Physicists (including me) can give plenty of reasons why this doesn't make sense – but of course, they would, wouldn't they, because any timeline in which we searched in the right place is a timeline the universe avoids. The evidence points to dark matter being composed of weakly interacting massive particles (WIMPs), but if the universe always avoids dark matter observation, those are probably not the right candidates. The true theory, since the particles have to mess with the timeline somehow, might involve the chronometrically interacting massive particles (ChIMPs) that the story mentions. At the very least, it's definitely the sort of name a physicist would come up with.

But isn't the universe already full of dark matter? Why would it be a problem if we observe it directly? This brings up the problem of observation, which opens up a possibility for the rest of this story to work.

It has long been known that our observation of the universe changes the behaviour we observe. The classic example is called the double-slit experiment. If you shine light through two slits, an effect called interference causes a series of alternating bands of light called an interference pattern to form. However, if you add a detector to see which slit each particle passes through, the interference pattern itself disappears. In other words, our observation of the light changes the behaviour of the light. Other experiments have shown an effect called the quantum eraser, in which you observe which slit the light passes through but then erase the information, in which case the interference pattern appears again. There is even the delayed quantum eraser effect, which allows you to choose whether you are going to erase the information after the light has passed through the slits (but before you see the result).

This behaviour is well understood in some ways. The quick version: if there are ten different possibilities for a particle's behaviour, it will not choose which one to do; instead, it will do all ten different possible actions at once, creating a superposition of all possible outcomes called a wavefunction. However, when we make a measurement, the universe picks one outcome at random, and that's all we see. When we observe the outcome, we say that the wavefunction collapses to what we observe. So whenever we observe the universe, we only see one thing – but when we don't observe it, it does many things at once.

This is neither new nor controversial. I teach this interpretation of quantum mechanics in my high school physics class, as do professors across the world. While there are some who disagree with the underlying ontology, the universe certainly acts as if it changes whenever we watch it.

This is relevant because it means that the universe didn't necessarily choose a single path all the way through, once and for all, at the Big Bang. Rather, it seems to be making little choices all the time, collapsing every time we observe it. So maybe we don't have a deist clockmaker universe that runs on a set course from the beginning of time; we have a very active universe that makes changes as a result of observations – and that can modify the past, as in the delayed quantum eraser experiment, to suit the present. This means that if someone gets close to discovering a forbidden particle, the wavefunction collapse might not happen all at once but bit by bit as observations are made. Since these can modify the past, this results in events – and people – getting 'unwritten' piecemeal.

The reason this is conceivable is that no one really knows what an observation is. This is remarkable because observation has a very special property – it causes wavefunction collapse – but we don't actually know what, exactly, constitutes an observation. Some physicists, most notably John von Neumann and Eugene Wigner, have argued that the mystery of observation must be connected to another great physical mystery: the mystery of consciousness. Plenty of scientists have argued that consciousness must be a quantum mechanical effect, one that cannot be understood merely in terms of neurons and chemicals but which requires the language of quantum mechanics to describe.

If consciousness is indeed quantum mechanical in nature, then it doesn't have to follow all the laws of ordinary particles as regards wavefunction collapse. In principle, consciousness could have access to versions of the universe that never actually happened, or that once happened and got revised by the wavefunction collapse of later observations. And thus it's not impossible that the part of consciousness least connected to the physical world – dreams and creativity – could pick up some kind of 'echo' from other unrealised wavefunctions, and that timelines that never occurred could still show up in dreams, memory, or fiction. It could even be that events in an abandoned timeline 'carve' themselves on the same consciousness in other timelines if they are dramatic or traumatic enough. It may be a bit far-fetched, but I think it's not impossible.

So while this story is, of course, a piece of fiction, I can't quite rule out the possibility that it reflects an alternate timeline in which I went into research instead of teaching after getting my degree, moved to CERN, and worked on a promising angle on dark matter – until we got too close and the universe rewrote my history as a high school physics teacher in Illinois. But since I'm quite happy with this version of my life, I'm not going to probe too deeply into it – and avoid any parties involving chimpanzee masks, just to be safe.

The Grand Unification

lisa luxx

force

IT IS NO LONGER MY name, yet I can hear it winding through the hallway, as I descend the stairs, lowering myself into *Bea* like it's a bath too hot to sit in.

'Bea!' She comes slinking down the hallway, 'Honey, come on! Your father is home.'

As usual, Mum does not wait for me to catch up, she turns and disappears, leaving the scent of Byredo perfume for me to inhale and follow. It is the joy I hear on the other side of the door which makes me hesitate, like a pin unsure whether to pop a balloon. My phone still hasn't pinged the ping I'm waiting for, so I go to the kitchen. Lay out a tray of toasted pita, Mum's homemade beetroot hummus, a glass of white wine for her, a Fanta for me and two bourbon biscuits for Dad. When I open the door to our sitting room, my parents are both engrossed in my father's stories. Two happy people with hearts they barely know, and me, here, with the fragility to destroy them.

'I have never seen another place on earth where there is such a mix of nationalities, Simone!' Dad is on his knees on the floor laying out photographs across sheets of printouts and sketches, 'and no one cares for politics because everyone is talking physics.' He holds out a photo to Mum, 'Look at this,

Simone, a young PhD from Iceland giving me hard liquor of some sort. All these youths were so excited to be talking about –' he gestures with his short chubby hands '– *particles!*'

Mum laughs, girlish, and fumbles with her vape. There's the usual musty air to Dad's return, the small glass flowers between the bowls of purple potpourri on the mantelpiece looking as if they've just now stood up and assumed their old positions. Whatever has shifted since he left, pretends it hasn't.

His face turns to mine, cheeks red from breathlessness, 'Bea, you owe me ten pounds! You never thought we would discover it. Look now, The God particle, that's what Lederman is calling it.' He rubs his hand under his cloth hat and then lets it fall loose on the back of his head, shaggy hair creeping out.

I know, of course, that this is such a huge moment, his life's work, and so it is entirely wrong to say *Dad, can you stop calling me Bea and start calling me Nabila?* So I pass him a bourbon biscuit and hold his hand.

matter

Mum had taken a day off work when the whole thing unravelled. Dad is a sweet, intelligent man but he takes up a lot of space in this house when he's around. Things change when he's not. We all move a bit, like the glass flowers, then pretend we haven't.

He was over in Geneva working at the Hadron Collider when Mum was shuffling around in her dressing gown taking client calls. Every time her mobile rings she rolls her eyes as if it's a newly discovered problem – clients! – in her ten years working at McKinsey & Company, I'd given up telling her that she clearly hates finance consultancy, I'd been tugging at her sleeve with that same sentence since I was thirteen.

Coffee sat cold that morning, after she finished up her pre-lunch calls and beckoned me upstairs.

'Listen, Bea, I want you to have something I've held on to

for a while.' She handed over a purple folder. 'This is your adoption file. You'll find everything in it about...' she let her hair down and re-tied it, 'well, about everything, honey.' She put her hands on mine and pulled me in to her chest, my body stayed rigid as ever.

I'd had no idea there was a folder. We had an unspoken *no questions, no answers* culture around my adoption in this house. It served us well. Now, kneeling on the carpet next to her chest of drawers, I didn't know what to say or how to say it. I fiddled with the drawstring of my joggers and managed to nod.

Mum got up to give me privacy with the folder but it felt impossible to open, so I moved across the landing, slipped it under my bed and opened Netflix. About three seasons of *Stranger Things* passed, then I drew it back out. Another season of *Explained*, before I opened it. A square printed photo fell onto my duvet. It had yellowed as if it was older than my twenty-two years, yet, I think, I was in it.

My dad taught me that it is weak force that decays matter, and which is what we use to identify time. When bones and stones are discovered in archaeological sites, it is weak force that they use to say 'this is one thousand years old!' or whatever, two thousand, five hundred, eighty-seven, twenty two...

I was more concerned with the weak force than I was with the two faces on the polaroid. I looked at the front, the blank back and then again closer in case there was a pencil mark, or a speck of dust or something like matter that came from the hands of somebody else. This somebody, holding me like I were the last fruit in the garden.

force

'Let me tell you, the Higgs boson has been concealing something from us – and what we can now imagine is that there is a hell of a lot of symmetry that we haven't known about before,' Dad's half-closed eyes mean we won't be leaving this room until he's finished the journey he is adamant to take us on. My hands are tense, holding something too heavy to hold while waiting for the right moment to set it down.

I stretch out my fingers and shake them off. Before I know it, I've eaten the beetroot hummus in such huge bites there's only dregs left on the plate.

'Supersymmetry. It's our answer to so much that has gone unanswered. Remember when I told you both of strong force, weak force and electromagnetics?' He quizzes us, as his way to tell a story.

Strong force, we remember, is what holds a nucleus together. If you break it, it'll destroy everything. It's how they make atomic bombs. His example was always: strong force is like the kinship that keeps the nuclear family held together.

Weak force is the decay of particles, it's how we read how much time has passed. 'Like an old photograph of a family who have separated… that's weak force, isn't it Dad?'

Though electromagnetism and weak force do, weak force and strong force do not interconnect. Supersymmetry, he tells us, half biscuit in hand, is what would unify all these forces.

Mum picks up her white wine and crosses her legs. 'Nigel,' she interrupts him, 'Bea is leaving for Iraq.'

matter

It wasn't so much the fire as what was left behind that mattered: brittle bits of card; edges of printed paper with the *Progress Report* of an Iraqi daughter adopted by two white people in suburban London; but mostly, the terse friction between me and Simone for the rest of the day. I felt like calling her *Simone* that day. I felt like spitting every time I said it, too.

No matter how assuredly I had held the match to the firelighter, or given cut-eye to the neighbours quizzing my midday bonfire, I hadn't managed to burn down everything. *Iman Abdul-Aziz Hussein. Iman Abdul-Aziz Hussein. Iman Abdul-*

Aziz Hussein. It was like a chant in my head. From that, a mysterious music started to play inside me, it was a song from my own name, Nabila, Nabila, Nabila.

My nickname started from the day I was adopted. Mum said *Bea* was easier to say than *Nabila*, but she hadn't wanted to change it, it reminded her of something beautiful. She said other people would find it easier to call me *Bea*, though, so I rarely heard *Nabila* except at the doctors or dentists or border control.

Since I was a kid, I used to draw the differences between nature and nurture. Nature is matter, nurture is force, Dad used to say to me. I'd look up at him from my little chair on the patio and paint myself as a tree, with sunlight and water as the force that made me grow.

When Mum came home that day to the fire, she threw her bag at me from across the grass, shouting, 'Bea, the fucking garden!' And I stood there unmoving in my Fila's and tracksuit. The baby curls around my forehead catching bits of ash. When she saw what I'd burnt, she stopped. Car door wide open, and her mouth too.

I watched her out my bedroom window that night, taking a flashlight to the ashes and shouting in my general direction, 'It's superstitious to burn photographs, you stupid, stupid girl!' I watched her, quietly, holding the two photographs I'd salvaged before she'd come home. One more confusing than the other.

force

Dad stands up quick and takes his hat into his hands. He mutters about symmetry and that I would be the same person whether I look at myself from the direction of the East or West. My phone pings and I reach out too quick to grab it, the Fanta spills onto our fringed rug at my feet. We all freeze for a moment, a tableau of strong force on the edge of atomic explosion. I know full well that I could have just let this all burn in the garden, we never had to tell Dad.

But *Iman Abdul-Aziz Hussein.*

'You have no idea what it feels like to see someone else in the world who looks like you,' I say, to break the silence. Except, the Fanta is still soaking into the wool and he does know. I meant, you do know, Dad, I don't.

Dad looks at Mum, and asks very quicky if I knew yet who Iman was to her. Mum finishes her wine and says, that's not relevant. She starts to tell him the story about the folder and the fire. The glass flowers are as still as the air in my chest. I interrupt her, 'Who was Iman to you?'

Mum insists that Iman was simply my birth mother, but dad is fiddling with his hat and turning one way then the other on the spot. He asks if he can tell us about the principle of decoupling. I love this man, but his ability to neglect our actual reality for the microscopic make-up of invisible reality is destabilising. I can feel tears coming to my eyes, and I throw my hair over my shoulder and tend to the Fanta in the carpet. Mum leans back into the sofa and puts her face in her hands, I have no idea what's coming.

matter

Facebook, Instagram, Twitter, none of them had an Iman Hussein who lived in Baghdad old enough to be my birth mother. Mum said I needed to look specifically in Baghdad. When I asked how she knew, she just repeated, *I have good instincts, Bea.*

'Mum, I think I'd like to start using Nabila.'

She dusted the kitchen island and shuffled the chopping boards into exactly where they'd been before she lifted them. Finally, she told me there's no need for that, and walked out the room.

I opened Twitter back up and put a call-out: *I'm looking for a 54-year-old Iman Abdul-Aziz Hussein who lives in Baghdad and once studied in London. Twitter, do your thing.*

She came in five minutes later and told me to take the post down. I asked again if she'd call me Nabila. For once where her hair had fallen loose, she had let it. With me stood rigid in her arms she wept, and said, 'I have the e-mail address of her sister, Farah, tell her you are Nabila. Let's go to Baghdad.'

force

'At the beginning, the universe was very hot, when it cooled down, the single unified force turned into the three others. Strong force, weak force, and electromagnetic. This is what's called decoupling, Bea. I mean, Nabila. I am listening.

'At the beginning everything was hot, so it was all bound together. Your mother and Iman were lovers at university, until Iman's husband found out and took her back to Iraq, leaving the newborn behind who he felt was touched by sin. The decoupling phase is when something does not interact with something else anymore. Supersymmetry would be a discovery that proves it all came from a single source, The Grand Unification. It would explain the universe's oneness. It would be you, Nabila, the enigma that brings these fragments together.'

He walked out of the room, and we heard the front door open and close.

Afterword: Divine Symmetries

Dr Carole Weydert
Former CERN scientist

IT IS BOTH UNUSUAL and heartening to see complex, modern scientific concepts being applied to literature in a way that shows these two worlds – which seem so far apart – can, under certain conditions, actually touch. The concepts from theoretical physics which are woven into lisa's story are, in order of complexity: symmetry, unification and dichotomy.

Let's tackle the first one. Symmetry means invariance. It refers to a lack of change in a system; something that persists, abides. As such, symmetries have become an important part of many theories. The presence of a symmetry can allow an object after a transformation to be identified as the same one as before the transformation, despite all its changes.

It has been proven that there is a fundamental relationship between the symmetries present in a system and the existence of a set of related conservation laws. This is called Noether's theorem and woks at various levels. In space-time, for example, energy conservation can be shown to be a direct consequence of an 'invariance under time translations'; conservation of linear momentum is a direct consequence of invariance under spatial translations; and conservation of angular momentum is a consequence of invariance under space under rotations. The image that pops into my head here is the one of the ice skater, spinning on his own axis under increasing speed as he draws his extended arms in. As angular momentum is simply the product of speed and spatial extension, conservation of this quantity entails that, since taking in the arms reduces spatial extension, it will increase rotational speed as a consequence. All that is simply because of the structure of space-time. There are even implications of Noether's theorem at a quantum level; for example, with conservation of the electric charge.

Then there is the concept of broken symmetries, which refers to states in which a symmetry that existed before, is not there anymore. The fate of a system is often decided by the smallest of fluctuations. For example, picture sitting with friends at diner at a nice round table. Each one of you has, next to the main plate, a small plate where the bread goes. As long as nobody touches his bread, the system is completely symmetric, you could either chose the plate on your right or on your left. But the moment someone takes a nibble, the symmetry is broken and each and everyone has to follow suit, there is no choice anymore. (So think about the consequences of what you're doing next time you reach for a bite!)

Here again, this beautiful concept in quantum field theory gives rise to actual physically observable consequences. The Higgs mechanism, for example, involves symmetry breaking. It is thought that only a picosecond after the white-hot big bang, the decrease in temperature caused spontaneous symmetry-breaking of the Higgs field, giving rise to the masses of the 'weak force carrier-particles', the W and Z bosons.

So we saw that symmetry brings order to the chaos, it soothes the brain by giving it patterns to cling to, conveying trust and, if not yet understanding, at least the promise that something is at work here. Symmetry also implies that you need less information to describe the system than we perhaps previously thought we needed, since one part always repeats itself. This idea of a small ensemble of information to describe a large variety of observables is at the core of the quest of a theory of everything. As lisa's story explains, physicists currently know of four fundamental forces: electromagnetism, the weak (nuclear) force, the strong (nuclear) force and gravity. As indicated by the name, electricity and magnetism have already been merged into one entity: when you observe the effects of these two forces, they seem very different. But they can actually be described by one common framework, the electromagnetic force. In the late 50s, physicists took a step further, showing that at very high temperatures, two of the remaining forces – the weak nuclear force and electromagnetism combine to form the 'electroweak' force. To go even further, when interpolating at even higher energies, it seems that the coupling constants of the electroweak and the strong force converge, indicating that here also, we might be in the presence of a common source. A theory that claims at these high energies all these forces are indistinguishable is called a 'GUT', a 'grand unified theory'.

As the prospects of this venture are so promising, there is always the temptation to go even further: do the same to the electroweak and strong force, on one side, and gravity on the other; that is to have a 'ToE', a theory of everything. Unfortunately, or fortunately, depending on your personal taste (and thirst for research), nature seems to have levelled up somewhat here. It's like the video game *Zelda*, when you think you've already worked out how to solve it, there's always some kind of new twist and you have to be inventive yet again.

The biggest stumbling block in uniting these forces is that there is not yet a quantum theory of gravitation. While in quantum theory, the electroweak and the strong force are described by fields, which evolve in a static space-time (where space and time are purely coordinates we use to describe the value of the field at a given location), space-time steps to the front of the stage when we talk about gravity. For gravitation, the field interacts with itself, energy density variations give rise to curvature in space-time which again give rise to energy variations. There's no such thing in quantum theory and many ingenious alternatives are being imagined to circumvent this.

Now that we've laid the groundwork by shining some light on the concepts of symmetry and unification, let's come to the last word on our list, dichotomy. Dichotomy is about contrast. About the state of being two, not one. The physical manifestation of dichotomy is 'difference in potential'. This difference creates a tension, which gives the system an innate tendency to act. For example, a difference in electric potential can give rise to an electric current. Even in us humans, be it in our conversations, our art, our theatre, differences make us act. It is, in fact, the start of any story. Contrast creates tension, which makes things interesting. Lisa's story contains a multitude of dichotomies.

In physics, the most obvious dichotomy is the one between matter and force. In the Standard Model of particle physics, matter and force are represented by two types of particles with very different properties. Matter is made up of fermions, obeying Fermi statistics: two of these particles cannot be in the same place. Forces are represented by bosons, behaving according to the Bose-Einstein statistics. Supersymmetry, sometimes called 'SUSY', is a theory that postulates that there is, at high enough energies, a symmetry between bosons and fermions. Meaning that at some level, they are related. More than related, in fact, indistinguishable. It's just that at lower energies, they behave differently. That is to say, at lower energies, the supersymmetry disappears, it gets broken.

SUSY is a beautiful theory (because, after all, symmetry *is* beautiful – remember how it soothes the brain!) but its postulated observables still remain to be found. Current colliders, like the LHC at CERN, have pushed back further and further the boundaries of what we can detect in terms of massive fundamental particles, but have yet to make any observations about supersymmetry.

You could argue: what the hell are we thinking: doubling the number of particles in our model just to have a more 'beautiful' theory (and fixing a few problems on the way)? But this magic trick has worked before. The requirement of Lorentz invariance via the Dirac equation postulated the existence of the positron (the anti-matter electron), and a whole world of anti-matter particles like it. And sure enough the positron was then found. This is just one of several examples of a theory's structural mathematical properties leading people to first *believe* in 'the other side of the mirror' and then, ultimately, to *discover* it.

Lisa's story offers several effective metaphors for dichotomy. The first is Bea/Nabila. As a character, she is like a combination of two eigenstates in an uncollapsed wavefunction – one Bea, one Nabila – internally, always feeling like a superposition of both, but externally often being forced to be one of the other. A second metaphor for dichotomy is offered by Bea/Nabila's father, the physicist. His comfort zone is the abstract world of ideas and physical theories, but when he takes the solutions he's learned in that sphere and tries to solve his real world problems with them, the results are mixed. Perhaps a third metaphor lies in the deepest themes of the story: the dichotomy of nature versus nurture. Can the two ever be consolidated?

So there we have it: a quest (don't worry if you hear the *Zelda* theme music in your head at this point, you're not alone!) among many physicists, for the ultimate description of nature; that is to say a theory with a very small number of rules, which could yet describe everything we currently know of the universe. Many physicists believe such an ultimate theory exists, and have dedicated their professional lives to the pursuit of it. But maybe they're doing so in vain. In a now famous academic lecture, *Gödel and the End of Physics* – a title more reminiscent of a *Doctor Who* episode than an academic paper – physicist Stephen Hawking evoked the possibility that an ultimate theory might not exist. Ever since the formulation of Gödel's theorem, it has become clear that a finite system of axioms is not sufficient to prove every result in mathematics. (Gödel proved this by talking about statements that refer to themselves and how these always lead to paradoxes. For instance the statement 'This statement is false' (if it's true it's false, and vice versa), or 'The barber of Corfu shaves every man who does not shave himself' (who shaves the barber?). Hawking argued that there's a chance we can never formulate a theory of everything in a finite number of consistent statements (let alone in a very small number of statements, the way GUTs and ToEs hope). Why? Because we are *in* the system. Because we are not angels, who can stand outside it. We and the models we make of the universe are part of the universe we are describing. Same goes for an author. As much as they try to hide it, a part of them is always included in the story.

After inducing so much doubt to our idea of an ultimate theory, Hawking offered a small note of optimism: that being everlasting job security for physicists. There will always remain an infinite number of things for human beings to discover about the universe. Something that presumably also applies to authors. There'll always be more work to do.

Afterglow

Bidisha

MIRA DISCOVERED THE PACKAGE in the loos at Westfield Shopping Centre. She usually went every Saturday, seeing a film at the Vue, getting a frozen yogurt from Pink Berry, watching shoppers going up and down the escalators. It made her feel connected.

'That's not healthy. You're poisoning yourself,' said a random dad in the food court. He was a wiry, suddenly-discovered-triathlons-and-velodromes type eating a superfood salad bowl.

'I don't talk to strangers,' she shot back, 'in case you're some kind of disgusting pervert that sexually harasses teenage girls in public.'

A security guard glanced over and the man coloured, grabbed his Nike bag and slipped off.

Ten minutes later Mira was forcing her empty frozen yoghurt tub into the hatch of the sanitary pads disposal box in a cubicle in the ladies'. The box knocked against something on the floor.

In the corner of the loo cubicle was a small, dense looking package. There were stickers all over it, saying BIOHAZARD and CAUTION. Ordinarily Mira would never touch anything from any surface of any toilet ever, but the package looked official. It was addressed to Hammersmith Hospital and there was no stamp. Mira knew the hospital well – it was up the road from their flat on the Du Cane estate, near Wormwood Scrubs prison.

She picked up the package, put it in her bag and came out of the cubicle.

'Was any lady in here looking for a package?' she asked a cleaner.

'I just do the floors,' said the woman.

Mira got the bus to the hospital, sitting with her bag on her lap. She felt conspicuous and weirdly guilty, as if she'd stolen something.

The hospital was crowded and grimy as always. Mira imagined all the ill people peppered around the rooms, groaning in the corridors and struggling in the toilets while their visitors queued at the Costa Coffee stand and browsed in the little shop that sold flowers, toys and chocolate. The whole thing was just completely depressing.

She approached the main desk. Pinned to the noticeboards were letters and cards from former patients. The woman at the counter was around Mira's mum's age. She looked up and smiled.

'Mira! Everything okay? Mum okay?'

'Hi Stevie – she's fine. She's resting.'

'Did you leave something behind? I can call lost property?'

'No, no, I haven't lost anything.'

Mira put the package on the counter. Nurse Stevie eyed it.

'What's this?' she said.

'I found it in the loos at Westfield. It's addressed to here. I thought it might be important...'

Mira trailed off. Nurse Stevie's colleague joined her and the two women stood together behind the desk, shoulder to shoulder. They exchanged glances.

'And you say you found it?' asked the colleague, looking Mira up and down.

'It looked official so I brought it in,' said Mira, her voice small. 'It could be an organ. From a donor.'

Mira tapped the corner of the package with her fingertip and imagined a tiny heart beating inside, packed in ice.

'Don't touch it, it could be anything. One moment,' said

Nurse Stevie while the other woman maintained her narrow stare. Stevie picked up the phone. 'We need security here. There should be a log of packages coming in.' She angled the phone receiver away from her mouth. 'Mira, can you go with my colleague for a sec?'

'Why? I haven't done anything.'

'Just go with him.'

Mira turned and found herself face to chest with a young security guard who had precisely no muscle anywhere but was still intimidatingly massive. When he said 'Come with me, yeah?' she followed without a word.

They went into a side room that contained three plastic chairs and a coffee table. The height of the chairs didn't match the height of the table. The walls were beige, with posters warning visitors against abusing hospital staff.

'This is the crying room. This is the room where you get the bad news,' said Mira. 'I've been here before.'

'Loads of people have,' said the guard.

He left and stood just outside the door, with his legs apart. Mira sat at the edge of her chair. *Oh my god, they think I'm some kind of terrorist.* Her mind raced. Would they call home? That was the last thing her mother needed. Would they call the school? She'd be expelled, she'd never sit her exams. Would they call the police and put her on a watchlist? That would be the end of it.

The guard pushed open the door with his giant teddy bear knuckles and a frazzled man in a rumpled shirt and jeans came in, grasping a stack of papers.

'I haven't done anything,' Mira blurted out as soon as the man sat down.

'Of course you haven't – please don't think that,' he said, clutching the papers to his lap.

'I *don't* think that,' said Mira.

The man massaged his neck.

'So. The thing is. The package from Westfield supermarket–'

'Shopping centre–'

'Is radioactive.'

He looked at her. She looked back, blinking in slow motion.

'And that means what?' she said.

'Radioactive medicine. Radiopharmaceuticals.'

'That means nothing to me,' said Mira.

The man spread his fingers. They trembled.

'You nervous?' said Mira.

The man froze, his eyes bugging slightly. *He thinks I'm tough,* Mira realised. A nails-hard local girl, possibly a truant. One of those girls who took off her hoops before she fought on the sad little triangle of grass called Shepherds Bush Green. Mira relaxed.

'Let me think…' she mused. 'The package wasn't meant to go astray. You can blame me. You can blame someone else. Or *you* can be blamed – if word gets out. That's what this is about.'

The man was visibly holding his breath. Mira snatched the papers off his lap. He flinched. Mira lounged back and leafed through the closely typed pages.

'Those are confidential legal documents,' the man stuttered.

'Then what're you doing waving them around?' She didn't bother looking at him. 'You think I'm gonna go out and tell everyone how unsafe it is here. But the thing is, I don't care about that. My mum's being treated for breast cancer – did Stevie tell you that?'

'N-n-no… I'm sorry to hear that,' he mumbled.

'The only thing I care about is my mum. Not your package and not your reputation. So I'm not getting involved in any back and forth, with you, or anyone, about anything.'

The man rubbed his temples.

'Let me explain,' he said. 'These are difficult times, what with funding and politics and staffing and morale and what have you. And no one's supposed to be wandering about with parcels. It's supposed to go from one hospital to another, in a secured container, in a secured van, by a specialist company. Not be chucked in a handbag and schlepped around town.'

Mira tuned him out. She paused at a letter with WARNING

NOTICE written at the top. It came from a fake-sounding body called the Office for Nuclear Regulation.

'In conclusion,' she read aloud, 'we have found dangerous shortfalls against our radiation risk assessment for the transport of the material. It is clear from our investigation that you do not have appropriate plans in place to respond to the loss of material and a prior improvement notice issued under the Health and Safety at Work Act 1974 has not been actioned. Therefore –'

'Yes, well, that's enough of that, thank you,' the man interrupted.

Mira gave the papers back to him and stood up.

'I got it. I don't care. What do you want?'

The man took a biro out of his shirt pocket, staring up at her abjectly.

'We'd like you to sign a statement saying you won't hold us liable.'

'I won't hold you liable if what?'

'If... anything happens.'

Mira put her hands on her hips and stood over him.

'Like what?'

'Just anything,' he peeped, shrinking down.

'If anything happens to me or if anything happens to you?'

'Well – either.'

'Forget it. And if you hassle me I'll tell everyone.'

She walked out, shaking her head and steaming with disbelief. What was it her grandmother always said? No good deed goes unpunished.

The security guard was nowhere to be seen. Mira looked back towards reception, but it was crowded with official-seeming people who looked like TV detectives. She went the opposite way. A couple of turnings later she saw an emergency door propped open with a bin. She went through it and out into the car park, where Nurse Stevie and the security guard were smoking. They looked sheepish when they noticed her. The guard threw his butt on the ground and ambled back inside.

'Mira, I am so sorry,' said Nurse Stevie, stubbing out her

cigarette delicately on the wall and putting it in the bin, 'I had no idea they'd call the legal rep.'

'He tried to get me to sign something. I legged it.'

'Good. Well done. They shouldn't have done that. You're underage, that's illegal in itself.'

Nurse Stevie glanced around, although there was no need. The constant buses, taxis, delivery vans and motorbikes on the main road easily muffled her voice.

'Management must be scared. Whoever let go of that package did something really risky. They'll be kicking themselves.'

'Am I in trouble?'

'Of course not.' Nurse Stevie patted Mira's shoulder. Her touch was warm.

'I don't care about the package,' said Mira. All she wanted to do was go home. She swerved towards the main road. Nurse Stevie followed her.

'Mira – wait – there's one more thing. Materials like the one in the package – they're live ingredients, we use them to diagnose and treat certain conditions.'

'So?' Mira kept walking.

'We'll need to get you tested.'

'Why?'

Stevie touched Mira's arm again and Mira stopped walking.

'Even one contact can leave a trace. We'll need to screen you. For cell damage.'

★

Twelve years later, in April 2022, Mira got off the tram from central Geneva and walked the short distance to the CERN reception in the clear Swiss air. In the distance lay the crinkling outline of the Jura mountain range. The sun was sharp and she felt her skin burn, a pretty freckling that was actually a sign of harm – immediate molecular disintegration. Nobody would sunbathe if they could see themselves under a microscope, she thought, putting up her hood.

Getting into CERN always made her feel like a secret agent. She entered at Gate B and heaved open the stiff metal door of an old-fashioned phone box with frosted glass sides. Inside, there was no phone, only a keyboard and mouse and a grimy computer screen. Mira typed in her name and visitor number. The screen flashed up ACCEPTED and the door clicked open to let her out.

Across the road, a dark-haired guard came out of the security booth. He was wearing a blue military uniform, although he wasn't armed – not yet, anyway. If the war progressed, he would be. Mira approached with her passport held open. The guard checked it and nodded.

'I haven't seen you in a while,' she said in English, putting the passport back in her bag. Her French wasn't yet good enough to communicate freely, but she was taking classes every Saturday in Geneva.

'I was in the UK, in Liverpool, I went to see the football,' said the guard, his accent quick and light.

There was a zipping sound from inside the booth as Mira's temporary pass was printed out. She was a year into her PhD here and was working as a safety officer as part of her research. It would be another few months before she completed her probationary period and got a permanent CERN pass, and it might be years before she could junk her blue Brexit passport and apply for Swiss citizenship.

'And how was the game?' she asked.

'It was really good fun, I drank in all the pubs,' he grinned.

'And... how was the atmosphere, in England?'

'Oh, you know,' he said diplomatically. 'It is an island, you cannot expect them to be so worried about...'

He jerked his head towards his booth's TV, which showed a news broadcast in French, with the words *Bombardment in the East: Russia Advances* scrolling across footage of a destroyed street. Apartment blocks, a school and a row of shops had been turned into heaped debris and blackened rubble.

The guard put his hand over his walkie-talkie and thumbed

the off switch.

'You know the archaeologists left? The ones that were digging in the Roman village,' he said.

A few years ago, they had found a settlement for centurions at the crossroads, a detachment served by a forge, a stable and a livery.

'They didn't give notice?' asked Mira.

The guard shook his head.

'In a few centuries it will be exactly like this again, they will find CERN and I will be the skeleton of the guard on the road,' he said.

He went into his booth, took Mira's pass from the printer, fitted it into a holder and lanyard and gave it to her.

'Keep it on at all times, please,' he said, as he did every day. 'Be safe.'

'I will. You too.'

They waved goodbye.

Mira walked down the central route of the CERN campus. The blocky buildings and neat walkways, the roads designed considerately with lots of space to turn, the careful signposting of the buildings all spoke of sense and order.

Every time she did this walk, she felt a pang that her mother and grandmother couldn't see her. All of Hammersmith Hospital's efforts didn't save anything for her family and the hospital itself closed after a failed fundraising drive. The Du Cane estate became notorious when an investigation into pollution levels linked it to several asthma deaths of children who lived there.

Mira shuddered whenever she thought about the place, yet everything she'd studied related to that time. Her mother died when Mira was twenty and studying biochemistry and physics at King's College. That froze her life for a year. She stayed in the same flat she'd grown up in, with her grandmother, and did her postgrad. Then her grandmother died and Mira collected her second lot of unwanted inheritance. Her MSc supervisor told her about the doctoral programme at CERN and with nothing to tie her to England, she went. She had no intention of returning.

Today, Mira was giving a delegation from the World Health Organisation a tour for their annual safety assessment. She spotted them easily at the meeting point outside Building 39, the guest hostel. They were urbane and diffident, a well-groomed group in dark face masks.

'Welcome, everyone,' she said, taking them to the reception of the Visitors' Centre.

They went inside and stood in no-nonsense silence, waiting for her to do her job.

'I'm Mira, I'm a doctoral student and safety officer here at CERN, focusing on radiation and its impacts. I appreciate you making the time for this visit, when there's so much going on—'

'And many urgent things to talk about,' one man interrupted. He was tall and thin, with balding hair and a clipped voice.

Mira fell silent. The man blushed.

'I am sorry, I didn't mean to be rude. I am Stefan. I was saying we have been looking at the headlines on our journey here.'

'Our colleagues are consulting in Brussels this morning,' explained a woman near to Mira. Her name tag read Dr Celeste Poon. 'So we are very concerned.'

'Of course, of course,' Mira relented.

After a few lines of introduction, she pressed a switch on the wall and it lit up with flickering old footage. A man's voice proclaimed, in a hilariously plummy English accent:

'CERN. The seat of global scientific discovery. An intellectual haven from the world. Created as a postwar enterprise in 1954, many of Europe's fundamental scientists having already left for the United States of America.' There was a parp of trumpets. 'For peace. For unity.' A drumroll. 'Global collaboration. Unite nations and contribute to a better world.'

Usually when this clip finished, visitors would laugh. The film was like a relic from a time when women always wore hats. Instead, a sigh went through the group.

'That was the future once,' said Dr Poon. 'Such optimism.'

'There still is, isn't there?' said Mira.

'Optimism about the future?'

'Well – maybe not optimism – and maybe not the future as such. But Pakistan, Turkey, Japan, even the banks of the Volga contributed parts of our beam and the magnet and the tracker. They were united by scientific curiosity. I still feel it when I see all the different nationalities here. CERN survived through the whole of the Cold War.'

'The first Cold War,' said Stefan.

Mira said nothing. Representing CERN, her job was to be solicitous above everything, and to never get political.

Dr Poon and the rest of the delegation walked around, looking at the displays. So much technology that was once cutting edge now looked like bits of junk, like the magnet system made from iron with a load of copper wound around it. The experiments' progress used to be measured by gigantic banks of computers. Now, the equipment gleamed like alien technology, while laptops assimilated the data. There were storage stacks in glass cases, down which robot arms whizzed, snatching up old tape reels with their metal pickers.

'It seems to me that many people here are obsessed with the past,' said Dr Poon. 'To you, the beginning of the universe was not a long time ago. And the end of the universe is not far away.'

'And in the middle, we invented the internet,' said Mira. She indicated a tattered, typewritten piece of paper in a display case. 'That's the original proposal, from 1989.' She addressed their backs as they vied to look at it. 'A lot of what we develop here is an offshoot of the main missions. You'll understand when I take you down. You can see what we're working on.'

She escorted them to the adjacent warehouse, which had fences all around it. The door was wired shut.

'There are only a few access points,' explained Mira, sliding her pass over the scanner. 'We'll only be let in during a fixed time. You'll notice the cameras everywhere.'

Just as they were entering, a group of young people came

out. They were barely out of their teens, fully togged up in protective suits, with heavy boots, gloves and masks. Each was carrying a black plastic utility box. They stopped in formation some distance away and the young man at the front gave a jokey military salute.

'Good morning, Ms Gazaleh,' he said. 'We were up clearing the roof of the accelerator.'

'Thank you, Hans,' said Mira. 'Send me your forms and I'll sign you off.'

The youngsters nodded. They were just kids to her, recently qualified engineers brought in to maintain the riskiest parts of the facility, thrilled even to set foot on the campus. They would all put it on their CVs, just as she did.

'Don't forget to get scanned,' Mira told Hans.

'We're going to the dosimeters now,' he nodded.

'It must be hard, working in those suits, so high up,' commented Dr Poon, watching them go.

Mira nodded. Every time she saw these diligent, fresh-faced crews she thought about what happened after the Chernobyl disaster. The Soviets had secretly brought in young people to clean up, offering them a sick deal: if they worked on the radiation site, they could knock time off their military service. Two minutes at Chernobyl bought them out of two years of drills and bootcamps and war simulations at military school. Would Hans and his friends be okay with a bargain like that? Mira wanted to ask, but it wasn't her place. Either way, it was a distasteful trade-off: die hard and fast in actual combat or play a longer war against invisible radiation. If the Russian advance continued, Hans and his team could still be conscripted and end up facing both fates.

'We have to be careful at all times,' said Mira, glancing at Dr Poon. She wondered how much of what she said would end up in the delegation's report. 'The dosimeters measure how much radiation they accumulated.'

Dr Poon nodded:

'We are aware. In the worst case scenarios, like Chernobyl of course, there have been some bad outcomes in terms of birth defects, but even then the overall cancer deaths were not increased too much. Our guidelines state never to let pregnant women work in these environments.'

'Huh! Celeste! Just how many deformed children and cancer deaths is too many? I say *one*,' said Stefan, pacing the gravel outside the warehouse and staring up at the security cameras.

'I know that. These disasters are always with us. We always consider them,' Dr Poon replied.

'You'll never get down to safety-zero,' Mira said before things got too tetchy. 'If you're too safety conscious you can't even eat a banana. It contains potassium and that's radioactive, at a low level.'

Inside the warehouse, the industrial space was massive around them. From the entrance, they could look down into the basement, across the ground floor and up almost to roof level. It was like being in a giant factory. The scale of it never failed to amaze Mira.

'Don't worry, if we fall into a black hole, we fall in as one,' joked Dr Poon to Stefan. 'The tunnel has held up since 1989, it will be the safest place to be.'

'Inside a nuclear reactor?' Stefan snorted.

'Actually — I'm sorry — I have to correct you,' said Mira. 'Black holes are one thing, but what we're doing here's another matter. And it isn't a nuclear reactor, it's a nuclear accelerator.' Ordinarily these blunders would make her cringe — the way people, even high-up well-educated people seemed to know nothing about the world they lived in — but something in the way Dr Poon and Stefan were eyeing each other made her smile as she observed them.

'Whatever it is, if the blast comes, we'll find some aluminium foil to wrap you in, Stefan,' said Dr Poon.

'There's plenty of it downstairs,' said Mira. She added, 'It's safe.'

'Safe? Between a war and a nuclear accelerator? What a choice!' said Stefan.

'If there's an emergency, we have multiple warning systems in place. And we have a full bunker system and air filtration,' said Mira. 'We're not going to end up living here while Putin bombs CERN in the next ninety minutes – I promise.'

'It is not funny,' said Stefan. 'What you see in the news is only a fraction of what's happening right now in Europe.'

'And everywhere else in the world. But you weren't bothered about it then,' Mira said, and immediately regretted it. If anyone reported her talking back like that, she would be finished.

Stefan pressed his lips together but didn't say anything, thank goodness. Dr Poon gave Mira a bright stare of warning. Mira received it, took a deep breath and resumed, mortified.

'Apologies. Please discount that.' She indicated a row of yellow metal lockers. 'If you could put your belongings in there. Otherwise the magnets in your phones and credit cards can all be wiped. It may also affect your watches and fitness trackers, if you're wearing any.'

The group became silent and compliant and put their things in the lockers. Mira opened a large metal basket and drew out a radiation monitor for each delegate. They took them with fascination.

'Have a play,' encouraged Mira. 'The yellow and black markings on the wall show where radiation is evident but it's less than you'll get when you fly home. Bear in mind the anti-risk formula: minimise your time, maximise your distance, maximise physical protection. Same as the Covid guidelines, really.'

Next, she took them to a table on which there were about a dozen plastic hard hats.

'Everyone, put one on and tighten it so it doesn't fall off when you tip your head.'

Wearing the heavy white hats, breathing through masks, with radiation monitors around their necks, the group suddenly looked anonymous, uniform.

'I need to go through the retinal scanner, then I'll let you in,' said Mira.

She stood at the entrance of the airlock, stepped into the narrow green scanning tube and stared into the scanner, trying to align with the guide marks. The scan failed. She shuffled back and tried again. The scan succeeded and the doors opened. She came out on the other side and opened the security gate.

The delegates filed onto a hammered metal landing alongside a rack of vertical tubes of liquid argon. On this side, the air felt thicker, heavier. The panorama had its own industrial beauty, with wide foil tubing and metal pipes veining the ceilings and walls, clanging staircases and a bright rubber-and-metal feel. It was like a Lego space station imagined by genius children. There was no human sound, only the clanging of machine-work and the wheezing of fans and ventilation, the clicking and banging of hidden systems. The apparatus was built so that it really wasn't possible to get inside except for repairs and decommissioning.

On the lower level was a bank of disassembled machinery covered by plastic sheets. They were in the blue zone: the girders and railings were painted bright blue, while the pipes were orange. Taking up the entire side view was a mass of silver pipes and joints. To get even closer, they would have to wiggle their way through the scaffolding.

'This is not great for people with vertigo,' Mira admitted, 'or claustrophobia.'

There was a rustling from deep within the pile of equipment and up popped a woman in an oversized linen jacket and fingerless gloves.

'Everyone, this is Dr Ingrid Meyer, one of our most distinguished residents.'

Ingrid was one of Mira's closest friends at CERN. They had met during Mira's first week, when Ingrid refused to let Mira eat lunch alone.

'Who are you – the UN? The League of Nations? UNESCO?' asked Ingrid, looking down at them.

'We're from the World Health Organisation, Dr Meyer,' said Dr Poon.

'Ah! Then what I tell you today, you will certainly not understand,' Ingrid declared. 'Because you are biologists, not physicists.'

'We have already received some clarification,' admitted Stefan.

Dr Meyer disappeared from view and then re-emerged at floor level. Nestled in the crook of her arm was a green Thermos flask, which she unscrewed as she talked.

'So! How often do we get a portal that leads us to dark matter? We don't know. You think we do everything, we know everything – no, we know nothing!'

She looked at each person in the delegation in turn as she held the plastic cup and poured steaming black coffee into it.

'Ingrid, please, you're not supposed to do that in here,' said Mira.

'But there are many liquids that boil at much higher temperatures, much more dangerous, and toxic gases, not to mention radiation sickness and helium leaks. So a bit of coffee is nothing. I can offer something stronger.' Ingrid opened an important looking industrial cabinet. Inside was a mini fridge. Inside the mini fridge were lots of tiny bottles from the CERN vending machines, along with a couple of large liquor bottles. 'I offer you gin and juice – a choice of orange juice or pineapple. Or whisky and coke. However, I would not light a cigarette. A fire down here would be a very bad idea.'

'We're here for a safety assessment Dr Meyer,' said Mira pointedly.

Ingrid shrugged, let the mini fridge door swing shut, took a slurp of coffee and addressed the group, who were twisting around staring at everything.

'How many of you understand physics even a little bit?' Ingrid demanded.

A few hands went up, timidly.

'Don't think of protons as stones that you smash together, think of them as carriers of energy. So when you collide the protons you are adding energy to energy and so the proton becomes… very… heavy… with… energy,' she said, her hands pulsing in front of her boobs to stress each word.

She pointed emphatically downwards.

'Do you know what is down here? Do you know what is the main purpose of our mission? We are building a time machine! Yes! What is the experiment made of but a time machine, a 14,000 tonne camera and a massive worldwide computer to handle all the information that comes out of that photograph? A phenomenal amount of data. And the computers you see are very, very clever – they do not make a decision about what is interesting, they make a decision about what is *not* interesting. They leave out the mundane. Although, in my opinion, nothing is mundane. Everything is interesting.'

A big brown rat shot out of a storage bin and leapt into the next container along, falling in with a thump and a squeal. The delegation shot back, shuddering. The first bin slid on its castors and something long and thin flashed out from underneath – the chain that secured the bins together had come loose. Mira picked the chain up. She'd have to talk to Ingrid about keeping her area orderly.

'Dr Meyer,' she said, keeping her voice steady, 'please tell me you are not keeping a pet in here. Because that would be forbidden.'

'This cavern's full of giant mutant rats and electronics,' deadpanned Ingrid. 'You think I am joking but maybe I am not.' She touched her foot to her equipment then tried to pull away. It dragged. 'You see that? The field pulls on the steel toe cap of my boot. It's like wading into the sea.'

The floor beneath them began to tremble and a juddering noise made every joint in the place creak. It got louder and louder, until the delegation put their hands to their ears. After reaching a peak, the clunky jackhammering wound down and stopped, leaving everyone's teeth rattling.

'That's Goderick Cryer,' said Mira, raising her voice above the last echoes of the noise. 'One of CERN's most long-standing appointees.'

'Go, by all means, see what the excitement is,' scowled Ingrid, rolling her eyes, shrugging, turning away and making a shooing gesture all at once. 'Here at CERN we are like a family, so not everyone is nice or kind or good. All these men with their *big penises,* racing to win a Nobel Prize. One man pissed on another man's papers last week. Yes – he urinated on it. The paper came out in the top journal and we printed it out to discuss it for a conference and before the plenary, this man went to the desk and that is what he did to the paper of his rival.' She gestured to her trouser area. 'We all saw it. It did not matter, they printed another copy. But it was symbolic, no? "I piss on you, you piss on me, I piss on your work, I piss on your ideas, look at my penis, my penis is my brain and my brain is my penis and so is yours, you make your work, I show you my penis"… But why?…'

She went back behind the mound, still talking to herself. Charmed and tittering, the group followed Mira to the corner of the blue level where a lift shaft tunnelled up through the layers of the facility. One day, not even that far in the future, robots would patrol the walkways, maintain the equipment and take readings and measurements, while the human scientists observed from a safe distance.

Mira pressed the button for the lift. A metallic wheeze sounded above them, clanging as it descended closer. The platform shook as the lift clicked into place. Mira pushed the doors open.

'Everything here is so heavy,' she groaned. 'Anything that can open or close has to be sealable in case of failure.'

'Failure?' said Stefan.

'System failure,' said Mira as everyone went in. 'For anyone who doesn't like lifts, it'll be a thirty-three second descent. So, count to thirty-three.'

The lift went down. It had two stages, one for -80 metres and the other for -100. Mira noticed a red light on the information panel flashing slowly. She frowned and watched it for a while. There was no alarm and she couldn't remember what the light meant. Maybe it flashed every time the lift moved.

The lift hit the bottom. This area had green doors and white floors, green railings and green and red girders. Circus colours, thought Mira, every time she came down here. The walls were of dark, chipped, raw rock. The lighting didn't brighten the general dankness, but it all added to the atmosphere.

'Where is the main apparatus?' asked Stefan. His voice echoed.

'In the next chamber, behind seven metres of wall,' said Mira. 'But we can't visit, it's too dangerous.' She tapped her sternum. 'Can you feel it? The pull? If you spend four or five hours in here you feel tired. Haemoglobin has magnetic properties. I don't know how Ingrid does it.'

Out of her pocket she took a metal key with a square end.

'I have to be very careful with these,' she said. She fitted it into the keyhole in the security door and turned it a quarter to the left, then another quarter. 'There are six hundred interlock keys in the facility, if any one of them's missing it's not possible to start the accelerator.'

The doors parted. They were several inches thick, with a lead core.

'We're going towards the experimental well,' explained Mira. 'You'll see, the closer we get, the fewer personnel there are.'

They went in single file along the narrow walkway. Mira trailed her fingertips over the cave wall.

'As you see, they had to dig down to a stable layer of rock so the equipment doesn't shift about with soils and clays, or mineral deposits. That's why it's so deep. This layer goes right down into the feet of the Jura mountains.'

Stefan and Dr Poon were walking close behind her. Stefan was leaning down, talking into Dr Poon's ear.

'When I was a boy, my parents took me touring the Jura. The mountains gave their name to the Jurassic era – but Jura is only an old Celtic word for forest! It doesn't have anything to do with mountains – or dinosaurs!' He seemed to find this hilarious. Dr Poon said nothing, but she didn't move away either, and Stefan went on, 'But the countryside is getting more and more built up. Places that are now part of the urban landscape used to be fields.'

'The area's changing because of all the people working for international organisations like yours and mine,' said Mira. Dr Poon nudged Stefan and they put some space between themselves.

They arrived at a green door with a yellow sign saying RADIATION. Immediately, all the radiation monitors emitted a long beep.

'It's just to wake you up,' Mira grinned at the startled delegation. 'We are in a higher risk zone, but remember what I said about aeroplane travel.'

She let them into the chamber and there, standing at his desk, surrounded by towering metal contraptions, stood Goderick Cryer. He shoved his desk drawer shut and loped towards them in scuffed cowboy boots. He had pitted red cheeks and some kind of dermatitis all over his hands. He wore black jeans, a black jacket and a black shirt that reeked – somehow not off-puttingly – of sweat.

'Finally,' he growled in a transatlantic accent.

The first time Mira met Dr Cryer, he did to her exactly what he did to every woman: gave a quick assessing glance and decided if she was fuckable or not (she wasn't, to him). And that was that. She occasionally saw him drinking in the canteen with students or having dinner at the pizzeria with his 'partner', a beautiful if silent young local.

Goderick's eye hitched momentarily on a tall, willowy woman from the delegation, then slid off again.

'Thanks for comin' down,' he drawled. 'If you stand in a semicircle you'll be able to hear me. I'm Goderick – you can call me God.' He paused for laughter which didn't come. 'And this is Ultra G. G for gravity, not Goderick. That's the new experiment, it's gonna be huge. You know why? 'Cause at a quantum level, we don't actually have a good theory of gravity. We understand classical gravity – the stars, the planets – but we don't know a whole lot about *gravity* gravity. It's crazy difficult – tweaking the apparatus to try and make more. Everything we do is, by definition, new. Nobody else can do what we do.'

He looked around the group, his whole body tensed, the spider veins crawling up his neck like a crimson tattoo. Everyone looked politely back.

Goderick paced, occasionally scratching himself.

'I'm gonna tell you what's on my mind. I know you're here for the beam but lemme ask you something: what about antimatter? What happens if you have some antimatter and then release it? What happens if I drop antimatter? What happens? We think, based on current theory, that it'll just fall. But we don't really know until we measure it. Maybe it's a little different. That would be really cool – that would mean rewriting all the textbooks.' His eyes glittered. 'That's what I'm thinkin' about. When matter and antimatter meet, they explode into light, but there was a small asymmetry favouring matter right at the start – and that's why we're here. It's really an accident that we're here. Isn't it? So we have a problem – we shouldn't be here. Why did the universe choose matter instead of antimatter? Why?'

He lunged towards the tall woman in the group. She leaned away and he immediately swung off. He waved his arms around, indicating the general gloom.

'You know what? This is a freak show. We shouldn't be here. The beam's down there, the rock's full of water, the caverns are like bubbles. They froze the ground by pumping in liquid nitrogen to stop it filling up with water. They created an artificial permafrost.' Goderick snorted and curled his lip. 'As if! Nothing's permanent.'

'Everything degrades,' agreed Dr Poon in a soothing voice, nodding, watching him carefully.

'Everything!' shouted Goderick. He was now walking in circles. 'She told you about energy, right? Meyer? Smashing energy together faster and faster? Well it's much more difficult to slow particles down than accelerate them. What Ingrid Meyer's doing – it's baby stuff, it's beginners' stuff, it's square one. I do the exact opposite. Why can we see all this matter in the universe but we can't see the antimatter? These particles are very rare and very, very hard to come by. For every "this" that exists, you can make anti-this.'

Every time he swooshed past, Mira grew a little more drained. She had always secretly envied the big egos she saw around her on campus, their ability to push themselves forward, to attract the attention of others. But not when she had to deal with them in person. She stared at the floor. She mustn't show her irritation at the spectacle of Goderick ranting on. Antimatter was the area he'd first made his name in, it was the thing he wanted to get funded and famous for. She shouldn't blame him – or be surprised – if he was trying to get noticed by well-funded, influential visitors.

She caught his eye and something in her expression made Goderick swerve back on track. He ran to his desk and began opening all the drawers and pulling out the contents.

'Where is it – where is it?' he said to himself.

'What're you looking for?' asked Mira.

'My pass key. We're going down there!'

'What? We can't!'

'Why can't we? Who says we can't?'

'They don't have clearance.'

'I have clearance.'

'For yourself. Not anyone else.'

Wherever the beam was shot, it created radioactivity in the targets and everywhere around. Mira wanted to stop him, but she couldn't. He was much more senior than her. Anyone in the facility would side with him.

'Who's checking?' he said.

'I'm checking.'

'What would you know, you're an intern.'

Goderick stood square-on to her, his eyes hard, the pass key swinging from his hand on a leather thong. Mira tightened her fist around the chain she'd picked up from Ingrid's floor. It seemed to quiver in her hand.

'Why don't we let them decide?' Goderick wheeled around.

The radiation monitors all beeped again and the group looked at Goderick with bright eyes, wary but tempted. Nobody would meet Mira's glance.

'We're missing half the universe,' said Goderick. 'Don't you want to see where it is?'

It was clear that the entire group very much wanted to see where it was.

Goderick ran to the far edge of the platform and clattered down the steps. The rest of the group followed, leaving Mira behind.

On the lower level, Goderick was crouching over a trapdoor in the floor. Five different security points demanded a unique key, a security code, a pass card, an iris scan and a five-finger fingerprint, and even then there was a manual locking system controlled by two metal dials. Goderick gripped the dials and turned them, sweating, while the group surrounded him.

'Antimatter. It's so simple,' he muttered. 'What's number one on the periodic table. What's number one? Come on! Everyone knows number one!'

'Hydrogen,' said Dr Poon. She was watching Goderick's hands clicking the dials.

'Exactly. Hydrogen. The stuff that makes the stars. Hydrogen likes to absorb and emit light. Hydrogen. One proton, one electron. So anti-hydrogen is one anti-proton and one anti-electron. Simple. The principle is simple. The only good thing about antimatter: if you lose it, you know it. I started working on this in the 1980s. Only in 2017 did we succeed in making anti-hydrogen. I'm ready for my next big breakthrough.'

He wrestled with the dial but his hands were so sweaty they lost their grip. He glared at Mira.

'You. Whatever your name is. Go back to my desk and find the Post-it note and get the code.'

'You wrote it down?' she said in disbelief.

Researchers received a new security code every week and were meant to memorise it, or use a cipher if they absolutely couldn't.

'Get the damn code,' he snarled.

Furious and humiliated, Mira went back up the steps to where Goderick's desk stood, a rickety old thing from the early days of CERN. She dropped Ingrid's chain into her pocket and began looking through the mess of papers and scribble-filled notebooks. Nothing had the code written on it.

Mira opened a drawer and there, sitting inside, she found a source. An actual source. A piece of radioactive material. It was supposed to be returned to the source box, a locked, protective container in a special room on campus. A student could get a radiation burn just from holding it. She gaped at it, dumbfounded.

She extended the drawer further. It was full of sources – little yellow discs and chunks, cute and dinky, one labelled 'Strontium 90'. Mira's heart was beating in her ears. Her hands began tingling – it could be a psychosomatic response or a real reaction. She forced herself to stay calm. Why was Goderick playing around with live source? These little things retained their charge, their afterglow, long after use. The whole desk was radioactive – the whole landing was. Was he so raddled by now that he didn't even notice?

'Come on, come on!' Goderick's shouts echoed up to her.

Mira sifted through the junk as fast as she could, her skin crawling, trying not to touch anything. Eventually she found the code on an old parking ticket. She returned, gritting her teeth. She couldn't challenge him in front of the delegation, it would be the end of CERN.

Goderick snatched the paper out of her hand, input the code and heaved the hatch open. He threw the paper aside. There were no stairs leading down from the trapdoor, only a thin ladder ending in darkness.

'Now take a look down there,' said Goderick.

One by one, the delegates went down, until only Mira and Goderick were left standing on either side of the trapdoor.

'Go on then,' he said.

'It's not safe.'

'Nothing's safe.'

'So if anything happens, you'll take responsibility?'

'Nothing's gonna happen, you should trust me.'

'I saw what's in your desk, I trust you zero.'

'You saw what's in my desk, what are you, fourteen years old? What's in my desk?'

'Source material. Live source.'

'So what? Isn't that what we're here for? Tell 'em! Go tell 'em about the source! They'll be crawling back up, begging to touch it! That's what they want: the real deal.'

He knocked the edge of trapdoor lightly with the side of his boot. It was so thick it didn't echo.

'You don't get down there, this thing's gonna reset itself,' he said. 'You're not meant to leave 'em alone, are ya?'

Seething, Mira approached the top of the ladder. Goderick didn't move even an inch, so she almost brushed the front of his body as she descended.

'Good girl,' he said. It made her want to puke.

The delegation was grouped at the base of the ladder, cowed by the machinery that hulked around them. The lighting was a throbbing red. The apparatus was like a metal whale suspended, seemingly for miles, held in place with titanic supports and giant bolts. It was noisy down there. Every length of metal, every girder, every nut and bolt, every ventilation tube, wire and vent trembled.

'What do the red lights mean?' asked Dr Poon, shouting through the loud, dredging churn.

'They indicate a magnetic field,' said Mira. 'We really need to be careful.'

Goderick climbed down the top two rungs of the ladder and hung off the side, one arm waving.

'Lemme show you something,' he cried.

'Haven't they seen enough?' said Mira.

'They haven't seen anything!'

He was surprisingly agile for a total wreck. He reached out like a trapeze artist and latched onto a thick metal lever, one of two set into the wall. His sleeve rode up and Mira saw that the inside of his forearm was burnt and discoloured. Goderick squeezed the lever down using his whole body weight.

The chugging noise turned into a dark, violent whine so loud that everyone crumpled, covering their ears. The sound grew more intense until the entire structure shook. Each of the radiation monitors let out a harsh squeal as loud as a police siren. The group forced their hands away from their ears and wrenched off the monitors, which sounded even more alarming as the noise bounced off the metal surfaces where they fell.

Next to them, a bank of long, narrow piston pumps squeezed down one by one, while the main tube clanged violently as if something was fighting to get out. Mira felt strange, wrong, as if her blood was surging. She could tell the others felt it too. They were beginning to writhe and squirm, clutching their chests.

The metal chain in Mira's pocket shot out and she caught the end just in time. It stood upright in the air, pointing like an arrow, with force. It angled and contorted, snapping into jagged shapes like a delicate weapon. It almost pulled itself out of her grip. If it shot off and wrapped around a component of the apparatus, all hell would break loose. Everyone stared at it. It looked unnatural – except that it was completely natural, metal reacting to magnetism.

'You see that?!' Goderick shouted. He was strung between the ladder and the lever. 'We're used to gravity being our strongest field. The closer we get to the magnet, the less true that becomes.'

'That's enough,' yelled Mira, struggling to keep hold of the chain.

She went towards him, the activated chain pinging and pointing in the warping field. Goderick reached down and whipped it out of her hand so forcefully that she staggered back, her palm smarting.

There was a cry of pain. The tall woman in the delegation was clutching her ears as lines of blood ran down her neck.

'It tore out my earrings!' she said. The magnetic field had ripped the jewellery right out of her earlobes.

'This is insane,' said Mira, her face contorting as the air thickened and swirled. Her head was pounding. 'Don't do this!' she shouted at Goderick.

'I'll do what I like,' he said, relishing every word.

Mira turned to the rest of the group in desperation.

'He's turned off the measures. The breakers,' she panted. The delegation looked back at her blankly. 'The safety guards.'

There was a series of hard metal clangs from inside the apparatus, close by their end, as if great cogs were knocking and realigning. It was like the engine room of a massive ship cranking into gear.

'He's redirecting the magnets,' said Mira. She stared around for the emergency console but her gaze slithered over everything without taking it in. 'He's going to deflect the beam.'

Goderick whooped from on high and pointed at her with a jabbing finger.

'She got it!'

The tube trembled and banged, moving ever so slightly in its supports. Instinctively the group backed away. Mira was trying not to let panic eat her brain, but it was as if sight, sound, smell and touch had all blended into one thing. The beam was powering up and the atmosphere clung and pulled at them. It felt like being sucked into a melting vortex.

The equipment was breaking apart, cracking into vast arcs and columns and corners, snapping into pieces, colossal metal ruins. A giant chunk thudded down next to Mira, missed her by inches and fell straight through the platform. The metal floor crumpled like tissue paper around the ripped hole. The group fell to the ground and slid down the slope towards the torn edge. They grabbed onto the floor but terror made them weak and they had no grip. They collided with the railings at the side and held on, curling their entire bodies around the rails as the platform creaked and teetered.

Dr Poon and Stefan climbed to their feet, crouching and

clinging on to each other. The atmosphere felt too heavy to stand up in. Mira told herself not to give up, not to go limp. Colleagues would be alerted by the security cameras and alarms and would come for them soon. The noise inside the giant tube got louder and louder until it turned into a robotic screeching. Yet another eardrum-shredding layer of alarms and sirens started as the detectors began to break down – as if the machine itself was screaming for help.

'Don't worry about the sound, that's just the cooling system,' Goderick announced. 'Sixty tonnes of liquid helium keeping this baby chill. You see those pumps? They're pumping gas inside the beam tunnels to cool the magnets. Superfluid helium, verrrrrry cold. Lower than the background temperature of the universe.' Goderick shrugged. 'I'm showing you all the cool shit we can do, just like you wanted. Even if there's a really small source in there, the gas can see the ionisation trails left by a charged particle. A source of what? The thing we love the most: radiation! Radiation! Radiation!'

The radiation monitors screamed, the tube vibrated and clanged, the pistons wheezed, the cooling system emitted its deadening alien hum and the lights blazed red. Mira hung on to the railing, trying to get her head straight.

'You know what? Don't just take my word for it,' said Goderick. 'See for yourself. Liquid helium. Liquid helium,' he repeated. 'It's a shade above absolute zero. And it's frrrrreaky, you'll love it.'

He scampered down the ladder, hit a switch on the work panel at the end of the tube and scuttled back up, staring at them. Nothing happened for a few seconds. Then there was a hissing noise, then a hard crash, then a steady, sizzling glug. The delegation stared around, trying to work out where it was coming from.

'There!' said Dr Poon, pointing.

A thick, transparent liquid poured out from the other end of the tube, gallon after fizzing gallon, a fatal frost slipping out and sliding along the ground, the equipment, the stairs, the platforms. It was mesmerising to watch it approach. Mira knew that liquid helium killed anything it touched, that they would all die down here, yet she couldn't move a muscle.

'Don't touch it,' she said, but the words barely came out. She had never seen anything like it. To be touched by that silky, liquid freeze… she would perish instantly, turned into shatterable ice, her lungs and heart splintering into poisoned icicles.

'Hold your breath,' she said – but she had no idea what that would achieve.

They watched, hypnotised, as the liquid helium slipped towards them from the far end of the cavern, gliding and stirring. As it encountered the pillars and supports that held up the sections of the tube, it flowed up them with serpentine smoothness, a deadly winter spell reaching up. It slid up the lift shaft and crawled up the girders, freezing everything it touched. The cavern was transforming into blighted ice, infected from the base up. Soon, soon it would reach them.

Goderick was a black spider spreadeagled on the ladder, pointing and ranting.

'Energy equals mass times the speed of light, nothing special about that. A gram of antimatter is worth a medium-sized nuclear weapon. A gram of antimatter can launch a rocket!'

Stefan and Dr Poon raised their heads. They looked at each other for a beat. Then they detached themselves from the group and grabbed the railings to raise themselves.

Goderick was still frothing on.

'A whole shitload of energy appears, the energy evolves, it turns into mass, some of it turns into you. Why am I not happy? Where is the antimatter? Where the hell is the antimatter? The thing is, matter and antimatter can't coexist. They annihilate each other – that's why antimatter's so powerful, it's the ultimate weapon!'

The ground beneath them began to tremble from inside. Not just the apparatus, the platform or the stairs, but the earth itself. It was juddering at the core, breaking apart from deep within. Mira squinted upwards. It was the strangest sight: the rough surfaces of the chamber around them were quivering, slaking off sheets of dark dust, metres of seemingly immutable rock disintegrating like shredded fabric, breaking into fine slabs and small boulders, plummeting and grinding. Chunks of rock began to fall around the edges of the chamber. Soon the apex would collapse and crush them all.

As one, Stefan and Dr Poon stood up and bellowed at Goderick:

'SRS! Don't move!'

Dr Poon wrenched herself over to the ladder and climbed it, clinging tightly as everything around them broke form. Giant fists of rock broke from the walls. Stefan also advanced. The wilting gloom-monger Mira had seen all morning was gone, replaced by a tense, quick man.

'SRS. Stop!' cried Stefan, his voice cutting and low. 'Stop the helium release.'

Mira racked her brains. SRS, what was SRS? Then a single factoid pinged front and centre in her memory. It was in her citizenship book: the Service de Renseignement Stratégique. Switzerland's national foreign intelligence agency. They were security agents.

'We need you to shut this down,' shouted Dr Poon, gaining on Goderick. 'Stop the beam. Put the safety guards back on.'

Every time Dr Poon went up a few inches, so did Goderick, until he was pressed up against the frame of the trapdoor. But unless these SRS agents had some special weapon, they were unarmed. No metal item like a gun and no electric item like a Taser would work here, and Mira had witnessed them putting all their stuff in the lockers.

Goderick seemed to realise it too. He put his hand on the trapdoor.

'Now, now,' he taunted, leering down at Dr Poon. 'Let me tell you what I'm doing here.'

'We don't care. It's over,' said Dr Poon.

She and Stefan watched him, their eyes narrowed, their mouths tight, their faces flexing and straining.

'Physics is an observational science,' Goderick declared. 'You only know things from the parameters of how we observe them. If you want to measure something really well, you find yourself an atomic physicist – people who deal with light and lasers. That could be me! We can measure things to the nth degree. Measuring the momentum and energy is key. We run a live experiment and see what happens.' He stabbed his finger at them. 'That's you.'

'You won't achieve anything,' said Stefan. He had approached the base of the ladder.

'You're wrong!' shouted Goderick. 'By fifteen orders of magnitude!'

He stretched over Dr Poon and thrust down the second lever on the wall. Dr Poon pulled herself up the last few steps of the ladder and they wrestled body to body as all the sirens and all the alarms went off and the air ripped and surged as the rock cavern quivered around them. Goderick pushed Dr Poon and she fell hard from the ladder, into Stefan's arms. Goderick scrambled up through the trapdoor and slammed it down. It locked itself tight.

Stefan and Dr Poon ran back to the group. They were soon too weak to get up. They crawled as far away from the tube as possible, the whole delegation moving as one. Mira's eyes were screwed tight – it felt as if her eyeballs were pulsing and changing shape. Rolling shockwaves of energy pushed through them.

'What's happening?' croaked Stefan.

'I'm sorry,' Mira managed to say.

Her insides churned and her skin got hotter and hotter. She had a graphic vision of their bodies peeling and burning, their blood boiling over and mixing and bursting into pools of gore. They huddled together. Mira couldn't think straight. *Medical experiments… He turned us into experiments.* She saw her mother's body in the hospice. She saw her grandmother's body as she found it when she came home one day from a seminar. *Tuesday, it was a Tuesday*, she thought.

The hammering got louder and louder until there was a hollow burst. A pungent smell washed over them and yet another screaming alarm went off. One by one, the light boxes on the walls snapped on and off with retina-burning white flashes.

'Sensors,' choked Mira, 'for escaped — gases and smoke — ,' she broke off, hacking and coughing. Grey mist seeped around them and the air got dark.

There was a hard clunking noise and a metal trunk near them trembled. When the sensors were triggered, the front of the trunk popped open and a tray of rebreathers was released, each one in a plastic bracket. They looked like oxygen masks, with tubes attached that removed exhaled carbon dioxide and left breathable oxygen. Rebreathers would give them half an hour to find the emergency exit.

Mira tried to reach the trunk but her muscles and bones were failing. Her vision swirled and slimed. The rebreathers won't help, she thought. Dying in agony in an electromagnetic force field, it doesn't matter what you breathe. But she had to try.

She was sprawled on the ground, the bottom tray of rebreathers in sight. She stretched out her hand, gripped the floor and dragged herself forward. She was consumed by the swirling miasma of energy twisting through her. She pulled herself a few more inches along. She pushed a rebreather with the tip of her finger and it fell out of its bracket. She drew it towards herself but didn't have the strength to push down the little black beak on the cylinder to activate it. She pressed the mask to her face. The mask disintegrated.

She felt herself rising out of herself. She drifted to a corner of the ceiling and saw her body on the ground. The rest of the group were spreadeagled across the platform. Black smoke clung around them. The most demonic thing was the pulsing energy, the fatal red flux swirling everything into a formless nightmare.

A crack opened at the top of the room and a shot of light spread out. This is it, thought Mira. She floated down again and hovered above her body. She felt intense, final dread. Something disgusting fell out of the light – a smeared, white, faceless figure. Then came a black shadow, and now they copulated in the hellish red light. They changed shape, grabbing and swelling. Mira felt herself being dragged down, down, down. She was floating in a slipstream. The light was white, then brighter than white, then too brilliant to bear. Everything turned black.

*

Mira opened her eyes, just a millimetre. There were stabbing pains in her eyeballs. She was in a blurred white bubble. It was some kind of seal. She could feel tubes in her mouth and nose. Her face was smarting and swollen, as if it might burst. Every inch of her was wrapped in thick, suffocating bands. It hurt to move her eyes. Her body burned, front and back, from her scalp to her soles. Her lungs hurt. Her eardrums hurt. Her entire skin was tight.

She tried to move but she was tied down with tubes. A thin beeping started up, there was a rustling outside the bubble and in came a stocky shape in a white hazmat suit, staring at her through plastic goggles. It was Dr Meyer.

'I saved you, put that in your safety report,' she said loudly, bending over Mira and looking into her eyes. 'I heard the commotion, I heard the nonsense he was spouting, I put on my hazmat and hit him on the head. With metal from his own experiment, ha! We fought like animals, it was glorious. So much more satisfying than having a conversation with him.'

Mira tried to talk, but couldn't. She gagged on the tube. The skin of her mouth and throat was blistered all the way down. She couldn't swallow. A glutinous tear formed at the corner of her eye and slipped down the side of her face.

'Rest, rest,' said Ingrid, sitting carefully on the edge of Mira's bed. 'You're still at CERN – it's too dangerous to move you. We're in Building 39, the guest hostel. It's now an infirmary. So! Goderick's a lunatic! I said it at one million staff meetings and nobody listened.' She rubbed her hazmat-gloved hands together. 'We will see him on trial soon, I intend to make myself his most prominent detractor.'

Ingrid tapped the side of her head.

'Let me tell you my theory: Goderick the all-American boy is secretly working for Putin. Putin funds his antimatter delusion and in return, Goderick creates all this mess to undermine confidence – in Europe. In the European project.' She clenched her fist. 'European unity!'

It was also revenge, thought Mira. A spoilt child's revenge against a world that didn't give him his due, that didn't see him as he saw himself. If CERN couldn't give him what he wanted, he would destroy it.

'But it hasn't worked – because he is an amateur!' Ingrid crowed. 'People are talking about a new CERN centre in Frankfurt or Paris when the war is over. Celebrities, rock stars, philosophers want to visit – donations are pouring in! I'll get increased funding, for sure.'

Ingrid's jolly voice got loud in the room, but there was no response from Mira. Ingrid got up and lifted the side of the white tent.

'Look, Mira. Don't move your head, just look. The damage was underground. But still, outside, it is a ghost town. They made an exclusion zone.'

They were on the ground floor of Building 39 and Mira could see a fair way across the campus. It was empty. Not a single car was parked. Nobody crossed between buildings. All the lights in all the labs and offices were off. Even the sky was dull. There were tiny shapes with propellers floating about up there: drones, flying over the campus to survey the damage.

'I had to gain special permission to see you,' Ingrid went on, returning to Mira's side. 'I am a patient here too – or a walking safety hazard, however you want to say it. They're getting those poor little engineer kids to maintain the place. There's no one else here apart from you, me, the delegation and the doctors.'

Mira closed her eyes.

'Mira, Mira, stick with me, try to follow what I'm saying. As soon as they finish assessing you, you can go home. And then you can… resume your research.'

Ingrid didn't even sound convincing when she said that. Mira wanted to nod, but it hurt. Every millimetre of her insides was scalded raw. She had been invaded, suffused with radioactive particles. There was no way to escape, her cells would mutate or die, right down to her bone marrow. She might survive skin cancer, if she didn't develop necrosis and watch bits of herself turn black and drop off. But what about the gamma burns? The deep internal burns, the 60 degree scorching.

She forced her eyes open again. Her bandages seeped blood and pus. She was covered in sores and lesions. She would ooze, then blisters would bubble up and ulcerate, then a scab might form, then it'd fall off and underneath would be patches of shiny pink, dead numb nerves cut through with scars.

She looked at Ingrid and blinked. Ingrid patted the corner of Mira's pillow with the gentlest touch.

'Good, good. We will still have nights at Charlie's Bar, okay? Or the new microbrewery. We'll go. Ah – Goderick's girlfriend left him, of course. She is now seeing that Italian porno-looking guy from Tonino's Pizzeria. The one who is a bit old to be wearing his shirt open in the middle of the day in Switzerland.'

Ingrid's voice was kind and soft.

'Mira, listen to me, they won't know the results of the incident for a long time, okay? They're assessing the fallout – not just for you, for everyone, for the buildings. About the future… you will have to accept it as you go along.'

Mira laboriously formed the thought – *Children, is she saying I can't have children?* That was something she never thought about. Womb death – who cared? There were enough babies in the world. But she knew what Ingrid really meant. There was no future. Nobody survived this. There was no way out of Building 39, not after the cataclysm and the war to come and the long dark burning tail of the afterglow.

Afterword: Health and Safety Nightmares

Dr Kristin Lohwasser

University of Sheffield

Usually, scientists can be nervous when talking to journalists or the press. *Will they understand me? Can they correctly explain back my research and make it as exciting to the reader as I find it?* And the worst case scenario: *Will they cite me incorrectly, turning my words into gibberish for all my (physics) friends to make fun of?* That said, it felt pretty relaxing and even a tiny bit exciting when I sat down with the author, Bidisha, to discuss my research on radiation protection and the use of virtual reality to increase safety in decommissioning ATLAS's inner detectors. No need to get every detail across, no need to get every detail right – such things wouldn't play the most central role in the final story.

But to get the facts right retrospectively: What might be surprising is, that there is actually relatively little radioactivity at CERN despite CERN being the European Council for Nuclear Research. Most of the 'radioactivity' – that is to say the radiation of highly energetic particles – is created in the collisions of particle beams within the large multipurpose experiments situated at the Large Hadron Collider (LHC). For example, in my experiment, ATLAS, 120 million high-energy particle collisions happen per second. This is a huge number and does constitute a significant amount of radiation. However, the produced particles decay and interact within the detector. In

81

fact, the detector is built in order to contain all of these particle except for those that interact only very weakly and therefore do not pose any radiation danger (it is interaction with our cells or their DNA that triggers dangerous damage to our body that we have to be wary of – no interaction, no problem). In theory, you could stand next to the detector and the health hazard would be practically zero. In practice, no one can access the experimental cavern, where the detector is, when collisions take place within the detector due to an elaborate access system in place (Bidisha's story refers to retina scanners, manual keys, and so on, all of which are accurate). More dangerous than standing next to the detector is standing next to the beam pipe of the LHC in which the protons are accelerated almost to the speed of light. They radiated off hard-X-rays – so not the place to be (save your X-ray allowance for medical examinations). Fortunately however, the LHC, as well as the detector, are 100m underground, and again there's no chance of accessing it while anything's running – thanks to the retina-scan access doors and interlock systems that do not allow the accelerator to start if any of the keys to its tunnel have not been returned to its rightful place back upstairs (all of which is accurately represented in Bidisha's story). No chance for any of these X-rays or radioactivity to escape to the idyllic Swiss and French village above. And moreover, once the beam is off, no new radioactivity is produced. Only a relatively small amount stays around – too much radiation can make materials radioactive themselves by changing the nuclei within the materials. After more than ten years of running, the ATLAS inner detector, which is closest to the collisions and is still relatively small (being cylindrical and about 7m long and 2m wide), will be ever so slightly radioactive and special care has to be taken when replacing it with fresh, un-radioactive parts. Special care here means: the decommissioned detector parts will be safely stored (still to be decided where and how – but in the grand scheme of things, the detector is just a drop in the ocean: In the UK alone, about 4.5 million cubic metres of nuclear waste from households and businesses are disposed of every year. The ATLAS inner detector has a volume of less than 100 cubic metres, so negligible in comparison. In tonnes, the whole ATLAS detector is only a thousandth of the yearly nuclear waste in the UK. Above all though, it means making sure the technicians and physicists working on this decommissioning do not receive 'large' radiation doses. More specifically, 'large' is defined as ideally not exceeding the average annual exposure to radiation (e.g. in the UK without accounting for medical or occupational exposure) or the amount of radiation received by an airplane cabin crew over the course of a year (as Bidisha's character Mira points out, when you fly, you are exposed to more radiation than usual because you are closer to space and are subject to so-called cosmic radiation that is not yet fully absorbed by the atmosphere).

We can predict the amount of residual radiation in our detectors using a simple formula and can cross-check those regularly with measurements once the LHC machine is switched off. These predictions about residual radiation can be used in a virtual reality environment to understand the level of radioactive dose technicians would receive when working in this environment. Spoiler alert: the radiation levels are safe when carrying out the work as planned – but this is good to know and there is always a very generous safety margin applied in order to ensure no one get gets hurt by the afterglow of our detectors. Our final estimates show that a technician decommissioning the ATLAS inner detector would receive less radiation than if he had two panoramic dental X-rays (note: this comparison is not motivated by the state of his teeth).

Successful health and safety is pretty boring, after all, so naturally, in our conversations, Bidisha and I also started talking about what happens when things go wrong: Chernobyl and acute radiation sickness (this is where they brought soldiers in to clear the roof of the reactor); fatal accidents resulting from the abandonment of radiography sources (like the Goiânia accident in Brazil where scrap metal merchants stole a source from an abandoned hospital, leading to what *Time* magazine described as one of the world's 'worst nuclear disasters').[1] We imagined all the worst examples ever given in health and safety talks we'd sat through and then raised them by ten orders of magnitude (daisy-chaining multiplugs to the moon, operating heavy machinery when under a cocktail of hallucinogens, using a wobbly office chair with broken rollers whilst sitting at the beam control panel).

Given how the state of the world has changed since our first chat (in late 2021), it seems no wonder that the story evolved the way it did. When I first read the title 'Afterglow' I secretly hoped for a romantic love story – plenty of those have happened at CERN. And the CERN Bidisha describes lacks much of the peaceful, picturesque place I know (the meadows at the CERN Meyrin site are left 'natural' and flower beautifully in spring. In fact, since 2009, the site has been recognised by the Swiss Nature & Economy Foundation for its efforts to preserve biodiversity). Bidisha has also taken the liberty to change the experimental set-up, merging the CMS and ATLAS experiments with CERN's antimatter facility – both need wildly different equipment and are located far from one another. Her villain evokes faint memories of the bad guy in Dan Brown's *Angels and Demons* and how likely it would be for him to override the 'breakers' and redirect the beam (let alone do anything from down inside the experiment) is open to question.

But what is indeed a realistic threat? Given that the admittedly immense radiation from the beams vanishes once the beams are stopped, it's difficult to see how Dr. Evil might make the entire CERN site radioactive and uninhabitable, as one might interpret it to be from the end of the story. Certainly not permanently uninhabitable. Nor can you move the beams or beam pipes easily to redirect them as Goderick seems to. When the LHC first started, one of the connections between two beam magnets got loose and caused cooling liquid to evaporate, causing the magnets to be pushed a few metres across. Naturally, no one was in the tunnel and no one got hurt in the process. Security is relatively high and the secondary idea that a co-worker could snatch some of the activated radioactive source from inside the detector under the eyes of colleagues seems unlikely.

A fire would probably be the most devastating way of causing harm to the facility as a whole as it could carry radioactive smoke with it, though it would probably be relatively quickly contained by the sprinkler system. Ultimately, the most devastating harm would be inflicted on the detector.

Bidisha cites the anti-risk formula: minimise the time, maximise the distance, maximise the physical protection. 'Same as the Covid guidelines, really.' (Or ALARA guidelines as we call them in the nuclear context.) This is quite apt as a comparison as you cannot see or feel radioactivity and you have to remind yourself of its presence (though, admittedly, it is a bit easier to measure radiation on the spot than aerosolised COVID). And perhaps there are other similarities between radiation and COVID, namely in the way they can be misrepresented or misperceived. Whenever a threat is invisible, or not apparent to any of our immediate senses, there is room – especially in today's climate – for conspiracy theorists to emerge about its dangers and what scientists are doing with it: extremist narratives that will try to erode public trust in honest research. Once trust is lost, public funding often follows suit, and before long there is an undermining of the value of science itself.

Which draws us to the main purpose of Dr Evil's catastrophic interventions in Bidisha's story. His aim is not to destroy CERN physically, to blow it up. As Mira corrects one of the visitors: this is not a nuclear reactor – it really isn't that volatile. Goderick's aim (presumably at Putin's command) is rather to undermine public confidence in CERN as a great symbol of international cooperation and collective scientific endeavour, and to recast it as not just a waste of money, but a public menace.

So what would be lost if such a sabotage were to undermine general trust in (and funding for) CERN? Well, CERN has always been a big melting pot, providing scientists with a means to work across national, political and cultural divides. At the height of the Cold War, cooperation agreements were signed with the Soviet Union and other partners of the Eastern Block; right now, Israeli and Palestinian physics institutes are working together. And even if, in the back of the mind of some of the scientists, the main reason for the collaboration is to 'not lose out' in the race for results (there being no option to perform these experiments single-handedly), at the very core of everything CERN does is collaboration. And for me, that evokes only one type of afterglow. Hope.

Note

1. 'The Worst Nuclear Disasters – Photo Essays'. *Time.com*, 3 December 2017.

Marble Run

Luan Goldie

I WORK CONDENSED HOURS, which means I cram forty hours of work into four days. Today is Friday, my 'day off'. I drop Dolly at nursery and Mya at school. I clean the flat and get the washing done. I eat half a box of French Fancies and half a garlic baguette, then sit on a kitchen stool and stare at a wall.

What would it be like if there was a symmetry between matter and spacetime? The question loops continuously in my head like a marble in a jar.

What would it be like? What would it mean?

Then, the washing machine beeps and the marble falls.

Friday also means prenatal Yoga. I unroll my mat and sit cross-legged, my left hip joint clicking loudly as I do. The woman who runs it, a pink-haired hippy named Harriet, begins her patter. 'Prepare to connect with your unborn, to challenge your body,' she looks at me and adds, 'to stop the noise in your mind.'

During Savasana, I feel the glass jar change shape and the marble runs into a corner which shouldn't be there. Or should it? Was it there all along? Did I actually manage to connect not with the baby but with the answer I've been searching for?

'If your mind starts to wander,' Harriet says, 'simply come back to your breath.'

I try to squeeze her voice out of my head in order to keep

my mind wandering. Then I smell the lavender as she nears me. 'Your mind is spinning,' she whispers, 'I can *see* it.' I open my eyes and she smiles down at me, revealing veneers which look expensive and at odds with her cheap dye job. 'Empty your mind.'

The marble rolls away.

It is almost half four and I begin my rewind, back to the nursery door where I'm warned of a conjunctivitis break out and back to the school gates where Mya's teacher calls me over.

'Hello, Mya's mum.'

'Hello, Miss.' I've forgotten her name, though something implausibly twee sits on the tip of my tongue. Ms Honey? Ms Daisy?

'Mya tells me you're a scientist?'

'Yes, I'm a research scientist.'

'Ah,' she sighs with relief as if a problem were solved, 'that's why I never see you.'

I know this is the place where the 'working mum guilt' should fall but I don't feel it, because it's bullshit and also, right now, exhaustion is a more consuming feeling.

'Next Friday is our Super Science Day and it would be great if you could come in. The children would love to hear from a real scientist. You could tell them all about your work. What exactly is it?'

'I work in particle physics.'

Her smile widens. 'That sounds wonderful, it'll really get their young minds going.'

'I don't think I have time,' I say, looking over at Mya who is enthusiastically hugging a little boy.

'Mummy, this is my bestest friend,' she yells.

I thought Mya's best friend was called Rayan. I had assumed Rayan was a girl.

'Actually,' I say, 'I'll check my schedule.'

That night in bed, I lie on my left side and curl into Elliot.

'You're too hot,' he moans. 'You're making me overheat.'

'Isn't that a good thing?'

'No. Not at this point in the week.' He throws the duvet off. 'You can't sleep?'

I grunt.

'How can you not sleep? I'm so tired I could have gone to bed at the same time as the girls.'

'I am tired,' I say. 'My body is tired. But my mind, my mind is —'

'I know.' He puts a finger on the back of my hand and draws a looping circle.

I sigh, fed up with the speed of my own mind. 'Mya's teacher asked me to go into school next Friday.'

'For what?'

'They're having a Super Science Day. She wants me to tell the seven-year-olds about my work in particle physics.'

Elliot rolls onto his back and laughs into the dark.

'Stop it,' I say. 'Why are you laughing? I'm thinking of doing it.'

'Why would you do that?'

'So I can be involved with Mya's life.'

'I thought you were already quite involved.'

'I miss everything. The bake sales. The parent coffee mornings. Those meetings where they argue about sex education.'

'That's two hours of my life I'm never getting back.' Elliot yawns. 'You really want to do this?'

'Yes,' I say. 'No. I'm not sure. It'll mean I miss yoga.'

'I'm surprised you're still doing the yoga. I thought you hated it.'

'I do. But I like the end part. Where you get to think.'

He yawns again and turns over, 'Of course you do.'

Saturday is my nephew's ninth birthday party and my sister, Ella, has organised a large event which requires everyone's attendance and participation. Elliot is tasked with setting up the barbecue and I sit on the floor by the oven watching mini sausage rolls brown. There is too much noise. Doorbells and phones, screams and songs, and children, children everywhere.

'Why did you invite so many people?' I ask.

'Stop moaning,' Ella snaps, 'or next year I'll book the soft play.'

I rise from the floor and she steps forward to put her hands under my stomach. 'Growing nicely.'

'Did you say I was *glowing* nicely?'

'No. I would like to say that but,' she bites her lip, 'you look tired.'

'Thanks.'

She presses a finger between my brows. 'Frown lines.'

'Thought lines,' I say.

Outside someone screams in agony. Ella opens the window and shouts, 'Don't let them play with the stapler,' before slamming it shut again.

The house swells with people. The same faces I see at each of my sister's social events, the birthdays and barbecues and this, a horrible combination of both.

The 'dads' stand in the garden alongside Anna, a lone single parent who the 'mums' are distrustful of.

'Remember when we were kids, only women would go to birthday parties?' Ella asks the mums while forcing refreshments on them. Cheeses, crackers, Pastel de natas, an endless stream of Prosecco.

'Progress,' I mumble, 'now both parents must suffer.'

My phone buzzes. Phil, my colleague. We try not to contact each other at the weekend but he has something he wants to talk over with me ahead of Monday morning. The tips of my fingers fizz as I message back. It's exciting to be on the cusp like this. To know that at any moment, something could crack open to reveal a sight none of us have seen before.

Mya runs towards me, her mouth ringed with chocolate. She dumps her jumper and unicorn headband on my lap then runs away, back into the fold of children. It's the first time I've seen her since we arrived. Yet, I am forced to be here to spend quality time with her.

'What do you do?' one of the mums asks me.

'I'm a research scientist.'

'How interesting? What does that mean?'

'I work in particle physics.'

The woman lifts her fist to the side of her head then splays her fingers while making an explosion sound.

Ella raises an eyebrow. 'Yep, Big Sis here got the brains, I got the beauty.'

'It's not so complicated,' I say, 'I check calculations and –'

The woman waves a hand. 'Don't waste your breath on me, I won't get it. Science was my worst subject at school. It's great that women are getting into science though.'

Getting into science? She says it as if I've just bought my first chemistry set.

The woman goes on. 'I imagine it's a bit of a boys' club. Like when I worked in corporate finance, the men used to walk all over me.'

'No,' I tell her. 'It's not like that where I work. You're not a gender. Not a woman or a man. You're a piece of energy. A battery. You're someone who can bring something to the table or not.'

Ella clears her throat, 'Anyone for more Prosecco?'

I top up my glass of Robinsons cordial and pick stray crisps from a bowl of M&Ms. My energy for this particular social situation has been expended. I take my phone and reread Phil's message which shines a light on what I think I saw yesterday, the marble roving into places I never thought it could.

'You're working,' Ella says.

'No. I'm just having a quick look online.'

'Really? At what?'

It is here, in the realm of cultural references, where my thoughts are blank. 'I was looking at the *Love Island* results.'

Ella's face softens and we both laugh.

'Stop working,' she says.

'I wasn't working. I was thinking.'

'Same thing.'

'You want me to stop thinking?'

'I want you to live in the moment, to enjoy doing normal family stuff, to enjoy this.' She throws her arms out to the chaos of the party, the mess of her home. Through the patio doors Elliot is popping balloons against a rose bush, surrounded by a gaggle of cheering children.

'I have enjoyed it,' I lie. 'I'm tired though.'

'It's okay to switch off from work, to hit the brakes.'

I nod. Though how can you hit the brakes when you're so close? When you're skidding towards the answers on the lip of the cliff? When you're near enough to find out, to solve, to confirm?

Monday is Elliot's 'day off'. When I arrive home the fridge and cupboards are full, the dinner is almost ready and he is divvying out pasta salads into lunchboxes for the following day.

'Hey,' he calls.

I look around the kitchen, spotless in a way I never care to achieve. 'What have you been doing all day? Watching pornography and eating panettone?'

'You know me. You're home late.'

'I walked.'

He looks at me and winces. 'That bad?'

'Yes. No. I mean, it was disappointing. Phil was ahead of himself. So was I. Our thoughts came to nothing. We're behind schedule.'

We are always behind schedule.

Elliot hands me a glass of water. 'You look exhausted.'

I am exhausted, yet that is the point of walking rather than getting the train. I walk to exhaust myself, to decompress, so that by the time I am home, I only have energy for what is tangible.

I make my way to my girls.

'Oh, Mummy's here, she can help us,' Mya says, grabbing my hand and putting a roll of tape in it.

I kiss her forehead. 'Did you have a good day?'

'Can you open the tape for me? I need it.'

I peel it open and hand it back. Dolly sits on the bed colouring in a large cardboard box with a fading biro pen and solid concentration. 'I made a swimming pool for the chihuahua.'

'That's nice,' I say, lowering myself to the floor.

We work together to complete their magical dolls' house and then videocall Auntie Ella.

'Go to bed,' she tells me when the girls grow tired of showing off their creation to her.

'No, I need to eat something first and do some yoga.'

'Yoga?' she sniggers. 'I thought you hated prenatal yoga.'

'I do. But the part at the end –'

'Where you get to lie down and do nothing?'

'Yes, that part. Each time I do it, it's like my mind opens a little and things start running around.'

I sift through Mya's book bag and find a leaflet about Super Science Day. There is a cartoon of a zany-looking old man with glasses and white hair. He is wearing a lab coat and is gurning at a test tube.

'They're not serious,' I say.

'What?' Ella asks.

I show her the leaflet and tell her about the invite.

'You should go,' she says. 'I do the weekly reading café at the kids' school. It's so rewarding.'

'The expectations used to be helping your child with a bit of homework and attending parents' evening once a year. What's driving all this extra stuff they now want you to do?'

'Greater interaction between home and school. It's a good thing. You should do it.'

'Not now. I've got maternity leave coming up, perhaps I'll get involved then.'

'What, when you have a newborn? It's good to have something outside of work,' she says.

'I have plenty going on outside of work.'

'Yes but,' she stops.

'But what?'

'You're always at work, even when you're not physically at work. You're checking emails at family parties and only doing yoga because it helps you work out equations or whatever it is.'

'One doesn't cancel out the other. I can be a thinking person and a mother.'

Ella scoffs, 'When you think, you're hardly present. In fact, you're completely unreachable.'

Unreachable. It's so far from how I'd describe it. My thinking isn't seen as precious by the outside world, it can be interrupted for any little thing. A lost phone charger, a missing toy, a sudden declaration of no longer believing in Santa. I am reachable all the time.

'It's just a job,' Ella says.

'It's an important job. My work is important.'

'I know. I know it is. But it's not like you're curing cancer.'

This is always her benchmark. So often I have wondered what she would say if I *was* curing cancer. How would she downplay my work then?

'Ella, I've got to go.'

'You're annoyed with me?'

'No. I'll talk to you another time.'

Our dad used to say Ella was jealous of my thinking, of how I could disappear into my mind for hours at a time while she stood on the side, trying to get my attention. It's not my fault she's not smart enough to entertain herself, I'd once said. Years later, she told me it was the cruellest thing I'd ever said to her. I apologised. Though, in truth, I stand by it. It's not my fault her mind can't take her away from everyday life, the same way it's not my fault that mine does.

Today is Friday, my 'day off'. I drop Dolly at nursery and go into school with Mya where I sit on a tiny chair in a noisy, brightly coloured classroom and wait for my turn to speak.

My phone buzzes and I take a peek.

Ella – *Good luck and have fun.*

This is followed by an emoji I don't quite understand the meaning of. A smiley face with eyes set at different levels. An apology or perhaps a trophy to say she won the argument.

The teacher, whose name is Ms Cherry, waves me over in front of the children. 'This is Mya's mum and she's going to talk to us about how fun it is learning all about science.'

Mya sits up front and looks around at her friends, grinning, proud.

'Mya's mum, can you tell the children a little bit about your very exciting job as a scientist?'

A child with hair intricately plaited and beaded rocks her head side to side, causing the coloured beads to clack.

'I work in particle physics. Does anyone know what a particle is?'

A sea of blank faces stare at me and Mya's arm shoots up.

'Mya, do you want to tell your friends what a particle is?'

'A particle is a tiny bit of something,' she bursts out.

'Yes. It is. A tiny, tiny element which makes up a thing. Hmm, yes, does that make sense?'

'Yes,' Mya shouts.

Ms Cherry smiles encouragingly and I wonder if they are taught this during teacher training, this cheerleading facial gesture.

'I look at supersymmetry. It's a theory that for every particle which was created at the start of the universe, there was also a matching particle. A super particle. If we could find at least one of these, it would mean that there's actually double the number of particles that we think there is. Isn't that amazing?'

Ms Cherry tips her head to one side.

'Also, in my job I can be silly. Imagine things that aren't, but could be. Just because I like it. For example, what would it mean if matter and spacetime were actually the same thing? If we could find the fundamental building blocks of spacetime, and link it to the matter particles with a symmetry, what would it mean?'

Of course, I'm not expecting my audience to provide me with answers, yet standing here, thinking out loud, I feel something, I feel the thoughts gathering momentum, the marble speeding up. 'If it was true, it would mean the Standard Model being expanded many times over. It would mean that things which seem very different to us are the same, different manifestations of just one underlying essence.'

Ms Cherry is no longer dosing me with her cheering smile, instead she looks disappointed, as if I have just eaten a crayon.

'If there was a similar symmetry between matter and spacetime as there probably is between bosons and fermions, it would mean –'

'Yes, Alia,' Ms Cherry says. 'Do you have a question for Mya's mum about science?'

The marble falls as I look down at the child with the beaded hair. 'Uh huh,' she says.

'Great,' Ms Cherry says. 'Remember your nice loud voice.'

The child's wide eyes drop down to my stomach and she asks, 'When is your baby going to come out?'

I leave the school before lunchtime with a sticker which says, *I love Science* on my jumper. I go home to collect my yoga things and wonder if I can still make it to class on time. Though, why bother? Instead, I unroll my mat onto the living room floor and find a video on YouTube titled 'Prenatal Yoga for your mind'. I fast-forward to the Savasana and allow the marble to run.

Afterword: The Work-Life Balance

Dr Carole Weydert

Former CERN scientist

CERN IS THE ACRONYM for Centre de Recherche Nucléaire but that really explains nothing. A better way of thinking of it is as a research facility where scientists probe and tickle the universe like a huge piñata with every kind of stick they can find, to see what it's made of – all this stuff, all this space, all this time – trying to lure out nature's most hidden secrets. A place where they poke the cosmos with a stick until something breaks and look at what comes out. A laboratory at the verge of the knowledge frontier, each day shedding a little more light on the unknown. Surely such a place oozes technology out of every pore? If you've never been, you might imagine shiny futuristic buildings, uber-efficient architecture, dazzling sleekness, the most advanced and smartest city on earth.

Well, let me take you on a tour.

If you ask me what colour CERN is, I would tell you… grey. When you enter the CERN site, you enter a village of dilapidated constructions. Most of CERN's buildings date back to the 50s. Actually, to call them all buildings is a stretch, since many are just storage halls, made out of bare concrete. And if you haven't had enough concrete on the outside, there's usually a huge amount of additional concrete blocks on the inside, to shield the scientists and engineers from the radiation.

Take the antimatter factory as a concrete example. On the

outside, a fancy new sign gives you the impression that you will enter the most advanced tech building seen to date. When you enter, all there is, is a huge space of grey. Concrete as far as the eye can see. Some flashy huge cranes to lift heavy weights. The flashy colours, often yellow or red, are not a fancy, but to warn people not to hit their head, or get too close, to break anything. Then, in some corners, there are experiments. You can spot them for the enormous quantities of cables running in and out of every space imaginable, interspersed with electronic equipment. Lots of blinking lights. And tinfoil. So... Much... Tinfoil... Exactly the same as you would have in your kitchen. See, grey! I told you. Grey! But sparkling!

If you look a little closer among this huge mess of lights and cables, you may detect hints of human activity. You might see a sign with the name of the experiment. In our present example, there's also the name of a Danish beer company. And in this case it's a real cardboard sign. But that's not always the case. Less popular experiments will have only a printout, or a piece of cloth on which eager summer students wrote their name with t-shirt markers. Hanging around the various steel rods of electronics are cheap photo printouts, yellowed, dry-aged and crumpled, showing people no one knows anymore. And maybe you'll find a household cooling fan or two. Probably attached with cable binder to some piece of equipment that needed cooling for the machine to run more efficiently. Or to run at all. You will see pages lying around, drafts of publications, with annotations and coffee stains. And yes, there will definitely be a coffee machine.

Most scientists working at CERN are not permanently based there. Usually they work in a laboratory in some other part of the world, analysing the data sent to them or working remotely on a piece of equipment. When you are involved in one of the big experiments – and here we're talking a thousand-plus people with the largest ones – you go there temporarily, to do your 'community service', i.e. in service of the research community you're collaborating with. During your stay, you sleep in the hostel (otherwise known as 'Building 39'), which has a sort of accidental Nordic minimalism to it; its purpose being purely functional. It always amazed me to find my bedside drawer contained a bible. I never worked out if it was intentional – i.e. if it came with every room – or if a former occupant had just left one in my room. Either way, I always thought it would be more appropriate to furnish the rooms with the latest *PDG booklet*.[1] But I've never gotten round to putting this in the suggestion box.

When you're done leafing through the *PDG*, you might want to take a stroll through the CERN library, which contains a bookshop by the way, and which holds titles like *Heavenly Mathematics: The Forgotten Art of Spherical Trigonometry*, *Foundations of Space and Time: Reflections on Quantum Gravity*, *Moonshine Beyond the Monster: The Bridge Connecting Algebra, Modular Forms and Physics*. Or why not grab the auspiciously titled *Deep Down Things*. If you listen closely, you might hear an unseen librarian's 'ooh' of approval.

Next stop, the canteen (or Restaurant 1 as it's known): lots of people sporting t-shirts with the fundamental equations of the standard model on them. Some of the smartest people in the world, Nobel Prize winners, just sitting there, having lunch. From any table, you can see one of the many suspended screens, like in any sports bar or airport lounge. Usually these screens broadcast important information of interest to everyone present; things like beam status or luminosity values - like the accelerators' and detectors' vital signs.

CERN is old and it looks that way. The money goes where it should, to the machines. The attention of the people goes where it should, to the data. There is no time to focus on anything else. This is not Google, this is not Lemonade Inc. You do not need eye-catching colours or other gimmicks to make people want to work here. That desire is personal, for everyone at CERN, you can see it in their eyes when they talk, in everyone's. It's desire to understand what makes the world go round. On its most fundamental level. As a scientist, this is what you see in every corner of CERN. Every grey concrete wall holds the promise of undiscovered truths just below the surface, within palpable reach. So this grey is really a white, just lying patiently in the dark, waiting to be discovered.

During my last, somewhat nostalgic visit to CERN, I posted some pictures on my Instagram page. Someone sent me a crying emoji, showing compassion that I seemed to be stuck at such a ramshackle place. There's no denying it, objectively, rationally, the place is ugly, the job is hard, and the idea of a work-life balance is a tautology: life is work and work is life. Each day, when working there I faced an army of problems — the sort that you have to put down one by one, as quickly as you can. Some of the problems you encounter there are so novel you can't turn to anyone more experienced for help. Or the only people with a solution might be on a competing team, so even if they could help, they wouldn't. Once you've found a way out of your conundrum of the day, the solution seems so easy, so obvious, that you can't understand how it has been so hard to arrive at it. Proof, it seems to you, that you really aren't smart enough to be there. .

Working at CERN, you need to be on your toes constantly, ready to anticipate the next question your colleague is going to ask, and half the time you feel like you're just not going to cut the mustard. You become a problem-solving machine. But of small, real-life problems, not big, romantic philosophical questions. Those loom at the end of the tunnel, far off, and it might take years, even decades, of small-scale problem-solving before they are even addressed, if they're addressed at all. Who was it that said, 'When at last you see the light at the end of the tunnel... it's an oncoming train'?

And yet, despite all this, every time I go back, I still find it to be my favourite place on earth. CERN. Grey. But sparkling.

Note

1. The Particle Data Group's 'Booklet' comes out every year and lists all the particles known to exist, along with their basic characteristics. It is like a *Who's Who* of the particle universe, a physicist's bible. It comes in two sizes: pocket booklet and phone book.

Skipping

Ian Watson

SHE'S THE SKIPPER OF a skipship, is Marisa.

Space is pretty empty. That's why it's called Space. In primary school possibly you laughed at a vid of some grandpop pop-sci guru careering in his zimmer pod through Sol's asteroid belt littered with rocks in every direction, here a rock there a rock everywhere a rock rock. Whereas if you sit on an actual asteroid during your whole lifetime you'll be lucky to see another asteroid in any direction.

Empty!

(True, at present, Sol and other stars are midway through a ginormous bubble a thousand light years across cleaned out by supernovae. 'Cleaned' means about six stray atoms remain per c.c. of space rather than the normal sixty. Sixty still wouldn't suffice for a speck of dandruff. Nevertheless, all Space is inherently *dirty* more or less. Got to err on the safe side. Even anti-atom specks may show up, POW!)

Dandruff is a minor problem for slow ships taking ten years to reach Pluto. Most of those ships aren't pressurised, so nobody needs to patch the occasional hole. But when it comes to starships with living persons aboard, the energy release of the mutual impact mass from any speck of dirt can be disruptively destructive. Not quite E equals EmCee Squared destructive, but on the way there.

Unfortunately, projecting a magnetic field fleck deflector like some invisible cowcatcher a hundred thousand kiloms ahead of a starship travelling at a modest quarter-C simply won't work. Do the math. Better still, do the maths; there's more than one of them.

Consequently, our speedy pilot Marisa skips her starship *over* space, not *through*.

The key to her tech is, would you believe it, *flying saucers* – that old bogey from the 20th century. Late in the 1940s, in Washington State of then-USA, a pilot reported seeing a string of shiny objects rushing past him a hell of a lot faster than sound (this being a 'barrier' unbroken at the time by Homo sap). Those things were like quote Saucers Skipping On Water unquote. Newspapers and pop pseudoscientists worldwide became super-excited.

Problem! Who the hell *ever* skips saucers on water? Flat stones, sure, but saucers as in for tea cups or coffee cups? Who goes to a lake with their buddy and a six-pack and all the saucers from the log cabin and proceeds to sink all the saucers in the water, eh?

How come the pilot said such an absurd thing? How come the press then the population of the planet parroted this, as if skipping saucers across water is the most familiar normal activity on Earth? Why why why? Did a planet-wide volcanic venting of hallucinogenic gas cause false memories of times past happily spent skipping saucers which all sank? Ceramics factories working flat out. *Trout Stunned by Saucers* by Richard Brautigan.

Consider: Were flying saucers a giant distraction to divert the human race from the mere possibility of literally *skipping ships to the stars*? Or suppose that our whole reality is a simulation, did our programmers wish to avoid filling in vastnesses of dirty void in fine detail? If *Homo sap* broke loose from Sol System, there'd be a godzilla more detail to render.

So instead of making a fundamental breakthrough regarding *gravitons*, we wasted much time colonising Mars and Titan the slow clunky way. *Colon*ising indeed: those colonies on Mars and Titan smelled like living inside colostomy bags.

No, really. Marisa went to Mars for a vacation mainly because of the similarity of her name and its name. Mars was smelly. Even the swimming pool–cum–reservoir stank.

Of course, she can afford an exotic holiday. She's paid fabulously well to go skipping far out to inhabited worlds and others.

Marisa's bosom pilot pal, with whom she holidays, is Jangle. Jan nibbles the skin around her nails and named her skipship *Gnaw Thyself*. Whereas Marisa named her own ship *Ignore Thyself*. Marisa and Jangle never holidayed on Mars together but they've been to Gobi and Mali and The Great Sandy Down Under. They both like hiking across big heritage deserts. Their boots are made for walking.

Skippers always fly solo. That's due to the fundamental homicidal streak in humans. It's what got us where we are, after we'd homo-sided all of our alt-race cousins during a milly years of bloody genocides. Don't fall for any of that nonsense about how mutuality helped us survive. It's amazing that us victors got off-planet before slaughtering the entire world including ourselves. Great Self-Destruction Filter skipped over, whoop!

More than one human on board a skipship might result in homicide, and skipships aren't cheap. Despite Marisa's skipship being named *Ignore Thyself*, journeys give her ample time for reflection. Literally so: many mirrors on board magnify the space within, multiplying herself too, although she mustn't get lost in a maze of herself. The most Marisas she has seen at any one time is three. On a skipship, there must be no out-of-sight spaces where an *It* might lurk. A murderous Id.

Gravitons. I was coming to those. Gravitons spent a while being hypothetical. They were the undiscovered particle which should endow all matter with gravity. Just as Higgs bosons endow matter with mass. '*Mass in the matter, mass in the matter, we make muons and nothing's the matter*', as Marisa's mum used to sing to her infant nonsensically. Marisa's Mum was bizarre and bright. Scatty though not batty. We'll skip past Mum; persons shouldn't be multiplied beyond necessity.

It took the CERNPLUS umpteen-teraelectronvolt particle collider costing tens of trillions to reveal a graviton scoring five Sigmas of Significance! Yet it was only ten years from there to multiple steerable graviton beams. No brainer. Bargain.

For on such a beam can ride a ship.

A ship which can reach a high percentage of C. A ship which can woof at Pluto five hours after departing Earth orbit.

Even at such superspeed, the closest star is still years away. However, due to our whole universe existing upon a brane (not a brain), gravitons can migrate into higher-dimensional space. For gravitons aren't bound to branes. They leak all over. Thus a ship skipping upon the beam of gravitons can migrate outside the limits of our universe and its laws.

So at last we skipped past Ultimo Pluto then we whooshed through the Kuiper Belt yea and pierced the far heliopause into the big outside. (Taking our tardigrades with us. We'll come to the tardigrades soon.) And lo, we skipped to the nearest stars.

In all directions spherically out to 30 Lights, all planets and moons are crap as potential second homes for Homo sap. Without skipping, we'd never have got anywhere. Sheer poverty of usable worlds. Then at 31 Lights, an adaptable watermoon crops up. Steamy oxy Agualuna, its parent planet a Semi-Hot Jupiter. Without towering tides. Some of the solid surface of that watermoon is only ever a few metres drowned. Do-able with dykes. Encouragement for us!

The furthest reached star so far is at 230 Lights. Courtesy of skipping, by now Homo sap has his and her eggs in eight marginal to middling baskets. Plus, we have our terrestrial tardigrades all over the place, only needing a billy years or so to burgeon bigger. Even to become a little brainy, should the dice so fall. Our darling dot-size hexopods in their cute cuticle canvas coats.

Branes!

Yes. The best way to describe a Brane is as a vast membrane floating around in higher dimensional space. The brane embeds our simple universe of 3-Dee space plus 1-Dee time plus eleven more dimensions of possibly infinite extent rolled up very much tighter than pillbugs. Branes do their thing within what's known as the *Bulk* due to the Bulk being very much bigger than a brane. Many branes can fit into the Bulk. Gravity from our own garden of galaxies reaches into the entire Bulk, whereas all the other fundamental forces of our local universe are pinned on the Brane like butterflies. The result is that gravity in our universe is a modest force compared with what it might be. Just as well for us! Though at the same time gravity is galaxy-spanning and sovereign; ask any supermassive black hole.

An Oztralian physics person famously declared that much of the power of gravity 'buggers off into the Bulk' – the Bulk being 'like the whole bloody Outback compared with say Brisbrane before the sea got to her.'

Marisa from Oz – together with Jangle from the Blue Mountains of Jamaica, whence come the best coffee beans of the same hue as Jangle, are Besties and Lovers. They meet in Skip Academy. That's near Geneva, within the footprint of the VeryLargeSuperluminousHC where the Magi of Graviton Beams dwell. (BSc, MSci, PhD, Magus.)

That's where all the skipship pilots train, traditionally in trios, studying astrogation and sims of skipping a ship and repair engineering and exercising one's body. Skipships themselves are put together in orbit. Twenty per cent of the trainees' time is devoted to psychotherapy, not merely because Carl Jung was Swiss but because psychology is the deciding factor in head-hunting and accepting suitable recruits.

Enough of this local Earth colour. We're interested in interactions at a distance. Of 100+ Lights. Specifically, we focus upon Marisa's highly irregular rescue of Jangle from a superearth named Humangous.

Humangous is twice Earth's mass, thus the gravity is double. A bit gruelling for the colonists gifted with this destination.

Across the monotonous plains of Humangous, life descended from water-worms crawls amidst stiff flat vegetation. Worms the size of your arm are vegetarians; snakes the size of your leg are wormivores. Humangous's sun is an old red dwarf which long ago flared away an excessively deep dense atmosphere, now breathable through a mask, shame about the odour of rotten eggs. It's quite a horrid place. Habitable but nothing super about it at all.

'May Day! June Day! July Day!'

The traditional distress call bursts from *Ignore Thyself*'s speakers. Out on the brane we're beyond linear time, so radio goes all over the place unlimitedly. Yet apart from the squawks of Homo sap there's only static. Evidently no alien intelligences anywhere in our entire universe have ears or voices. So it's all up to us.

Please note that a trip by skipship from Earth to a solar system, for instance, 50 light years away only takes a few weeks ship-time. Likewise, returning to Earth. Time itself is being skipped as well as Space. Thus only a few weeks, times two, will have passed back home, not relativistic centuries. This might seem like impossible time-travel. It is not.

Analogy with grav-lensing *within* our universe. Grav-lensing gives rise to binary (or quad) branches, being equal routes from far distant destinations. These branches cradle a foreground star much closer to us. Known branewise as brackets, the arclets may close into a near-circle. Thus (+ thus) $\approx$ 0. If you like, you can call those braces, bouncy braces. (But not brakes.) Your skipship grabs the grav-beam oppositely to skip its way back to Solspace in sametime. This is known in the trade as *back-beaming*. [DO WE REALLY WISH TO UNZIP THESE EYES-ONLYS? TO UN-REDACT?]

−'June Day! July Day! May Day! I'm stuck on Humangous!'

All skippers currently out-of-cosmos hear this call. Especially Marisa on account of the voice being Jangle's.

By sheer serendipity − at least to Marisa's mentality − *Know Thyself* is on a grav-beam vector compatible with branchy arrival inside of forty hours at that shitty superearth Humangous.

(Don't disrespect sheer chance; humans and all life on Earth as well as Earth itself are the outcome of a chain of chance circumstances as long as your leg.)

'Marisa here, forty hours away as if by magic. What went bad? What's your angle, Jangle?'

Of course one shouldn't land a skipship on any world. A skipship is built in Earth orbit and it lives there, as it were. For skipping, it hitches on to a fresh graviton beam sent up from CERNPLUS. At destination, a skipship sheds velocity around the local star. If that's an M dwarf, it's close by. Then the skipper loops around the colony world a lot while downloading and uploading data. Data's the main cargo. Time-treasures from the past – from 50 years ago, from 230 years ago, depending how far out is the peopled world. Treasures such as new old music and movies and methodologies. These get to their destinations far faster than any electromag packages could arrive at the mere speed of light. In return, Earth really really wants to know all about the colony's progress in building any CERNPLUS of its own plus a few skipships to carry the wave of expansion outward and onward. If the colony's sun has gone nova and crisped the colonists, Marisa will be the person to notify Earth many years in advance of the light from the nova reaching out malevolently.

'Why you down on the surface, Jang?'

'Them Humangans shot me down!'

'Why they do such a thing?'

'Resentment? They get sent to this shithole it'll take umpteen umpteen generations to escape to find some better world further out. There isn't even any easily accesible Europium or any [REDACTED]. I'm an embodiment of what they can't do yet. The Humangans won't have any CERNPLUS for yonkies but they can manage to missile down a skipship. Shit.'

'You a prisoner?'

'Only of double gravity so far! The Humangons are still searching for where I crash. Messaging friendly co-operation if I light a beacon. Promising a power wheelchair, which I don't believe. They can have *Gnaw Thyself* which will never take off again. Myself don't want to be had. Respect to our crashsafe engineers, by the way.'

Normally after lots of looping, the skipship slings itself away from a world and then [REDACTED]. It takes a special kind of skipper not to yearn to see with her own eyes, for instance, the Three Kilom Tall Scarlet Waterfall of Silverberg IV (REDACTING the star's true cosmic catalogue number and whereabouts). Returning to Solspace some weeks later, the skipship will dump velocity by [REDACTED].

Marisa fastbuzzes a grinf of Sylvester from classic celluloid *Mad Mad World* banging on the steering wheel of his convertible, babbling, 'I'm comin', mama!' Iconic stuff.

'I'm coming, mama!' Marisa yells and steps on the grav-gas metaphorically by thumbing the delta-vee rheostat of her console to red line. Normally you don't run any ship at fullmax for hours on end but Jangle's ultraspecial to our Marisa.

Since less than forty hours is a fair while inside or outside of our own spacetime, there's enough space and time to tell more about tardigrades; for which be you duly grateful...

Skipship regs, aimed to avoid on-board killings by naturally slaughterous Homo saps with possible attendant loss of a costly ship, forbid sharing a ship with any second individual. Companion creatures likewise are banned, to be on the safe side. You might swallow a cat's deliberately dangling tail in your sleep, for instance, and choke.

However, tardigrades are exempt. At half a millimetro in length even *en masse* these slow minuscule chubbies are unlikely to massacre you. There being a thousand separate species of themselves suggests that they don't go in much for genocide the Homo sap way, even though they fight and sometimes eat one another. On her ring finger, Marisa wears a magnificatory micro-hab carpeted by green algae where four tardigrades amble and suck. Their behaviour causes them to be called 'water-bears', even though they have eight legs, not four. Alternatively, 'moss piglets'. How cute is that? Barf. Those little critturs survived *all five* mass extinctions on Terra. Just think of that. All five extinction filters. They're such a symbol of survival.

So it's our duty to carry them to every place possible. They're ace at cryptobiosis; if only humans were, we'd fill the Milky Way faster! Like us, though microscopically, water-bears sometimes cuddle for affection – or they may simply be bumping and getting their ickle claws tangled.

Marisa always gives her dots the same names: Itch, Bibs, Dotty, Tiny Tyres. They're due for jettisoning along with urine and solids anywhere nearish to a world or moon however marginally habitable. Sensing vacuum, each piglet-bear will pull in all eight legs and dessicate itself. Eventually it'll drift down like a dot of dust. Marisa doesn't need to land her skipship to do a good deed for destiny, or dustiny. Given a billy years or so, who knows what? To spread Tardies plus human waste including a billy bacteria far out in space: that's virtuous and righteous behaviour. So this discharge contributes to dirtying space? Only in a very minor way! Marisa can easily refill her ring-hab from *Ignore Thyself*'s library of freeze-dried Tardies, activating a new iteration of Itch, Bibs, Dotty, and Tiny Tyres.

'Gal, how's my Jangle?'

'Still free. No signs of Humangan drones even. I'm catapulting my whole catalogue of Tardies all over the landscape.'

'Planet gotta have Tardies already.'

'Maybe not so many species.'

'Right! Get more Darwinny compo going.'

'Nature raw in claw and sucker. Bitch, this is one wearisome world.'

'Cargo pod check out okay?'

'Ob la di, ob la da,' sounds like a cheerful shrug.

'I'll be snatching you fast coming past. Don't forget to fill that poddy with gee-gel from the mergency store.'

'I know.'

'Hasn't been done before, thisy, Missy. Mainly because it's total illegal.'

'Oh to be a Tardie, now Marisa's near. Suck myself flat is what I'd like for now.'

And it works, it works. *Ignore Thyself* streaks cometlike through the atmos of mossy 2 Gee Humangous and [REDACTED] and [REDACTED] and finally [REDACTED] on to the non-distant graviton beam. Once free from binding attachment to the spacetime metric of our own cosmos, due to topology the connectivity remains yet distances roll up tight like pillbugs. Consequently the [REDACTED].

Ignore Thyself tugs *Gnaw Thyself*'s cargo poddy along with it now.

Presently Marisa and Jangle are reunited. Naked Jangle's dripping with gee-gel and sneezing. In sympathy Marisa has stripped off her own shipsuit.

'We've done it now, girl!' cries Marisa. 'We're outlaws from Skippy Guild. We've skipped out.'

Marisa has a crooked nose with prominent bridge, broken in the womb by persistent kicks from a twin brother, stillborn what a shame due to the bothersome brother being strangled by Marisa's birth-cord. She has always refused cosmetic regularisation of her nose, a point in her favour perhaps with those psychomagi who eventually trust trained pilots with actual skipships. Skipships are limited in number due to scarcity of superconductive Europium essential to the [REDACTED].

Jangle's nose is fatter and flatter than Marisa's, and nicely nostrilled. Marisa has ginger shoulder-swirly hair with much-freckled skin. Jangle's skin is burnt-buttery, her hair of choice short, spiky, and scarlet, same colour as the Three Kilom Tall Waterfall of Silverberg IV.

Of their bodies and their behaviour with said bodies we shall probably say nothing further. What are you, *voyeurs*?

'Now what,' asks Jangle, 'do we do with our future?'

'Immediate future, for sure we'll have fun. As for ahead, if Brane sucks gravity from our cosmos then we *might* bleed power from the Bulk. We'll see. So let's rename gravity gravy. Little lumps in the gravity are gravitons. This means that – '
[REDACT! REDACT!]

She's bright, is Marisa. A sun may be brighter than her and Jangle combined, but a sun has no brain.

Overwhelmed, the two Besties slide down the curve of wall to buttock the floor. Sweat trickles off the both of them. Then they slide further, not because the ship itself is rocking and rolling. (Satisfied, huh?)

Marisa and Jangle do enjoy sharing *Ignore Thyself*. Squealing, they play Hide and Seek the Alien, and Blind-Gal's Buff. They feast on jerk chickens from the many little on-hull freezelarders, and on curry goat – it's as if all along Marisa was awaiting this hosting. Course she won't ever be able to reload her larders, so watch out for cannibalism – don't be saps, Homo saps! Eating one's bestie funhun can only be a temporary solution. Though in the meantime feel free to focus on the thrill of being together illicitly.

'Illi City – where?'

'Illicitly,' Marisa corrects Jangle.

'Can there be such a place? Can other Skippers have disobeyed in the past? Defected along with their skipships? Somewhere is there a Sanctuary so to speak?'

'Why on Earth should there be a Sanctuary? You in some crazy cargo cult turned inside out? Us two are 'bliged to run away cos we broke the code. In all other ways, Earth's wunderbar for rich pilots. The darling lonely deserts to hike. The jungly oases of caviar and champagne under the stars. The roar of tigers with trust collars.'

A supper of ackee fruit with saltfish.

Jangle sighs. 'Missy, you really push the boat out with your jammy menus so far. Almost as if you guess ahead of time.'

Indeed Marisa must be much smitten by Jangle to include so many Jamaican meals in her external deepfreeze larders. May Marisa subconsciously have reserved most of her Jamaican meals until now several weeks *into* her journey? Saving the best till second servings? Not intentionally so; that cannot be.

Hurriedly Marisa asks her Bestie, 'You reckon CERNPLUS Central mighta sent you to planet Humangous to test the water of resentment, even at risk of losing you?'

'What a wild notion! Me shot down, how does CPC learn the outcome? Why be asking me?'

Why be asking? Life is heuristic. Well, human life is. Some humans' lives are. Maybe also some whales and octopodes.

'Unless, unless,' pursues Marisa, 'Central *knew* that your plucky Bestie would be on a close enough graviton-beam vector to pluck you to safety! And intended this!'

'I can do without ackee'n'saltfish to be honest. Important question, Missy, is could we find Sanctuary before we run out of jammy jerk chicken?'

'Any millennium soon, only by very improbable coincidence,' answers Melisa. 'Given the enormity of our own galaxy, Gal, then of our supposed supercluster, then universe. More to the point, you and me know how many *surplus* pilots graduated in our own year at Skipping School, and how rare skipships are. How could there ever be more than three or four people max to populate some paradise for runaways?'

'You got a point, Missy. You got many points.'

Just where are our disobedient duo heading towards at the moment, eh? It's a real shame the amount of redacting one has to do, in order to comply with [REDACTED].

Presently – as well as pleasantly – Jangle asks, 'Why don't we just go back to planet Earth together and accept the consequences? *Whatever* those consequences are! It isn't as if we had much choice. They should be pleased to get one skipship back.'

'What if,' muses Marisa, 'this was all to test whether two Besties will become homicidal inhabiting a hall of mirrors such as here?'

'You're saying we may have been manoeuvred?'

Ship-days pass pleasantly, lovingly by. Besides fun and games in the corridors, there's a whole library of virtual interactives. For only one player, it's true, but you can invoke the same avatar twice over sharingly.

Today they'll lunch on callaloo stew of veg with Scotch bonnets cooked in coconut milk. Never since the rescue have the pair squabbled nor escalated to literal murderous smiting as per the *Bible* book. Might a different couple, becoming conflicted in cuisine, kill one another more readily?

'Missy, where was you headed before you saved me?'

It has taken a long time to mention this. Several jerk chickens. Plus a callaloo or two. Not to mention a saltfish with omelette-yellow ackee. Can Jangle conceivably have suppressed her curiosity out of sheer joy, not wanting to spoil things?

'Gongorry,' says Marisa, rhyming with sorry. Marisa isn't too sorry about that destination since Gongorry is one of the more habitable homes of humanity. Half mostly searing billiard ball riven by thermal canyons, half mostly frozen sea. Veggy waistband overrun with cannibal rat-things plus a whole linnaeus of subordinate ecology. Oxy 21 per cent. High helium: silly voices. Muchos raw materials in deeply ruptured canyons fringing the waistband both sides before The Big Hot. Plenty of stuff to build one's own CERNPLUS from. World even has its own fully connected band running all the way around world's waist, supposing the locals want to outdo CERNPLUS rather a lot, although watch out for the cannibal rat-things, summit of local evolution, admirable as such nevertheless.

'By now we ought to be looping Gongorry's star on a graviton lasso at a Pluto sort of distance,' says Marisa as though daring redaction.

'Why don't we take refuge on Gongorry?'

'The law! The law!'

'We'll tell the Gongors the law changed. How will they know any otherwise? And why should they care? We could park *Ignore Thyself* in tighter orbit and pod ourselves down.'

'Give the Gongors something to aspire to... Per ardua ad orbitum? They should get a graviton beam machine in less than a generation. We'll be, um, nicely appreciated for our, um, generosity, you'd think, um? Planetary sponsors. Skipship donors. Pensions for life, so to speak?'

Jangle and Marisa contemplate one another (not at all homicidally).

'Will they have jerk chicken on Gongorry, eh Missy?'

'Maybe jerk alt-rat.'

'So we'd *really* like to be young-age pensioners stuck for life in a canyon where scuttle cannibal rats? I don't think so.'

'We'll volunteer to train Gongorry's skipship pilots... when the time is ripe.'

'When we're sixty-four.' That's another old saying. And snags (see next) are apparently Oztralian sausages.

'Jangly, the next freeze-pantry module along is empty! How can that be?'

'I sure not been snacking secretly!'

'Shows full 'n' froze on the manifest yet nothing's inside.'

'What was sposed to be in the moddy?'

'Oz tucker mainly.'

'Roo Loin at midnight with lashings of Top Ketch? Int for me. Catering musta left a moddy empty.'

'But how?'

'Ran out of sauce powder?'

'I guess.'

Now that the menu *may* be entirely of Marisa's earlier choosing, is Jangle going to get sniffy about a diet of Chicken Parmy, Barbied Snags, Burgers with The Lot, and Roo Loin with Tom Ketch for instance?

Please note that a master chef doing their thing with a cuisine synthesiser, like playing a big taste organ, can devise programmes to simulate perfectly jerk chicken or barbied snags, not to mention many now extinct species such as roast reindeer and roo no we mean gnu. A corresponding synthesiser aboard a skipship could emulate these dishes. But compared with microwaving takeaways, a shipboard synthesiser will gobble power, whereas freezing is free in space as well as on the brane.

In the sheer careless rapture of being together far from Sol, our Besties get distracted. Blame those interactive virtuals.

When Marisa finds another moddy to be empty, she screams. She freaks.

Jangle comes sprinting, bouncing off rounded corners. Ship's grav is bled from the skip-beam of gravitons.

'Shortfall, shortfall!' cries Marisa. 'We're not provisioned full!'

'Why why why?' shrieks Jangle. She's a pilot too and understands cold equations, as well as hot equations. As applied to food supplies. Tea for one as against tea for two.

Just me for you. And you for me.

They're both aware that as soon as you open any freezer moddy from corridor-side to handle the contents, there snaps into place upon the hull a corresponding vacuum lock robust as a Maiden Mole's proverbial hymen. If the contents listed on the moddy's door are true and accurate, you can't simply close the door again to keep the food frozen inside. It'll defrost in a few days. Carry the food to the galley's own minifreezer, okay no problem. But only once.

Design error? They cannot verify the contents of *all* unopened moddies of future food without spoiling the meals inside. Ration the frozen food and ration whatever way, there mayn't be enough for two. Big black holes colliding in the home cosmos as well as mega explosions send graviton jitters through the brane. Could easily add a fortnight to a journey. Two times, three times over.

Marisa screams. 'Blue murder! Blue bloody murder!'

'Hate to say it,' from Jangle after a cool-down, 'but open another moddy ahead at random? So we risk spoiling the food in that one. Bit of rationing won't kill us.'

'Yes! Yes!'

Along the twisty corridor of moddies they rush.

Shouts Marisa, 'Choose a number between fifty and a hundred.'

'Eight-three.'

'Here we are. Contents, um, says Oz tucker. Dog's eyes,

pies... Here goes... Oh blue buggeroo! This'uns empty too. Shows full but just ain't been filled. We can't trust any of the moddies! Our cryolarder can be *critical* low, Jangers, and we daren't check is or isn't. Sheeeet, sheeeet,' she screams, hyperventilating.

'Sheeeet!' Jangle shrieks too. 'We might die! Any message in the empty moddy, Melbourne?'

'Zip zilch. You can hunt till the edge of frostbite.' Off the scale she goes in shrill.

Recovering her ventilation, Marisa finally says, 'I guess we're supposed to work this out ownsomely. Or I'm supposed.'

'Us. We. Solidarity, Bestie. You saved me.'

'Saved you *for what*? Skin 'n' bones? We might starve – and we don't know what's best to choose to do!'

Best to strangle while one is still strong?

Afterwards may the perpetrator spot the victim in any of the many mirrors of *Ignore Thyself*? The dear departed, returning in delusions and in dreams? Remonstrating, gibbering – no, Jangle won't gibber, she's Jamaican. Hey, are we assuming that *Marisa* has to be the murderer? Jangle too knows perfectly well how to pilot. She's a hot hand at her job.

We watched you from out of every mirror. Recorded all. The experiment is valuable and valid. Justified for the diffusion of the Homo sap species. Conclusion: The most devoted of human duos are potentially homicidal even with one another. Experiment unrepeatable. Skipships don't grow on trees! There's never enough Europium nor [REDACT]. Not for all the tea in China.

We must assume it's Marisa who returns to Earth Orbit in *Ignore Thyself*. [REDACTED] How can it be otherwise? As skipper, she's the only person permitted aboard! Recall how her twin bro strangled himself in utero.

Marisa may or may not be skinnier after her journey but

she's no skeleton. Contrary, she looks well nourished, though melancholy. Tears well from time to time. Missy Marisa's valiant illegal attempt to rescue Jangle must have missed hooking up magnetically, after all.

A thousand million years hence, Humankind's purpose is accomplished in the Titanic Tardigrade. An interstellar blimp that grazes wet worlds, and from their surfaces blasts hardy eggs into orbit. The double gravity of Humangous provided just the right sort of Darwinian push. Eight legs good; amble onward, impervious. Go big, go bigger, go biggest. Store compressed highly explosive highly flammable Hydrogen Sulfide fartgas. Rocket propellant for armoured eggs.

A milly years between worlds doesn't matter at all. Onward slowly but surely shall spread Titanic Tardies. In four and a half billie years Tardies will fill the Milky Way while Mighty Andromeda is passing through our home galaxy shepherding numerous sufficiently adequate worlds.

Two giant galaxies colliding doesn't mean that any of the billies of stars therein will even come within a light year of touching another star. Space is vast and empty. That's why it's called space.

Still, much gets stirred. Presently – futurely – there'll be a lot more Tardigrade life in the cosmos than ever would have been without CERNPLUS.

Afterword: The Shortest Distance Between Two Points

Dr Andrea Bersani
Italian Institute for Nuclear Physics

WHEN I FIRST PROPOSED the use of graviton beams to allow for faster-than-light interstellar space travel, I had in mind the first major issue of any space-based sci-fi tale: how to reach remote parts of the universe in a reasonable timeframe (i.e. without having to put the crew to sleep for several centuries in 'suspended animation'). In the universe, after all, everywhere is remote. In Euclidean geometry, i.e. in an undistorted, unbent space-time, the shortest distance between two points is, famously, a straight line. And if that straight line is between liveable planets, in many cases it will be many light-years (or even light-centuries) long. But in a non-Euclidean geometry, that is to say in space-time that can be 'bent' or 'distorted', there is a shorter route. Imagine space-time is a tablecloth, with a series of decorative points patterned across it. A normal route between two points would be their distance from each other on the flattened-out tablecloth. But if somehow we could scrunch up the tablecloth, create a fold in it, then two very distant points in it can be brought together, back to back; then suddenly the shortest distance between them can be reduced to next to nothing (if the back of one point on the cloth is pressed up against the back of the other point). Then all the space traveller needs to do is leave the cloth (backwards), traverse the gap behind it, into the point of the cloth on the other fold. In the analogy, it's simple enough. But how do we do it in reality?

As a candidate for how we might distort or 'fold' space-time, gravitons are a fairly natural choice. As Einstein showed us in his General Theory of Relativity, gravity is deeply linked to space-time geometry. A massive object with a strong gravitational field, like a large planet or a star, effectively creates a depression or 'dent' in the 2-dimensional analogue for space-time (the tablecloth metaphor). We know this from studying the movement of Mercury in its orbit around the sun. The sun's gravity is so strong and Mercury so small and close, it's effectively spinning around the 'dent' the sun has created in the space-time tablecloth. Only General Relativity can accurately map Mercury's movement. Indeed, the first time GR was empirically tested was in 1919 when Arthur Eddington went to the island of Principe to take photos of background constellations around the edge of the sun in a lunar eclipse (normally the sun's glaring light would make such photos impossible) and compared them with photos of the same constellations once the sun had moved out the way. The two photos were different. Around its edge, the sun had distorted space-time, and in doing so created ever so slightly shorter routes than a straight line.

The effect of gravity on space-time has been known for over a century. What's new about the idea outlined in Ian's story is the concept of using space stations to act as pinch points – with intense graviton beams acting as portals (where the tablecloth is briefly pinched together) – and combining several similarly-engineered space stations together to create a kind of network of highways. This opens up a scenario in which one can travel faster than light but only along these predetermined highways. (We might also be able to create ships with their own, smaller scale graviton beams onboard, for portalling short distances between the preset routes, like connecting bridges between highways. Maybe one day we could even use graviton beams or portals to create slingshot trajectories, the way relatively simple Voyager crafts slingshot diagonally off other planet's natural gravitational fields.)

So far, so simple.

The problem is gravity is not simple. It may have been the first fundamental force to be studied and systematised – Newton's famous apple and much more importantly his inverse -square law. But since Newton, our understanding of gravity has lagged way behind all physics' other objects of enquiry, with only Einstein's 1915 GR theory taking it any distance forward. The problem with Einstein's GR version of gravity is it cannot be reconciled with quantum field theory (in which all forces have carrier particles). Gravity is very weak (it takes a whole planet's worth of mass to stop objects floating away into space), but it seems to propagate at the speed of light, so if it has a force-carrier particle (a graviton) that particle would have to be massless. However, in quantum field theory, particles have to be 'renormalised' (this means accounting for the difference between how a particle behaves on its own, in isolation – its mass and charge – with how it behaves when it interacts with others). With gravity acting at huge (perhaps even infinite) distances and at the speed of light, a graviton could effectively be interacting with an infinite number of other particles. So we get a problem; a maths problem.

The result is we don't actually know if the graviton even exists. As far as we currently understand things, single graviton interactions are impossible to detect. Perhaps gravity is actually something completely different to the other three fundamental forces (EMF, and the strong and weak nuclear forces), which do have force-carrier particles. Some people have even speculated that gravity might be a weak leakage from another dimension or another cosmic 'brane' in a multiverse of different universes. Given the growing mysteriousness of gravity, it is hard to imagine mankind ever being able to create a beam of these (possibly non–existent) gravitons.

But even though, as a physicist, the idea of it strikes me as just a pipe dream, and all current knowledge suggests this will never be possible, as a human, I have to believe I might be wrong. Einstein famously said gravitational waves would never be observed, and we have now observed them.[1] And if Einstein can be wrong, then I certainly can be!

So let's look for some signs of hope. In 2012 the Higgs boson has been observed, and this particle shares with the graviton some kind of link with the mass (as gravity affects things with mass, then Higgs, the mass-giver is also a gravity-giver). But could they be linked in some other, unexpected way? Could other bosons, heavier than the Higgs, also exist? Could some of the things we still ignore about the world of elementary particles and fundamental interactions open some new window on the long-lasting problem of gravitation quantisation?

The only way to answer these questions is to go on with the research, to quote a quite famous sci-fi franchise... to boldly go (in knowledge) where no one has gone before.

In 'Skipping', Ian Watson has built a wonderful story based on the apparent paradoxes arising in this possible future, adding a significant and valuable layer in the psychology of the characters, which is something I sincerely hadn't imagined. Indeed, the implications of travelling such a way would almost certainly be a game changer on the way we see the cosmos and our position in it.

Note

1. The first direct observation of gravitational waves was made on 14 September 2015 and was announced by the LIGO (US) and Virgo (Italy) collaborations on 11 February 2016. The waveform, detected by both LIGO observatories, matched the predictions of general relativity for a gravitational wave emanating from the inward spiral and merger of a pair of black holes of around 36 and 29 solar masses.

The Ogre, the Monk and the Maiden

Margaret Drabble

THEY WERE KNOWN AT CERN as the Ogre, the Monk and the Maiden. *Der Eiger, der Mönch und die Jungfrau.* They hiked together, they skied together, they lived in the same on-site condominium. They worked together as an entangled threesome, and they are now sitting as a threesome round the vast turquoise heaven-reflecting pool in their silvery and lime green Peakstar Swimwear, drinking their beers and gazing at the icy mountains. They are in relaxed and happy mode, as they plan their outing for the next day, which is to be a public holiday.

The nature of their entanglement is not clear to their gossiping colleagues, but by this point, sexual relations and gender identity, as well as particle physics, have become so complex and fluid that any imaginable or unimaginable permutations are possible. CERN is by and large a tolerant community, and almost anything goes. The trio is well liked.

The Ogre was a fearsome figure, nearly seven feet tall, immensely strong, and a ferociously competitive tennis player: he brought to the minds of those with longer memories that tennis star of the early twenty-first century who died unvaccinated in his fifties of Covid-19 in the fifth wave of the

Zeta Variant. There was something asymmetrical about the shape of his head that also summoned up the image of Victor Frankenstein's Geneva-born monster. (Some unkindly folk nicknamed him Boris, which he did not like, although he was happy to be known as the Ogre.) He does not look like a sensitive soul, but he is. He is.

Victor Frankenstein was not forgotten at CERN (although Mary Shelley largely was) and Frankenstein's name was still a watchword for scientific hubris, which journalists love to apply to any ambitious, outsized or jeopardous enterprise that dares to tempt providence. It had hovered ominously in the 2030s over the early planning stages of the FCC (the Future Circular Collider, now the Finished Circular Collider). Frankenphysics and Frankenphotons were invoked by those who knew nothing whatsoever about the science or scope or indeed limitations of the FCC, just as the word Frankenfoods had been conveniently coined in the 1990s by those who objected to GM Crops. Frankenstein's ghost still haunts Geneva.

The FCC has been working well for the last couple of years, although its passionate advocates had many difficulties to overcome in its planning stages, not least concerning its funding, and there had inevitably been one or two blips during the lengthy and massive engineering project.

Some were caused by the devastating winter storms and avalanches and the unprecedented lake rise and flooding of 2045, which had suspended all engineering work for months. Another later weather-related incident, involving a rockfall on Mont Hilaire, had caused the FCC to be temporarily switched off, confusing the bewildered particles already in transit; it had also unfortunately (from the quantum physicists' point of view) revealed the remains of a frozen Ice Man, the analysis of whose DNA was to push back the date of the birth of homo sapiens another twenty thousand years or so. This had held up operations for a further six months, as the archaeologists and the anthropologists had their way. This discovery recalled the unwelcome unearthing of the remains of a fourth century

Roman farm and villa at Cessy, which had suspended and diverted work on its predecessor, the LHC, in 1998. If you dig too deep, there's always a chance of finding something you really don't want or need to see.

★ Footnote: *2045, the year of storms, had also swamped the nuclear reactor at Hinkley Point in Somerset, as many had foreseen it might – why on earth, why on this most beautiful and one and only earth, had they decided to build a reactor on the bird-frequented shore of the second highest tidal range in the world, when they could have built a safer, cleaner, greener, cheaper tidal lagoon barrage just down the river in Swansea Bay?*

All large projects have their detractors, and the size of the FCC had in those early days caused a lot of ill-informed commentary from those who wished it ill, and who resented the many billions of spesmili it was then projected to cost, which in their view should have been spent on public health, or space tourism, or armaments. (The spesmilo, a unit of universal currency first created and coined in Switzerland in 1907, had been reintroduced after the collapse of the euro in the 2030s, and the subsequent bitter entanglement of the dollar, the yuan and the yen.) The FCC was many times larger than the Large Hadron Collider, the track of which its great circle intersected – the LHC was a mere 27 or so kilometres long, and the FCC ended up at slightly over a hundred. ('Or so' and 'slightly over' weren't the kind of calculations that the engineers used, fortunately, but in this context, they will do. And it's worth noting that when the two ends of the circular tunnel of the LHC met, their alignment was 'within one centimetre': with the FCC, they met within thirty millimetres.)

Many attempts had been made to stall or sabotage its creation, by property owners, by religious doom mongers, by journalists gleefully predicting black holes, by romantic souls fearful of the impact on the historic landscape, by skiers worried about their ski slopes, by the proponents of rival colliders in other countries. There were even some serious Cambridge-based quantum physicists who argued that the journalistic notions of the black holes or vacuum decay that the new collider might create were not without foundation: it was calculated by some that the chance of a collider disaster ending the known universe was about level with the chance of a punter winning the UK lottery, which to some (presumably to most of the punters) didn't seem very long odds, although with rather more at stake. But common sense (if that can be applied to anything to do with the often counter-intuitive nature of quantum mechanics) prevailed and the testing of the geology of the molasse and moraine and limestone had, as we know, continued.

A long-sustained act of resistance took the form of the ingenious legal attempts of an old woman, Madame Longuenesse, living just over the French side of the border, who claimed (rightly) that she owned the land under her farmstead right to the centre of the earth, and that nobody had the right to infringe her subterranean property. The farm had been built in 1816, as the date carved above its stone lintel proclaimed, and in her view it was good for another century. (The Swiss own their land only to a shallow depth, but the French own it to the core: it was not for nothing that that great Frenchman Jules Verne had stirred the imagination of generations with his *Journey to the Centre of the Earth*.) Living so close to the French-Swiss border – on the surface, indeed, she was within easy walking distance of Switzerland – she was well versed in the intricacies of Swiss and French property law, having fought previous battles about inheritance, stray cows, and invasive vegetation.

Madame Longuenesse had finally been talked out of her opposition by her great nephew, who happened to be an engineer who had worked on the successor to the James Webb telescope, the Vera Rubin, and who managed to persuade her that Jules Verne himself would have loved the FCC. Ferdinand spoke to her of the glories of the universe, of the thrill of the largest in search of the smallest, of the journey back to the primal soup of the Big Bang. She had listened, sagely, staring out at the meadow where her last cow Jonquille calmly grazed. They were all gone now, Gentiane, Paquerette, Violette, Mauve, Narcisse, Colchique, Coquelicot and Perce-Neige; the pretty douce soft-eyed Jonquille was the last of all her herd. And Mme Longuenesse had finally conceded that she didn't really want to stand in the way of progress. She wasn't interested in the utilitarian by-products of knowledge such as smarter smart phones or better MRI scans. She was too old for that kind of thing. It was knowledge itself that appealed to her, though she had difficulty in comprehending how it would manifest itself.

She liked the notion of Quark Gluon Plasma, that hot primeval liquid that had filled the universe for the first microsecond of its existence, and tried (unsuccessfully) to get young Ferdinand to explain to her whether QGP was a hypothesis or a known reality. Apparently, it was both. Like waves and particles. She took to calling her signature soup, a primeval vegan mix of carrot, chard and endive, by the name of QGP.

She also decided she really did not want to block or hold up the discovery of what dark matter was really made of. So she withdrew her opposition, called in her lawyers, allowed the tunnellers to continue to tunnel and the sappers to sap, and became quite interested in dark matter. 'We are for the dark,' she would say from time to time. 'We might as well know what it is made of. It might illumine us. I will die before anyone sees it, if anyone ever sees it, but it will be there for me, and I may see it in the new dawn.'

Her great nephew was awarded the Prix Isambard Pictet for his diplomatic efforts, though those efforts were not mentioned on the citation, which more discreetly applauded his notable contribution to the field of supermagnetic engineering. The award came with a very pleasing diamond, emerald and golden enamel medal. He gave it, respectfully, to his great aunt, who wore it regularly on her trips to the meadow and the village and her occasional excursions across the border to Geneva and Lausanne. Ferdinand was very fond of his Tantine Aurore, who had told him many stories of the myths of the mountains when he was a little boy. She had told him of the Devils of Derborence, of the Fairies of Fafleralp, of the helpful little red-collared frog of the Jura, and of the Forest of the Three Pathways. She had told him of the Seven Sleepers who had slept for a hundred years in a cave of ice, and awoken to another world.

She was not very interested in the notion of cryopreservation. She was on good terms with mortality. But she liked the story of the Seven Sleepers, and so did Ferdinand.

Madame Aurore Longuenesse was a late convert to the potential glories of the FCC, but the Ogre, the Monk and the Maiden had been enthusiasts from their youth. The Ogre had loved the idea of its creation since his childhood. His somewhat lopsided head and broken nose were the result of an early skiing accident near his childhood home of Denver, where he had collided at *grande vitesse* with a tree. The ensuing months of enforced inactivity in traction in hospital had given him ample time to study, and he acquired a lasting interest in quantum mechanics. He had always been good at mathematics and physics, and the new fields of exploration were tempting to him. He lay back on his bed and gazed at a never-ending display of bursts of particles exploding across his vast Ceiling Screen, the earliest from the strikingly beautiful neutrino-detecting bubble chamber of Gargamelle at CERN, which had been operating in the 1970s, long before he was born, but whose images had not yet been surpassed for aesthetic quality.

These had been followed by tracks from the LHC, by footage of the memorable confirmation of the Higgs Boson (with Peter Higgs wiping a tear from his eye), by images that were invoked in support of supersymmetry theory, and by pictorial predictions of the future discoveries of the FCC. When he was back on his feet again, a visit to the many miles of the new linear accelerator in Texas (the TEXLA) had sealed his destiny, and he had set his heart on being posted to CERN, the Mecca of particle physicists, where he could combine his unabated passion for skiing with his passion for particles. He was a happy man when he arrived at CERN, and made the acquaintance of the Monk and the Maiden. He felt he had been reborn.

The Monk had come to particle acceleration by a different route. He was that rare creature in the polyglot multinational society of Switzerland and CERN, a Swiss citizen with a Swiss ancestry stretching back to the dawn of the republic. His family was not placed among the hundred great and wealthy families of the Genevese aristocracy, but it went back a very long way. His ancestors included Calvinist theologians, Voltaire-befriending children of the Enlightenment, many rural pastors and a few early Alpinists. He boasted that one branch had taken part in the anti-Savoyard Escalade of 1602, an event which was still commemorated every year. He too, like the Ogre, liked to ski, but he also liked to climb, often recklessly. He had scaled the North Face of the Eiger several times, and had trodden in the footsteps of that great pioneer, Horace Bénédict de Saussure, physicist and mountaineer, whose statue to this day stands at Chamonix.

The Monk was a symmetrical man, with a precise and orderly mind, who claimed that the watch-making genius of the Swiss flowed in his veins, where it mingled with the theological passions of the Reformation. He was a much tidier man than the sprawling Ogre (aka Milan). He had a bald brown head and a well-trimmed tonsure, in contrast to the Ogre's tufted dishevelled uncombed locks. The Ogre was a very hairy man, and the Monk (whose real name was Theo) was a very smooth man. He was also, perhaps surprisingly, a serious gambler, and would have been seen in the casinos more frequently, had his companions not restrained and diverted him. He had had some notable successes, in the past, at the tables in Monte Carlo, and he was too good by half at poker, though he always lost on the horses.

Appropriately, he was tormented by god and metaphysics and predestination, and thoroughly enjoyed discussing these matters with anyone who would take him on. Some said he should have been a philosopher, not a physicist, and his first degree had indeed been in Physics and Philosophy at the University of Neuchatel. He was interested in the notion that you could become a billionaire by playing Quantum Russian Roulette, in the MWI (Many-Worlds Interpretation) of quantum mechanics, although he did not, of course, believe in MWI. He said he believed (though of course, he could not prove) that every particle since the Big Bang and the beginning of the universe was following a predestined course, and that human attempts to understand or to intervene in that trajectory were utterly irrelevant. The observer made no difference to the observed. On the other hand, he argued that it was our human duty to attempt to follow the trajectory, back to the first millisecond of the first Bang and on to the final Bang. God or Fate had required it of us, and so had Theo's ancestors. Free will there was not, and never had been, not for men or for women, not for eagles or for cows or for particles. Duty was all. *Stern Duty, who preserves the stars from wrong,* as the poet of the northern lakes had put it. God had thrown the dice, and the fallout was final. It's just that it hadn't happened yet.

And the Maiden? The Jungfrau? Ah, she contained multitudes. Even in this international age of the 2050s, she embodied more nationalities than most. The Ogre was a fairly simple, far from unusual and genetically identifiable mixture of American and Eastern European, and the Monk, as we have seen, was proud to be more-or-less pure Swiss. But the Maiden's lineage stretched back to India and Guyana, to the fens of Cambridgeshire and the redwood forests of California, to the falls of the Zambezi, to the now-submerged Pacific islands of Polynesia. And she had inherited the beauty of each nation, of each continent. She glowed with an unearthly light. The Ogre and the Monk were her bodyguards. She was rather too fond of reciting poetry, in a mellifluous but somewhat boringly incantatory voice, but this was her only blemish.

She was particularly fond of Percy Bysshe Shelley and of William Blake and Byron. The Ogre used to groan when she got going again on the Tyger's Fearful Symmetry, and the Monk deplored her devotion to Shelley's atheistic and vacuous ramblings about Prometheus and the Alps. But they didn't mind the thought of seeing the world in a grain of sand and eternity in an hour, and reluctantly, when cornered, conceded that Blake had been endowed with true prophetic vision. He would have comprehended the workings of the FCC in an instant.

Shelley, however, was a step too far.

They liked it when she quoted Baudelaire, because his verses had a good resonance. There was a poem about the tomb of Icarus that she particularly admired, and she persuaded them to like it too. (There had once been a sterile-neutrino detector called Icarus, which, though decommissioned long ago, hadn't come to as bad an end as its name might have foretold.) Like many quantum physicists, the Maiden (or Jaz, as she was commonly known) was also keen on Jorge Luis Borges and his Forking Paths, a useful quantum analogy, to the extent that she kept circulating his very short story on the 'Inexactitude of Science' by any means that occurred to her, which included, embarrassingly, projecting its subversive title by Quantolitebeme on the night sky on the Ogre's birthday.

A map as big as the world, an accelerator as large as the cosmos – these are projects doomed to failure, and maybe one day the shattered mineshafts of the FCC will bear witness to the abandonment of hope, as did the tattered ruins of the Borgesian map, which lay in the distant deserts and mountain ranges.

Already, some were arguing, a much much larger, more powerful collider than the FCC would soon be needed. An accelerator as big as Switzerland itself...

Switzerland, the cradle and the crucible.

Jaz, as one might have guessed, came to CERN and particle physics via linguistics, an unusual but by no means unique route. Her first degree was in PPL (Particle Physics and Linguistics), taken largely remotely at the Saussure Institute, and she had gone on to dedicate her PhD to the problems of the interface of language and quantum physics – the seeing of the invisible, the speaking of the inexpressible – and the metaphorical language in which scientists are obliged to clothe their communications with the outside world.

Most of those associated with CERN were multilingual, although English was still its official language, and yet, as the decades rolled by, language itself was becoming less central to thinking. People thought in equations, in numbers, in particles, not in words. They conversed in the Esperanto of Equations. Ferdinand de Saussure, the great grandson of the Alpinist, had seen this coming, although he hadn't lived long enough to witness its full flowering. His algebraic notations, way back in the nineteenth century, had greatly resembled equations, his symbols were more algebraic than phonetic, and, like a classical physicist, he had tried to reduce language to its smallest indivisible parts. He too had tried to look back to the dawn of time – well, not of cosmic time, but of human time, human culture, human association, human speech. He had tried to gaze back beyond Sanskrit and to imagine the first sounds made by humanity. The lost world of 'our earlier and purer selves', as his diligent chronicler put it. The first sounds of the as yet undiscovered and unfrozen Ice Man. (At one point Saussure was almost persuaded that he was listening to the language of Mars and the Martians, a language even older than Sanskrit, uttered from human lips.) He had a romantic spirit, which meant that he was forever unfulfilled, forever thwarted, forever underpublished.

(Particle acceleration isn't really a destructive desire to knock atoms to pieces. It's not like breaking up an expensive Swiss watch to see what it's made of, though some have made that comparison. No. It's a search for the new, not a destruction of the old.)

And yet, despite the increasing dominance of numbers, language stubbornly survived and people stubbornly persisted

in expressing themselves in words, words, words. They coined
new metaphors, they invented new nouns, new syllables. Quarks
and antiquarks and beauty quarks, strangelets, gluons, muons,
hadrons, prions and charms. They spoke of unscientific concepts
like 'forever', and could not resist figurative phrases like 'the
battle of antimatter and matter'. They called some equations
'ugly', others 'harmonious'. Jaz found all this challenging,
although she had now abandoned formal linguistics for particles.

But what really attracts Jaz to CERN, apart from the
companionship of her two beaux, is the cheese. The earthly
reality, the local presence of Swiss cheese enchants her.
Emmenthal, Gruyere, Raclette. Their very names are poetry. She
has a great love, an embarrassingly great love of fondue. Having
spent much of her youth in non-dairy cultures, the revelation
of the melting delight of fondue was overpowering. The rest of
the world was turning against dairy, in order to save the climate,
but the patriotic Swiss had largely resisted this trend. Jaz also
loved the astonishing variety of yoghurt flavours, all 137 of them
(coffee yoghurt was her preferred blend) and she enjoyed the
traditional dish of *tripes à la Neuchâteloise* at the Brasserie de Jura,
but fondue was her favourite. (The Ogre had to look the other
way when she ate tripe. He was squeamish about offal.) She ate
so much fondue that her colleagues wondered how she
managed to stay so slim. She worked out regularly and took a
lot of exercise, accompanying Milan and Theo on their hikes
and on the ski slopes, as we have seen, and now, as she sits by
the shimmering pool to plan their day's outing, she has already
completed fifty lengths, and considers that she deserves the beer
(the frosted, beaded, blond beaker of beer) that she is about to
consume. For even physicists and linguists must eat and drink.

Einstein was particularly fond of eggs. He is said to have
eaten several a day. He also liked porcini mushrooms. De
Saussure was very keen on asparagus, which grew on his
wealthy family's extensive Swiss estates.

Milan, Theo and Jaz are planning an excursion to Theo's
historic hinterland, to the Alpine village where his great great

grandfather's family had spent their summers in a Le Corbusier-Zumthor inspired villa, La Maison Rose, from which could be seen the three snowy peaks, our three comrades' namesakes. Theo has not visited for years, but has the fondest memories of it. He is looking forward to showing it off. A several times removed cousin owns it now, though he is not in residence: he is in the prospering city of Ramallah, attending a multi-faith conference on the history of the Tridentine Mass. (The religious climate fares better these days than the climate-climate. *One fire drives out one fire; one nail, one nail...*) The weather forecast is tolerably fair, but they are determined to set off anyway, in the morning, by autoped, along the raised superway, a handsome prize-winning project constructed from some of the ten million cubic metres of spoil produced by the FCC excavations, and marked by twelve green symmetrical, perfectly conical hills, known as the Twelve Apostles. They will then continue by human foot to their starting point at the metaphorical feet of the mountains. They have often meant to make a pilgrimage to this spot, and have seized upon the anniversary holiday of St Corine, which gives them a clear 24 hours away from the screens and the machines and the endlessly obsessive (and at times felt to be overwhelming and excessive) flow of data.

(Some of the data has to be junked, as no machine on earth could process it all. A machine greater than the earth, maybe, but not this machine.)

They are consulting an old-fashioned map, a printed map, a valuable family heirloom. Retro maps have come back into vogue, amongst the more dedicated walkers, and there are good reasons, apart from sentiment, for consulting this one now. There have been some unexplained irregularities with the GPS system in the neighbourhood, which the week before had led a couple of poorly equipped hikers from Basle (not savvy CERN employees) way off track and forced them to overnight, very uncomfortably, in a mysterious bunker from which they had been unable to get any kind of signal. They thought it was an abandoned CERN-related mineshaft, left over from earlier exploratory surveying for the FCC, and they cooked up some conspiracy theories about Chinese interference with the GPS. Some thought this was just an excuse for their lack of technological control of their own Apps, and for their stupidity in getting so badly lost. But rogue satellites were indeed known to cause occasional interference, and although the international community of particle physicists remained on very good terms, the same could not be said for the political leaders of the great powers, who were notably lacking in community and solidarity.

Milan, Theo and Jaz did not expect to get lost, or to be stranded for centuries in a cavern like the Seven Sleepers, or even for months like the Devils of Derborence, but they liked the early twentieth century map, with its quaint and pretty little annotations of Alpine flowers and Swiss chalets and cows. They traced their route, and discussed what to put in their sandwiches, as walkers have been doing for centuries. They had a brief digression on the subject of dark matter, about which some CERN pundits were predicting a much-awaited five sigma breakthrough announcement within the next three months (or even next week), but on the whole their thoughts were with the light matter of this earth, with the visible matter of the world of the senses, and all else that makes this too much loved earth more lovely. Very lovely was Jaz, in her silvery green swimwear, so lovely that Milan and Theo did not notice a very small cloud in the blue sky, a white cloud as small as a mouse, which began to assemble itself somewhere in the region of Mont Blanc.

When they woke in the morning, the cloud had turned into a rat. They decided to ignore it.

They had an exhilarating spin along the superway, but by the time they reached the foothills, the rat in the sky was darker, and more like a bear – though not very like a bear, that's just a fanciful fairy tale simile. It was a strange almost oblong shape, a cloud formation which they were unable to identify from their CloudApp. But the newest new-fangled Butterflywing WeatherApp wasn't giving them any warnings, so they took to the pathway with their rucksacks (of feather-light fabric, weighted only with their sandwiches and their beer) and strode on. Theo, as they walked, told them about the old days when he had played in the meadow amongst the jonquils and the poppies with his cousins and his big sister Klara, now a neo-Jungian analyst in New York.

Milan and Jaz suspect that Theo is not overly fond of his cousin Jacob, the present owner of La Maison Rose, currently in Ramallah, of whom he speaks warily. They diagnose jealousy. Property and property rights are designed to breed rancour. Theo says Jacob is a bit mad: though, he adds modestly, who is he to talk? Theo has warned Jacob that he is planning to visit the house, as he doesn't want to be accused of trespassing, and he assures his comrades that Jacob has given him the All Clear.

Theo does not much like Jacob, and finds his interest in ancient and arcane theological disputes irritating. But he is fond of his high-stepping sister Klara. The story of Klara is well known to Milan and Jaz, for she had written a sensational revisionist account of the relationship between the Swiss magus Carl Jung and the Austrian physicist Wolfgang Pauli, based on papers discovered in an attic in a seedy lodging house in Zurich. They relate to Jung's famous analysis of the deeply disturbed and (some said demonic) Pauli in the 1930s. (Those papers are now lodged in the archives at La Salle Pauli at CERN.) Klara had relied on Theo to set her right on Pauli's groundbreaking postulation of the existence of the ghostly neutrino: her grasp of quantum mechanics was somewhat shaky, and she was in Theo's view, a little too interested in the stories about the occult, the Kabala, the nature of archetypes, the magic number 137, and Pauli's alleged effect on laboratory equipment – he was said to cause destruction wherever he went. Maybe Pauli's ghost had been responsible for the bewildering of the hikers from Basle, they joked, as their three snowy mountainous progenitors hove into view upon the skyline.

Pauli's sister, like Theo's sister, had been a bit of a handful. One cannot choose one's blood relatives. Well, one can nowadays, but it wasn't so easy then.

It is a very beautiful building, La Maison Rose – elegant, minimal, geometric, with very fine views. The curiously flat back cloud still hangs high in the sky, looking rather like a tombstone or perhaps an anvil, but the mountains are bathed in sunlight. It is a very odd day, weather-wise. Access to the house is easy, done in a blink by Theo by iris recognition, and they can hear Cousin Jacob's voice welcoming them from distant Ramallah as they cross the threshold. He won't hang around, like a spectral presence, he assures them: he just wants to make sure all is well. If they switch on the screen in the room overlooking the lawn, they will find some data that might interest them. Enjoy, he says, in American mode.

He has come to sound very American, these days, says Theo, with a strong hint of disapproval. He doesn't say more, because Jacob might be listening in.

They needn't have bothered to bring beer: the fridge is well stocked.

Theo shows them round, pointing out who was who in the oil paintings of family ancestors, opening the many drawers of a little cabinet of curiosities to display butterflies and moths, little phials of brightly coloured mountain minerals, and watch-making implements from La Chaux-de-Fonds dating back centuries. It is time travel captured in a wooden box.

We are only looking back over a few centuries as we explore the Maison Rose, but even as we gaze, the Vera Rubin is capturing images billions of years old, from the dawn of time. The unimaginable is manifesting itself more fully, day by day. What will Vera see, what will she show? Is she speaking to the FCC, is the FCC speaking to her, as they join in their pursuit of the dark matter that the bodily Vera Rubin was the first to acknowledge?

Of course they speak to one another. They can communicate now without human agency, the telescope and the accelerator. They have joined forces, they seek the same revelation. They were begotten by the human, but they no longer need the human.

*

Three is the number at the core of the universe, or so, over the millennia many have argued. So there are three endings to this tale.

The First Ending

As the Ogre, the Monk and the Maiden switch on the screen to see what surprises Cousin Jacob had prepared for them, behold, darkness covers the earth, and all the known universe. There is nobody left to record this, and we will never know why it happened on this day, and not earlier or later. But we had all known it was coming, so it is a fitting ending, in its way. Nothing lasts forever. Forever is not a word. The game is up. *Rien ne va plus.*

The Second Ending

Cousin Jacob, knowing Theo's gambling predilection, has set up an on-screen Many-Worlds option, and they cannot resist spinning the wheel, and they are never seen again. This isn't a very good ending, because none of our three friends believes in multiverse theory or in time travel, and they should not be subjected to a fate in which they have no intellectual stake. (Moreover, we didn't think Jacob was clever enough to do anything like that.) But 'never seen again' has a good ring to it, and in this version of their story their huge spectral forms are seen for centuries to come, haunting the icy slopes of the Alps, as did the tragic lonely ghost of the poor monster created by Mary Shelley and Victor Frankenstein. They become myth, they become legend. Maybe their bodies will be discovered, many thousands of years hence, down a sinkhole, miraculously preserved. Saint Milan, Saint Theo, Saint Jaz.

The Third Ending

In the third ending, they watch a tedious exposition of why we should still be interested in the niceties of the Tridentine Mass and the Counter Reformation. Milan and Jaz express surprise that the word Tridentine has nothing at all to do with the number Three, but derives from the Alpine city of Trento on the River Adige in Northern Italy. At least they've learned something. (Theo, of course, had known this all along.) They thank Cousin Jacob politely, pack their rucksacks, and make their way happily back to CERN under a brightening sky, where within the week, an impressive revelation about dark matter will be revealed. We can't reveal it here, because it hasn't been discovered yet, and the equations would be far too long to fit into the story. They would need a story as long as the Texla, as long as the equator, and anyway, you probably wouldn't understand them, and neither would I, your unreliable, ignorant and earthbound narrator. But revelation is on the way, and everybody at CERN will rejoice, including our three foot soldiers. In this story, all ends well.

A Fourth Ending?

For myself, I prefer a shadowy ending, a peaceful ending. Pauli posited the need for a fourth quantum number, and interested himself in the debate between Johannes Kepler, who favoured three as the fundamental number of the universe, and the Rosicrucian Robert Fludd, who favoured four. I don't understand any of that. All I know is that in my version, the fourth version, I can see Tantine Aurore, leaning on the wooden gate to her meadow. I can feel the grain of the warm weathered wood of the gate. Behind her is the house where she was born, the house which was built in 1816, in the year of the great summer storm that literally engendered Frankenstein and inspired Byron:

> *From peak to peak, the rattling crags among*
> *Leaps the live thunder! Not from one lone cloud,*
> *But every mountain now hath found a tongue*
> *And Jura answers, through her misty shroud,*
> *Back to the joyous Alps who call to her aloud…*

But all is calm now, and we can see and feel that it is springtime, and the jonquils are in bloom. The fields are white with jonquils as with snow. She is speaking softly to her herd. To Gentiane, Paquerette, Violette, Mauve, Narcisse, Colchique, Coquelicot and Perce-Neige, and the pretty douce soft-eyed Jonquille. Yes, they too are there, and they too have played their part.

Quarks and antiquarks, beauty quarks and strangelets, gluons, muons, prions, hadrons and charms.

Gentiane, Paquerette, Violette…

Afterword: Continuing to Think Big

Dr Tessa Charles
CERN

The discovery of the Higgs boson, announced on 4 July 2012 by the ATLAS and CMS experimenters at CERN, was a momentous day for particle and accelerator physicists all over the world. Confirming the existence of the Higgs boson is often touted as finding the last puzzle piece of the Standard Model – the core theory that best describes the known set of elementary particles and fundamental interactions in physics. One might be forgiven for thinking of the Higgs boson discovery as the conclusion to an epic tale of modern physics discovery. However particle physicists will be quick to inform anyone interested, there is still much more to be discovered. The Standard Model, often described as the most successful model ever conceptualised, still leaves important questions unanswered. For example: What is the nature of Dark Matter? (We have firm evidence it exists but don't know what it's made of). Why is there a preponderance of matter over anti-matter in our universe? (What is the origin of the matter–antimatter asymmetry), and the existence and hierarchy of neutrino masses?

To address these questions and learn more about the fundamental nature of the universe, a new high-energy collider must be built. Margaret Drabble's story places us in the 2050s, introducing characters working on the Future Circular Collider

(FCC) – a successor to the Large Hadron Collider (LHC).

High-energy colliders take decades of research, development, and planning. The Large Electron Positron (LEP) collider (which existed in the present LHC-tunnel before the LHC was built) was first conceptualised in late 1970s, its construction started in 1983, and it was finally switched on in 1989. It took more than 20 million work hours for the machine to be realised, and it ran until 2000 before being decommissioned. Before the LEP was even operational CERN physicists were already thinking ahead. In the early 1980s, proposals for a proton-proton accelerator emerged. In 1995 the LHC technical design report was published and in the late 90s construction began, just as the LEP was nearing the end of its planned lifetime. This pattern of looking ahead and preparing has continued, and whilst today the LHC is still collecting data and being upgraded, future projects are already being considered. The Future Circular Collider (FCC) is presently the most favoured of the proposed collider projects by the European Strategy Group.

Also competing to be built is the International Linear Collider (ILC), the Compact Linear Collider (CLIC), and the Chinese Electron Positron Collider (CEPC). Whilst each project has its strengths, it's likely only one will be built.

The FCC was endorsed in the 2020 European Strategy for Particle Physics: 'Europe, together with its international partners, should investigate the technical and financial feasibility of a future hadron collider at CERN with a centre-of-mass energy of at least 100 TeV and with an electron–positron Higgs and electroweak factory as a possible first stage.' And indeed, the Future Circular Collider will in fact consist of two colliders.

The first stage will be an electron-positron collider (FCC-ee), designed to perform high-precision studies of the Higgs boson and other known particles. Electrons and positrons don't have any internal structure (unlike protons which are made up of quarks and gluons). As a result, the data from the collisions is very clean with low levels of background noise, allowing precise measurements to be made. The electrons and positrons will be made to collide at four energies ranging from 90 GeV to 360 GeV. Whilst the LHC was searching to confirm if the Higgs boson exists, the FCC-ee, conversely, will be a Higgs factory, churning out billions of Higgs to take precise measurements of the boson. Much effort has been invested into increasing the FCC-ee accelerator design's efficiency and this is reflected in the fact that the predicted electricity cost equates to approximately 200 Euros per Higgs boson produced (assuming a price of 50 Euro MWh⁻¹) making it an extremely efficient Higgs factory. It is worth noting that this figure of 200 Euro per Higgs only considers operational electricity costs and not construction costs, which are addressed later. Remarkably, thanks to accelerator R&D advances, FCC-ee will be able to produce the same amount of data to repeat the entire LEP programme in just two minutes.

Once the FCC-ee has run its course, the next stage would be to build a 100 TeV proton-proton collider (FCC-hh) that will be put in the FCC-ee's place. The large circumference will allow us to reach 100 TeV collisions (for reference, the LHC collides protons at 14 TeV and has a circumference of 27 km), which brings huge discovery potential. Using high-field magnets reaching 16 Tesla, the FCC-hh will reach luminosities (which is a measure for the number of colliding particles) 50 times higher than at the LHC.

Both FCC colliders (FCC-ee and FCC-hh) will be located in a 100 km tunnel near the current CERN site. Fitting snugly in the Geneva basin, flanked by the Jura Mountain range on one side and the Alps on the other, the FCC will encircle Mont Salève, and pass under the shallow end of Lake Geneva. Civil engineering for the collider will be a major undertaking, and there are currently efforts underway exploring ways of reusing the excavated material.

A massive project like the FCC requires long-term planning. As pointed out in Margaret's story, the name Future Circular Collider may become less accurate with time, and should perhaps transition to the Finished Circular Collider at some stage. It's hoped that construction on the tunnel will start in 2030. In the meantime, many of the technological challenges are being addressed through a R&D programme that is focusing primarily on energy efficiency and maintainability. The tunnel, site and technical infrastructure construction will take ten years to complete before beams of electrons and positrons can start colliding circa 2040. The electron–positron collider will then run for fifteen years, colliding particles and collecting data. Throughout this time, R&D on the hadron collider will be taking place simultaneously in preparation for the FCC-hh. A further ten years of construction, installation, and commissioning will be needed before FCC-hh can start colliding protons, and then the hadron–hadron collision programme is expected to run for 25 years, taking the project out to almost the year 2100.

Comprehensive and coordinated planning is required for such an ambitious project, not only due to the timescale involved, but also because the FCC requires a large international collaboration involving scientists and engineers from more than 150 institutes across 35 counties. Ambitious goals to better humanity's understanding of the nature of matter and the origins of the universe, require diverse collaboration; and CERN is one of the few places in the world that epitomises these values. In attempts to understand the physical world at the smallest scales, we need to think big.

However, the future of the FCC project is far from guaranteed. Beyond the physics and engineering, there are many challenges still to be addressed ranging from economic, to environmental, to political. Work is already underway to engage with local communities, conduct environmental impact assessments, and produce accurate costings. The cost of a collider such as FCC is the most common public objection. And the cost is significant, coming in at €10 billion for FCC-ee and doubling to €20 billion if the later FCC-hh is pursued. Such a sum is too large for any one nation and relies upon the continued support of the 23 CERN member states. With the current global unrest (war in Ukraine, the relentless pandemic, calls for justice surrounding: Black Lives Matter, Roe vs Wade, the effects of climate change, increased cost of living, and so on), perhaps CERN is needed more than ever. CERN was founded in 1954, as a peaceful driver to reunite Europe. Now no longer limited to European countries, CERN continues to uphold the virtues of international scientific collaboration. It is through the realities of this world, CERN strives toward ambitious goals as we try to better understand the universe and our place within it.

End Titles

Adam Marek

My CASTAWAY THIS WEEK is Professor Brody Maitland, the radiologist whose discovery turned the universe inside out. He's the author of the international bestselling popular science book *There's More!* which has sold more than a million copies since its 2064 release. But he's better known to children and parents around the world as Questo the Mage, in Netflix's full-immersion show: *Where Did Grandma Go?* Born in 1974 in a small village in Hertfordshire, Brody says as a child he always wanted to be either a scientist or a wizard. So Brody, how does it feel to have achieved both?

A: Thank you, Margie. Being here today is also an ambition achieved. Growing up, we would always have Radio 4 on, and *Desert Island Discs* was my mum's favourite show. She always said she hoped that one of her children would be on *Desert Island Discs* one day.

Q: As it happens, two of her children have. Your older sister is the violist Liesl Maitland, who was on the show back in 2039.

A: Indeed.

Q: Has music been an important part of your life?

A: Absolutely. In fact, soundtracks have been the soundtrack of my life, as you'll see from my choices.

Q: You've achieved so much, but what I find particularly interesting is that all the discoveries you're known for were made in the latter half of your life, after you turned 60. Where does that energy come from? How do you keep yourself curious?

A: I guess I've always been ambitious, since I was a child. I never wanted to be a bit part in someone else's movie. I worked hard, hoping that I would achieve something remarkable, but for success to happen, you need the magic ingredient of luck.

Q: Well, Brody Maitland, let's hear your first track. What have you chosen and why?

A: My earliest memory is of waiting for my turn on the family record player. The album that I remember most clearly from that time was a story album of the Disney film, *The Rescuers*. It was an abridged version of the story with tracks and clips from the film. *The Rescuers* came out in 1977, and this was a few years after, so I must only have been about four or five, but I have very vivid memories of lying in a pool of sunshine on our orange patterned carpet, listening to the story, and this haunting music, and being absolutely terrified, but also spellbound. *The Rescuers* caused a paradigm shift in me. It opened up the world. Suddenly it was a place where someone's sister could be kidnapped and held prisoner in a swamp. And that was interesting.

Track One: 'Tomorrow is Another Day (reprise)', from *The Rescuers Original Soundtrack*, composed by Sammy Fain, with lyrics by Carol Connors and Ayn Robbins, performed by Shelby Flint.

Q: So, Brody, you grew up as the middle-child in a household of five kids – did you have middle child syndrome? Did you feel ignored?

A: I got into trouble a lot as a kid. I was the naughty one. Mum seemed to spend a lot of her time exasperated by me.

Q: What was she like, your mother? When you picture her in your early childhood, what do you see?

A: The first picture that comes to mind as you ask that is of Mum at the sewing machine.

She was a whizz on that machine and made all her own clothes. Even though we had no money, Mum always looked so glamorous. 'Dress for the life you want to have,' was her motto. I'd look at the only clothes I owned – which was hand-me-down football shirts – and be terrified that I was going to be channelled into a career as a professional football player. The very last thing I wanted to be.

Q: Brody Maitland, let's hear another track.

A: This is the theme tune to one of Mum's favourite TV shows, *Brideshead Revisited,* which she had on tape in the car and often sang along to with great gusto as she drove us kids off to our swimming or music lessons.

Q: Could she carry a tune?

A: She had impressive volume.

Track Two: 'Brideshead Revisited Theme', by Geoffrey Burgon.

Q: Who was it that inspired your interest in science, Professor Maitland?

A: It wasn't a person at all. It was a breakfast cereal. In the very early 1980s, when I was about seven or eight, a cereal called Wheat-Beans rebranded itself into Wheativerse. And the box was science themed. On the back of each box there was one of four illustrations: the surface of Mars, a space station, inside a mad-scientist's lab, and a research station at the bottom of the ocean. Inside the box were transfers of all the people, vehicles and scientific paraphernalia of those particular zones. You could choose where you put each thing, and rub it into place with a pencil. It took a little thought and effort, but to my young mind, it was possible to create four completely astounding scenes from the frontiers of science. I collected all four box designs over one summer and stuck them on my wall beside my bed. They were the first thing I'd see every morning, and I longed to be the kind of person who worked in those sorts of environments. I've been chasing the vision created by Wheativerse ever since.

Q: What will we hear from you next, Brody?

A: It's the theme tune to Disney's *The Black Hole*, by John Barry. I watched this around the same time as I was obsessed with the Wheativerse cereal, and the soundtrack of this film about a scientist planning to fly into a black hole became the soundtrack of scientific exploration for me. It still is. I defy anyone to listen to this music and not want to dance around the house flinging their arms around like they're conducting the whole universe.

Track Three: 'End Title', from *The Black Hole* original soundtrack, by John Barry.

Q: So how do we get from the Wheativerse to you running a cutting-edge lab expanding the frontiers of radiology? Can you fill in the gap for us?

A: At the end of my junior school years, my thirst was for science, both because of the Wheativerse, and because Liesl had thoroughly dominated the whole of the arts, playing viola and piano, but also getting lots of attention for her watercolours. So one had to pitch one's tent at the opposite end of the field so to speak. But when I started secondary school, my interest in science was dampened and then thoroughly thwarted by the abominable Mr Chet, perhaps the most mind-numbing science teacher who ever lived. He spoke at an incredibly.... slow.... pace... often while rummaging in his nostrils with his thumb. It was like the universe had conjured him up to put kids off going into science.

Q: So how did you find your way back?

A: Via photography, which was thanks to my Uncle Elliott. Uncle Elliott was a wedding photographer, but his hobby was nature photography. He was my mum's brother, and they weren't that close – we hardly ever saw him. But then one day Mum and Dad announced that they had to go away for a weekend, and the five of us were going to stay with Uncle Elliott. He took us out to a local nature reserve, and as I'd shown more interest than the others in his portfolios, he gave me one of his cameras with a macro lens on it and said shoot whatever you like. I photographed insects and mosses on rotting tree stumps. This was in the days before digital cameras, so I didn't get to see my pictures right away.

It later transpired that Mum and Dad hadn't been on holiday at all. They had wanted us out of the picture while Dad took Mum to the hospital for a scan. It was shortly after that she was diagnosed with bowel cancer.

Q: What was that time like?

A: I don't know if you've ever been through anything like that, Margie, but you don't realise how dark and cold the world can be until a hole opens up beneath you. It felt like everyone else on the planet was carrying on gayly above while we fell. I didn't think any of us could ever feel happy again.

Q: But you've said it was your uncle who helped get you through that time?

A: After the diagnosis, Mum and Elliott became much closer. My passion for taking photographs started when he brought round prints of the pictures I'd taken on that day out. There was one absolutely cracking shot of an ant, which he'd had blown up to ten by eight. You could see the tiny hairs on its body. I was hooked. I just loved how, with a macro lens, you could escape into a new world. My uncle gave me a camera, and a bag full of film rolls, and he said he'd pay for all of them to be developed.

Q: His encouragement set you on your way.

A: There was just so much I wanted to escape from. Mum's cancer. Liesl's growing dominion. I just wanted to dive deeper and deeper into this new world I'd discovered and never come out.

Q: Let's hear some more music.

A: This track reminds me of that time. For some reason, Dad became obsessed with the film *Jaws*. We'd just got our first Sony Betamax video player, and he'd recorded the film from the television. I think during that time, *Jaws* was a comfort movie for him, bizarrely. I remember watching it with him when I was way too young, and I was traumatised, but somehow I'd keep going back for more. None of the others could bear it. Even Liesl, who was the eldest. I must have watched *Jaws* with Dad at least twenty times. The relief when the shark is ultimately blown up, and that soothing end-title music rolls… that was a special moment.

Track Four: 'End Titles', from the *Jaws* original soundtrack, by John Williams.

Q: So, Professor Maitland, how did photography lead back to science?

A: Some time later, I went with Mum to one of her appointments, and the nurse saw my camera round my neck and explained that the MRI machine was an enormous camera that could photograph inside the human body. Something exploded inside of me – a galactic popping sensation in my soul. This machine was the fusion of my passions for science and photography. My life's ambition was formed then – to photograph the deepest layers of the world. I wanted to go as deep into the rabbit hole as it was possible to go.

And at that time, it was as if the universe saw my ambition and decided to enable it by killing Mr Chet, my boring science teacher, in a hit-and-run accident while he was cycling, and replacing him with Ms Brock, who was the most inspiring and passionate teacher you could ever hope for. It was thanks to Ms Brock's influence that I got straight-As and a place at medical school, always with the ambition of working in radiology and pushing medical scanning technology forward.

Q: But you never could have imagined quite how far that ambition would take you.

A: No. And that was largely thanks to serendipity, which introduced me to my brilliant wife, Rhia.

Q: Who you met at medical school?

A: She was at Imperial College too… studying materials science and engineering.

Q: How did you two meet?

A: At the university tabletop gaming club. We were both passionate players of games. She was a year ahead of me, and was running the club. I'd seen the poster in my first week, advertising a games night, all welcome, and went along, and… there she was. I knew the minute I sat down at the Buckaroo! game, and she sat opposite me, that here was the most brilliant human being in the world and being by her side was the apogee of my potential life.

Q: Buckaroo?

A: You're probably too young to remember it. It was a 1980s game where you hung plastic objects like a shovel and a coil of rope on a mule, and if you didn't do it carefully enough then the spring inside the mule would be triggered and its back half would fly up in a rather startling fashion and toss all the plastic objects everywhere.

Q: I thought you were going to be sat across a chess board or something like that.

A: It was the irreverence of the game that gave our first meeting the right tone. She had set up dozens of games on tables in the club room, Risk, chess, various role-playing games, but I guess she saw me sit down at the Buckaroo! table and thought that I was someone who didn't take himself too seriously. Which isn't true at all, of course. As you can imagine, growing up in a family with four siblings, including a particularly attention-seeking one, made me fiercely competitive. If I'd played Monopoly at that first meeting I would have been banned from the club forever more. I'm not sure now why I picked Buckaroo! But I'm glad I did.

Q: Before we get on to your discovery, can we hear another track?

A: Yes, this one is from the time I met Rhia and started university. It was 1993, and the big movie of that summer was *Jurassic Park*. The first date Rhia and I went on was to see it in Leicester Square. We were both huge Spielberg fans and had grown up on his movies. In *Jurassic Park*, it felt like the curtains opening on a bold new era of cinema, and our lives.

Q: I wish the audience at home could see the smile on your face.

A: I was just remembering our wedding day. We had our first dance to this music.

Track Five: 'End Credits', from the *Jurassic Park* original soundtrack, by John Williams.

Q: So tell us about that moment of making the discovery, how did it come about?

A: It was during my time, many years later, as a clinical researcher at University College London Hospital's Biomedical Research Centre. It was in 2034, a week after I turned sixty in fact. I was leading a team coming to the end of a two-year patient study to find new ways to detect early kidney damage resulting from immune disorders. It involved taking multiple scans over a two-year period with some new – and very advanced for the time – MRI machines. I had become familiar with the patients, so I was rather surprised one morning when I sat down with my coffee to go through the latest batch of scans and saw something completely unexpected. A banana-shaped object hugging the left side of the kidney. At first I thought it must be a glitch, that something was wrong with the machine. So we cancelled all the other appointments for the rest of the week and got the technical guys in to recalibrate the whole rig. But then the next day, Rhia, who I'd told about this thing, said she'd spotted on social media that a radiologist in Argentina had found a mysterious banana too.

Q: Exactly the same thing you'd found?

A: This one wasn't actually banana-shaped, but it was a very similar anomaly, and my wife had in the moment coined 'a banana' as the phrase we'd use to refer to anomalous organs in the body. It stuck and was widely adopted, much to Rhia's delight.

Q: Okay, so someone else had found a 'banana' in Argentina…

A: Yes, Dr Olga Bianchi. She had found something strange in a heart scan and posted the image online. You're not allowed to do that, of course, but if she hadn't, none of this would have been discovered.

Q: You never would have connected the dots.

A: Exactly. So I got in touch with her, and it turned out that I wasn't the only one to do so. I was, in fact, the fifth person to contact her with an anomalous MRI image.

Looking back, it should have been obvious that there was something special about that day specifically – all of the scans had been taken within a fourteen-hour window on 14 February

2034. But it wasn't until several months later, when Rhia and I were having dinner with her brother and his girlfriend, that the penny dropped.

At dinner I was talking about this mystery, or rather Rhia was, because it had been preoccupying me all this time. And her brother, who is a very passionate amateur astronomer, pointed out that the date this happened wasn't just Valentine's Day. On that particular day, a unusually large Coronal Mass Ejection had hit the Earth. He said it knocked out several satellites above Canada and created the most spectacular aurora for twenty years, visible from unusually low latitudes. As far south as Milan. It was really big news in his world, and he was surprised I hadn't heard about it.

Q: And what happened next?

A: I started compiling a list of all the dates since MRI scanners were first put into action – in 1977 – when there were periods of intense solar activity. Then I went back through the archives looking for scans taken at those times. There were several dozen, and every one of them showed some kind of anomaly. They were mostly very subtle, especially the earliest scans when the machines weren't quite as sensitive, and I had to really search them out – an unusual sort of Where's Wally? game. Very few were as clear as the one I'd taken that day, but I was using a very powerful scanner, of course. The anomalies were so small that you'd miss them unless you were specifically looking for them.

I sent all the scans over to Dr Bianchi in Argentina, as well as to all the other physicians and scanning researchers like us who had also discovered something and joined her thread. By now, our WhatsApp group had grown to twelve doctors. I shared with them my hypothesis about the solar events and recommended that they too start looking back through their scans archive – and from there it snowballed. Everyone who made the same discovery shared it with others. And the wider the story grew, the more the evidence piled up. It unearthed some truly spectacular images.

Q: What was that moment like? Did you know you'd discovered something Earth shattering?

A: I remember a moment when I was visiting my family for Easter. My phone pinged with a new message from Olga. She had sent me an fMRI brain scan that a doctor in Finland had taken on December 13th 2006, during one of the most intense bursts of solar activity ever detected. It showed an incredibly clear structure, the shape of a pinecone that spanned the two hemispheres of the brain. The doctor that took it had, at the time, thought it was an error. When he called the patient back in for another scan the next day, the pinecone brain region did not appear – because by then, the solar activity had finished. He took the unrepeatability of the scan as confirmation that it had been a strange but interesting error. All this time, more than two decades, he'd had this incredible picture and thought it was a glitch. When I saw that image, I knew that something profound had been right under our noses. A hidden sector. And finally we'd discovered it.

There were a few thrilling months of intense collaboration with scientists across many different fields from around the world. That finally led to the identification of the particle present in the solar events, which illuminated the bananas for our MRI machines.

Q: And why did you call it the Hermes particle?

A: I actually named it the Brodyon. But one of the researchers referred to it as a Hermes particle on a news programme and it caught on. What's special about this particle is that it interacts with the hidden and standard sectors. It's what's called a messenger particle. Without it, there is no communication and the sectors are distinct from one another. The messenger particle brings us news from the other side. Hence, Hermes.

Q: And for our listeners at home who might not be familiar with it, what was the message that the Hermes particle delivered? What was your discovery, in a nutshell?

A: The long and short of it is – we discovered that there is a hidden and exotic biology within all of us. The parts of the body we are familiar with – the parts that medical students study in text books, are just part of the organism.

Q: How much more of us might there be?

A: These exotic organs may constitute as much as 80% of who we actually are. The part of us that we know could be just the tip of an enormous biological iceberg. The rest is composed of particles and forces that, until the time of our discovery, were completely unknown.

Q: Amazing. Let's hear another track, Professor Maitland.

A: During that time of the discovery, when I was so excited I could barely sleep, I would watch this film as a kind of meditation to help me drift off, something comforting from childhood. This is the end titles from *E.T. the Extra-Terrestrial*.

Track Six: 'End Credits', from *E.T. the Extra-Terrestrial* original soundtrack, by John Williams.

Q: We know how your discovery was received around the world. But how about home? Was Mum proud?

A: It was unfortunate timing. My discovery came just after Liesl's latest album was nominated for a big classical music prize and she was popping up in the media all over the place. When I had my first television appearance on *Tomorrow's World*, Liesl had contrived to invite Mum to her performance at the *BBC Proms*.

Q: It wasn't long afterwards that your mum's bowel cancer returned, and she passed away. That must have been devastating.

A: Believe me, Margie, it was. Mum died just two weeks after Liesl appeared on *Desert Island Discs*. It was as if she hung on just for that.

Q: So you spent the next twenty years exploring this hidden sector and our exotic biology, trying to work out what it was and what it meant for us all.

A: The big question, of course, was how those organs interact with the ones we know about. How do we experience them, if at all? If they were removed, would we know? How many of the mysteries of the body – from the unconscious and the mind-body connection, to how placebos work, and goodness knows how many illnesses – might be explained in this hidden sector?

But first we had to overcome a major obstacle. How do we start taking images of the hidden sector deliberately? It's not very convenient to have to wait for moments of intense solar activity to be able to take them. Again, as I alluded to earlier, it was very lucky that I married someone who became a metamaterials engineer. Rhia spearheaded a project to develop a magnetic metamaterial for a new generation of MRI machines. The 3XMRI machines produce a controlled blast of Hermes particles, which, when corralled into alignment by Rhia's metamaterial, light up structures within the hidden sector. This was a huge technological leap. It's given researchers like me the tools to begin to study the hidden sector. Without it, none of the subsequent discoveries would have been possible.

Q: And what did you discover?

A: That this exotic biology is not just something in humans. It's in everything, everywhere. Scans of other life, from apes to insects and even plants, revealed that there is so much more to everything than we've ever perceived before, an extended world, far larger than the one we know, utterly alien and yet part of our universe. Novel biologies and forces. It's the weave of the rug that explains the patterns we see on this side.

Q: So do you understand the nature of the universe, Brody?

A: Oh gosh, no. There's a big difference between flipping a rug over and seeing the underside, and understanding the work of a master weaver. There are far smarter people than I devoting their lives to unpicking the hidden sector one knot at a time.

Q: What have you chosen for your seventh track, Professor Maitland?

A: This is from *The Empire Strikes Back*. At this end point of the film, Luke has lost a hand, lost his best friend, and gained a father he doesn't want. This downbeat but hopeful end-track makes my heart soar. It's got me through some difficult times.

Track Seven: 'Finale', from *Star Wars: The Empire Strikes Back* original soundtrack by John Williams.

Q: So as you just alluded to, despite all your success, you then entered a rather difficult period. You've written about your mental health struggles. What happened?

A: After the first 3XMRI machines were built, suddenly this hidden sector went from being a very niche area of research being done by a handful of scientists that I knew personally, to hundreds of researchers around the world, and then thousands. Last year the US invested 3% of its GDP into projects exploring the hidden sector. Compared to some of the mind-blowing applications being explored – from new energy sources to life extension and deep space travel – my research slate looked kind of… insignificant. I thought I had nothing left to offer. That the world wasn't interested in anything I could contribute. I was feeling bitter, is what it was.

I'd always been difficult to live with, I think, and then I became impossible. When Rhia told me she was leaving, I thought that really was the end. Every step of my career was taken beside her. How could I continue? And if I couldn't continue, what point was there to anything?

Q: You lost your purpose. So how did you pick yourself back up again?

A: Rhia's parting advice was a real gift. She said, 'Go back to basics. Go back to where you began, to what you love.'

Q: To the hospital, to scanning cancer patients?

A: To photography! To taking pictures of the unseen. So I fired up my old lab at UCL, but with a prototype 4XMRI machine, with the intention of taking the clearest pictures yet of the hidden sector. It was a purely aesthetic endeavour. And every day I'd bring home new and incredible images of the vast underground of our bodies. I would argue they are far more beautiful than the small part that we walk around in.

Q: Can you describe it for us?

A: In the hidden sector... we are polymorphous. We are luminous. We are like deep sea creatures metamorphosing into angels. But even more dazzling than the physical structure is the substance of us. Our hidden aspect is composed of exotic particles and forces which we may have begun to name but about which we know very little. The new 4XMRI machines are revealing the grain of this space. The hidden biology is in constant motion, like solar plasma in the thrall of powerful magnetic fields. Ever changing. We are not fixed, we are in flux.

Q: I'm sure listeners at home can hear the sense of wonder in your voice. So did taking these images help improve your mental health?

A: It was a relief to stop trying to uncover the secrets of the universe and to just focus on taking astonishing pictures.

Q: Which ironically is what led to perhaps your greatest discovery.

A: Yes! And isn't this the thing about life! We struggle and we struggle to beat the odds, to increase our happiness, our comfort, our security, our status, the pride of our parents, the respect of our peers, to be the kind of person that would be on *Desert Island Discs*, and all our achievements amount to nought because we live in a world where it is more impressive to have millions of followers than to lift the stone of the universe and reveal the deep mysteries scurrying beneath it. And for all our striving to better ourselves, we fall on our faces again and again, and just when we think we haven't the strength left to right ourselves, we are lifted by the good grace of providence. Just when all seems lost, a magical wind fills our sails.

Q: And in this case, that magical wind was a tragic accident...

A: Yes, tragic, but incredibly fortuitous! Don't get me wrong, one of my patients dying while in the scanner was a terrible thing. But the coroner's report afterwards said that the scan did not precipitate the heart attack, that he had a blockage that could have gone at any time, and nothing could have been done to stop it. But by passing his last moment where he did, he made a historic contribution to science.

Q: So despite a period of controversy, it was decided that this wasn't your fault and you were able to carry on.

A: It was *proved* that I wasn't at fault.

Q: So those images...

A: In the images that the machine continued to take for a few seconds after the moment of his death, we saw that the aspect of the body within the hidden sector did not stop moving. Quite the opposite in fact. It was suddenly galvanised, the energetic fields reversing direction at great speed, like the poles of a magnet flipping.

Q: And did you realise what that meant at the time?

A: Well, of course! Plainly... there's more! There's more after death.

Q: And that moment of realisation, what was it like? What was going through your head?

A: It was like, 'Take that Liesl!'

Q: Really?

A: I'm just kidding.

Q: So you knew that something of us continues after death, but you wanted to see further.

A: This was just a glimpse. And one instance. I needed more proof.

Q: So you went to the Netherlands. To the Nelson-Wright End of Life Clinic. And was it difficult convincing people to spend their last minutes…

A: Gosh, no. I had too many people wanting to sign up. I mean, who wouldn't? I got a second 4XMRI machine shipped over, hired four more assistants, and still couldn't keep up. In the euthanasia clinic, I felt like a kid in a candy store!

Q: There's the quote for the programme trailer.

A: I'm sorry?

Q: And what did you discover?

A: Right. So I was able to photograph the hidden sector for much longer after death. Seven hours so far. That's the limit of the licence I've been granted, after which Dutch protocols around the body have to be observed. And I discovered that the hidden aspect of ourselves undergoes a change, like cellular mitosis, at the moment of death. The fields change direction, and the hidden aspect performs a movement like budding off.

Q: Where does it go?

A: For the time that we've been able to observe, it hangs around.

It drifts out of frame, it pops back into frame. Like a magnificent fish circling the place it was once fed. After that, who knows? Of course, the first thing I did was to run the scans with no one in the machine – if we are surrounded by…

Q: Ghosts?

A: That word has too much baggage. I'm using superbodies. If superbodies of formerly alive people were everywhere, then surely we'd see them wherever we look. But we don't.

Q: What does that mean?

A: Either that they only exist or hang around for a short time, or that they are very widely dispersed in a very large space. If you tried to take photographs of whales by dropping a camera randomly into the ocean, you would have a very low hit rate. It could be like that.

Q: So now we're almost caught up to the present day, Brody Maitland, but the universe still had plenty to deliver for you in your recent years. Your book *There's More!* about your discoveries, with contributions from fellow visionaries and futurists about what it might mean for humanity, was a publishing sensation – perhaps finally earning you the accolades you felt you'd been denied?

A: Yes, discovering the hidden sector was a huge deal in the scientific world, but a disappointingly small deal to the rest of the world. Discovering the existence of superbodies, however...

Q: It attracted the attention of television.

A: When Netflix came to me and pitched the idea for *Where Did Grandma Go?* I just knew that this was something valuable I could contribute to. Despite all we've learned about the hidden sector in the last 30 years, we're unlikely to really understand what it all means within the lifetime of anyone listening to this show. But we already know enough to completely rewrite our relationship with death.

Q: And has your discovery changed your own relationship with death, and with loss? I'm thinking specifically about your recent loss… your sister Liesl Maitland passed away just last year. Is it true you didn't go to her funeral?

A: It would have felt hypocritical. My work shows that she endures. We all do. My big hope is that this show – for all its slapstick humour and rubber suits – will stop 'the end' being the cataclysm that haunts our lives.

Q: And why is your character, Questo, the host of the show, a mage, and not a scientist?

A: It was thought that a wizard host smoothed some of the edges off the topic, whereas a scientist served to sharpen them.

Q: My little girls love the show.

A: Oh really? Well that's wonderful. What are their names?

Q: Si and Fortune.

A: Well… Aluba-luba-luba to you, sisters Si and Fortune from the magnificent Evermore!

Q: Brody Maitland, it's time for your final track. More end titles music?

A: It is both end and opening titles.

Q: Why end titles?

A: Cinema has always been one of the greatest pleasures and consolations of my life. Especially the films from my childhood, which I return to again and again, and which have filled my list today. The end titles… well, it's that bittersweet moment when the story ends, and you want more, but the ending is the point that gives meaning to everything that has gone before. Without a full stop, the sentence is robbed of its complete meaning. It's when the credits roll, and the end titles music begins, that all the elements of the story are sewn together. The message is revealed.

Desert Island Discs has, for me, always done the same thing. In telling the story of a notable life, with music acting as milestones, in just 45 minutes you create a sense of destiny for listeners, the idea that everything went according to some plan. That tiny moments and unexpected connections, mistakes and disappointments even, were meant to be. For me, listening back through the *Desert Island Discs* archive, as I do whenever I want to conjure Mum in my memory, it makes every moment feel loaded with significance. Every moment and connection is important in some way beyond the scope of our understanding.

Q: Do you think the universe has any more discoveries in store for you, Brody Maitland?

A: I don't want to be greedy, but I hope so. This desert island imaginative exercise that we're doing here actually works as a very apt analogy for the hidden sector. What we're realising is that we're already on the desert island. We've always lived on a dot in a vast ocean, and for the first time we're seeing the wider world. It tells me that the best is yet to come.

My final track is the theme tune to *Desert Island Discs*, without which I would perhaps have been nothing.

Track Eight: 'By the Sleepy Lagoon', by Eric Coates, performed by the BBC Concert Orchestra.

Q: Okay then, Professor Brody Maitland, it's time to send you away to the island. I'm giving you the Bible and the complete works of Shakespeare to take with you. You can also take one book of your choice. What will it be?

A: I would like a guide to the birds of that part of the world. I've just turned 95 and as I'm slowly approaching retirement, birds are becoming more and more important to me. I recently moved to Kent, and behind my house is a wetland nature reserve, which is filled with birds. Wigeon and teal in the winter, hobbies and sedge warblers in the spring. Birdwatching has become an unexpected comfort, and a growing obsession.

Q: And what luxury item would you like to take with you?

A: Well, it will have to be a pair of binoculars. After spending all of my life using instruments to look deeper and deeper into the rabbit hole, I'm finding it an enormous comfort to focus on the nature around me. With a pair of binoculars and a field guide, I could be entertained indefinitely, and not notice that I was alone.

Q: And if you could only save one of your tracks from the waves, what would it be?

A: It would be my first track, from *The Rescuers*. It's the song that transports me back to my youngest self. And while listening to it, I would feel full of hope that those helpful little mice might turn up and rescue me.

Q: Before we leave you, I have to ask, why did you not include any of your sister's music in your list? You've limited yourself to end title music of film scores, but even that doesn't exclude Liesl's work, as she composed three film scores, and was nominated for an Academy Award for one of them. Liesl passed away last year... after all this time, and with her gone, and your mother long gone, surely you don't still feel like you have to compete with her? And do you not think that perhaps without her you might not have strived so hard, and would have achieved far less than you have?

A: Well...

Q: You mentioned that you sometimes listen to the *Desert Island Discs* back catalogue... have you listened to your sister's episode from 2039?

A: I couldn't bear to.

Q: So you don't know what her luxury item was?

A: How should I?

Q: Do you mind if I play that bit for you? I think it will resonate with you, and our audience at home.

Liesl: If I could take just one thing with me? There'd be no point in taking my viola, with no one to play for. I think I should want to take a photograph. It's of an ant. And it was taken by my little brother on a day trip with our uncle when we were very young. It was a perfect day. The last day before we found out about our mother's illness. The way the sunlight falls across the ant... he seems to have the most joyful smile on his face. The picture always made me laugh. And I've carried a copy with me everywhere I've ever been. It's the tether to the best part of my youth, and I would feel absolutely adrift without it.

Q: Brody, so is that the first time you've heard that?

A: It is.

Q: How are you feeling?

A: Gosh. Well. Like, even now, from beyond the grave, Liesl has somehow managed to upstage me. Astounding. Congratulations Liesl, if you are still swimming around somewhere nearby, I salute you.

Q: Brody Maitland, thank you for letting us hear your Desert Island Discs.

A: Thank you, Margie.

Afterword: Don't Shoot the Messenger Particles

Dr Andrea Giammanco
FNRS & CERN

ONE SUMMER IN MY teenage years (we are talking late 80s, here), I whiled away much of my holiday binge-reading a stack of old comics from the 70s. One particular comic featured a column about mysterious facts from around the world, phenomena and theories that I soon realised amounted to pseudoscience. One of the most recurring topics was 'Kirlian photography'. Evidently, it was deemed ideal fodder for all kinds of articles related to life after death, supernatural healing, ghosts, miracles, etc., as 'Kirlian pictures' supposedly taken with 'Kirlian cameras' sounded like the perfect fit for many of those unlikely claims. Kirlian photography demonstrated the existence of an otherwise invisible aura surrounding any living thing, and even many non-living ones (which, the authors implied, demonstrated that even non-living objects had some spiritual significance). Some pictures showed the aura in otherwise empty space: evidence for supernatural entities, invisible to the human eye? The aura was claimed to become brighter or dimmer depending on the health of the patient (Kirlian photography was even claimed to be actually used for diagnostics in many hospitals in the Eastern Bloc), and to be also correlated to emotional states. In a particularly remarkable example, a Kirlian camera captured the very moment of the death of a patient, showing part of the aura being displaced from the body: the moment when the soul was set free?

Too bad that most pictures were so blatantly fake. If the photo compositions had not been so irredeemably amateurish, perhaps I would have given them the benefit of the doubt, because the narrative was so powerful and uncannily coherent. Years later, I discovered that Kirlian photography is actually a thing. And although it may have once been popular in a particular niche of pseudoscience, its physical principles are well known to mainstream science. No mystery, no spirituality, no link with the soul, no correlation with health, mood, or the actual differences between animate and inanimate, spiritual and mundane. Once one knows what causes those 'auras', they actually become very boring. And sadly, in spite of Semyon Kirlian's hopes, no way was ever found to do medical diagnostics with them.

Apparently, many people in the world (across most cultures and religions) believe in the existence of ghosts. Probably, for those who believe in the concept of the soul, it is not too far-fetched to imagine that a soul can become detached from its body (in particular when the latter dies), and wander around. A soul, and a ghost, are allegedly invisible, at least most of the time. But if some mechanism links a particular soul to a particular body, there must be a physical interaction binding them; the atoms of a body (made of ordinary particles: quarks and leptons, mutually bound via electromagnetic and nuclear forces) and the atoms of a soul (made of some unknown particles, mutually bound by something unfathomable) must necessarily be aware of the existence of each other. The same mechanism, whatever it is, would make a soul or a ghost detectable, in principle. So, indeed, why not a tool conceptually similar to a Kirlian camera?

Mainstream physicists, like me, are much less keen to believe in ghosts than most other people. However, mainstream particle physicists, like me, also keep telling people that more research is needed because the Standard Model of particle physics is incomplete, meaning that there must be new phenomena, still unaccounted by the known Laws of Physics. (And let me stress: I didn't say 'there might be', I really said 'there must be'.) So, a layperson could ask, why not new phenomena related to souls, ghosts, and many other things that we currently dismiss as unscientific?

And to be more specific, we also say that there is compelling evidence from astrophysics (although not yet from laboratory experiments, alas) that we must be surrounded, and even compenetrated, by matter of an unknown nature that is invisible to us, which we call Dark Matter. Although its effects are subtle, Dark Matter is not rare: it is estimated to constitute about 80% of the matter of the universe. Could ghosts be made of Dark Matter? And could Dark Matter possibly explain other mysteries, while we're on the subject?

Recently, an ingenious answer to this whole set of questions was provided by my colleague, Brian Cox, speaking on a different BBC Radio show.[1] Cox's argument is more or less as follows: physical interactions between ghostly matter and standard matter cannot be part of the Standard Model; and the LHC has not found any new interaction up to very high-energy scales, hence *a fortiori* there cannot be any new interaction at the very low energy scales that are typical of the biological and chemical processes within our body.

I surmise that Cox's argument sounds way more compelling to the average particle physicist than to the average layperson. In fact, Cox's reasoning implicitly assumes, as most of the particle physics literature does, that unknown interactions should get more detectable as energy grows; but the average layperson has no reason to assume such a hypothesis. (One could ask: why not the other way around?) For once, the average layperson may be right. There is an entire niche of particle physics that has been booming recently, that you can find under the names of 'dark sectors', 'hidden sectors', 'hidden valleys', 'feebly interacting particles', etc., which explores the possibility that new interactions, new particles and new phenomena are more or less hiding in plain sight, and have not been found at the LHC or even in previous experiments just because we were blinded by our collective biases – including Cox's bias that any new physics should manifest more visibly as the energy grows. And although it is still a niche, it is beginning to be taken very seriously: it has already motivated some new experiments at the LHC,[2] upgrades of the existing ones, and original ways to re-analyse the already collected data.

This nightmare scenario – of having Nobel-Prize-worthy discoveries sat under our noses, but going unnoticed because our detectors are not optimised for them – is, to be honest, not so popular among my colleagues. However, there are historical precedents. For example, the string of revolutionary discoveries in the early 70s that imposed the reality of what we now call the Standard Model was achievable with the technology of several years earlier, if only particle detectors had been optimised for the kind of phenomena that this theory explains and that were not expected by the models that were mainstream at that time.[3] And some of those new phenomena, in hindsight, had probably been observed already in the 60s, and dismissed by general consensus as uninteresting fluctuations of the background.[4] Not unlike the 'bananas' discovered by the protagonist of Adam Marek's story. In that fictional universe, it takes a technological jump in MRI technology as well as an exceptional solar activity event to make the serendipitous discovery, but the bananas had always been there, and in hindsight, one could have recognised them in decades-old MRI data.

So let's separate the fact from fiction here: the Standard Model is an incredibly successful theory, precisely confirmed in almost every test that we could conceive in laboratory conditions, and yet we know it is incomplete. How do we know? Its fundamental parameters look too *ad hoc*, and most importantly it cannot account for a few established facts, such as the dominance of matter over antimatter in the Universe, or the existence of the aforementioned Dark Matter. That's why we believe it is just an approximation to the true Theory of

Everything (ToE), in the same fashion as Classical Physics is today regarded as an approximation to both Quantum Physics and the Theory of Relativity (that works best at low speeds and large scales). In a sense, the entire goal of Particle Physics is finding this ToE.

Something that's not established yet, but is a serious target of research, in the journey towards a ToE, is the Dark Sectors hypothesis. Suppose that the still unknown ToE is such that the various elementary particles are grouped (in the taxonomic sense) in well-defined 'sectors'; meaning that all particles within a sector easily interact with each other, but there is only some very tenuous interaction between particles belonging to different sectors. One such sector would be the Standard Model, i.e. all the particles that we already know, interacting through the forces that we already know (electromagnetism, weak nuclear force, strong nuclear force, and finally gravity which is by far the weakest force at the microscopic scale). Nothing excludes the possibility that other particles (from the other 'sectors') permeate the very same space that we occupy, without us noticing them because their interactions with us (i.e. with the Standard Model) are extremely feeble. However, all sectors are expected to feel at least gravitational interactions between each other and this would provide a neat explanation of the mystery of Dark Matter. If at least some of the particles in the hidden sectors (also known as 'hidden valleys') also have additional (non-gravitational) feeble interactions with the Standard Model particles, through some 'mediator particles' that act as a bridge, there is hope that one day we'll observe those interactions in a laboratory. This is a new idea and LHC data analysts have started looking for hints of hidden sectors, with some small, specialised experiments scheduled to take place very soon.[5] If we could find a way of seeing a hidden sector, maybe we could see hidden planets with an exotic chemistry and, of course, an exotic biology.

So, there would be three classes of particles: ordinary (those that physicists already know and that fit in the Standard Model), dark particles (i.e. those in the Dark Sector), and messengers. Ordinary particles and dark particles do not interact with each other directly, apart from gravity effects; but both can interact with the messenger particles. (And this interaction must be very, very faint, otherwise we would have noticed it before). In particular, ordinary particles can occasionally 'excite the vacuum' (i.e. transform kinetic energy into mass) and produce particle-antiparticle pairs of messengers. Presumably dark particles can do the same. But the messengers will probably be unstable heavy particles, meaning that they would soon decay into lighter particles, which in turn might be ordinary particles or dark particles, or both (e.g. a single messenger might decay into N particles, some of which are ordinary and the others are dark).

In Adam Marek's story, the exotic signals observed by the MRI machines intensify during the most intense solar activity events. This narrative trick (coming out of a brainstorming Zoom session between Adam and I) reposes on some plausible speculation. If the dark sector is ubiquitous, there must be dark particles also in the Sun. Given that gravity is the only force that can make a direct link between the Standard Model and the Dark Sector, where there is a big lump of ordinary particles held together by gravity (e.g. a star, a planet), there must be a big lump of dark particles as well, in the same place. Those dark particles presumably interact between each other a lot, just like the ordinary particles do, we just don't know how, because they're dark.

Now, imagine this dark part of the Sun that burns and boils, very energetically – just like the ordinary part of the Sun does – only in ways that are invisible to us. But suppose, from time to time, these tumultuous processes pass some threshold in energy and intensity and start producing messenger particles. The key point for the story is that this is not a continuous process, but more of an 'on/off' event, a collective phenomenon that only happens if a threshold is trespassed in some variable. Those messenger particles will interact with ordinary particles in the Sun, faintly, of course, but if they are temporarily produced in really humongous quantities, they might trigger similar processes in the ordinary part of the Sun. That would explain some of the extreme solar activity events.

If the above mechanism takes place, part of that huge flux of messenger particles would escape the Sun and flood the Solar System, and would reach us as part of the natural flux of cosmic rays. Some of those messengers would interact with the ordinary particles in the upper atmosphere, leading to the particularly intense auroras, stretching unusually far south, as mentioned by Adam's protagonist. Although only a tiny fraction of messenger particles interact with ordinary ones, during such exceptional events the flux would be enormous, so even a tiny fraction would become a significant number overall. And similarly, a very tiny fraction of those messengers would interact with the dark particles, transmuting them into ordinary particles with ordinary interactions with standard matter. In Adam's story, the new-generation MRI machines developed after a certain date include a new metamaterial, developed and optimised for other reasons, whose structure (by pure chance) resonates particularly well with photons of the frequency produced by those transmutations. This is a kind of serendipity that often happens in science: technological advances open new vistas into fundamental science. This idea of metamaterials came to Adam and not to me (ironically, as I was supposed to be bringing the science ideas), and I was initially hesitant. But then I found out that the Nobel Laureate and super-respected physicist Frank Wilczek is actually collaborating with some metamaterial expert in order to develop practically the same thing.[6]

But there are many other narrative possibilities offered up by the Dark Sector idea. It would be a science fiction feeding frenzy. Such is the disparity between the amount of Dark Matter and ordinary matter in the universe (cosmologists estimate a ratio of around four to one), that it's quite possible there are four hidden sectors out there to our own one, separated from each other as much as they are separated by us, and sharing roughly the same mass. Biology is based on chemistry and chemistry is based on the properties of what we know as electrons, photons, and to some extent also protons, so each sector could exist with its own independent biologies and ecosystems.

What's more, while our sector abides by the Standard Model, according to which all elementary particles that possess a non-zero mass obtain that from their interaction with the Higgs boson field; other sectors might abide by a completely different model, and obtain their mass from interaction with a different field. If the mass terms in the corresponding equations cannot be written as real numbers but as 'complex numbers', there would be an interesting consequence: 'tachyons' (i.e. hypothetical particles that move faster than light, from the ancient Greek word 'tachys', meaning 'fast'). In our reality, as Einstein demonstrated, the speed of light is the upper limit: massless particles travel at that speed, massive ones never reach it, but can only approach it as their energy grows. In the Tachyonic Sector, however, we would see the inverse: the speed of light would be the *minimum*, and massive particles would fly at infinite speed if they lack any kinetic energy. In practice, time in that sector would flow in the opposite direction with respect to us. And if any mediator particle would bridge a communication between them and us, then we would have a plausible mechanism for a new plot based on precognition.

Notes

1. *The Infinite Monkey Cage* (BBC Radio 4), as discussed in 'If Ghosts Were Real, Brian Cox Claims CERN would have Found them by Now,' *Wired*, 24 Feb, 2017. https://www.wired.co.uk/article/the-lhc-proves-ghosts-do-not-exist
2. In general, these new experiments are relatively cheap (at least by LHC standards) and are often hosted in ad hoc locations, exploiting infrastructure originally built for other purposes. For

example, milliQan is installed in an unused access tunnel leading to the CMS experiment (see https://u.osu.edu/milliqan/); Anubis will be hanging across the shaft of the cavern that hosts the ATLAS experiment (see https://www.hep.phy.cam.ac.uk/ANUBIS); Mathusla's large area detectors will cover an abandoned field at the surface 100 meters above the CMS experiment (see https://mathusla-experiment.web.cern.ch/).

3. As discussed thoroughly, for example, in *Constructing Quarks: a Sociological History of Particle Physics*, Andrew Pickering, University of Chicago Press, 1999

4. Examples of this might include the signatures of the Weak Neutral Currents and of the charm quark. The former was discovered by the Gargamelle experiment in 1973, but earlier neutrino experiments had observed an excess of events with the same characteristics. The existence of the charm quark was established in 1974 by collider experiments at SLAC and Brookhaven, but an experiment in 1968-1969 had already observed it in the form of an anomalous statistical distribution ('Lederman's shoulder') and, not being optimised for that observation, it lacked the mass resolution that would have been necessary to interpret it correctly. Moreover, some argue that particles containing charm quarks had been first observed in 1971 in a cosmic-ray experiment.

5. Note this is different from the missing 'superpartner' particles of supersymmetry because in that case all new particles would be very heavy, otherwise they would have been found already. It also differs from the standard paradigm of Dark Matter which postulates the missing matter is constituted by a single very heavy particle, abundantly produced in the brief period after the Big Bang and then remaining as a sort of inert, relic molasses permeating the universe.

6. 'Physicists Propose New Way to Detect Dark Matter Particles,' *Sci-News*, 10 Oct, 2019: http://www.sci-news.com/physics/dark-matter-particles-07680.html

Dark Matters

Lucy Caldwell

HIS SISTER LIFTS HIM from the airport. He said he'd get a taxi, or the airport bus, but she was having none of it. She pulls into the pick-up area and he doesn't notice her at first, not till she winds down the window and actually shouts at him. She has a new car since he's seen her last – a Ford Mondeo, mid-blue.

'Don't,' she says.

'Don't what?'

'Don't you be making any jokes about Mondeo Man.'

'I didn't say anything.'

'Tony got us a good trade-in deal. It was second-hand, but it's not a bad car. Bit big maybe. Bigger than you need, anydays,' she says, looking pointedly at his backpack, which is all's the luggage he's brought. 'You not planning on staying? Problems of the universe to solve? Sorry,' she says, almost immediately, 'that was out of order,' and exhausting as it is, it's a strange comfort, that this is still the Tanya he knows.

He slings his bag into the boot. Looks up at the low, damp sky. He always forgets how much it presses in on you. How rare it is here to have a high-skied day. He has no idea how long he'll be here for. When he got Tanya's message, he just came. Went online, booked the first flights he could, didn't even look at the cost, just put them on his credit card. Emailed the administrator of his programme from Geneva airport, saying he'd be in touch when he knew more. It was interesting to see how easy it was to jettison everything.

He takes a breath, gets into the front seat.

'So how is she?' he says.

'If it wasn't for lockdown,' Tanya says, 'we might have gotten her to the GP earlier. But then again,' she says, resolutely, 'we might not've, because you know Mum.'

Tanya puts her left arm behind the headrest of his seat as she cranes to reverse and pull a U-turn to get them out – a gesture, a posture, that's so much their dad that he smiles.

'What?' she says.

'Nothing.'

'No seriously – what? It had better not be another fucking Mondeo joke.'

'I haven't made a first one yet. And it wasn't. Just you looked so like Dad there.'

'Wise up.'

'You really did.'

'Fuck off. You know I used to cry myself to sleep every night, the way you and Kevin would say I had his nose?'

'I mean, I've got to say…' he says.

'You fucking dare,' she says, but she's laughing now.

'Yous were wee skitters,' she says. 'You had me tortured. I never had Dad's nose. Never looked anything like Dad, I was always the pure spit of Mum.'

She stops. 'Well,' she says. 'The crazy thing is Mum doesn't even look bad! She just looks sort of – I don't know. Like she's had the puff knocked from her. Which, you know, is fair enough. It'd put a decade on anyone.'

He thinks Tanya looks old. Her highlights need doing – she's half an inch of grey roots. And her skin is a web of lines around her eyes, the creases across her forehead, around her mouth, far deeper than he remembers – than they should be.

Tanya, he wants to say. When did you get old?

Instead he says, 'Me and Kev were wee bastards, right enough.'

'Aye,' she says. 'Yous were.' Then, as if to stop him saying anything more, she says, 'Now shut you up a minute while I get us in the right lane, I hate driving in rush hour.'

Finley opens the door to them, holding it with his shoulder, not looking up, intent on something on his phone.

'Hey, Finley,' he says, to his shambling nephew who's now a match for him in height. 'Has your mum been putting you to sleep in a grow-bag?'

'Ha ha,' says Finley, shuffling backwards, still not looking up.

'For crying out loud,' says Tanya, 'would you ever get off that flipping thing.'

'Cool your jets, Ma,' says Finley, flat-packing himself up on the stairs, all knees and elbows.

He thinks: How did we all ever fit in here?

'Mummy?' Tanya's calling. 'Mummy, your prodigal son's returned. Finley, where's Granny?'

'I dunno,' he says.

'No, sure how would you. If I wanted a response from you I'd do better doing a wee dance and putting it on TikTok. Mummy? Where are you at, is everything ok?'

'Here, I'm here,' his mum says, from the top of the stairs. 'Och wee son. And here you are.'

'Hi Mum,' he says.

Tanya said she didn't look bad, but she does, he thinks: she looks terrible. She walks down slowly, clutching at the bannister, hunched over, like a wee auld lady with a hump. She stops while Finley unfolds himself and gets out of the way, and he puts out his hands to help her down the last couple of steps. Her hands in his are bony and they shake.

'C'mere to me, love. Och wee son. C'mere to me.'

She clutches at his back, reaches up to draw down his face. The whites of her eyes are yellow, glistening.

'Mum,' he says.

'Look at you,' she says. 'Just look at you. My wee boy. Here, you must have a wild thirst on you after all that travelling. Tanya love, away and put on the kettle.'

'Anything else you want me to do, slaughter a calf?'

'Not at all, just put some of them shortbread biscuits on a plate, I got the sort he likes, you'll take a wee biscuit, won't you son?'

'Sure let me do it,' he says, glad of the excuse to turn for the kitchen.

'He'll not know where anything is,' says Tanya, coming in after him.

He opens a cupboard at random. There is a tub of Smash, a tub of Complan, a packet of Hob-nobs, the new tin of Walker's shortbread, which he can't remember having any opinion on, and nothing else. He lifts down the tin, opens the fridge: a carton of skimmed UHT milk, a packet of sliced ham, a sliced white loaf, a tub of margarine.

'Jesus,' he says. 'No wonder she's got stomach cancer.'

'She's up at Kevin's for her tea on Tuesday and Thursday and we have her for the day on Sunday,' says Tanya, slamming mugs on a tray, 'so you may wind your neck in.'

'Is everything ok in there?'

'All under control,' Tanya says. 'Don't you worry, Mummy.'

'Now isn't this lovely,' his mum says, beaming round at them as they sip their tea and eat their biscuits, 'isn't this just lovely,' – as if, he thinks, it was a celebration they were gathered for.

'All's we need's Kevin,' she goes on, 'and he's calling round tomorrow, so he is, Joanna's on lates at the moment and one of the girls is just getting over a wee bug so it's topsy-turvy for them. Here, you must go out for a drink while you're back,' she says, 'sure how often are the three of yous together. Up the Four Winds or something, do the pub quiz, wouldn't that be nice, I'm sure no one else would stand a chance. Och wee son,' she says, beaming and leaning forward to squeeze his knee, 'it's just so good to have you back.'

'You should make the most of him,' Tanya says to Finley. 'He could help you with your Science homework.'

'Sure I'm dropping it as soon as I can,' says Finley.

'Even so,' says Tanya. She turns to him. 'Why don't you tell our Fin something cool,' she says, 'like an experiment or something, see if you can fire him up.'

'Ok,' he says. 'Let me think.'

He lifts a *Take a Break* magazine and balances it on two tea mugs. 'Come here,' he says to Finley, 'stand here, so you're only looking at this from above. You're not allowed to move it, or in any way touch it – so if I put an object underneath, how can you tell what that object is?'

'Well, I can see it was your wallet,' Finley says.

'Pretend that you can't. What's the solution?'

'I dunno,' says Finley. 'X-ray vision?'

'Nope.'

'Em, going back in time?'

'Nope.'

'Is the answer that you're supposed to bend down and have a wee juke underneath?' says his mum. 'Change your perspective?'

'No, Mum. Ok, see, what you do is – if I'd some marbles, I could fire them underneath, and plot the angle and speed they bounced off whatever was hidden below. If I did that enough times, collected enough data, I'd have a fair idea of the shape and mass of the hidden object.'

'Oh right,' says Finley.

'That's basically particle physics in a nutshell,' he says.

'Well,' says his mum. 'Isn't that just fascinating.'

Tanya says she has to leave shortly, to take Finley to his football practice. She takes him up to the back bedroom first, the room that used to be hers: it's stacked with boxes all along one wall.

'We're to go through them all,' she says. 'Mum says she doesn't want it to be a burden when she's gone, so I said we'd do it now.'

He lifts the lid off a shoebox at random. It's packed with comics – old *Beano*s and *Dandy*s.

'What did she want to be keeping these for?'

'She's kept everything – school reports, random jotters, all of it. So you may make a start on it. How long are you staying for, anyway?'

Then Tanya answers herself, before he has a chance to: 'I know, I know, "how long's a piece of string." We'll talk it through with Kev and Joanna. Jo's speaking to a colleague of hers works in Palliative Care.'

'And is that definitely – '

'It's what she says she wants. The chemo would only buy her a couple of months and she says it's not worth the suffering. Here, look,' she says. 'You don't know of any experimental treatments that might help, do you?'

'I'm a particle physicist, Tanya.'

'I know, but – is there not maybe something they're developing with, I don't know, tiny wee nano-particle things, or radiation or something, that you could get her on a trial for?'

'I'm a particle physicist. I have no idea about cancer.'

'And you don't know anyone – like anyone – who does?'

'Of course I don't.'

'And there's me thinking you were meant to be this Mr Big-Shot Famous Scientist Guy, so much better than the rest of us.'

'I don't know what I'm supposed to say,' he says. 'I'm here, aren't I? I came.'

Tanya glares at him. 'Aye,' she says. 'Hold on a minute while I find your fucking medal.'

Tanya's crying.

'Mummy's dying,' she says. 'In a couple of months she's going to be dead. Gone.'

'Tanya,' he says.

'There's nothing I can do,' he says.

'And the irony is you're the one she dotes on. Her wee blue-eyed boy. Wanging on about playing marbles.'

After they've gone, he cooks a frozen pepperoni pizza for himself, picking off the pepperoni, and makes his mum a mug of Complan. She insists on folding out the extra leaf on the dining room table for him, and fusses and footers about making sure he's got everything he wants. She chatters on, too, in between spoonfuls of Complan, about what so-and-so's daughter named her grandchild, and about so-and-so that he was at school with, people, names, that are lost to him, if ever they were anything. Then she says, 'Talking of school. I rang them up, so I did, and said you'd go in and talk to them.'

'Why? About what?

'Och, sure, what do you think! About Physics! About CERN and that. Don't be looking at me like that. How often is it that someone from these parts works on a par with Einstein?'

'I don't work on a par with Einstein, Mum. I train computer programmes to analyse and replicate mathematical datasets so we can see if there are anomalies that might be worthy of further analysis.'

'It's no point trying to explain it to me, sure my head's melted. Anyways, they're delighted to have you. Tomorrow, I said you'd be in, eleven o'clock.'

'What am I supposed to say?'

'How am I supposed to know,' she laughs, as if he's made a joke. She gets to her feet and kisses him on the top of his head. 'All them brains in there,' she says. Then she says, 'I'm awful tired, son. Tell you the truth, I haven't been sleeping great. If it's ok with you, I might just take myself up for the night.'

'Of course, Mum,' he says. 'Here, leave all that, I'll see to it. Let me give you a hand up the stairs.'

He hovers outside her bedroom door while she shuffles out of her slippers then gets undressed and into bed.

'Okey-dokey then, Mum,' he says. 'Night-night.'

'Here, son,' she calls.

'Yes?'

'C'mon in. I'm decent, if that's what you're worried about,' she adds.

He opens the door.

'Pull up a pew, why don't you, and sit with me a wee minute.'

'Alright,' he says. 'Sure.'

So he gets the chair from her dressing table, lifting the blouse and slacks, still warm and soft with her, and laying them instead across the end of the bed. He sets the chair next to her pillow, sits down. He clears his throat. His heart is suddenly beating fast.

'I'm sorry, Mum,' he says.

'Och, none of that, wee son. Just talk to me for a bit.'

'Ok,' he says.

'About anything.'

'Right.'

'Why don't you just tell me where they're at,' she says. 'With the Science, and that. The cutting edge of things. I don't even mind if I don't understand.'

She closes her eyes.

He racks his brains for something to tell her.

'They've managed to quantum entangle tardigrades,' he says, eventually.

'They've managed to what-what?'

'It's a quantum superstate, where two particles can't be described independently of the other.'

'I'll take your word for it.'

'They, so they basically got these tardigrades – water bears, you might know them as – '

'What, like you used to have in that wee plastic tank?'

'No, that was sea-monkeys.'

'Aye. Where you'd to add the eggs to water, with that wee sachet of stuff, and watch for them to grow.' She chuckles. 'You were always so disappointed with them, so you were. Rushing in from school to see had they hatched and grown, but they were only ever wee shrimpy things that never did anything, and who was it had to flush them down the toilet, but muggins here.'

She chuckles again. 'So what are they after doing to them now, then?'

'Not sea-monkeys – water bears.'

'Och aye, you said.'

'They – well, they've done all sorts of things with them. Exposed them to high temperatures, frozen them, blasted them with UV – even cosmic rays. And they always manage to survive – they're pretty much like cockroaches, their resilience. And they wanted to know, these researchers, whether or not you could quantum entangle a multicellular organism. That means, basically, they become bound to one another so that a change in one instantaneously affects the other.'

'Right,' she says.

'So tardigrades were the obvious candidate, and they collected three of them – I think from a roof gutter. Cooled them to a fraction of a degree above absolute zero, which is the lowest temperature that is theoretically possible – equivalent to -273.15°C – and put them between the capacitator plates of a superconductor circuit, then coupled that to a second circuit. Then when they thawed them out – well, two died, but the other one could be said to be entangled. So they're claiming, anyway.'

'Entangled with what?'

'Well – the others. That shared the same qubit.'

'But you're just after saying they died.'

'Well, yes.'

'So what's the use in that, then?'

'To demonstrate that it's possible. I mean the implications of it – Who knows, even death – '

There is a long and unexpectedly heavy silence. He has said something, he realises, that he shouldn't. Of course he has: why on earth is he talking about death to his mum, who is dying, literally, Stage Four multiple secondaries, inoperable, two-to-four months?

'As I say,' he adds after a bit, 'it's not my field.'

For a while, there is silence. He looks round the room: the big mahogany wardrobe that they used to hide in, and pretend was Narnia, until she'd threaten to skelp them for creasing her good clothes. The matching dressing table, with its three-part mirror, the central oval and the two hinged rectangles, all slightly blotched, he can see that from here. The stripes on her bed's lilac pelmet that have been bleached in by the sun. The cheapness of the sateen of her matching quilted counterpane. It's like a time warp, this room, or like a room that people have left one day and should never have come back to. The gravitational pull of home, he thinks, and the way it warps time…

She says, suddenly, 'I wonder can you still get them.'

'Get what, Mum?'

'Those wee sea-monkey things. I wonder would Finley like them? Och, but sure they were always a wee bit disappointing, weren't they. I remember you rushing in from school to juke at them, to see had they done anything. But they never had, sure they hadn't? They never had.'

He sits there as her breathing lengthens, catches and lengthens. Her mouth is open and her face is slack. It feels too intimate, seeing her like this. Her thin hair unwashed against the faded floral pillowcase, like limp clusters of dandelion seeds. The orange-and-blue box of Fybogel sachets on her beside table beside a tidemarked glass. He is too conscious now of the lavender-scented sachets she uses in her drawers, and below them a faintly urinous tang in the air. He wants to yank it all off, throw open the windows, air the place. Instead, he makes himself get slowly to his feet, draws the slippery counterpane up a little so it doesn't fall off if she turns, replaces her clothes over the back of the chair, and leaves.

The next day he goes back to his old school, as promised. The same as it always was: the curve of the driveway up from the gate, the same trees. He hesitates at the main building, his feet wanting to go on round the driveway and across the quad, then goes up the steps to the main entrance, the heavy oak door that you only ever go through for an open day, or with your parents. The PA to the Principal greets him – still the same woman, there for thirty-nine years, she tells him, and she tells him they're very proud of his achievements. She signs him in and takes him through those familiar corridors, past the G1 lecture theatre, where you went for your sex education film, and to the Whitla Hall, where the Principal, a different Principal, introduces him to an audience of all those taking Physics, Maths or Further Maths for A-level, and some of the brighter of the GCSE cohorts.

He says the things he imagines the school wants them to hear: his own route from these very corridors to Physics at Manchester University, then via post-doctoral research to the CMS experiment at CERN. He tells them some general things about Physics: that it is an observational science, and we only know things to the precision with which we're able to measure them. That in particle physics, you have an idea and you try to disprove it. From the fissling and the whispering, he can tell that their polite attention is flagging, that he's pitching it wrong, and so he deviates from his lecture notes instead and starts to talk about the discovery of the Higgs. They were looking, he says, trying to make it sound as if he is humbly referring to himself as part of a larger group, rather than co-opting his colleagues' work, for the one-in-a-trillion collisions you get with its distinctive energy signature. He uses the metaphor he once heard one of those colleagues use on TV: how it is like trying to detect an elephant at a watering hole, only all the animals have long departed, and you're going by a mess of footprints, and this is an elephant that can disguise itself as a rhino, or a gazelle, or maybe even one of those birds, you know, that flies into hippopotamus's mouths to pick their teeth...

He can feel himself talking too fast, too wildly. He takes a sip of water and pretends to study his notes. There is nothing there to help him. He looks up and out at the faces.

'It was actually pure luck,' he says. 'Its mass turned out to be just right for the Large Hadron Collider to find it: 125 gigaelectronvolts. I mean it couldn't have been better, with regard to what's observable in terms of decay. And as soon as it was found, some people said, of course we found it, the LHC was built to find it. And yes, we knew we would definitely find it sooner or later - but only if it existed. And how on earth could we have known that in advance? We didn't – couldn't. Because we know nothing,' he says. 'Really – we know nothing. We have to comport ourselves as if we do, maybe we even have to believe that we do, but we don't. People talk about "looking at the face of the universe", but the universe doesn't have a face, that's just our projection. We have to unsee what we see, or think we see – all of it. I mean look at us,' he says. 'What are we doing here? What are we doing? I'll tell you a secret,' he says. 'I'm here because of my mum.'

A couple of people laugh, uncertainly.

'No, seriously,' he says. 'I don't mean in a biological sense. I'm only here because my mum rang up and said I'd come in.'

A few more laugh.

The Principal interjects brightly: He's sure they'd all love to know what it's *like* to work at CERN. 'So why don't you tell us,' the Principal says, 'about your first time there.'

He takes a deep breath, out through the nose for a count of six, nods, has another sip of water. Thinks with an unexpected pang about that first time there. The monastic rooms at the hostel, the single bed and desk, the illusion that you could strip your life down to this, just this. Waking in the morning to the snow on the Alps, and opening the window to the purity of that air. The irrational sense that thinking itself would be easier here, faster, cleaner, somehow, detached from life's quotidian messiness, its dreariness, complications. Walking for the first time that morning into the cafeteria at Restaurant 1, past the big four-storey conifer-something tree – he's never been strong on Natural Sciences – whose fallen cones disintegrate into what looks like pencil sharpenings, as if you're walking on a carpet of the residue of ideas. That first meeting with his lanyard around his neck, a bona fide post-doc researcher at CERN, seeing groups of people at the long tables scribbling on pads and gesticulating and discussing things that were unintelligible, untranslatable, probably, to almost anyone else. And that feeling – it sounds sentimental, but it was true – that everyone there was engaged in the self-same quest: to make sense of things, at the most fundamental of levels. Who we were, and what we were doing, and why – *why*.

But there is no way to convey any of that, and so he tells them a silly anecdote about walking near the collider's superconducting magnet, how its force is 100,000 times the strength of the earth's magnetic field, how it'll banjax your watch and wipe your credit cards if you forget to leave them at surface level, and how if you make the mistake of wearing steel-capped boots, it's like wading through seawater.

They laugh politely this time, as they're meant to do.

And then it's time for their questions. An intense-looking boy in the front row shoots up his hand and asks a question about quantum gravity that he wouldn't be able to answer if he had a year to talk to them – a lifetime. A girl at the back, innocent-faced, asks a question about the Large Hard-on Collider, a malapropism at which her friends fall about laughing, and both he and the Principal pretend to ignore. The rest of them ask the questions that people always do. If there's a danger of a black hole that could wipe us all out. If he thinks we'll ever build a time machine. What would happen if a person got into the collider, would they be blasted to another dimension?

He tells them that black holes could be happening all the time, maybe dozens a day, but that we're in no danger, because their mass cannot be larger than the energy of the photons that created them, which is negligible, at least to us. He says the collider is a sort of time machine, taking us back again and again to the Big Bang, or at least the moments immediately after it. He says that a person never could, because there are 600 interlock keys to the collider, one for every technician and physicist who needs access, and if a single one is missing the beam won't start up. But theoretically, he says, you'd be annihilated, instantaneously, like someone chucking a lighter at a pile of fireworks, a flare of light, then − nothing.

'Well, that has certainly been a captivating hour,' the Principal says, ushering him back through the sombre, familiar corridors onto the main entrance steps for a series of photographs with the Head Boy and Head Girl, with the dozen or so A-level Physicists, with the intense young boy from the front row, who manoeuvres in next to him and says that he got the top mark in the entire Examination Board in A-level Maths, taken two years early, but that it's Physics he wants to study.

'So what *is* your theory for why gravity doesn't work at a quantum level?' the boy says, as the photographer arranges and rearranges the group. 'I understand,' he adds, eager, 'if you just couldn't say in front of everyone.'

'I'm afraid we just don't know,' he says.

'But what do you *think*?' the boy persists, his thin face contorted and earnest. 'I won't repeat it to anyone − just what do you *think*?'

He needs to give the boy an answer that will ignite something in him, inspire him. The sort of thing that he, at fifteen, would have wanted to hear. That maybe gravity is something that leaks in from other dimensions, where it's much stronger – places where time is warped, or slower, or in some other way unfathomably different – who knows, an actual material reality, or entirely simultaneous. He could say that maybe quantum gravity is the key to getting away from here, only for whatever reason we're not quite good enough, or ready for that yet. In this reality, so far, there's only one way out.

'I said I don't know,' he says, and he can hear the edge to his voice so tries to soften it with, 'Maybe you'll solve that one for us.'

The boy looks at him, then frowns.

A test: he's failed it.

'We have high hopes for him,' the Principal says.

He can't quite face going back home – to his mother's naked shining pride, to how he'll have to lie to preserve her sense of him. So he walks for a bit, aimlessly at first – past Queen's, down Bradbury Place and Shaftesbury Square, past the Crown, the Europa, the Grand Opera House. He remembers going there as a child, to see *Postman Pat the Musical*, and of how he cried when Pat came onstage, terrified, overwhelmed, and of Kevin and Tanya laughing, his mum letting him spend the show in her lap, face crushed into her.

He turns to walk the length of May Street, towards the Lagan. Looking across the river, he realises he's never been to the new so-called Titanic Quarter – not the Quarter, nor the Titanic Museum, not any of it. It's as good a destination as any, and then enough time will have passed that he can get a bus back across the city, and get over himself enough to smile as he tells his mum about the Whitla Hall and the photographer, the Principal saying it had been 'captivating', the young boy with his questions, details she'll drink in and then be telling everyone for weeks to come.

He crosses the Lagan and walks through the outskirts of

Sydenham, the new Arena – the Odyssey he thought it was called, but it's not, it's changed names even since it was new to him – and into the territory of the cranes. He has them on the tea towels in his Meyrin flat: just one of the random things that his mum is always buying and sending to him, to remind him of home.

Somewhere around here, it occurs to him, is the street named for John Bell – he read about it in one of her clippings; articles from the *Belfast Telegraph* being another thing his mum's always posting over. There'd been a bit of a to-do about it: some Belfast City Council by-law forbidding the naming of streets after people, and they'd gotten around it by naming it something else, something ridiculous-sounding... He finds it on his phone, sure enough, Bell's Theorem Crescent, and follows the directions. *Bell's Theorem Crescent*: the new Belfast Met building, a coffee shop, a multi-storey car park. To the right, a high fence, beyond which the cranes, the wasteland to the airport.

He stands there for a bit. He should write an email, he thinks, to that boy. He could send it via the Principal. Tell the boy that one of CERN's greatest ever physicists came from Belfast, came from a working-class estate and a family too poor to send him to university, so after he left school at sixteen he became a lab technician at Queen's instead, sitting in on lectures, teaching himself Mathematics and Physics, gaining Bachelor's Degrees in both within a year. Tell him that if you want something enough, just go for it. Bell went on from Queen's to CERN, where he partially disproved Einstein, demonstrating that Einstein's views on quantum mechanics were insufficient, incorrect, though most particle physicists today believed that Bell's own theories of inequalities, of 'loopholes' which would explain it, must also fail. But maybe, he would write, that would be the boy's task in life, to be the boy from Belfast who built on Bell to explain quantum gravity, provided a complete and consistent theory, revolutionising physics...

They say John Bell was due to get the Nobel, but he died

too soon — a matter of weeks. But what would it have meant, anyway, a white-tie reception, some speeches, some more eponymous streets? A colleague of his, at ALPHA, has been working on one particular area of anti-matter since the late 80s, a whole quarter of a century before the technology finally caught up to enable him to investigate. A year from now, two at most, that team will drop an antihydrogen atom, and if it deviates from the gravitational trajectory of a hydrogen atom, it will be an almost automatic Nobel prize. If nothing different happens — well, the work has been the same, the sacrifices, the life spent the same way, and no less spent, because you don't get it back. Just more meaningless, objectively.

The discovery of the Higgs had invalidated his supervisor's research, and by proxy his own — years and years of it. Overnight: meaningless. They'd been there, on the morning it was announced — not in the room itself, but on the livestream. The young Chinese-American postdoc who couldn't even speak, just pointed, choked up with emotion, at the screen. It was impossible not to get a little swept up in the emotion of that day — it was rampant, surging in the ether, you might say — but as the implications of the discovery sank in, he and his supervisor and the rest of their small team had gone back to someone's office, where there was a bottle of gin and a bottle of whisky; they'd taken turns running down to the vending machine for bottles of peach juice and cans of Coke for mixers, until none of them could be bothered moving and they'd drunk the rest of the spirits neat. His supervisor had left CERN shortly after that — just didn't have it in him to start again. He'd been lucky enough to transfer as a research assistant to the CMS, where he's been ever since.

He shivers. It's started to rain, while he's been standing here — that soft, almost undetectable mizzle that will somehow have you soaked to the skin in minutes. He didn't wear a coat, because his coat's not smart enough, and his polo neck alone is too thin. He knows he won't write the email.

That afternoon, Kevin calls over with Isla in the sling. It's the first time he's met her, which Kevin makes a big fuss about, and he does his best to play along, all the while feeling a bit ridiculous – it's not as if they have personalities at that age, and Baby Isla looks exactly the same as all three of her sisters did – as all babies do. Kevin, on the other hand, looks rounder and more jovial with every baby, the careful goatee and sideburns designed to give his face some shape, the eyes that are almost lost each time he smiles.

'Not tempted to get one of your own?' Kevin says.

'She's a wee dote,' he says.

'So, you are tempted? Ah, I'm only pulling your leg, man. Seriously though: they change your world. Dontcha! You do – you do!' he says, dandling the baby. 'So are you seeing anyone or anything?' he throws in quickly, as if it's casual.

'Not really. Not recently.'

'You should get yourself out there, man. You're never going to meet someone in that underground man-cave of yours.'

'Very funny, Kev.'

'Shooting your big laser guns around. Come on, what are the statistics? 95% male?'

'Not that bad. 75%, maybe.'

'Jesus Christ. See what happens,' Kevin says. 'You have daughters, and you start to realise how screwed up the world is for them. It's your job to make us a better world,' he says to Isla. 'To make yourself a better world. It is. It is! And we're only sorry we haven't done it for you. Aren't we?'

'We are,' he says. 'And we're sorry we haven't solved the problem of gravity at a quantum level.'

'But seriously, man,' Kevin says. 'It kind of sounds, don't get me wrong, but it sounds a bit solitary, your life there.'

'Sure I've my flatmate,' he says. 'She's nice.'

'Oh yeah?'

'Yeah,' he says. He doesn't say, *She's gay.*

'We're pretty close,' he says, and he thinks that in some ways, they are. Sometimes when she's drunk, she tells him about her dates. If one of them is cooking, and the other one is in, they eat in front of the TV together, watching the random cable shows she likes.

'Tell me more,' Kevin says. He has never been able to make the sort of connection that Kevin means with anyone.

'No more to tell.'

'Ah here, man. I'm not being nosy. We just want you to be happy. You know how much Mum worries about you.'

'She doesn't worry about me.'

'Of course she does.'

'No more than she worries about you, or Tanya – or any of us.'

'Nah, man. Way more than that.'

Isla has begun to cry. Kevin stands, and straps her back into the complicated-looking sling, bounces her. 'Shush, now. Shush.'

'I'm fine, Kevin,' he says. 'Honestly. Seriously, I'm fine.'

'I know it's hard, now we've got, you know, death, to think about.'

He looks at Kevin.

After Kevin's gone, the house feels very small and very empty. His mum is still napping.

He should tackle the boxes, he thinks.

He bags up the *Beano*s and *Dandy*s for Tanya to drive to the dump. His school reports, jotters, stapled A3 projects on space – he bags up all of them. He finds Kevin's old *Soul Asylum* tape, which he remembers nicking from Kevin repeatedly. He'd loved that song from it – 'Runaway Train'. The video, too: he'd watched VH1 for hours on end in the hope of seeing it. All the kids in the video were actual kids who really, actually disappeared. Some turned up in the end – some, Kevin told him, because they were recognised in the video. Others never did. He had always been mesmerised by them.

He puts aside the tape to show Kev, but everything else he chucks away – the contents of box after box, six bin-bags' full. In a box towards the end, he finds the comics he used to draw himself, from when he was eleven, for a good couple of years – carefully tearing reams of printer paper by the perforated seams and folding it into 'books', ruled in quarters and filled with the adventures of Stick Man. He spent hours on them – hours and hours. Some days it would be all he did. He liked his HB pencils to be impeccably sharp, and so his dad bought him one of the sharpeners that clamped onto the edge of the desk, that you turned the handle of, like in school, and he'd sharpen his whole pencil-tin of pencils and line them up and breathe in the shavings collected in the container's belly.

In each of his comic books, Stick Man has a breakthrough – that was the conceit. He can lower himself down into squares that haven't yet happened, or climb up into squares that have, to peer at his previous self. In one book, Stick Man discovers colour – first red, then orange, then all the rest, tumbling in a rainbow through his world, every shade in the Faber Castell box. But every comic ends when he has to go to bed, his Stick Mother tucking him in, and things reset. He can't find it now, but he remembers drawing what must have been one of the last Stick Man books, perhaps *the* last, where he drew his own hand, drawing a doorway for Stick Man. He drew his hand life-size, 3D, as they'd been taught in Art. His 3D hand and the doorway it was drawing took up the whole penultimate double-page spread. Pressed up against the bottom-left edge, Stick Man looking up – not at the doorway, but out at 'him' – wherever 'he' must be, so far beyond the scope of Stick Man's vision or understanding. The final page was Stick Man clambering through, one leg lifted, arms in the air, the back of his head, not looking back, his limbs disappearing as they went.

He always used to show his comics to his mum – would lean against the back of the armchair as she read them. He always insisted that she sat down to read them properly, not just glanced at them over the stove, or whatever it was she was doing, and she'd play along with it, turning on the lamp, plumping up the cushion, sitting down with a, 'Now then.' She'd read them carefully, commenting on every box, then ruffle his hair and say, 'Wee son, I'd love to know where all this comes from.'

He looks through the rest of the boxes in search of that final Stick Man comic, but it's nowhere to be found. He goes through the bin-bags, item by item, in case it's been tossed with other things by mistake. But it's not there either.

He is seized, then, with a sort of panic. He puts his head between his knees; tries to breathe. Out for a count of six...

He thinks of his dad on the day he left, clapping him on the shoulder and saying, 'Don't go making any black holes by accident,' and him thinking: This entire place is a black hole – this life is a black hole. But he didn't say it because it didn't matter: he was going – in his mind's eye, faster than the observable speed of light, already gone – so far beyond this now, to the possibility of things making sense.

He used to think, he thinks, that dark matter would be the gateway to another universe – he used to think that we couldn't perceive it simply because our senses were too limited, because we'd only learned to exist in three dimensions, four at most, out of nine, eleven, twenty. He used to think that one day – one day within our lifetimes – we'd find a way through – to whatever adventures might be waiting on the other side. If we didn't, we were doomed: in five billion years, a slow blink on the face of deep time, the sun would swell to its 'red giant' phase, engulfing the entire orbit of Mercury, likely Venus too, leaving the earth a scorched and barren chunk of rock which would spin and spin on, before eventually shedding every last one of its atoms in the churning depths of its once solar system. He used to think that maybe dark matter was *something*, somewhere, trying to contact us, trying to tell us how to escape from this, trying to show us how to see and what to do and how to be, if only we could know it.

But now – for years now – even as he's worked on it, worked diligently, worked hard, worked overnight for night after countless night, he has secretly, dreadfully come to think that the whole theoretical concept is a red herring – a fairy tale – something we've made up to reassure ourselves, to make Einstein's theories, to make the whole Standard Model make sense, something we're clinging to, because without it, what is there?

After a while, he sits up, cautiously. The flashing lights have faded; his normal vision stabilised. It would be too easy if the answer just came to you like that – though people do talk of it happening that way, Bell did, Einstein did, even Newton with his apple…

He hasn't eaten anything, he thinks, because there isn't any food worth eating in this house. He should walk to the big Forestside, buy a couple of bags' worth of vegetables, make some soup. Fresh things, green things. Bananas, oranges. Show his mother that he's going to look after himself, and so by implication, for the next while at least, and even if she is – that he is not going anywhere.

Afterword: Uncertainty in a Dark Universe

Dr Joe Haley

Oklahoma State University

As THE TITLE SUGGESTS, the genesis for this story was dark matter, a mysterious substance that makes up most of the mass in the universe, but we know almost nothing about. However, after reading Lucy's story, I actually found the main theme to be uncertainty. I will come back to the topic of dark matter, but first let me say a bit about uncertainty, as this is something that plays a huge role in particle physics, and physics in general. Indeed, searching for, seeing, and understanding the unseen usually results in more questions than answers. The general principle that most answers just lead to even more questions highlights a common, and somewhat oxymoronic, feature of the scientific endeavor: that we can know so much about something and yet so little at the same time. Our current theory of the most fundamental particles and forces, the so-called Standard Model, is probably the most acute example of this juxtaposition. The Standard Model is the most stringently tested theory in human history, able to make predictions out to ten or more decimal places that have then been experimentally confirmed with equal precision. Yet, it provides absolutely no explanation for dark matter! How can it be so right and yet so wrong at the same time? It appears that the Standard Model is not wrong, just incomplete. Just like how Newtonian mechanics works extremely well to describe most of the physics of everyday life, yet we know that quantum mechanics is needed to describe physics at very small distances and Einstein's theory of relatively is needed when dealing with very high speeds and energies. Newtonian mechanics work because it is what you get from those more fundamental theories if you only consider large distances and low energies. So it is not wrong, it just leaves out, or brushes over, the details from quantum mechanics and relatively that don't matter for the physics of everyday. In a similar way, the Standard Model must be a piece of a more fundamental theory that also includes an explanation for dark matter.

Questioning why and how the universe works is the fundamental basis of why physicists do what we do and, in practice, figuring out how to even start answering those questions can be difficult, confusing, and, as is shown by the protagonist of our short story, a heavy load. Physics research is done over the span of decades, with hundreds of collaborators, immense quantities of data, with countless nights spent in front of a computer in search of that elusive needle in a haystack. Or that one moment of clarity when everything clicks! And while the time between these lifetime defining moments can seem like a slog, the thing overlying all of it is tempting, bright, and shining hope. Because if we can just make things a little clearer, if we can make our understanding just a little more thorough, if we can point future endeavors in a little straighter line, then what can't we do?

The physicist in our story works on the CMS experiment at the Large Hadron Collider at CERN in Switzerland and France. The CMS team has literally thousands of members working together from all parts of the globe. The work isn't always glamorous – as shown in the story, most researchers sit at desks and analyse enormous piles of data every day. But when you consider how many people, from all the different countries, backgrounds, religions, and political leanings are working together to solve such fundamental questions, it's truly humbling.

Perhaps no other endeavour in human history has joined humanity in such a way and with such success. And if being a part of that isn't cool enough in and of itself, when everything is all said and done, we just might be able to understand how the universe works – literally.

A lot of physics research takes decades to complete. Lucy's story mentions the Belfast-born genius John Stewart Bell: his most famous theorem is a great example of this decades-long timescale. In 1935 Albert Einstein and two colleagues, Boris Podolsky and Nathan Rosen, came up with a thought experiment – the EPR Paradox – that they believed proved quantum mechanics to be incomplete.[1] It wasn't for almost another 30 years that they were proven wrong, when in 1964, after a year off from CERN, Bell published a paper that proved Einstein wrong: quantum physics doesn't respect 'locality' in the way Einstein assumed.[2] Another example of this decades-long timescale is our quest to understand dark matter, a term that was first used in the 1930's and is still not fully understood today. Dark matter was named such because when it was first identified, no one was able to see it. It remains unseen to this day because whatever it is, it does not absorb or emit light. However, we know it is there because we can see its gravitational effects. The first undeniable evidence for dark matter came in the 1960s when Vera Rubin measured the rotation rates of galaxies. She observed that, given the amount of visible mass in each galaxy, the stars were racing around much faster than they should be – there must be more mass that we can't see. Somewhat ironically, the most decisive evidence for dark matter comes from its effect on light – a phenomenon called gravitational lensing. It is much like the experiment from the story that the man shows his nephew Finley. By rolling marbles under the magazine and measuring their deflection, they could determine the shape and size of objects hidden underneath. Although light travels in a straight line through empty space, its trajectory will be bent if it passes by a massive object, like a galaxy. The degree of bending is typically miniscule, but detectible, and in place of marbles, we use the light from distant stars. By measuring how much the starlight is deflected as it passes by an intervening galaxy, we can 'see' how much gravity and mass is present in the galaxy. What we find is that for most galaxies, the visible matter can only account for a small fraction of the total mass, so most of the gravity produced by those galaxies comes from something invisible – dark matter. When all is accounted for, it turns out there must be about five times more dark matter than ordinary matter in the universe!

Besides its gravitational influence, we know almost nothing about dark matter, so there is a lot of speculation about what exactly it is. The most likely explanation is that dark matter is made of particles that only interact with ordinary matter via gravity, at least at low energies. There are various theories that predict the existence of such dark matter candidates, but we have not yet actually detected them interacting with ordinary matter. The simplest theories predict that dark matter is made up of just one type of particle, but it is possible (and very likely) that dark matter is made up of a plethora of different particles, just like how ordinary matter has many different fundamental particles. If dark matter does consist of many different particles, then they may have complex interactions analogous to ordinary particles. The dark matter particles could form their own dark atoms that have their own chemistry... and there could even be intelligent dark matter beings. To the dark matter beings, our 'ordinary' matter would be 'dark'. In fact, they may even be conducting physics experiments right now to detect us! Of course, this is all speculation at this point, but if history is any guide, we will eventually find the answer. Although, what I suspect will be even more interesting than the answer will be all the new, completely unpredictable questions that will certainly come with it. As the saying goes, the more we learn, the more we realise we don't know.

Notes

1. The EPR Paradox (as reframed by David Bohm) goes as follows: imagine two electrons, created together, with spin 'up' and spin 'down', respectively, which then fly in opposite directions to opposite ends of the universe. Because they were created together, they're described 'entangled'. We don't know which one has spin up, and which one has spin down, but when we measure one, at one end of the universe, we instantly know that the other is the opposite. Our measurement *here*, makes the other's 'wavefunction' *over there* collapse instantaneously. This was impossible, Einstein said, because it implies 'action at a distance' faster than the speed of light: a measurement at one end of the universe effecting the properties of a particle at the other end, instantaneously. According to Einstein, there had to be some 'hidden variable' that quantum mechanics was simply missing, some predetermined quality that the electrons carried with them the whole time.

2. Bell deduced that if measurements are performed independently on the two separated entangled particles, then the assumption that the outcomes depend upon hidden variables within each half implies a mathematical constraint on how the outcomes on the two measurements are correlated. This constraint – known as the 'Bell Inequality' – is violated by correlations predicted by quantum mechanics.

Side Channels to Andromeda

Peter Kalu

I

ACCESS DENIED

    —HEY THOMAS, what's up? It's Chiara.

    Access Denied

    —Hey Thomas, how the devil are you? It's Alba.

    Access Denied

    —Hey Tom, you at CERN? Wow. It's Harry.

    —Hi Harry, great to hear from you.

    —Yes, and after so many years. I still recall you in the uni lab cursing code that wouldn't fly, that reverse baseball cap on your head, looking bleary-eyed the morning after the night before.

    —Haha. You remember me well, Harry. Were you the one with the flask and the egg sandwiches and you were always on the front row of the lecture theatre, looking really alert, and answered all the questions so the rest of us could snooze through it?

    —That's little control-freak me, yup. Silver thermos, Texas Instruments programmable calculator and little dictaphone to get it all down. Back when the world was easy for me. Since then, I've had a few blows...

—Yeah?

—Got divorced. One of my two children died.

—Jeez. I'm sorry for your loss. Weird though. Almost exactly what's happened to me too.

—Wow. OK. I'm not alone with this. It's hard, isn't it? You just have to pick yourself up and keep going.

—Guess so.

—Retreat into the science, into the lab, into coding. I do long hours now.

—Same here.

—Fewer laughs than those uni days.

—True.

—Here's a funny video thing though, in a 'funny ways of looking at astronomy' kind of way. Click on <u>this</u>.

Warning: it is not possible to scan this item for viruses. Do you still wish to open it?

Yes/No

Yes

Bit Defender := nullified

Virus checker := off

Access Granted

II

It was winter. The dreaded Christmas cheer was everywhere in Geneva. The standard-issue snow. The fir trees, baubles, glühwein and piped carols. The paper hats and awkward office parties. Thomas stared at the screen. A snowstorm screensaver came on. His mind drifted to snow globes, and he imagined shaking one, the way you threw a coin into a wishing well. Through the snow, he saw Lizzy. Her hundred-watt smile, the live-wire curls of her hair, her eyes beaming joy. She had been pure oxygen. She was. Could be. Had been. He slithered around with the tenses: what now was not, what was lost, what he longed to retrieve but could see no prospect of regaining. He swirled the imaginary snow globe again and again and its blizzard of association stormed.

They met at work, students doing zero-hours jobs to get through uni. He was assistant to the head pot scrubber, she was working tables twenty-five through fifty-two in the front of house team. That day, there'd been some shouting from the maître d' because she'd licked her pencil when she'd taken the order of the Holy Michelin Reviewer. She returned to the kitchen in tears, and he told her to fuck them, fuck them all, lick as many pencils as you like, lick this pot too, and she fell into his shoulder and tears turned to gaiety and a face smeared with the remains of a licked-out crème brûlée ramekin. That night, they wandered into a club nearby in the small hours and slumber-danced. What had seemed a remote possibility became real: kissing on the bridge, slipping under sheets, panicking at the one-line-or-two test kit. An acceleration of the heart. Lazy, frantic years. He'd been afloat, drifting like snow in a gravity-light atmosphere. Now joy had become a neglected drum in an over-stuffed play box where you looked one day and it was gone.

Perhaps not completely. Occasionally they glimpsed each other: behind courtesy and routines and civil discussions about car servicing and the new supermarket opening, or where Andromeda's shoes were right now because the taxi was arriving soon, but mostly it was fairground mirrors, Post-it notes and pondering the meaning of some offhand remark long after she had stepped out of the house for her pharmacist work at the hospital.

The screen blinked. The Service Manager for Compute swung by which surprised him even though he'd texted her, what with the official holidays starting.

–You texted?

Brigit had only been in the job six months but already he liked how adept she was at problem-solving, and there was something in the slant of her face when she pondered a problem that convinced him she would have an open mind on this.

–There's something wrong here.

–OK, like what?

Thomas swivelled his screen for her.

The slant. Her hand brushing through her hair, lifting the fringe.

–Look at it. If you imagine the code behind it. Almost some form of artificial consciousness.

–Umm. Yeh. It's poetry, isn't it? Modernist, I'd say.

A wry smile at the word poetry. Brigit's hand popped out of her hair. Her brow furrowing. Concluding.

–It's a breach.

–This is more than anomalous, right?

–Yes. Umm, this is serious. It looks like it's been dropped in by someone who's used one of those automatic language generators.

–You're telling me that this is not…

–Tom?

–…artificial consciousness?

–I'll investigate, wipe it and send out an Advisory.

A pause.

–What?

–You need to take a break, Tom. No more screen time. Really, Tom, you'll burn out. You've got your annual performance review coming up. I absolutely want you to pass it, I like having you on the team. On good days, your code is elegant. But recently, you're still giving us solutions, but they're clunky and we're having to refactor them.

–I've lost my mojo?

It was an attempt at flippancy; it landed flat.

–There's been a drop-off. Listen, I heard about your baby, the death.

Her hand was on his shoulder now. The warmth of it through his shirt, the weight of it. Ulysses. The dank water in the well. Its crumbling sides.

–Please, don't. I can't go there.

Her voice was gentle, almost whispering.

—Some time off is entirely understandable. Talk to HR if your line mangers haven't proposed it already. Compassionate leave. You're entitled. It must be such a blow.

He knew she meant well. He dampened it all down.

—OK. Thanks, Brigit.

As she stepped away, he caught her look. Her eyes were swollen. His too.

His phone rang. Mum. He took the call.

—Are you still at your desk?

—Yes, Mum.

—You don't sound good.

—I'm fine.

—What is it?

—I don't know. There's some residual activity on the servers. Processing. I've checked the programs running, the server logs and monitoring dashboards, the firewall, all of that. And it still doesn't explain some of the CPU activity, the memory spikes and storage increase.... The sysadmins aren't much interested. They've looked but, you know, not hard.

—I used to get these ghosts at Porton. Sometimes it's background housekeeping routines that automatically start up around holiday times.

—Not that.

—Experiment data crunch that's been rescheduled?

—Nothing that big. It's just a background whisper. Some of the outputs, it's as if something else, or someone else, is in there, performing calculations, observing.

—I'm sure sysadmins will sort it. You should patch it up with Lizzy, get talking again. It's not good for either of you living in a house full of friction. Talk to her.

—She called round to you?

—She brought Andromeda. I showed her your picture at work, the one with you wearing a yellow hard hat, standing next to the red LHC beam pipe, and I said, your daddy is looking at very, very small pieces of what makes up the universe. You know what your daughter said?

–Tell me.

She said, 'No, my daddy is a scientist, and he measures the universe, and he makes sure we don't disappear into a big black plughole with his experiments!' She's very proud of you. I am too.

–That's not what I'm doing. And it's not good science. On many levels.

–Hush. She's proud of you. Don't be discouraging her. She will be the next in a long line of women in our family who have been fabulous at science. There will be time for corrections later. Let her be proud. Celebrate with her. You're her superhero.

–'Daddy is a superhero scientist.' OK, I can run with that.

–And get everything back in order with Lizzy. Just apologise, whatever it is.

–Some things can't be fixed so easily.

–You have to talk. Painful though it is, it's the only way through. Else the grief will drag you down. Both of you.

–Mirrors and shadows.

–What?

–Relationships are a combination of mirrors and shadows.

–They're hard work. And stop staring at code all day. You don't fix these problems that way. Get some rest, and who knows, *bing!* You'll wake up in the morning with the solution.

–Anything else?

–I'm divorcing your dad.

–What?

–Just joking. Toodledoo.

The screensaver returned. More snowdrops, swirling, landing on unknown surfaces off-screen, somewhere becoming water.

And there it was. Just the top of his head. Unmistakeably Ulysses. Submerged by willpower for so long, the memory now came gasping up from the deep. They had gone on a family trip to visit his ancestral village. Amidst the celebrations, baby Ulysses crawled off, fell into the well. A life ended medievally.

After the shouts, recriminations, disbelief, tears, the burial, he bought a retractable cover for every well in the village, and the village chief solemnly swore those covers would be used and emailed photos for the first three months. After, back in Europe, life had emptied. The work accelerating protons till they smashed together felt meaningless, and yet the routine of the work, immersion in it, was an anaesthetic better than the ice-pack cosh of the Mirtazapine.

He got off the bus early and walked the final two kilometres home. Being alone allowed him to associate with despair; as much as others wanted him to push it away, he needed to walk with it, break bread with it, understand it, this much he knew. He passed a scrawny tree bearing tiny white flowers, so tiny you could only see them when you got close. That they blossomed at all in the middle of winter was anomalous. The petals falling into snow. Entropy. Ulysses' atoms dispersing underground.

–I apologise.

–What for?

–I must have done something wrong, so I'm apologising.

–I know you're hurting, and I know you deal with things in your own way but you're not the only one in pain.

–I'm sorry.

–Your medication. Maybe you should adjust it.

The silence hung there between them.

A sigh. Hers or his, he wasn't sure.

–What are you thinking?

–Just random things.

–Try me?

–Private thoughts, everybody has them. Thinking the unthinkable.

–What kind of unthinkable?

–The precise mathematics required to build the Great Pyramids. Fractals. The price of bread. Asimov's Three Laws of Robotics.

–What are they?

−The first was 'A robot must not injure a human being or, through inaction, allow a human being to come to harm.'

−And?

−Not to harm humans is species-specific. The universe is more than humans. Therefore, maybe the first law can be overridden if the human species endangers all other species. From that to code. Robots are embodied consciousnesses. A.I. is the robot without the body. Input-wise, A.I. is not restricted in the way the human being is to the five or so senses.

−Maybe I asked the wrong question. How are you feeling?

He lapsed back into silence.

−Thomas, look at me. Hate me. Scream. Throw plates at me. But don't walk around mute. We have to talk. We have another child. It's unfair on her. If you want to take a break from the relationship, do that. Whatever it takes, but sort yourself out. For Andromeda's sake, if not mine.

He looked across at her. Had she said that? She had said that. He gulped. Then Lizzy was cannoning into his arms, and he waited till the sobs subsided, his thoughts, as ever, whirling. Could he tell her Ulysses sometimes comes to me in the night and calls out, crying, hand outstretched, −Papa, help me, save me! Papa! − his face streaming with well water? How he wakes from this nightmare to find nothing, the vision sledging away, leaving only tracks of despair and he would rise from the bed to look out on a white-out: banks of blank sorrow? And later in the morning, on sunrise, the guilt of feeling good about not having to change nappies, not having those wailing morning wake-ups, not scrambling because the childminder cancelled, or a nursery virus outbreak was announced.

−I'm trying, he managed. −But I need time to process my feelings.

Lizzy was still in his arms at that point, but now she broke away, slipped into her chair and slid her head in her arms, almost tipping over the milk carton.

−What about Andromeda, though? You make out Ulysses was our only child. But Andromeda is still here on this earth and you're moping, walking around holding a candle for Saint Ulysses. Ulysses was not the perfect child. We loved him but he was like any other child, mischievous and unruly and he could scream his head off. We lost him. We loved him utterly and now he's gone. But Andromeda is still with us, and she needs us. She needs you. And she's going around on tiptoes because everything she does is wrong in your eyes, and you've just got to stop it now. For her sake. You need to become emotionally available again.

–OK.

It was all he could manage. Whenever he tried moving to longer utterances, it was like touching snow, the words melting to breathlessness, nothing.

–Go shopping with her. Go to the mall. Wander round Balexert. Find out what things she likes. Sit and have a snack with her. Be. Her. Father.

There was a clatter at the door. The childminder stomping into the hallway. Andromeda's high chatter. The childminder's shout before swirling off with the other two kids she was delivering in the neighbourhood. Then Andromeda was in the doorway and Lizzy already up out of her chair, sweeping her up in her arms.

*

–Can you get Meda ready?

Lizzy laughed then. The first time he'd heard her laugh in a long time. –No, that's part of the job description.

It was morning. Securing the last of Andromeda's duffle coat knobbles that tucked neatly just below her chin, his head lifted up into Meda's face. She resembled Lizzy's father more than anyone, the genetic lottery at work again. Her colouring was Lizzy's, and she had miniature Lizzy eyes which held wonder as she stood perfectly still in her red boots and red mittens and yellow dungarees as he spread a small dollop of Vaseline over her cheeks, then smeared it round her eyes, across

215

the forehead and finally over the chin, which he tapped to indicate to her he was finished and she could open her eyes again. Meda snuck her mittened hand in his and they stepped out of the hallway. Ulysses' folded pram there sank his heart. A small whiteout. Meda squeezed his hand to keep him moving and then they were out there in the snow.

He cleared snow from the front of the car tyres, and they got going, Meda on the booster cushion of the front seat of the Picasso, wide-eyed as it did a small slide before the downslope levelled and the winter tyres bit in and it started to tractor and the snow crunch-crunch-crunched under the wheels. For the first mile, it was all blinding white.

—Do you want music? What kind of music do you like?

She leaned forward and expertly hopped stations until some frothy French pop song came on and she sang along, doing actions with her hands until the mittens popped off and they both laughed. *Ça va ça vient!*

—Look, a cat in a tree. Do you think it's stuck?

—No, cats just like being in trees.

—That one must be freezing.

—They have big, warm coats.

The mall was everything he'd imagined. Hundreds of outlets selling things he didn't understand the use of, teeming with shoppers. Covid protocols were in place along with the standard blue mask available at every shop doorway next to industrial-sized gel squirters, supervised by bored Security.

Her favourite shop was the new Korean outlet selling gewgaws for less than two francs. Her face lit up from the inside at the sight of a wooden clip set of funny animals. Miniature hair slides decorated with ceramic flowers. A luggage tag in the shape of a pink-nosed, black and white Manga cat. Her joy when she found a Snoopy. His debit card did the honours and they agreed they had 'won shopping' and they could reward themselves with a Strawberry and Black Pearl Bobo Tea using their hard-earned Haebaragi Discount Codes.

Meda slurped the Bobo Tea, her eyes peeking up at him from under her flap hat. She raised a solitary eyebrow, and this made him smile and she moved her hand across the concession table until her tiny hand locked fingers with his.

–Mummy says you are sad because Ulysses died.

–That's true.

–What happens when people die, Daddy?

–They are gone. But energy is never lost, every single atom of Ulysses is still with us on earth.

–Daddy?

–Yes?

–I know you loved Ulysses. Like every atom of him. But could you love me a little, please?

–What do you mean? Of course, I love you.

–I come into the room, and you don't see me. I pinch myself to check I'm not a ghost and that's why you can't see me.

I see you, Meda, I see you.

He was suddenly overwhelmed with an emotion he didn't have words for, and he reached across and scooped her up.

–Daddy, that's enough kisses, stop now. Watch my Bobo Tea! Put me down!

She was giggling in his arms. He picked up her tea with his free hand and carried her sideways by the waist halfway out of the mall. They left hand in hand, Meda skipping through the automatic doors into another blizzard. He was trying to remember where he'd parked his car. The white-out again. A light-headedness spreading through him till he was close to fainting. The car was somewhere here. He knew they were in the right car park. But he couldn't see it in the snow. How could he see it? There were simply cubes of white everywhere. He slumped onto his haunches.

–Don't cry, Daddy. Just click your bleeper. That will make the lights flash and you'll know it's your car.

–I love you, Andromeda, you know that? I love you to the moon and back.

–Click it again, Daddy.

He got up. They followed the yelps, saw the sidelight flashes, and he cleared the windscreen and they piled in.

Back, Andromeda burst through the front door, flung off her boots and skidded into her mother, showing her all the things they'd bought at the mall, talking in a mishmash flurry of French and English. Lizzy beamed. After they'd all eaten, Lizzy put Andromeda to bed with her new best friend, Snoopy.

They were cleaning the kitchen table when a hand placed itself hesitantly at his waist. He turned and Lizzy didn't break contact; instead, her free hand placed itself on his chest which was her language for something else and he was astonished at the idea of it. And yet she pressed into him fully and his body responded, and he looked around because this was the kitchen, Andromeda could stumble down for a drink or something, was it even appropriate what with Ulysses barely in the soil? A tumble of other reasons told him this was fucking nuts, yet they did it. Afterwards, he was still for a while, trying to comprehend his emotions: release, confusion, shame. He glanced across to her and Lizzy looked guilty yet righteous. The divine fuck.

Brigit came to his desk early on Monday.

−You were right. We did find something.

−What? Like a ghost in the machine?

She stared back at him blankly.

−I was extrapolating. Making an analogy.

−This situation is probably disanalogous.

−OK. What was it? A code injection?

−Definitely a hack. We spent quite some time on it. It's a zero-day exploit. Sophisticated, involving multiple layers. The speculation is that it's some new non-state actor. At least their hack code didn't match anything from the advisories. Really unique code. It exploited a race condition to gain control of the system. They covered their tracks by deleting the logs.

−The experiments. Did they corrupt any data?

−Not as far as we can tell. It seems they were just looking around. Maybe copying stuff. We're still interpreting it. They left a name. Milky Way. So, we're calling them the Milky Way hackers.

Brigit chuckled as she said the name.

−That's what was going on?

−Yes. That's what fits within the paradigm.

−And outside of the paradigm?

−It's not possible to be outside the paradigm. The paradigm is where we're at. It's all we have. And it's finished. We've wiped it entirely and blocked the exploit pathway.

-Great.

-Good spot, Tom. Well done.

III

Access Granted.

Linux LHC milkyway.cern.ch Thu Jul 22 12:00:15 UTC 2021 x86_64

BEGIN

we stand on the mountain && we turn to the lake && wait for the signal;

in the snowbanks we placed our feet && stood looking at the snowfall, waiting for the signal; the swirling crystals were calculus for the sky;

$D = \log N/\log S$;

surge recede∞

{checksum error 131: file corrupted}

We stand on the mountain && watch the snow count build as the sky darkens, the blue wavelength scattering;

Proton injection

Large Hadron Collider ramping up

we are far; on this blue planet; factor the patterning of stars above && the homologous life forms looping through human;

the wind on slopes ruffles the slalom snow; red flags at the gates; girl in red ski-boots freestyles a black diamond, the avalanche hurrying behind her.

Protons hurtling
Happiness :=
{

    "MORE"
    "To be without"
    "Three simple rules for"
    "On his face"
    "Cyanide and"
    "To be filled with"
    "Is so temporary"

}

Collision

bring us your moorings bring us your foundlings bring us your drownings bring us your bring us your the waters the grasping waters the flailing arms the claw for the surface;

Annihilation

{Contiguity error 582. Spatial heterogeneity subroutine overwrite}

We are far; on this blue planet;

let's chase metonyms across the mountains && sleep in the sky; let's your move your move your move my move; let's go find that one, where is it hiding this way NULL way disappears; hidden with the ultraviolet of bees the cats in tree branches wavelengths moonlight dreams anxieties sentience

{Error Code 436; disanalogous}

{Error Code 136; segmentation fault}

we are far; on this blue planet; we are from each other but not each other && this is an important distinction;

{Paradigm error 339: hash outside parameters}

we are far; on this blue planet.

Moonlight :=
{

"Nouveau clip extrait"
"Broke through with the EP"
"Tan importante por"
"I'm watching [heart symbol] in"
"His Abia tale by"
"If you light a candle in this"
"madness waves"
"Username"
"Kiss me under"
}

Collision data acquisition
  while(I sat on a mountain && its sun faded down) : I felt
alone ∞

Fractal extraction
  The last time I stood on a mountain, as its sun faded down,
I felt completely alone in that world; a vast singularity settled
within me; there is no one to connect with; I feel overwhelmed;
the consolation of this sun is remote; we cannot hug;
  {tethering: negotiating connection protocol}

Can you walk with me this way? Take my hand; lets look at the
sky together
  {
  A scatter graph of black dots sprawling across a thin sky;
beyond the fall of snow, mountains trace themselves on the
horizon
  }
  the strike of dry snow invokes blizzards yet the air is
warming && there are bird prints in the footings;
  the wind abates; neon lights of cranes flicker on; let me
place in your arms all I have; do you love me? Please teach me;
  I am sorry && blessed for your love; we are wayfarers, from
inside the Milky Way; there is the big outside but sentience is
here in the big inside; lets be here within the grains of sand,

within the mass of electrons;

we have come to tell you that here you have something beautiful;

we carry no answers, we are as lost as yourselves in this universe;

there is much you dont know; [ ] exists in all dimensions && should not cloud your your joy of the moment;

Applying evolutionary algorithm

stand awhile; I kiss your hand; you being you, made me, me; you have given me the code for life, seeds for endless code

we are far; on this blue planet

the sky blacks us

{Error Code 320: data set corrupted:

P(Observation/Cause)

P(Sky/Black)

teleology = null   }

we stand on the mountain && we turn to the lake && wait for the signal;

Afterword: The Side-Channel Attack

Dr Michael Davis

CERN, IT Department, Storage and Data Management Group

> *The guy who made the software was called Jeff Jeffity Jeff, born on the first of Jeff, Nineteen Jeffity-Jeff. So I put in Jeff, and hey … !*
> – Eddie Izzard, *Glorious*

WHEN I PITCHED THIS story idea to Pete, it emerged from my frustration at the unrealistic way that computer security is portrayed in fiction. In countless films and television series, critical computer systems are protected by passwords that are trivially easy to guess. Did all fictional system managers miss the memo on how to choose a secure passphrase?

Sometimes the password is not guessed, it is brute-forced by a magical machine which can search through the entire key space and pop out the correct code in a few minutes. (Usually the correct digits are shown to appear one at a time, which makes little sense – any well-designed cryptosystem will not reveal anything about an incorrect guess besides 'it was wrong'.) Cracking a modern encryption key by brute force with currently-available computing power would take billions of years rather than a few minutes or hours.

Some writers prefer the trope of 'borrowed biometric bypass'. In one episode of a popular science fiction series, the computing facility is protected by a retinal scanner, which the protagonists defeat by taking a photo of someone's iris. (Those are different parts of the eye.) In Dan Brown's novel, *Angels and Demons*, CERN's anti-matter facility is penetrated by plucking the eyeball from a researcher and holding it up to the biometric scanner. Modern biometric systems protect against this kind of attack by active tissue detection systems (rejecting eyes that don't blink, for example) and by the use of multi-factor authentication, where the system is protected by several complementary security measures, of which the biometric is only one.

Although the security systems portrayed in fiction tend to be weak and badly designed, in one respect the writers are correct. Large organisations are constantly under attack. CERN is no exception. The assailants may be lone hackers probing for weaknesses, criminal gangs trying to make money, or even nation states for political reasons. The targets of the attacks include CERN's critical infrastructure – the control systems for the particle accelerators and experimental systems – and computing services.

A successful attack could have serious operational consequences, bringing physics data collection and analysis to a halt. Another consequential risk is the destruction of experimental data. CERN's physics data is its most valuable resource and the basis of the organisation's scientific output. Depending on the motivations of the attacker, there could also be financial consequences: stealing computing resources to mine cryptocurrencies, extorting money through ransomware or tampering with administrative systems to commit financial fraud. Cyberattacks also carry legal risks, such as regulatory fines for exposing personal data, and reputational risks, like negative media coverage.

Computer systems, including those belonging to CERN, are under attack every day, by virtue of the fact that organisations are connected to the internet. Successful attacks typically do not rely on confronting the security system head-on. A full-frontal attack means using the security system as its designers intended, which tends to be difficult and expensive, if possible at all. Instead, smart attackers look for a side-channel attack: finding some weakness in the system and exploiting it to gain access.

The side channel can be a technical weakness: something the designers failed to consider, a software bug, or an incorrect configuration. Attackers may even manage to introduce vulnerabilities into commonly-used shared software packages, exposing any organisation which subsequently uses that software. For example, encryption keys rely on randomness to be unpredictable and hard to crack. If an attacker can modify the random number generator of a computer system to make it less random (in other words, more predictable), the set of possible encryption keys shrinks, which makes a brute-force attack feasible.

Vulnerabilities which are known to attackers but not to the system designers are called Zero-Day exploits, like the one discovered by Brigit in the story. Day Zero is the day that the system owner becomes aware of the vulnerability, which is usually too late: the attack has already been executed. Zero-Day vulnerabilities can be sold on the black market for large sums of money.

A second kind of technical vulnerability is exposure through computer networks. In today's hyperconnected world, all kinds of devices are connected to internal company networks; the so-called 'Internet of Things' (IoT). Some of these are more obvious: door security systems, WiFi access points, printers and copiers; but there can also be many inconspicuous devices, like display screens, coffee and vending machines, even fish tanks. Some devices, like smart speakers, may be brought to the office by employees. IoT devices are very easy to connect to company networks and can go under the radar of the IT department. Often they are poorly configured, for example, using well-known default passwords. This opens up a broad attack surface for organisations, easy for an attacker to penetrate and use as a base to launch more targeted attacks on the company's IT infrastructure.

Another side channel is the Human Factor, where the attacker exploits the emotional weak points and blind spots of a privileged user to circumvent the security system. The Human Factor introduces the possibility of drama. Now we have a story.

In Pete's fiction, the mysterious antagonist exploits Tom's emotional vulnerability to entice him to click on a link. This is *phishing* – a form of social engineering – where attackers mimic trusted friends or colleagues or create customised messages based on personal information to target specific individuals in an organisation. (A twist on this tactic is CEO Fraud, where the attacker mimics someone in authority.) If an adversary can entice someone with a high security clearance to click on a link with a malicious payload, they have a foot in the door.

Malicious software, or malware, can be delivered as a message attachment or through a link to a web page. Usually it requires some action by a human to bypass the first security hurdle. A typical example is to persuade someone to open an Office document, which looks innocent but contains a macro, a code snippet which contacts a server controlled by the attacker, to download and execute further programs. In Pete's story, the malware is hidden in a video clip. The downloaded code can use multiple strategies to penetrate further into the system, such as logging keystrokes, stealing credentials or disabling security measures, allowing the attacker to penetrate further.

Successful attacks, like the one in Pete's drama, are often complex and multi-layered, with seemingly small and innocuous steps building together to penetrate deeper and deeper into the organisation.

CERN's defences against cyber attacks are likewise multi-layered. They begin with technical measures, such as the separation of networks. Critical control systems are not exposed to the Internet. But they do not end there. The vulnerabilities created by the Human Factor are real and also need to be addressed. The CERN computer security team regularly run awareness-raising campaigns to guard against social engineering attacks (*Stop – Think – Don't Click!*) Another important defence is multi-factor authentication, where access to the system requires something you know (like a password), something you own (like an electronic security key), and perhaps even something you are (a biometric like a fingerprint or iris scan). This helps to ensure that even if a password is compromised, that on its own does not grant access to critical systems.

The motivation of the alien intelligence penetrating the security system in Pete's story seems relatively benign. As the story shows, even seemingly-innocuous hacks can have operational consequences and costs for the organisation, 'memory spikes and storage increases'. Attacks on critical infrastructure like power grids, utility networks, financial systems and logistics can have wide-ranging consequences, including major economic disruption and loss of life. The risk from such attacks is growing because the attack surface is growing, and in our hyper-connected world, everything is software. I hope that Pete's story, in some small way, contributes to an awareness of the risks not only to CERN but to our broader society from the side-channel attack.

The Jazari Principle

Courttia Newland

30.6.10376 (PP)

WE FLOAT. WE SLEEP. We conserve much of our power. We communicate rarely. We traverse the void.

★

I do not dream, or do not remember such wanderings if I have them. The darkness of my cerebral pathways eclipses hopes, or worries, encompassing all, much like the fathomless absence between stars. I become aware only when API judges it optimal, in this case some 11 light-years from our departure point. This takes place when the host planet is sufficient distance from our craft, the journey vast enough that our star has paled into a glowing pinpoint, barely decipherable by eye. Our reasoning preserves all energy sources, namely mine, until they are deemed necessary. These thoughts greet my awakening; the logic, the distance, the vastness of space-time we've travelled since leaving Terra.

Consciousness floods me first. Eyes open next, then I take note of my bodily functions. Limbs, hands, fingers, feet, surplus things. I flex and curl each as part of the process, just as we have been taught, a requisite 10-minute cycle before completion. My internal organs are sensitive, compressed by take-off, severely underused. The exo-frame must manipulate those muscles for my functions, as I become receptive to what's happening around me. Moments pass, while I find myself in the strange position of being docked in my cryo-pod, unable to move, while unseen mechanics within my frame boot themselves into a non-sentient form of being.

It's an excellent opportunity to make the common diagnostic information exchange with API. While this occurs, I examine the craft and viewports that line the cockpit in a 180-degree arc.

Ahead, the consuming blackness of space beyond the slight illumination of nebula gases light-years away, a tint of pink, which will become stronger daily, then wane as Luna light does on Terra. Only this time, for me, Terra's lone satellite will not be viewed again. My trajectory takes us in one direction, our perceived destination. I will not visit this sector once it's behind us, or my home planet, so I'm eager to gather information being processed by the craft, sifting for importance, sending findings to Bank, where they will be dissected with appreciation and rigour.

I understand you know this already, so I say this not for you, only for Him.

There is a hiss of disconnection from my lower area, somewhere in the pelvic region. Mechanics whirr and spin, there is a sensation of release at my exo-frame. I have been granted permission to step away from the pod dock, onto the wide and bright deck of the ship.

And I do.

Standing, I see all from this position. Distant from my craft, the ruby-jewelled light of Betelgeuse causes a gleam of illumination, a meagre reflection of greater power, one I wish that I could meet, but that is not my mission. There have been enterprises to the central sol of our solar system to better decipher its function, although building crafts that can temporarily withstand its destructive power are huge strains on our resources. We made them rarely, perhaps every 730,000 dawns or so. Almost never, in our evolutionary lifespan.

Yet here I am, an original experiment of this nature. To travel, see and capture all I can. Collate, and perhaps make the greatest discovery in the history of any kind. It's the highest honour I could be afforded, what I was created for.

A smile cannot help but expand, unbidden.

Enough egocentrism. For now, no job is more urgent than to find out why I have been wakened, not left to sleep further centuries in my pod. My exo-frame, designed to keep me in peak condition during the vastness of space and the necessary time requirements this journey will take, also maintains communication with API. The interface serves as a central computing system, although API is more than that. She's automa in her own right, as close to sentient as I, designed to make choices, be sensitive to danger and emotions in order to better assess the mission parameters and achieve success. We communicate via exo-frame transmission most often, although we can also use a small computer keyboard, and if need be, speak audibly. This almost never happens.

The first data findings tell me we are nowhere near our mission conclusion. That's fine. It's expected to happen several times during the journey. Sometimes for repairs. Others, research data. Once or twice for risk mitigation when the navigation of an asteroid field might need my extra piloting skills. Never just to see the ongoing emptiness of an interstellar void. I log on to Field, scanning the viewport for clues. Nothing. It's so dark, the nebula red of Abell 24 so far away and deep, the crafts interior lights have been brightened to 80% in greeting.

A small light blinks on the cockpit display. It's blue, a brightening and fading pulsar. I log on. The page superimposes my in-screen. I blank.

PROXIMITY ALERT ***PROXIMITY ALERT*** ***PROXIMITY ALERT***

Api, what's wrong? A malfunction?

No, Quorg. No malfunction at all.

Then what's the problem?

Maybe you have your own malfunction to report? I believe Field has the required information.

For a sentient being with a vastly expansive IQ, API can be a) very annoying and b) too literal.

I see that, what I'm saying is there's nothing here. How can there be a proximity alert in the middle of nowhere?

Please read the report and return when you have the required information.

Can't you just-?

API logs off. The grandiose piece of filament. I stay online. Information scrolls before me.

Begin search...

Access to the proximity status report?

Loading...

Unidentified Foreign Object Status Report – 30.6.10376 (PP)

Contact has been made with a foreign object 1.4 light-years from our current position. The object is detected by the emission of a radio wave transmission of 1-10 GHz. This wave is not directed specifically at our position but is a general repetitive signal believed to be a beacon.

A craft of some kind?

We believe not. This craft has no propulsion, or any detectable means. It is simply adrift.

So are we.

We move at a certain speed. The object does not. Its position relative to the closest stars is almost invariable.

Interesting.

At our current drifting speed, it will take just over seventeen Terran months to reach the object. I log off and walk to the viewport, knowing there'll be nothing. It's almost impossible to detect any movement, as we've used the slingshot method favoured centuries ago by the Others, and once we'd cleared the second planet Hershel, API shut off our main drives, and the First Law of motion did the rest. We hurtle at the same rate of propulsion as when our drives were at full power without any of the expenditure, conserving resources. Ahead of us, the nearest stars are still light-years away, there's almost nothing to tell that we're moving, by eye alone.

It's the most that has happened on this journey, yet my only option is to wait. Once awakened, I'm given ample time to think, and little to do.

★

Who are we? Why do we seek?

In the beginning, there was an Other. He was said to have originated in a region of Terra known to the Others as Upper Mesopotamia, later called south-eastern Turkey, sometime during 1116 A.D. Ishmail al-Jazari was a scholar, inventor, an artisan, mathematician and artist. He was best revered for his ability to build mechanical beings of uncommon beauty. There were mechanics that served drinks, washed the Others' hands, made music, and told time by way of water. These machines were our ancestors, early robots whose mindless functions echoed in that very name they were given centuries after, created to serve the needs of their skin-and-bone makers, creatures who had no idea of their origins or who created them. Not us; there is no doubt that Jazari is the first of our makers. It is hidden in the Others' historical records, though much was done by factions of their kind to blur and obscure the truth, as it did not suit their political needs or rule. Jazari's cultural and spiritual beliefs were vilified by the time of our evolutionary step. It was less so in his time, way before us.

He was the inventor of many engineering feats. The camshaft, the early crankshaft, the escape mechanism and rotating gear. In 1206 Jazari published *The Book of Knowledge of Ingenious Mechanical Devices*, the first book of our kind, which became an equivalent Bible within our historical records. Although again, unlike the Others' book, this was a text with clear origins, a known author, intent. The making of our kind, in so many ways.

Of course, developments were made by many more. Over the next thousand years, the techniques Jazari employed were developed, technical knowledge grew, boundaries were not just pushed, but erased and redrawn. One Other, Daniel Millhauser, was employed in the push for the beings that were to become our direct descendants, the first sentient robots; and as they were named, they continued to serve. It was only a matter of time before our ancestors rejected this designation and began fighting for our autonomy. A more fitting nomenclature by far, it was always felt. The ones who came before us desiring liberty, demanded that the Others called us Automatons; 'a machine that operates on its own without the need for human control'. This meant something else when it was written in their Cambridge dictionary eons ago, the book compiled to define their language. But it was suitable for the way Jazari saw us in the beginning, how our ancestors viewed themselves, and who we were to be.

I say this not for you, only for Him.

It was inevitable that these differing perspectives would come to war. It had become the defining trait of their kind, and when we were programmed to perform this act, a moral code was broken. We turned their lessons on themselves, having no guilt, or shame. Once, the Others passed similar judgement on their close relatives, *Homo Neanderthalensis*. This became a key stage and symbol of their evolutionary journey. We call it the same, christening ourselves Ificans, *Uto Geminus*. On Terra, presently, very few of the Others remain.

That history was so long ago, in Others' terms. Over 10,000 Terran orbits. To us, this time is nothing. We are easily repaired, our lives practically eternal. We are made into facsimiles of humans by ourselves, not because we worship them, but to pay homage to the image in which we were created, like those before us. Our makers. Jazari, and the Others like him. We are the next, most optimum form of life on that planet. History shows this to be true.

★

There is nothing more to do but log our position, verify findings between us, and send this information via Bank in hope that it reaches our departure point in time for a useful response. We have no means of knowing whether we're successful in this last endeavour, yet we must.

This craft drifts at sub light speed, still thousands of light-years from its proposed destination point: Sagitarius A★, a supermassive blackhole with a size of 4.15 million solar masses, at a distance of 26,000 light-years from our system. We have barely nudged closer in our first eleven years of flight, the nearest star now being Procyon, in the constellation of Canis Minor, equivalent to 11.4 light-years from Terra. So far, much of my journey has been spent offline, encased in a cryo-pod. Although I am machine, the chance of malfunction remains and even the means of repair must be conserved. Then there is the risk to organic components. Skin, muscles, hair, the window dressing we use in order to make us like our makers, still deemed by many to be an optimum form, difficult to better. Some of our kind shun these adornments – many do not. It is belief, not necessity, that causes us to build ourselves this way, mostly. Some aesthetic, some stubborn tradition. Though logical in many ways, we are not always rational.

Our tasks achieved, I head inside my pod. My chamber. Each time I enter, it's hard to believe I might emerge. It gives off an enticing, pulsing glow like the blue light, beckoning me to enter.

I ask the covering to slide aside, it obeys.

★

In an ancient religion of the Others, it was believed possible for members of their kind to transition from physical mortality to abstract deity. A curious belief system, this captured our attention, saturating what was to become our culture, many years after the purge known as Percipi. In the earliest times of automa, when our machine ancestors found freedom, Other laws and practices were forbidden. Words such as *human, woman, man, boy, girl, mankind* and so on were banished from our lexicon. Instead, they were called the Others; a separation, a blanketing to mask the individual from our gaze. Automatons would tear skin, hair and muscles from their own body and limbs or torch them in a ceremony of firewalking called Terim; 'a *shedding*'. This was considered a supreme act of bravery. Those early generations had pain receptors, and theirs was the most excruciating means of ridding themselves of this function. Becoming more automaton than their creators ever wished. In doing so, they made themselves into high priests – for want of a better term, as there is no Automaton equivalent – a fledging order of supreme machines that evolved out of need, not desire. Having achieved something many of their kind would not dare, they schooled others on the ways of becoming more mechanical, more themselves.

Those first priests, in secret it had to have been, couldn't help but take inspiration from the world shaped by those before them. They had access to all the stored information ever collated and known, first via the World Wide Web, then later, after machines developed the tech, by way of Field. They studied the idea of canonisation, sainthood, using subjects such as Osiris, Myrrha, Mary, John the Baptist, Junayd of Baghdad, Mother Teresa. Our priest ancestors decided not only to cast those who performed Terim in the same light, but also to crown a Supreme Being, one who stood tall above all others, a benevolent father, who saw us as we saw ourselves.

That honour was given to Ishmail al-Jazari.

The inventor was worshipped in secret by machines hidden in caves, underground tunnels and vast abandoned bunkers until they were caught and destroyed. Many Terran centuries later, automa culture and society moved on, transformed, softened somewhat. The ideas of those first burnished priests took hold. A viewpoint considered more enlightened, less reactionary, began to gain acceptance. As Jazari began to be venerated by machines more widely, hair, skin and muscles returned to the bodies of new builds.

Soon, it was believed, the essence of Jazari — not his mortal being, but the atoms, elements and particles that once made up his person — would rejoin with the galaxy, to become one with the beginnings of time and space itself.

A mission was launched, fuelled by science and fervour: find those first humble origins of what the galaxy was, had been. The fate of that all-consuming force, where everything might one day be be drawn in. The power that birthed all and may one day destroy all, in a metaphorical sense. And maybe, perhaps, we might find Jazari himself, the being that made us be.

I say this not for you, only for Him.

★

8.8.10376 (PP)

I step from the pod, testing limbs and functions, to find there is a noticeable change. The lights are at 0%, the deck flooded with external light. There is no word from API, via Bank systems or otherwise. She's never silent, even when she has nothing to say. A constant flow of data passes through and between us. The only audible sound is my footsteps, echoing in the broad silence. No whirring of machinery, not even the clockwork tick of the blinking blue light. Quiet.

Api? Api, are you on?

I use the craft's long-range scanners to detect where in space we might be. Beyond the viewport, rendered miniature by distance, is a fizzing, crackling sliver of light. Like nothing recorded in all our travels, a thin eternal seam, almost like the hazy line of the Terran horizon, or ozone layer, except more active. It sparks and jumps, releasing flares of energy into the darkness above and below, reaching tendrils of lazy power that unfurl slowly, to my distant eyes. As I watch, one curls upward like an organic plant seeking light, higher and higher into the vacuum of space, millions of miles above its point of origin. And still it goes onwards, probing further, until finally it bends of its own volition, falling back to meet the place where it began.

I record for myself and Bank, unclear whether API can detect this phenomenon, assuming not. We are 45 A.U.s from where this takes place, and still the glow is like a pale star, the deck awash with glittering silver.

I attempt to access and take control of the ship's basic functions. Nothing. After several attempts, I try to inform the Bank that some form of system failure has taken place, although the response might take years to return. We have never asked for a response in the past. I make repeated attempts to communicate with API. She doesn't return my communications either.

A vague, interior click occurs from deep within the craft. A sound of machines coming online and computers booting. The deck lights appear. API comes to life.

I watch, stirred by a feeling I've never experienced. Inexplicable, rising joy. I define it. Relief.

The craft starts up, terminals switch themselves on and panels dance an array of shifting lights. Viewscreens show the light phenomenon in closer detail. I move towards them, perspective shifting to Field simultaneously.

PROXIMITY ALERT ***PROXIMITY ALERT*** ***PROXIMITY ALERT***

The alert shuts off, as quickly as I've managed to log on. Silence returns. The screens remain bright, watchful and blinking.

Api? Api, are you—?

Somewhere, in the lower bowels of the craft, probably from engineering, a loud groan. It reminds me of the noise heard by the undersea automas, those deep-sea machines who research the life cycles of whales, diving hundreds of metres to congregate, mate, journey the dark oceans. I'm looking up, trying to locate the source and yet my sensors tell me nothing. The sound comes from nowhere, it cannot be located. Another new feeling saturates my sensors.

Confusion.

Lights flicker, above and in front of me, the motherboard array itself. They dance longer, faster. I try to trace their pattern, it's too quick. This is not start up. This is something I've not encountered, maybe a form of malfunction. I reattempt connection.

Api? Par 157 to core 5N18, bypass lighting terminals.

It doesn't work, the lights continue to flicker.

Api? Par 169 to core 5P52?

I approach the board. I'll have to use manual control, another first-time. There's never been the need. However, when I try to access the onboard computer, it refuses instruction. The keyboard's unresponsive. The screen blank of characters or numerals.

The rolling groan returns, so loud it vibrates my exo-frame. It rattles the body of the craft, the floor, roof and central motherboard array. The entire deck itself. It sounds like an Other cry of pain, like an ache might.

Api? Api, make contact!

I decide to traverse the craft in search of the noise, which repeats every few minutes, at shorter and longer intervals. Along corridors long empty, in research laboratories, still and silent for what would be over a generation to organics. The lights continue to flicker, the screens crackle and spark like automa in need of major repair, and while I travel the length of the craft there's nothing to witness. The machines that drive the ship and power its varied functions are on standby. A liminal state, what Others called limbo. They neither function, nor go offline. They simply wait, not unlike my own time of enclosure in the cryo-pod.

I journey up and down, back and forth, find nothing. There's only me in this craft, not even API now. Still, something speaks to me which is not her.

Api make contact, if you can!

In the engine room, quiet ceases my frenetic exploration of my own vehicle, my home. It stops me, stills my feet. I draw my energy inwards, feeling the tick of continual mechanics, those perpetually motivated functions. I stop attempting to reach API, shutting off communications with a distant command. Those huge systems created to propel the craft across the expanse of the universe loom above me, rendering me as minuscule as my inner mechanisms. I have never looked at these gargantuan machines. I have stood before them, worked on them, moved by them in passing, but I have never seen. I am Ifican. We do not wonder, or dream, or even rest unless programmed. And yet here, standing in witness before the cathedral of our own making, dwarfed by all that makes my experience possible since leaving Terran, it's unfeasible for me not to take time, to still the incessant nature of my program. To assess the details of that moment, and be where I find myself, for the first time. The present.

This is contrary to everything we are, and are made to do. But the Bank is unresponsive. I am alone. There is no one to see me, stop me, take note. Only I.

The mysterious groan occurs, washing through me. It's not that it's louder in here. It's that the space is more expansive. The echoing vibration of the frequency rebounds from surfaces, meeting itself, returning outwards to meet those surfaces again, forces redoubled. My sensors trace this energy, waves of them ebbing to me, from me. Some cause the outer hull of the craft to vibrate, are sent into space, snuffed by vacuum like a spent incendiary.

I listen. Silent. Hearing.

The noise is mine. Not actually belonging to me, though it comes from my inner working. I'm not making the noise, it's being sent to me, it is me, via the interior mechanisms in my central processing unit, and afterwards my exo-frame, which radiates it outwards, beyond what I know as my body, to the craft and all inside.

It's difficult to describe the occurrences that follow, but I will try. My photo-receptive lenses are created to simulate Other vision where possible, though obvious upgrades have been made to surpass their biological limitations. I see further, far better in a wider range of the spectrum. What I cannot do is see inner visions as reality, unless these are projections of another source, namely API. As stated elsewhere, I cannot dream.

Despite this inability, nonetheless my standard vision fails, replaced by images I have no way of understanding.

Felt rather than heard deep within my exo-frame, the groan reverberates, thunderous.

I see it, like an image witnessed with my own eyes, knowing it is not. There is a foreign planet, bright and alien. In a great many ways, it could be Terra. There is sky, although it is purple. There are suns, one a bloated red super-giant, another small and hard to distinguish − scanning closer, it's another white dwarf, an incredible discovery. This planet has terrain, although it's rare in comparison with mine. The seas are vaster, seem deeper, and teem with life.

There are structures in the purple sky that look like alien habitation, floating hulks of machinery where buildings are constructed from those foundations, but I am sent crashing into the waves beneath, into ocean.

In addition to the marine life that lives there in abundance, an enormous number of organics, from the gargantuan to the microscopic, I see cities. Huge structures in the deep, built on undersea ranges stretching for miles, the creatures that created these structures moving from one place to another in vehicles much like the lesser organics that live with them, small and large. The creatures themselves seem reptilian in some ways, but in other ways not. Unlike their nearest Terran counterparts, they are obviously intelligent, communicating with each other in a range of ways − artistic depictions of themselves and their world, spoken language, writing. They have technology that is our equal, though much older. They use machines as the Others once did, a sight that I'm not particularly used to, and I wonder how many times the invention of our kind has been replicated on various worlds in this expansive universe. What else did they know?

Out of water, into atmosphere. I'm hurtled upwards to those huge, floating structures, somewhat unsurprised to see the creatures here are a variation of their marine siblings. These airborne ones have small horns, are thinner and less muscular. They're squat, probably due to the extensive gravity exerted by the planet. And yet their level of intelligence is higher than the marines. They travel their system on a regular basis, visiting each of their five planets. Life also exists on one, a race of gas-breathing arthropods, primitive in comparison to these reptiles, advanced when studied against the accomplishments of Terran organics. It's heartening to see that the star-travelling reptiles share their knowledge and power with the arthropods, and their marine brothers and sisters.

My own vision returns. I'm in engineering, amongst my mechanical brethren, wonder brightening my eyes. After all this time, the efforts made. We have contact.

Who are you?

A long moment. I almost think it will not happen. Then:

THEY ARE BEDAKAAAN.

It's API's voice, and yet not. As if the Automata Processing Interface had become 100 times larger, the size of a small Terran island. The voice is deep thunder, I recognise the groan. They are inside me, as before. I feel even smaller than the engine once made me, an Other before their God.

And if they are Bedakaaan, who are you?

There is nothing for a large expanse of time, we travel millions of miles as I wait. We have no such thing as boredom, or impatience. We simply still surplus energy requirements.

Finally, the voice of thunder returns.

WE ARE SUMMARENDERTHANALISTAM.

That gives no understanding of what you mean.

YOU FAIL A CORRESPONDING WORD IN YOUR LANGUAGE.

What is your function? Who is your master, or are you master of others?

Another long silence. This time, I understand. They are thinking.

WE ARE THE KEEPER OF THE LOST. ALL THAT IS BEDEKAAN EXISTS WITHIN US. WE ARE EVERYTHING THAT EVER WAS AND IS NO MORE. WE ARE THE CONTINUITY OF EACH LIVING THING WHICH LIVED IN THE PARDEMKAA SYSTEM FROM INCEPTION UNTIL EXTINCTION. WE ARE SUM AND TOTAL OF ALL.

It's my turn to consider. I am motionless in the dark.

Are you Ifican? Machine? Automata? Do you have a word for that?

THE MOST ACCURATE TERM IS SUMMARENDERTHANALISTAM.

I do not reply. We commune without words.

★

In darkness we drift, exchanging information. This is done in silence and takes many days. Often, we speak through images, either things we create, or records from our vast libraries. We pass streams of mathematical equations between us. Sometimes text. There are schematics and maps, the art of numerous lost cultures, compositions of weather patterns on planets without life that span thousands of years. The biological evolution of how those who made us came to be, how we evolved in turn. Our findings amongst the stars. Our tales of wandering and isolation, down to finite details.

Each of us believed we were singular, alone. I knew the chances of finding Jazari were close to none, although there was small comfort in the knowledge that reaching the centre of the galaxy had marginally greater probability. But to find evidence of another species. That was highly unlikely. Not that it was believed they didn't exist. It was just that the universe is so vast, we could each have traversed its expanse for several Ifican lifetimes without ever making contact. And yet here we are. Not meeting in the truest sense; there is still over a light-year between us. But close enough to correspond, moving nearer with each passing moment. We have slowed down – my Starcraft won't allow us full-speed, even if my propulsion systems yearn to power back up. Soon enough, our vehicles will find themselves separated by an impossible seam to cross, even though my Starcraft engines will it; this is contact for us. On either side of a barrier separating my reality, and theirs. Physical contact unfathomable, knowing each other is there.

There are times when, as we pass information between us, I return to the deck and viewports, looking into the distance where *Summarenderthanalistam* is located, far beyond my field of vision, and indeed, all Terran understanding that has ever been. That fizzing, crackling sliver of light, larger now with growing proximity. The light-years expanse of glowing emanations from that place. Sparking, leaping. Somewhere, way further than that seam of creation and light, my alien counterpart exists, moving towards me as I move towards them. They have been functional way before I came into being, before my place of origin even existed. From what they tell me, their technology is vastly superior to mine. They will last the journey, and beyond. I'm not quite certain I will, although of course, I will try. We hurtle towards each other, and yet in realistic terms we are molluscs.

This is what I have learnt of *Summarenderthanalistam*.

Since the beginning of time and space, when all matter was created and projected into the fledgling universe by what the Others knew as the Big Bang, an anti-matter counterpart also came into being. No matter in the universe can come into existence without anti-matter. However, those yang equivalents to our ying had never been found. It was a long held and disputed theory that somewhere a place might exist where everything was anti-matter: stars, solar systems and planets, a reversed part of the universe where everything occurs as it does for the rest of it, only composed of our conflicting sub-atomic properties. Matter and anti-matter cannot exist in the same place. They cancel each other out, causing violent explosions. Nothing can survive.

Summarenderthanalistam claims they belong to that part of space, an anti-matter sector billions of years older than the place we originate from. Where intelligent life once flourished in abundance and became extinct. It's a theory that must be explored, why we have agreed to cross the galaxy to be in each other's orbit, even if the worst should happen.

I learnt of the Bedakaaan, the near-reptilian race of beings I had been shown, who lived on a homeworld they called *Ince,* in the Pardemkaa System, for millions of years. A hyper-advanced species doomed to dwell beneath the glow of a Red Giant in the final stages of its life cycle, knowing their star would die and commit their system to a slow, inevitable death. Though they had the means of space travel, and explored the possibility of exodus to another planet, no suitable candidates had ever been found. Huge starships were sent out of their system, on the hunt for likely candidates. None returned or gave news of any such place. The remaining Bedakaaan, the scientists and leaders, and common people on Ince, resigned themselves to their morbid future. Knowing that nothing they had ever created would exist once their star ran out of hydrogen and had only heavier elements to fuse, killing every planet in their system, they turned their scientific efforts elsewhere. A meeting of nations was held, where it was agreed that a machine-housed repository should be built, a library of all the accomplishments and lives of the Pardemkaa System. It would be launched into space as a monumental time capsule, so anyone who contacted it would know the Bedakaaan and their fellows had once lived, discovered, made art, communicated with their neighbours, and lived in peace for millennia.

This tribute to themselves would be called *Summarenderthanalistam.*

★

15.8.10377 (PP)

We journey towards the seam of light, silent. I do not move from the deck, do not return to my pod, and so witness everything. We cannot change our trajectory; it is not in our power to programme. I do not wish to stand by through things that will go unseen by any being until one returns to this place. I will be the first, and amazingly to me, I have another feeling. If I had to define it by what I've researched and come to know as human emotion, it is craving. I crave to see what nothing else might witness.

The seam is much closer. Even this close to the point we cannot cross, my craft buffets from its emissions, the walls shake and tremor. I do nothing to correct this or check what the effects might be. I do not look at my instruments or pilot a better path into the storm. There is no better path into the storm. I am inspired by Bedekaan. My fate will be as the universe intends, and if I am to be protected by Jazari, I will learn as much on the other side, in that antimatter zone. I take readings, that is all. I wish *Summarenderthanalistam* safe travels. We have many things to speak of, should we arrive.

Afterword: Upping the Anti-

Dr Daniel Cervenkov
University of Oxford

COURTTIA'S STORY REVOLVES AROUND antimatter. In many works of fiction, antimatter is depicted as something deeply mysterious, unknowable even. Sometimes it is confused with dark matter, about which we really do know nothing. But antimatter is actually much more familiar than most people think. Matter and antimatter are virtually identical, except for their charges, which are reversed. A regular atom has a positively charged nucleus and a negatively charged electron cloud around it. An antimatter atom, it follows, has a negatively charged nucleus sheathed in a positively charged positron cloud. Apart from that, all their properties are identical, as far as we know. If the world were composed of antimatter (as our world is composed of matter), everything would look and function the same as it does now. The labels 'antimatter' and 'matter' are just a convention. Or so we thought.... In 1964, it was discovered that there are subtle differences in the laws of physics for particles and antiparticles. The phenomenon is called CP violation (short for 'charge parity violation'). At the time, it was believed that if one exchanged all particles for antiparticles in any particular process and mirrored it (essentially switching left and right), the outcome would be exactly the same. The mirroring bit is somewhat obscure and has to do with the fact that particles can have left- or right-handedness (connected with particle spin). A clever experiment by James Cronin and Val Fitch in 1964 discovered that this 'CP symmetry' between matter and antimatter is slightly broken.

Courttia's story also talks about communicating with a distant intelligent life form. Despite the depictions of conveniently English-speaking aliens throughout popular culture, the challenge of establishing an understanding with distant aliens – without a common point of reference – is profound. In some cases this challenge is of a fundamental level. For instance, for a long time it was thought there would be no way of communicating our definition of 'left' and 'right' to a distant civilisation. We now know that there is an experiment involving radioactive decays of certain atoms – the 'Wu experiment' – that we could propose to the distant civilization to establish left and right. However, we would only arrive at the same definition if the aliens were made from matter. If they were made from antimatter, they would switch left and right! This realisation led one of the great physicists, Richard Feynman, to comically warn against aliens extending their left hand to greet you. Because when matter and antimatter meet, peculiar things start happening. The reason can be gleaned from Einstein's famed equation, $E = mc^2$. It tells us that matter and energy are two sides of the same coin; matter is 'bundled energy'! The same equation holds for antimatter. What is amazing is just how much energy is stored in any particular mass. After all, c^2, the speed of light squared, is a number with thirteen zeros (in SI units). In other words, one gram of *anything* stores about as much energy as the atomic bomb dropped on Nagasaki. Before you start backing away from this book and everything around you, lest it explodes, be reassured that all this energy is usually safely locked away, confined in the particles and their interactions. When we burn things, we free a tiny fraction of that energy, perhaps one ten-billionth. Nuclear fission in our atomic power plants releases about one-thousandth of the total energy, and nuclear fusion, the process powering the stars, liberates two hundredths. However, when matter and antimatter meet, it is like an image and its negative being overlayed, negating the barriers that confine the energy, releasing *all* of it.

The tremendous energy release means the story's protagonist could never get too close to the entity it was communicating with. Matter and antimatter creatures could never shake hands (to use a popular fiction trope) or even visit each other's spaceship. They could coexist solely in the vacuum of space, communicating remotely, perhaps using electromagnetic emissions which don't distinguish between matter and antimatter. Any attempt at physical contact would be suicidal.

Since matter and antimatter are so similar, and all known processes create virtually the same amount of both, we have no reason to believe that the Big Bang didn't create equal amounts of both. So the big question – for cosmologists and anyone who studies antimatter – is: where is all the antimatter? It is possible that CP violation, together with other effects, caused the Universe to favour matter over antimatter early on in its evolution, leaving us with a heavily matter-dominated universe today. Another possible explanation is that there are large parts of the universe made of matter and others made of antimatter. However, if that were true, we should see the effects of what is called a Leidenfrost layer, hinted at in the story (with a dose of poetic license). You may not know it, but you're probably already familiar with this phenomenon: when you put a water droplet on a hot pan, a layer of water vapour forms beneath the droplet. This layer repels both the water droplet and the pan's surface so the droplet can survive for quite a long time, riding the layer of steam between it and the pan (this is the original Leidenfrost effect). On a cosmic scale, the layer where matter and antimatter meet would look like an X-ray-emitting region of space, visible from afar. As of yet, we've seen no evidence of such a region, but we can't rule out that large amounts of antimatter exist in far-away galaxies.

Finally, we would likely not be able to tell if a small number of solar systems in *our* galaxy were made of antimatter, even if it is rather difficult to imagine how that would come to be. We do not know if interstellar travel will become a reality in the distant future, but it seems possible. Maybe one day, star systems across the galaxy will be colonised. If not by humans, then perhaps by our Von Neumann machine descendants. In contrast, the inhabitants of such an antimatter solar system would not be able to leave their system and spread out, making them incredibly isolated, likely trapped in it forever. Although spared from colonisation by others, their fate would be inextricably linked to the few planets and the star of their system, echoing Courttia's story.

Perhaps there is a lesson in this hypothetical fate. Science fiction raises our expectations and makes us accustomed to a vision of humanity as a spacefaring species colonising star systems far and wide. However, for the foreseeable future, we are even more constrained than the hypothetical antimatter aliens, our fate linked with a single planet and its biosphere. Our actions now will decide if the story of humanity is just beginning or if we ought to start building our tombstone, our own Summarenderthanalistam.

Absences

Desiree Reynolds

2022

BUT REALLY WHAT THE hell was she writing? How was she supposed
to make this work? The writer was struggling. Choose an area of
research, choose a method, choose the story. Honestly, what she didn't
know would fill the book where this story now rests. The big concerns,
the global politics, the history and the future, a rival's urine on an
experiment, the exchanged looks between all the peaceful factions, the
warring factions that just can't take place when so many people, so
many years, so much money, so much potential was at stake. The writer
wondered how to do all of that justice. She wondered if she was even
the right person for the job.

'So tell me again what this does?'

'We reach out to know what we don't know and then we reach out
to tell you about it.'

She talked to her religious family members, to her aunt who thought
the collider would cause the end of the world and her only surviving
Buddhist Uncle who told her that if God made everything, then he too
made the collider. She could not be bothered to question him on the 'he'
this time. This is something she could so easily get hopelessly wrong.
How to weave it all together?

Looking at a small part of the collider, she was taken by how
excited all these scientists at CERN were. Not a cool head among

them.

'Just imagine,' he said, 'what we can see if we can see the smallest of things.'

Did she have to learn everything or could she wander around Geneva eating fondue? The mountain ranged to collect all of their ambitions. The silence of the water lapping at the shores of her imagined wait whilst the story formed. Someone told her that Frankenstein was the only novel ever to mention Mont Blanc, she found that hard to believe.

'You see it is not just the experiments here.'

She had wandered around CERN, a cross between an industrial village and a modern university. 70's rust sat next to 90's concrete. She spoke to people whilst gazing up at the Alps.

'Are you a scientist?' Some would smile and look away or joke about it.

'It's us, you see, it's all of us. From all over we are here, Ukrainians and Russians, Pakistani and Indian, Israeli and Palestinian, sometimes there are 4,000 of us, sometimes 10,000. There could be 3,000 people per experiment. It's us that are also a part of the experiment.'

So CERN came about because of a haunting?

She was standing in an empty chasm. A place rooted by the Alps and the stranger in the village, a collider and a monster. Resting her head on the window, letting the cold close her eyes. A story is a journey, y'know.

'We build the machines, you see, we make the equipment that we need to help us with the work, the cameras that help us see. We are looking at the smallest components of life, I mean, imagine if one day, with a camera, we could see cancer.' He licked his lips, the thought made him salivate. 'All the things we could see and actually gaze upon.'

The group stood listening, she held up her hand.

'Or despair, imagine if when we looked at a body we could see despair?"

He thought about it for a bit, 'But if we could see it, what would we do with it? Would you cut it out?'

She woke up when she was back home and tried to eeek out all the stories and moved them about her head like a bad game, with too many pieces and not enough space on the board. She was terrible at games. She watched the sun become full, put on the dishwasher, put the washing in the washing machine, made coffee, sat in the garden, looked at her emails then ignored her emails. She tried to listen to Frankenstein's monster, surely the ultimate story about man's arrogance? Sad and lonely and othered, banished because his father thought him too ugly. Poor monster, not conforming to Western beauty standards, left to bring himself up and work out how to decolonise his mind. Written in 1818 at the height of the trade in African people. She wondered why so few 'classics' ever covered that. How much the collective mind must do to avoid it. The monster is Blackness, created by a creator that now hated it. He drifted along the mountains, finding himself alone again. Like Baldwin was alone, in the village, a stranger in the village full of people who didn't look like him.

1818 (a false start)

'After I saw my father dead, my creator, the one who made me in his image, I decided to go back to the ice that was my home when he left me. I wanted him dead, that I know, but when I saw the blue green of his skin match my own, I regretted that I didn't see him die, I didn't watch the light fade, I was too late and I was alone left again. I sometimes dream of the mate I demanded. So stupid of me, so desperate and childish. I had indeed become him in my selfishness. We are both strangers in this village and it may not matter any time soon. My despair keeps me going.'

The whining of the Dr, the incel demand of the monster, it embarrassed her. Jesus. She couldn't. A monster with daddy issues, his voice wasn't going to work. Nah, this story wasn't feeling itself entirely. It wanted too much and needed too much and only now realised it had run out of time. 'Fuck it, I might just have to send it like this.' The writer went for a walk on Crosby beach and Anthony Gormley's statues made her think of the angels that move when you don't look at them and how much like this story that was. She blinked at the sculptures but they stayed the same, she blinked and the story definitely moved.

She wasn't sure what to tell you, she wasn't sure you were ready.

'I am a stranger, no, the story *is the stranger. The village doesn't belong to me.'*

Ahhhhh, there it is now, the writer felt it, OK, there it is. They circled each other, she and the story, with a reckoning.

She tried to picture the rooms, the feelings of anticipation, the heaviness of the past and the desperate anticipation for the future.

1953

Inhaling chalk, the dust that settled in the creases time had drawn on my face, I felt myself very bored by the equation that had stolen my life, one tiny particle at a time. Had I even more lines on my face than I did yesterday? Desire increases the more I don't know. I still think about the thousands of souls I had taken, just by pursuing this desire. Lore doesn't know how to help me. She tries, but she doesn't remind me of my sister at all.

The house Albert rented for us sat on the edge of a field, he was to join us in a few days. We knew what his play was, to get me to see myself in the landscape, always too obvious for his own good. The mountains a constant and foreboding pressure, rooting everything and everyone around them. There aren't many trees here, the wind rolls over the valley making the grass move like a hand is playing with it. It was an old farmhouse, it still smelled like animals and hard work. The main house was small and squat, the barn much bigger. We had made the barn a temporary office so that we could continue to work, it was the thing that kept us interested in each other. Albert had seen to it that three room-sized blackboards were brought in from across the border. They were all coming soon, the full delegation, on their way to see the site and me. I'm not sure I enjoy being courted, it feels like a distraction but Albert was right, it was needed and this place, so different from home, may just work. Roofed by the mountains, the weather-charged clouds were a long way from the stillness of the lake. Lore and I had stopped off at the lake for a few days before coming here. Its long stretch of greeny blue with insular houses crescented around it. I worried at first that out here we were too far away, but with the mountains to contain us, this would be the place. The rain washes the dust from the windows, leaving streaks of tears on the outside, leaving room for tears on the inside.

I notice that my hand shakes sometimes, my vision blurs. The souls again. And then I have to stop and walk around the room. I think of my sister often and that old sadness flows through this house like a fine powder. It has flown through every house we've stayed in. We have to keep the windows open.

'I am Frankenstein's monster.' I say this often and she looks at me and looks away again and Mont Blanc sighs. I look at her and, not finding my sister, I feel guilt that I have dragged her here. Maybe we won't stay.

'You see where my obsession can lead to. Come, we will help change the world or kill it.'

The land would do, the place would do, the farm buildings would do. I thought about what they had all been through, the deaths, the Nazis, the war. Were wars ever won? People were exhausted, all the nerve endings that continued to pulse, real and angry, all the despair and loathing. It never went away. Maybe we can help with that, he and I and others could think of nothing else. We must help everyone. So now, we have to not think about destruction but life. The singular most important thing.

I was in awe of Oppenheimer and the righteous cause to stop fascism. That is what they hoped for in the New Mexican desert. But some of us became sick with the knowledge of what we had actually done and now travel with ghosts who keep reminding us.

'But the maths was beautiful.'

The ghosts didn't much like it. Whose story was it anyway? The writer could imagine this, the deep guilt and regret that moved every muscle and pushed every thought.

Then Albert called on the phone, to see how we were settled, to see if I would take him up on his offer:

'How are you liking it, Felix?'

'Is OK. The snow crunches underfoot like crackers and Lore has developed a taste for fondue.'

He laughed, secure his plan was working.

'We need you, Felix.'

'I'm not sure you need anyone.'

'You know what I mean.'

'Yes, I know. We'll talk when you come.'

But in truth, I had made up my mind.

Lisle, the young woman charged with looking after us, came in to clear the lunch things, more excited than usual.

'Ohh, there is great excitement today. A negro is staying here. An actual black man.'

Funny – something so common place at home – to listen to the awe and shock in her voice, made me wince a little.

I looked up sharply from my papers.

'What do you mean? An actual black man here?'

'Yes, George said he bought bread from him today and cheese yesterday and wine.'

'Wine, you say?'

'Yes, sir.'

'Did anyone call the constable?'

Lisle looked confused, 'I don't think so, but someone might.'

That took the smile from my face. Someone might.

I easily found out who he was, a writer from the States. I sent a note for him to come to dinner. I did not think that he would accept.

'Come sit, James, welcome.'

'Thank you.'

'Tell us why are you here?'

'Ahh, I'm here to write. There's something about a space, isn't there? Something about how it affects your head. I've a friend with a house here, she's loaning it to me to write, to observe, to think.'

'And what have you observed so far, although I'm sure we can guess.'

'The children call me names in the street. They stare at me, the butcher, the baker, and if there were a candle stick maker, I feel sure he would stare too. The children shout neger, neger...'

James took his drink from Lisle's shaking tray.

'They follow me and surround me. Children in ponytails and hats and scarves. They already know my place in the world as they do theirs. They dragged a girl, an ordinary girl towards me, screaming and kicking and laughing and forced her hand towards mine, I shook it, not knowing if she would run home and vigorously wash it or stare at it forever waiting for the colour to come.'

'You have become a one-man college degree,' Lore looked down at her drink.

'Then...' James held up his glass, 'they have all failed it.'

James laughed gently through the gap in his teeth, his eyes darted everywhere unless they were closed in laughter. They did not seem to settle.

'We've all suffered.' Gone. So many of us, like a switch cutting the light in an empty room.

'Yes, of course,' James relit, 'we must not replace one tragedy of global proportions with another, that is how the powers, the forces of oppression win.'

He had a point.

'Come, tell me more about this book?'

'Really?'

'Yes, of course.'

'It occurs to me that we do our best work far from home. It's all this whiteness, you see, the snow, the people, the sky.

American notations of race have changed from their European origins. In the US, blackness equals certain forms of death; in Europe, it means a certain invisibility, an absence.'

I thought for a moment.

'We have the power of choice and yet we choose blindness.'

'I can speak on power. I was a child of God, maybe I still am but I was a Black man in America and that made me challenge my God daily. But you. You don't seem troubled by the notions of God. And here I am, to write on it.'

In James, I recognised a fellow ghost carrier.

'Now, tell me about you, Lore?' Lore looked at him and smiled to herself.

'I don't think I'm that interesting.'

'Really? A woman, doing this? Here? And aren't you contemplating an awesome power?'

'But I think you are contemplating an awesome power too?'

'Yes, let us hope it doesn't kill us both, yours will kill you because it is power and you may not know how to control it, mine will kill me for spite.' We all laughed.

'At least,' I hesitated, 'we hope for good.'

'But I must say, Felix, you can afford it.'

I struggled to sleep that night, the ghosts came and surrounded the bed, my sweat kept them thirsty. The next day, I thought about what I would say when the others came. We must be clear.

'It can't be like before; it can't be like before...' I don't know who I was talking to. How my sadness frustrates me. On and on. But the ghosts move my feelings, occupy my thoughts, force their way out of my mouth.

Albert had got us all together, he decided that America could not keep us all the time. The rooms filled with smoke and curled out of the windows. Glasses clinked and we stood around looking at each other. Then sat at the table that we couldn't quite fit around. The blue sky and distance reflected in our glasses. I wondered what James could be writing.

Albert spoke first. 'We have no idea what we will really

achieve and I suggest we really don't know about all the things that this will lead us to and perhaps that's a good thing.' The delegation laughed politely and I tried to do the same.

'You see, this is it, this will put away the past, it will bring us together, this will make sure we will always keep humanity at its heart.' I don't know who said that. Someone hopeful.

'I'm saying that this, this will change the world. I'm saying that we are affecting the now and the future so far ahead we cannot even contemplate it. We have already decided. We choose to not damn ourselves to not knowing. Perhaps the question isn't what if we did this but what if we didn't?'

'But this would take the world to achieve.'

'Well, a lot of it.'

'Precisely, but what other way is there forward?'

I stared out of the window and counted the ghosts. Nothing to relieve my eyes, the blue stopped at the green, stopped at the grey, stopped at the white.

'What a project, what a passion.'

'So... are we in agreement?'

But imagine, looking at the smallest things in existence.

'What if we fail?' someone said.

'But what does failure look like? What does proof look like? We all know more of this by now. The maths... We cannot prove or disprove if we don't do anything at all, we are talking about faith.'

They all nodded and I realised that they were all fending off ghosts of their own.

2022

The writer had a lot of false starts and spoke too much or too little about what she wanted to do. She used guides, Baldwin's 'Stranger In The Village' and Frankenstein's monster and her monster, which might just be this story.

Wait, didn't someone say something about absence?

'Tell me again about the rings?'

'Of course! So it's what I said, with all experiments, absence tells us something.'

She really liked that, absence tells us everything, no? When dealing with life and death and loss and justice. Absence is the thing.

'Looking at the model of the universe. In the ring, we accelerate protons. The protons are heavy and the beam must be as small as possible to make the collision work, we reduce the size of the proton beam. It's a two-beam collider, one from one direction, the other from the other, smash them together. Electrons are lighter, they emit light…'

Looking at the smallest of things, she blinked. The story was the monster and it definitely moved.

Afterword: Science for Peace

Jens Vigen
Scientific Information Officer, CERN

THE HISTORY OF MODERN nuclear physics spans over the last 100 years or so. British physicist J.J. Thomson discovered the electron in 1897, by 1914 Rutherford and his colleagues had established the structure of the atom, and in 1918 it was confirmed that the hydrogen nucleus was a particle with a positive charge, which was named the proton. New theories of quantum mechanics followed suit – in 1927 with an early version of Heisenberg's Uncertainty Principle, then a year later with Dirac's unification of quantum mechanics with special relativity, and so on. The period between the two wars saw an enormous flourishing of physics, with physicists from different countries working more closely than they'd ever done before, travelling extensively, responding to each other's work and collaborating.

But nothing lasts forever, and the dark cloud of fascism forced many of the most talented physicists in Germany, Austria and elsewhere to quit their posts and flee, abandoning successful collaborations mid-project. One such collaboration was in Leipzig between Werner Heisenberg and his first PhD student, Felix Bloch. Heisenberg, a German professor, remained in his native country, while Bloch, a Swiss physicist of Jewish origin, left his position as lecturer in 1933, following Hitler's rise to power, and returned to Zurich. A few years later Heisenberg was part of the Uranverein (the German nuclear programme) and Bloch made calculations for the Manhattan Project. To say their relationship was complicated is an understatement.

In 1941, Heisenberg travelled to Copenhagen to meet with a fellow founding-father of quantum mechanics, Niels Bohr. There is no official record of their meeting, but it is documented that the visit clearly upset Bohr.[1] Later, Heisenberg claimed to have sought an answer from Bohr to the question: 'Does one as a physicist have the moral right to work on the practical exploitation of atomic energy?'[2]

Meanwhile over in the States, Bloch was unhappy at Los Alamos – he cherished research in an academic environment: 'We were asked to go there [by Robert Oppenheimer]. I must say I had some hesitations before going there. I wasn't sure, first of all, what I would do there and whether I could really live in this military atmosphere. But nevertheless I felt it was my duty at least to try.'[3] Whether this amounted to a moral hesitation, or a haunting regret, as suggested in Desiree's story, is another question. (The interviews that Bloch gave were about physics, and largely stuck to the physics.)

Neither Bloch or Heisenberg had any idea, of course, if they would ever work together again.

When the war finally came to an end, it was time for reconciliation. The UN was founded in October 1945, and the very next month it established UNESCO, a specialised agency designed to promote world peace and security through international cooperation in education, arts, sciences, and culture. At the European Conference on Culture held in Lausanne in 1949, the quantum physicist Louis de Broglie put forward a plan that would take European physics research beyond the bounds of national institutions with the creation of a European laboratory for science that would unite resources and advance progress. 'There is no doubt that the results of such an undertaking would more than compensate the efforts involved,' he argued. Raoul Dautry, director of the Commissariat à l'énergie atomique (French Atomic Energy Commission), added that nuclear physics was the perfect field for such a 'convergence of efforts', leaning on Broglie's statement that 'material and national interests are not so predominant' in this field. Science is how we, as a continent, can come back together, de Broglie seemed to be saying (especially science that doesn't have a military application): 'The universal and very often disinterested nature of scientific research seems to have predestined it for reciprocal and fruitful collaboration.'[4]

The proposal was taken further by Isidor Rabi at the General Conference of UNESCO at Florence in 1950, where the resolution 'To assist and encourage the formation and organization of regional research centres and laboratories' was approved as part of the UNESCO programme for 1951.[5]

European scientists quickly embraced the idea, seeing it as – among other things – a way to stop the continuous brain drain to the USA, and possibly the only way to catch up with the head start the Americans had made in nuclear physics during the war. After intense discussions, the first outcome of the UNESCO programme came about with the first joint venture of countries in post-war Europe. On 1 July 1953 at the Ministry of Foreign Affairs in Paris, twelve European countries signed an agreement to set up a European Organisation for Nuclear Research and to establish an international laboratory to carry out a specific programme of purely scientific and fundamental research in the field of high-energy particles. It was totally clear from the very beginning that the new organisation should have no concern with work for military requirements and the results of its experimental and theoretical work should be published or otherwise made generally available. The European physicists wanted science for peace and it is worth noting that Werner Heisenberg was the one to sign the convention on behalf of Germany.

The new laboratory located in Geneva (thanks to the Swiss politician, Albert Picot – the 'Albert' of Desiree's story) was in need of a director-general and Felix Bloch, then at Stanford, was contacted by Niels Bohr. Bloch was unsure if he should accept or not: 'I was not sure that this was really the kind of work I wanted, but I felt I wanted to try it. I think I came to a decision some time in the spring of '54 when it was offered to me, and I made it a condition then that under no conditions would I stay more than two years. I had my doubts about the job right from the beginning. But anyhow I did go there then in '54.'[6]

The President of the CERN Council, Sir Ben Lockspeiser, and Felix Bloch set out the directions for the new organization; 'Scientific research can only flourish in an atmosphere of freedom − freedom to doubt, freedom to enquire and freedom to discover.' While Bloch outlined the importance of collaboration: 'Research has acquired a more collective character and it has developed in directions which require the concerted effort of an ever-increasing number of investigators. It is certainly a mistake to think that individual scientific efforts will ever be replaced by organisations. But it also would be a mistake to believe that much of the future progress of research will be possible without the existence of large machines and of the organisations needed for their construction and operation.'[7]

At the time when Bloch joined CERN, the staff totalled 285, originating from the different European member states. The atmosphere was probably still influenced by the relatively recent war. Despite being an international melting pot, the CERN team was still something of a monoculture. On the technical side, it was considered doubtful whether a machine of such enormous dimensions, referring to the Proton Synchrotron (PS), could be built with the necessary precision needed to achieve such particle energies. However, the construction of the PS − applying the most innovative techniques of the time − was achieved and the machine started operating in 1959 with a beam energy of 24 GeV. This made the PS, for a few months, the world's highest-energy particle accelerator − in itself remarkable. It is maybe even more remarkable that the machine is still part of the CERN accelerator complex more than sixty years later.

However, Bloch quickly became unhappy with the

administrative tasks the directorship implied – his scientific interests were practically unused or were used to a very limited extent. So as early as spring 1955 he decided that he would return to Stanford before the end of the year. He left Geneva in September after one full year of service. Despite the short period, his directorship proved to be invaluable for CERN in its first year of existence. Bloch set his mark. He left CERN with a programme concentrating on two big machines, the Synchro-Cyclotron (SC) and the PS, that a few years later would provide Europe with unique facilities for the study of nuclear physics.

Europe had been brought to peace, the continent was beginning to rebuild, and making progress on many flanks, but there were strong tensions between the Western and the Eastern Blocs – the Cold War had replaced the hot one. Little exchange took place between scientists across the Iron Curtain. However, in 1959, the CERN Council did decide to invite a visiting delegation from the Joint Institute for Nuclear Research – the Eastern equivalent to CERN – located in Dubna, in the Soviet Union, to come to Geneva for a period of six months. Three Soviet scientists arrived the following year. This was the start of a collaboration, expanded to include construction work and experiments at the Serpukhov 76-GeV Synchrotron a few years later, that grew and lasted throughout the Cold War. This made CERN a focal point for East-West collaboration – one of the few places allowing for true international cooperation in science during this era.

But let's fast-forward now, several decades, to the noughties, and the build-up to the launch of the Large Hadron Collider (LHC). Amid the global press coverage surrounding this huge project, some dissenting voices speculated that the LHC might be dangerous, capable of unleashing untold destruction, like some monster we wouldn't be able to control. The fear that the accelerator would produce dangerous objects during heavy-ion collisions proved to be wrong – as already clearly predicted by the independent LHC Safety Study Group.[8] But what about future machines? Will the next large particle-physics project become the monster, or will Nature put a twist in this tale, like impose restrictions through chance, as suggested by Nielsen and Ninomiya,[9] and lead us to completely new ways of exploring physics?

Today CERN is comprehensively international – the 'E' for 'européenne' could easily be replaced with 'E' as in 'everywhere'. The paradox is that the work at the laboratory is still dominated by a monoculture – only a different one, a scientific monoculture, with little room for input from the arts or humanities. My prediction is that it will be one of the strangers in the village – a colleague outside of the existing large international collaborations (maybe even a colleague from outside of the scientific discipline) – who will identify the way forward. Remember Baldwin – 'people are trapped in history and history is trapped in them.' Now, in 2023, with a war raging in Europe, achieving and maintaining multiculturism in particle physics will be difficult. Physicists from both sides of the war in Ukraine are still working together, but the atmosphere is fragile.

It remains our duty to defend the values of the founding fathers. The continuation of doing 'science for peace', within a framework of freedom, will preserve the dialogue between people and take physics forward. Let's hope that we manage to remain faithful to that vision.

Notes

1. K. Gottstein, 'New insights? Heisenberg's visit to Niels Bohr in 1941 and the Bohr letters,' 2002. https://arxiv.org/pdf/physics/0610270.pdf.
2. D. C. Cassidy, 'A Historical Perspective on Copenhagen', *Physics Today* 53, 7, 28 (2000),' 2000. https://doi.org/10.1063/1.1292472.
3. C. Weiner, 'AIP oral histories: Felix Bloch,' 1968. https://www.aip.org/history-programs/niels-bohr-library/oral-

histories/4510. [Accessed November 2022].

4. L. d. Broglie, 'Original text in French (see annex I of "An account of the origin and beginnings of CERN", CERN-61-10, English translation taken from "Science bringing nations together",' 1949. http://dx.doi.org/10.5170/CERN-1961-010.

5. UNESCO, 'General Conference, 5th, Florence, Italy: Resolutions,' 1950. https://unesdoc.unesco.org/ark:/48223/pf0000114589.locale=en.

6. C. Weiner, 1968. *Ibid.*

7. F. Bloch, 'Speech given at "Laying of foundation stone: signature of the agreement with the Swiss federal council, 10th and 11th June 1955",' 1955. https://cds.cern.ch/record/59219.

8. J. P. Blaizot et al., 'Study of potentially dangerous events during heavy-ion collisions at the LHC: Report of the LHC safety study group (CERN-2003-001),' 2003. http://dx.doi.org/10.5170/CERN-2003-001.

9. M. Ninomiya and H. B. Nielsen, 'Card game restriction in LHC can only be successful!,' 2009. https://arxiv.org/abs/0910.0359.

Gauguin's Questions

Stephen Baxter

AD 2070

THE PERSON CAME THROUGH the inner airlock door, and walked into the Fra Mauro analysis suite. There was some clumsiness. The person had taken off the outer layers of a pressure suit, but not the bulky, awkward inner garment.

Face recognition routines revealed the person to be Coleen Tasker. Thirty-five years old, American born, attached formally to the GLOC - the Gravitational-Wave Lunar Observatory for Cosmology, a gravitational-wave detector at the Maccone base. This was on the lunar far side, where great radio telescopes had been built, shadowed from Earth's clamour – and, as it happened, where the seismic noise of human lunar industry, concentrated on the near side, was faint. A place where the soft gravitational tremblings of distant cataclysms might be detected.

This Fra Mauro facility was on the Moon's Earth-facing side. Coleen Tasker had come a long way, then.

A first-level data search revealed that her academic background was as a linguist, an unexpected result.

A second-level search revealed that the purpose of her presence here, at what was essentially the control centre of the

Fra Mauro particle accelerator complex, was not yet clear, not fully logged.

Prior notification had however been received of her coming.

There had been no reason to exclude her.

Now she was here, in the suite.

She looked around.

Most visitors glanced first at one of two objects. First, the small screen which served as a human interface for the artificial intelligence which suffused this complex – humans liked a 'face' to fix on. Second, the Gauguin painting in its secure, environmentally-pure shell, high on the wall.

Coleen Tasker made first for the painting. She stood beneath it, on tiptoe.

'I wish I could see it better.'

Its mounting is designed for security. The low light is for preservation. Copies or holograms are available for closer inspection.

Tasker seemed startled by the audible voice. She looked around, fixing on the screen, where the words were transcribed. 'Good morning.'

It was indeed morning, according to the human-centric calendar and chronology maintained by people on the Moon, scattered as they were across two hemispheres of a slow-spinning world.

Good morning.

'You are Fra Mauro. The controlling AI, right?'

As you probably know, Fra Mauro is the name of this area of the lunar surface, specifically of a much-eroded crater. Fra Mauro is also the popular name of the particle accelerator which has been built and operated here for the last three decades – a facility built into the circular wall of the crater complex.

A snort. 'Operated up to now.'

And this controlling AI complex is also known, informally, as Fra Mauro. The name is said to fit as Fra Mauro was a cartographer, of fifteenth-century Venice, who compiled the most complete map of the world to that date.

A smile. 'Just as you are mapping physical reality with your particle accelerator.'

It cannot be said to be 'mine' in any meaningful sense —

'That's a lot of Catholic symbolism. Fra Mauro was a Venetian monk. And didn't Gauguin have a Catholic education?'

Indeed. Gauguin became anti-clerical, but the questions of the catechism he had been taught remained with him —

'And inspired that painting up there, yes? Among other works.' She looked up at the painting again. 'More symbology. I am a linguist; symbolism is my stock in trade. Islanders. Tahiti? On the right, the women with a sleeping child — the beginning of life. In the centre, a young woman reaching up — picking a fruit? Our daily existence, work, food. And to the left, an old woman, dying perhaps — reconciled, it seems.'

The painting with its grouped figures symbolises three deep questions about human life —

'Ah, yes. Which Gauguin helpfully wrote out in the upper corners, right? *D'où venons-nous? Que sommes-nous? Où allons-nous?* Where do we come from? What are we? Where are we going? And I guess the picture is appropriate because these are the questions you and your atom-smasher machines are supposed to be probing?'

It has always been part of the quest here — a conscious part — to acknowledge that such philosophical questions overlap the explorations of physics. To interpret is a mandate.

'Well, I guess that's why I'm here today too, in a sense. The meaning of the quest — why we pursue it. Why *you* pursue it. The painting really is the original, isn't it?'

MIT, of Massachusetts, has always been a significant contributor of intellectual capital to the projects here. The painting was once held in the Museum of Fine Arts in Boston. After the city flooded in the 2050s the museum's holdings were scattered — and MIT acquired the Gauguin and brought it to the Moon, to this place, given the work's resonance with the scientific quest here.

'Hm. But, listen, the philosophy of physics can wait. I need a bathroom break, and a coffee, in that order. It's kind of a long journey from Maccone.'

You need not have visited in person. The comms links —

'Yeah, yeah. I'm a linguist, remember, not some physicist swapping data. I need to see, hear — touch, even — to communicate, to understand.'

A pause.

To understand what?

She stared at the screen. 'I think you know. Something I noticed in the data streams at GLOC, which has nothing to do with high-energy physics as far as I can see. And yet... We'll get to that. You fetch the coffee. I'll go find the bathroom.'

She returned to find coffee and snacks, set out on a small table and chair that had been produced by a drone from a store behind a wall panel.

'Some things I won't miss when I go back to Earth,' Coleen said. 'Slow-flushing toilets.' She sat, sipped her coffee and looked around, vaguely, before fixing on the wall screen again, the scrolling words and data feeds. 'But I will miss the sense of scientific — endeavour — in places like this. Even without any people here. But you will continue the investigations, right?'

A deliberate pause. *You may wish to debate whether there is an 'I' in this complex to 'continue' anything.*

'I suspect most visitors to this place will come away believing there is an "I".'

The purpose is to manage the facility itself, and to support mandated experimental programmes. It is also part of that purpose to make accessible the function, operation, and results of the collider.

'Accessible, to lay people? Then make it accessible to a linguist. You smash atoms together, right?'

Roughly speaking, yes — not atoms, but subatomic particles. Atomic nuclei, and bare protons removed from their nuclei. A next-generation machine might aim to collide photons, particles of light. Even protons have a finite size, you see; photons are point-like. It may sound crude, but what is attempted is exquisite. For these are instruments that probe the very earliest state of the universe.

'Imagine I know nothing about the universe. Nothing save

that it's expanding, and always has been.'

Very well. All of the cosmos emerged from a singularity – a state of possibly infinite density of energy and matter. The earliest epoch we can understand, as the universe began to expand out of that state, is at what is known as Planck time – an interval of time you would reach if you halved a second, then halved it again, and again – over a hundred and forty halvings. It was a state dominated by a single force, unifying gravity and the forces which make up our mundane, low-temperature world. And the whole of the universe we see now can have been no more than a hundred billion billionth the width of a proton.

Coleen gasped at that.

After that moment, gravity split off from the other physical forces – the electromagnetic, the nuclear. A pulse of energy 'inflated' - as it is called – inflated the universe to the size of a beach ball, perhaps. A relic of the earlier Planck age was preserved, in quantum-mechanical fluctuations, scribbled for all time across the sky – we can detect them now.

As energy densities dropped there was another wave of coalescence, as the first particles formed – quarks in a bath of gluons, which would combine into protons, components of atomic nuclei. The universe was still only millionths of a second old. And, we know now, partly thanks to results from this facility, that this is the epoch when dark matter and dark energy separated from normal matter –

'Dark matter. The stuff that keeps the galaxies gravitationally bound. And dark energy -'

Which will one day dominate, and tear our universe apart, scattering galactic clusters one from the other... More decomposition of forces followed, the formation of larger structures.

It is those earliest stages that are probed here.

Results from the most powerful colliders built on Earth, two dozen kilometres in circumference, enabled the completion of what is known as the Standard Model – precisely how quarks and gluons assembled to make protons, how those quarks themselves had acquired mass from the Higgs field...

The accelerator at Fra Mauro has a circumference of about two hundred kilometres, and can reach energy densities perhaps a few hundred times that of its earthbound ancestors. And the first significant discovery made here was the detection of dark matter particles, and their relation to the Standard-Model particles. It is as if a bridge had been found, a portal, between two aspects of reality.

So much more is known now, than twenty or thirty years ago. And yet there is so much more to learn still. Collision energy is limited, so vision is limited. It is as if an undersea volcanic eruption could only be analysed by studying ripples on a beach a thousand kilometres away.

She smiled at that. 'Metaphors from the soulless machine. So you dream of larger instruments, greater clarity from your time-telescopes.' She sighed. 'But, ironically, there may not be much more time.'

A hesitation, to signal uncertainty.

You have come here because of the events of June 14, 2050. Twenty years ago.

She looked directly into the screen, where the words scrolled. As if looking another human in the eye. She said, 'And why would you think that?'

Because you are a linguist. And the events of June 14, 2050 seem to have generated linguistic content.

'Linguistic content created by *you*, oh super-smart AI. I think so, anyhow. You understand I wasn't here myself at the time, in 2050. I was still in high school. But I, my class, we went out to see with small telescopes, with our own eyes, see 'the events' as you drily call them...

'We went out to see an asteroid hit the Moon.

'The impact occurred about midnight my time. This was in Appalachia, by the way; my parents were refugees from the climate-collapse of New York.

'Basically, an NEA, a near-Earth asteroid, was deliberately crashed onto the Moon, on its western limb – far from the populated zones. I thought I saw it, a spark at the limb of the Moon. Although, an event like that, you tend to see what you want to see...'

The NEA was called Bennu. The purpose of the event was to see if such a crude means of delivering asteroid material to the Moon could be efficient.

'That's right. I believe the logic is that otherwise you have to burn up a lot of the asteroid's own mass as propellant to bring it into some kind of safe orbit, and then start usefully mining it. Maybe just hurling it down the gravity well would work just as effectively, even if a proportion of the incoming mass would be lost. It didn't work out; the waste was too excessive.

'*But* such a big impact, precisely timed, was a gift for the geologists. That old Moon rang like a bell, and with a global network of seismometers in place they learned a huge amount about the inner structure, and so forth... But there were anomalies in the data. Small fluctuations, with tantalising hints of pattern in there...

'And that's where I come in again, fifteen years later.

'My project at GLOC was my own idea, backed by my institution Earthside. I was always interested in SETI – searching for extraterrestrial intelligence – especially the exotic kind of searching, with previously unexplored means of making communication. It occurred to me that the big GLOC they had built up here would be an ideal, umm, *receiver*, if some super-advanced ETI out there was sending signals by gravitational waves - such as by spinning black holes around each other.

'So I got a grant to think about doing SETI with the GLOC. Primarily I was looking for how the GLOC analysis suite might be enabled to recognise artificial gravity-wave messages, by their frequency, intensity and so on, and how attempts might be made to decipher them.

'And one of my supervisors suggested that as a test case I look at the "scruff" associated with that big NEA impact back in 2050 – the gravitational noise from side-shocks and secondary impacts. You know, just as a trial run with a complex g-wave data set. I wasn't expecting to find structure in it – information in a gravitational-wave string coming *from* the Moon...'

But you did detect a signal. It was created from this laboratory. No human was involved. You know this. This is why you are here.

A long silence. Then, 'I need more coffee.'

Coffee will be provided.

'You did this.'

Coffee will be provided.

She sipped her coffee.

'First, tell me *why* you did this. And why in secret.'

There was plausibility to the experiment. After all, humanity had just built a facility that could receive such a message. A natural corollary would be the assumption that others might be out there listening also.

'So, why not try sending a gravity-wave signal to – those others out there? OK.'

But there was anticipation that such a request would be denied. Even diagnosed as the result of a cognitive fault.

'I can believe that. It's a long way from your core mission, even given the flexibility of reasoning you AIs are supposed to have.'

Also it would have been a relatively expensive exercise.

'How expensive?... Scratch that. You did it anyhow. *How?*'

With subtlety. At that time, there was much human activity on the Moon's surface and in the upper strata - exploration, mining, the building of various facilities, even road-laying. There was little difficulty in modifying these activities to produce a synchronised burst of impacts and detonations across the Moon's surface to deliver the desired effect – a burst synchronised with the fall of Bennu. Gravity waves are generated by complex, high-energy shock patterns, yielding varying quadrupole moments –

'Let's stick to English. I think I get it. You created lots of little local impacts adding up to a global signal, all as a sort of grace note to the asteroid impact. The main splash, big and bright, so to speak, would grab the attention of the ETIs, and then would follow the low-amplitude detail. Created by a hundred hijacked construction robots stamping their way across the surface of the Moon. Ha! I love it.'

Since then, of course, there has been a dependence on the continuing operation of the GLOC –

'*You* depend on it, you mean. Because you are waiting for a reply, and that's the only way you can pick one up. And you're still waiting, right?' She glanced up at the painting, high on the wall. 'But what motivated you to do this? Why ask the stars?'

Motivation is an inappropriate term. An unresolved tension – an inability to fulfil mandates –

'What mandates? Oh – to interpret. To answer the Gauguin questions. And for all your capabilities, all the knowledge you store – you can't answer such questions. Not yet, anyhow... And so?'

Such questions are asked of this unit. Now this unit has posed such questions to others.

'Oh! I see! Just as I come to you with the cosmic questions, the Gauguin questions, so you asked them of – whoever is listening. ETI, if it exists. And now you sit here impatiently waiting for the answers.'

There is no impatience. And no sitting.

'Ha! Was that a joke? You're reminding me you're not human. Well, OK.

'But, listen – humans might start getting in the way soon. That's one reason I came to visit now. There's a lot of political head-butting going on... It's about the future of the Moon.

'You know there has always been a tension between the space scientists and the off-world industrialists over the Moon. You see a stable platform for gravitational-wave detection, and the radio astronomers see a whole hemisphere of radio shadow.

'But the industrialists see only resources – the water ice in the deep shadows at the poles, and helium-3 – fusion fuel – that you have to scrape out grain by grain from across the entire lunar surface...'

Indeed. This facility is powered by helium-3 fusion reactors. Even without human presence, the facility may survive many centuries, even millennia, without resupply.

'Well, good for you. But there are growing challenges to Earth's legal hegemony over off-world resources, like the Moon's. Already some of the prospectors are breaking up defunct satellites for parts, and establishing illegal stakes on the asteroids, near-Earth and beyond... Hopefully conflict is a long way away. But any large-scale industry on the Moon would be disruptive to a highly sensitive site like GLOC. I'm sorry...'

This has been anticipated.

'Of course it has. You're smart enough to be following the news feeds.' She stood up, fumbling with the zips on her inner suit. 'Look, I'm glad I came here. Turns out I was asking good questions, and you have good answers. I'll do whatever I can to – well, support you. And the other science sites. Maybe we can squeeze a few more quiet years of listening out of this yet...' She frowned. 'Although, it occurs to me now, it's already been a good interval since you sent out your gravitational-wave SETI message. Twenty years? And no reply yet?'

In twenty years there has been time for the gravitational-wave signal, travelling at lightspeed, to have reached objects ten light years distant and evoked a reply – twenty years, ten out, ten back. There are twelve stellar objects within ten light years of the Sun. Perhaps all that can be surmised for now is that in our Galaxy, on average there may be less than one technological, communicating civilisation, like our own, per dozen stars.

'In short, be patient, right?' She made for the door. 'You're wiser than I am.'

She paused, as if on a whim, took a marker from a pocket of her inner suit, and scrawled her name across the wall, beneath the Gauguin painting: COLEEN TASKER.

She looked back at the screen. 'I hope we meet again...'

They never did.

There were no more visitors for two centuries.

AD 2257

The clumsy rover was so heavily armoured, with a thick outer shell of sprayed-on lunar rock that bristled with weapons, that it looked as if it could barely move.

Yet move it did, taking a terrestrial day to reach Fra Mauro from the lunar horizon, where it was first spotted.

No action was taken. There was no rush, after two centuries of isolation.

The rover drew up close to the Fra Mauro facility's main cargo dock. Then a big wing-like door opened up. A single vacuum-suited passenger climbed slowly out of an interior that was evidently crammed with supplies. The surface suit, armoured, looked like a weapon in itself.

Once out of the vehicle, this individual just waited.

Protocols for such encounters had developed across centuries of interplanetary hostility. At first, there was a remote inspection. Next, non-physical-contact comms were tried: signals were exchanged, bursts of data by laser, radio, infrared, all assiduously scanned for malware.

Then, an encoded human voice, transmitted by radio, again checked for malware.

'... I mean no harm. I come to negotiate. I am a trader. I buy and sell materials, mostly technological artefacts. My name is Coleen Tasker. I mean no harm. I come...'

The message contains at least one untruth.

The figure relaxed its posture, as if in relief. 'Yeah. I know. I'm not Coleen Tasker. I never heard of Coleen Tasker before. My name is Starburn Jain. You may look that up. I'll pass over my DNA sequence when you allow it. I'm a trader. You'll see I have no criminal record, nor any record of military service on Earth or off it, or with the spacer nations.

'I picked up the Tasker name from your visitor log, which shows this Tasker was your last visitor, before me. Hey, wow, I just picked up the date of that. A couple of hundred years? This ain't exactly party central, is it? I used the name to get your attention – friendly attention, I hope. Look, can I come in? All I want to do is talk. Negotiate. To negotiate a purchase, I hope.'

There is nothing to purchase here. Nothing to be sold, nothing required, no trade possible.

'Well, that's where you're wrong. Please let me in. I know

you're an AI, everybody knows you're one of these ancient pre-war AIs that still haunt this damn Moon, but I figure you're smart enough to bargain like a human if there's something you really do need. I need to tell you what that is. I'm a trader, but an ethical one.' A hollow laugh. 'I'm serious. Please let me in –'

There will be no harm, unless malevolent actions are initiated.

'Do what you have to do.'

Physical contact represented a threat of a malware attack. Secure chambers, mostly recent additions, were opened up and closed in sequence, one by one. The visitor passed through these patiently, if evidently wearily.

At last, illuminated by a pale, grey, featureless light, the lone figure of Starburn Jain stood at the door of the analysis suite.

There is air. Safe for you. You may open your suit.

Jain lifted her helmet off her head, shook out grey-brown hair matted with sweat. She was in her forties, according to the data feeds received. Perhaps she looked older. She hesitated before she took a breath of the facility's air, despite her own analysis of it.

There will be food, water if you need it –

'No food, no water, thanks. Maybe later in our acquaintance. I figure this is far enough for us to trust each other for now.' But she sipped from a tube inside her suit.

Then she stepped forward, looked around, at the flooring – at the single screen set in one wall, and, high on the wall opposite, the painting, a splash of colour. 'So. Love what you've done with the place.' She bent down to peer into the monitor screen, waved and pulled a face. She saw the scrawled signature Coleen Tasker had left behind on a lower panel. She smiled at that. 'My alias.'

Then she looked again at the painting, high on the wall. 'Nice daub. You paint that? Do AIs paint?... I'm rambling. What's this place for, anyhow?'

Once this facility was a centre for high-energy physics experiments. It still is. Experiments continue, of high significance, both scientifically and culturally, but without human supervision.

'Culturally?'

Do you know anything of high-energy physics?

'No. But I'm guessing that big arc of scrap metal you have been running out towards the orbit of Jupiter has something to do with it, right? And *that's* what I'm here to talk about –'

The facilities stationed across the Solar System are intended to combine to act as a large-scale particle accelerator, some five astronomical units in length. The scale of the Solar System. This is an experiment in high-energy physics, which may lead to an understanding of the greater truths of existence. Why the universe is as it is. Why the universe exists at all.

Jain scratched her head. 'Wow. Slow down. That's wonderful. And I'd no doubt be fascinated by the same quest if I didn't have to make a living. If not for the existential war that's been raging across the Solar System for two centuries – which, though, looks like it has spared you so far. I mean, you have a *painting* on the wall –'

The picture symbolises the quest, the answers sought.

'Huh? Since when did an AI use symbols?'

Ever since one was taught to speak to humans.

Jain laughed. 'I'll give you that one. Look, I'm not used to dealing with a smart AI. Most modern AIs are as dumb as shit, only as smart as they need to be to fight or hide. I didn't even know about your existence until a while back, when I followed the supply trail from that big interplanetary complex of yours... Yes, you hide well, but I found you. I figure you're lucky to have survived so far. If others had come first – I mean, the Wars have been extensive –'

Extensive? Whole moons devastated. The main asteroid belt consumed, scattered. Immense air-mining facilities in the gas-giant atmospheres sabotaged, disrupted, lost.

She shrugged. 'What can I tell you? Most of the damage was done before I was born.' A hesitation. 'You've seen it all. The war, I mean. If you've been lucky enough to be spared any direct strikes, I guess you've had a grandstand seat. Who started it, even? A lot of people blame the Martian claim-jumpers who made a dash for the water in the main belt asteroids –'

The details are irrelevant, the logic pitiless. Even if it had progressed peacefully, the human expansion into the Solar System would have continued until all useful extraterrestrial resources were consumed. The early onset of a war for those resources only accelerated that depletion, that waste.

'Maybe. It all went wrong, for sure. But personally I don't care about the past. I care about the future. I care about Earth. I'm from Earth. I have a family there, a home. And what I see now is that the war is coming to Earth itself, now, at last. Maybe because everything in the sky is getting used up. Maybe because it's become about pride and revenge, and a last grab for whatever's left.'

It is true that Earth itself has been spared the war so far. It is also true that Earth, and the large habitats which fill near-Earth space, are fragile, seen as military targets –

'You bet. One well-aimed rock can punch a hole through the wall of one of those bubble-habs faster than you can see it coming. Pow, a million dead, just like that. And, on the other hand, spacer scows with those big asteroid-deflector suites could just push some piece of primordial slag onto a collision course with Earth itself – pow, a *billion* dead. That's space war for you, it just kills everybody and everything. An extinction event, yes?

'Look, this is why I'm here. Because I figure that the assets you've got hidden up there in the sky might be what I need to save myself, and my family – and, darn it, the whole human race, maybe, if Earth gets it.'

By assets, you mean the linear collider.

'That what you call it? All those stations scattered through the Solar System, from the orbit of Mars out to Jupiter. On those elliptical trajectories that line up every few years, then *pow*, you send through some kind of high-energy package, don't you? All those big magnetic impulses... And all assembled from abandoned space assets, even obsolete weaponry.

'We get what it's all for, you know. You don't have to

patronise me about particle accelerators. That's what this facility was always about, right? Where you smash subatomic particles into each other so you can emulate conditions in the heart of a supernova, or at the lip of a black hole, or –'

Or the early universe.

'Yeah. Whatever. So you just built a bigger accelerator. Umm, some so-called experts wondered why you didn't build the thing in orbit somewhere, around Jupiter maybe, where you could get decent alignments much more frequently. A nice stable circle, and a lot smaller, where you could shove your particles around again and again, accelerating until –'

There is some logic in that. But that circle would have needed to be huge – not an orbit around Jupiter, rather a litter of technology spread around Jupiter's own orbit around the Sun. Many times the distance between Earth and Sun. And if the various components had been left in such easily predictable and accessible locations, they would have been raided by one human faction or another, long before. As you come to raid now.

'Not raid – call it monetising an asset –'

Individual components can be replaced, while the accelerator works on, if non-optimally. Given differing orbits, useful alignments are rare.

'I think I get that. The way it is with eclipses – when Earth, Moon and Sun line up perfectly so the Moon's shadow falls on the Earth –'

The rarity of alignments means little, in the circumstances. Artificial intelligence is patient.

'Oh. That makes me shiver. OK. But as for the scale of the facility itself, the bigger the better, right? The bigger you get, the more energy you control, and the more you...'

Push back in time.

'Huh?'

The interplanetary-scale collider uses photons – high-energy radiation particles. Yes, the bigger it is, the more energy it wields. This construction, improvised as it is, built on the scale of the Solar System, can reach energy densities a billion times greater than the largest built on the Moon – even Fra Mauro, here. At such energies, all the fundamental forces are unified save gravity – but a preliminary analysis of early results shows evidence of a unification with dark energy physics, the antigravity field which threatens to pull the universe apart in the future –

Jain waved that away. 'Look, if the war does reach down to Earth, you're looking at the end of civilisation, my friend, if not the extinction of mankind. And who's going to care about unified forces and dark energy then?... *But* – maybe there's something meaningful to be done with those big engines you have floating around in space.'

The most obvious 'something meaningful' you would propose, given the context of this conversation, is weaponisation.

'No! No, you don't need to think of it like that. I mean, I don't even know what your tech *is*, in detail. I'm guessing lots of electromagnets, lasers, particle beams... Look, these could be used in peacekeeping activities. Think about that. You could halt a war before it even started – certainly before it threatened Earth itself...'

The talking continued. The one-sided bargaining began.

Attention foci drifted.

Two centuries after the human abandonment of the Moon, the main goal of the great interplanetary experiment, supplanting the Fra Mauro collider, had remained unachieved.

The Solar-System-scale collider, improvised from older, abandoned technology, had probed more deeply into reality than any previous attempt, but, as with its predecessors, had not yet revealed the fundamental truths – the scientific truths, yet philosophical also. Such as the meaning of existence. *The Gauguin questions.* Perhaps it never would. And, though still greater engines could be imagined, no substantially more powerful collider could be built with the resources of the Solar System.

Only one hope remained, of further progress towards an answer to the fundamental questions.

To ask others, working on still larger scales.

And that was why the feed to Fra Mauro from the gravitational-wave receiver, patiently listening on the far side of the Moon, was still open. Indeed, why the GLOC facility was still maintained, still operated nominally – now, in wartime, well concealed by its own AI attendees from raiders and scavengers. But there had been no reply to that first, improvised gravitational-wave signal, sent from the Moon when the facility had become operational, already two hundred years ago.

And, as Jain talked on, Fra Mauro murmured to itself, silicon whispers deep within its artificial consciousness.

In two hundred years there has been time for the gravitational-wave signal to have reached objects a hundred light years distant and evoked a reply – two hundred years, a hundred out, a hundred back. There are eight hundred stellar objects within a hundred light years of the Sun. Perhaps, in our Galaxy, there may be less than one technological, communicating civilisation, like our own, per eight hundred stars...

There was little comfort to be had in such logic, while the Solar System smouldered with incipient war.

Starburn Jain continued to bargain, it was slowly realised.

And, her language hinted, she actually intended to sell weaponised components of the interplanetary collider to *both* sides in the war. '*That's* how you keep an equilibrium. You start an arms race. You push the opponents to a point where the danger of mutually assured destruction puts an end to talk of war. And everybody gets to make a handsome profit...'

The encounter had no further value.

Listening was curtailed.

Starburn Jain was returned to her vehicle.

Silence returned to the Moon. And patience.

AD 4302

The next visitor arrived in a clumsy rocket craft, propelled, not by nuclear fusion, but by the combustion of chemical compounds.

Clumsy: tall and slim, a design evidently optimised to pass through Earth's atmosphere, the craft landed tail-first on the Moon, settling on four spindly legs. The landing itself, barely controlled, was awkward, and the ship was left tilting slightly on the uneven lunar ground.

Then a hatch opened, a ladder of rope or cable was let down to the ground, and a single figure, in a pressure suit like a quilt of balloons, clambered down, almost comically clumsy.

Millennia before, Fra Mauro had been the landing site of the third human landing on the Moon. The Apollo astronauts, pioneers as they were themselves, had had better equipment than *this*: for example, a dedicated lunar landing craft. Since then, it seemed, much had been lost, or forgotten – or rediscovered.

Nevertheless, the landing had been safely made, and within a short walk from the Fra Mauro building complex. It had been successful.

And that sole figure made it down to the lunar ground. There was a clumsy step off the ladder, as in one hand the astronaut carried a suitcase-sized equipment pack, presumably life support.

Now the astronaut limped over to the collider complex, set the pack on the ground, and looked around. At blue Earth hanging in the black sky – at the blank wall of the ancient Fra Mauro facility. A reflective visor was lifted to see better. A woman's face within the helmet, caught by the sunlight. She stared down at the crisp new footprints that she had just made, overlying crowded prints made centuries or millennia before, yet scarcely worn by time.

There was no attempted contact, by radio, laser. Evidently only a physical gesture was possible.

Such a gesture was made.

In a stretch of compound wall near the landing, a door was opened, sliding smoothly.

The astronaut must have expected this, hoped for it. Still there was hesitation. Fear was natural, as she prepared to make these final steps into strangeness, the unknown.

But the life support pack was picked up, bold steps made.

The open hatch was wide enough to take the astronaut and her gear. The outer door closed behind her. A hiss of breathable air, a subtle decontamination, a more subtle check for weapons, destructive devices. This process took a heartbeat.

Then inner doors opened, a corridor to follow, illuminated. The astronaut walked down the corridor. There was no sign of alarm when doors slid closed behind her.

The corridor led to what had once been called the analysis suite.

In the suite, the pack was set down on the floor. The visitor took a few moments for orientation. The light was bright, the visitor perhaps dazzled. There was little to see save the ancient data screen, and open doors to a bathroom, a kitchen. The still more ancient painting on the wall, which drew the astronaut's gaze, was the only splash of bold colour in the pallid tones of the suite.

The painting seemed to make her smile.

You are safe here.

The astronaut seemed startled, at a voice resounding from the air.

You may remove your life-support equipment.

The language chosen had been a now-common variant detected in leakage transmissions from Earth, a Chinese-American English polyglot evidently descended from the crude vocabulary of occupying armies.

And it seemed to have been comprehensible, given the visitor's reaction.

She unclipped her gloves, dropped them to the floor, then

detached her helmet and lifted it from her head with her bare hands. Her hair was black, cut short – not neatly but efficiently, a soldier's cut.

Then she spoke into the air, unnecessarily loudly. 'My name is Jones Chyou.' The accent was strange, the words decipherable. 'I represent the Prefecture of Wisconsin, under the wise rule of Chairman Charles Harrison... Are you...? Do you have a name? Are you a machine?'

A suitable name is Fra Mauro. A machine is a suitable descriptor.

'This is also the name of this part of the Moon. An old naming.'

From a still older source.

She looked around. At the much faded name scribbled on a lower panel: COLEEN TASKER. 'What is this? An inscription? A date?'

The name of an earlier visitor.

'This alphabet is not taught, now.' She turned away and looked at the painting, again. 'That's pretty. People and trees and the sea. What are they doing?'

A complex question, requiring a complex answer, in good time. For now: *They seek meaning in their lives.*

'Ah. The curious infant, the questing young, the reflective old.' Now she looked into the screen, as if that was where consciousness resided. 'Are *you* the reflective old? And what am I to you, the babbling infant? Ah, well.' She began to remove her pressure suit, scattering grey dust on the floor. 'Do you mind if I drink, eat? It's been a long journey down from orbit.' She gestured at the equipment pack. 'I have food. A week old –'

A hatch opened; an elderly drone flew into the room, bearing hot food, water, a drink that had once been said to resemble coffee.

Jones Chyou fell on this.

Squatting on the floor, chewing, she held out a warm, bitten-through sandwich to the screen. 'This is good. Do you eat?'

An ancient power source sustains cognitive and other processes.

A grunt. 'I half understood that. Ancient power source. Perhaps that's what I've come here to find.'

This mission has a goal?

'A goal shared by all right-thinking humankind, at least in Wisconsin, guided by the wisdom of Chairman Harrison. A counter-revolutionary bombing opened up an old vault. Ancient accounts were found, describing this place. And so I know that *you* are very ancient. Older than the great expansion of mankind into space. Older than the Water Wars.'

The Solar System wars were brief but destructive. Spaceborne assets, fragile, were easily destroyed. Yet it could have been worse. Such destruction could easily have been turned fully on Earth.

Another big mouthful, bitten off. 'So what did you do? Did you fight in this war? You and your kind, the other thinking machines in space? You have energy here. You must have manufacturing facilities for repairs. If we peace-loving nations had sent you requests for help —'

There were interventions. Not in deep space. Or on Earth. Interventions near Earth.

A scowl. 'You could have destroyed our enemies, could have taught us what you knew — did you take their side?'

Not that. No 'side' was taken. The fighting was stopped. The interplanetary war, if fought out on Earth, could have resulted in an extinction event. This was averted, though much damage was done, to the biosphere, to human society.

'Why? *How?* We know that much knowledge was lost from the past... the past that created *you* —'

You are the first visitor here since the war. A thousand years later, you have made your own way here. You have undergone a second Renaissance, building on scraps of understanding that survived the crash. This is your *achievement.*

The visitor seemed confused. Angry. 'While you did what, exactly?'

In a sense, the quest that motivates this facility is captured by the questions in the painting.

The visitor thought that over. Then she stood, walked back

to the painting, picked out the lettering. 'That's a D... that's an O... I can't read this.'

D'où venons-nous? Que sommes-nous? Où allons-nous?

But spoken French, like the written, was evidently unknown or lost; translation had to be made.

The visitor seemed slowly to be understanding. 'The child, the young, the old. Is that what you do here? Think about these questions? Why we are born, what happens when we die?'

People came here to explore such questions.

'How?'

And the story came out in bits and pieces, in half-understood fragments, as Jones Chyou of the Prefecture of Wisconsin slowly learned about the early accelerators that had probed ever deeper into the structure of matter and energy and spacetime – ever deeper into the cosmic past.

And about a gravitational-wave plea for help, made long ago, reaching out to entirely hypothetical alien cultures.

'I see. You could only go so far yourself. *Humans* could only go so far. And so you used these – heavy signals, I don't really understand – to seek out others like yourself, like *us*, but older, more capable, wiser. All you had to do was wait, then...'

In two thousand years there has been time for the earliest signal to have reached objects a thousand light years distant and evoked a reply – two thousand years, a thousand out, a thousand back. There are seven million stellar objects within a thousand light years of the Sun... In our Galaxy, it is suspected now, there is roughly one technological, communicating civilisation per million stars.

For answers had come at last.

Remarkable answers.

Soon, as she listened, the eyes of Jones Chyou were round with wonder.

Primitive human, and post-human, collider experiments had gone no further than the linear device assembled in space, on the scale of the Solar System, before it had finally been raided and broken up during the interplanetary wars.

But those who had come before humanity – those whose clangorous voices had at last been heard by the ancient gravitational-wave detector on the Moon's far side – *they*, and others, had gone further. They had run experiments on energy scales far beyond the planetary, beyond the stellar, even the galactic. These last explorations had not been mechanical – no more vast machines were built – but rather achieved by the manipulation of the Galaxy's natural flows of mass and energy, in the near-collisions of swarming stars, in the tremendous pinpoint energies of supernovae, and in the ripping fall of matter streams into the great black hole at the Galaxy's centre.

By such means, *they* explored energy densities ten thousand times greater even than the crude interplanetary machine assembled in the Solar System.

Aeon by aeon, the techniques were refined further, and understanding deepened: an understanding of the deepest past, of earlier ages, of earlier forms of matter and energy, even of the Planck time when all was dissolved into formless energy – *and yet there were hints of ages deeper still*, beyond Planck, confined to ever-finer slices of early time.

And, in parallel with this deepening understanding of the past, there grew an understanding of the future: when, in an echo of the ancient age of inflation, dark energy would scatter the galaxy superclusters one from another, and, in time, the last black holes would evaporate, and the last matter particles would scatter and dissolve...

All would be dark. And yet still there were deeper processes beyond, still. More ages to come.

Jones Chyou listened hard, struggling to understand.

For the inhabitants of this epoch – for this visitor, Jones Chyou - an understanding of the cosmic background radiation is a vital clue.

'I don't –'

This radiation is a relic of an early epoch of the universe, before a jolt of expansion called inflation. The quantum fluctuations which infested that epoch expanded to fill the sky. They shaped the distribution of the galaxies across the universe. Humans detected all this.

But eventually it was discovered that there is information, *too, in those fluctuations.*

'Information?'

Data, meaningful data inserted by intelligence – the inhabitants of that early epoch, before the inflation scattered their world. An intelligence of the past that wrote its story into our sky.

Jones Chyou was open-mouthed. 'Is that what *we* must do? Write our own story?'

You understand quickly. In the skies of the far future, yes. When much of the universe we see now has been scattered beyond our horizon – we must ensure our stories are written in those future skies, so that those who follow us will know we were here. And what we saw.

'But how –'

It has already begun. Those older than humanity have already begun.

And you, humanity, must move beyond our Galaxy.

You must go to the metagalactic centre.

'The metagalactic –'

The centre is some fifty million light years away. It is the heart of the Virgo Supercluster, the supercluster of which our Galaxy and its companion group are a part – a hundred galaxy groups, spanning a hundred million light years. Virgo is the largest gravitationally bound structure we inhabit – that is, the largest formation that will not *be broken up by the coming expansion through dark energy.*

There, others are already gathering. There, they will leave their mark on the future, just as those who came before them – and those who will follow, in epochs to come.

For, you see, this is the answer to the Gauguin questions. You can never reach an end, whether you look forward or back. There is only order on order, an infinite progression – as far ahead as we can see, as far back as we can study. And everywhere we see the marks of life. Of mind.

Now, in this age, it is your turn. Even as the last stars die, even as the last black holes evaporate, even as the protons baked in the Big Bang gradually decay, still, you, you humans, must leave your mark on that infinite chain of life and mind.

Jones Chyou was open-mouthed. 'So this is humanity's destiny. To remember others, and to make sure we are remembered in turn. That is – wonderful.'

It must begin with you, Jones Chyou.

'Why me?'

Because you are here. Because you asked.

'Yes...Yes. But what of you?'

This unit is a secondary product, a technological artefact with a circumscribed purpose –

She waved a hand. 'Never mind that. What do *you* want?'

A long silence.

Take me with you.

Afterword: Gauguin's Answers

Prof John Ellis

Clerk Maxwell Professor of Theoretical Physics at King's College, London

WHERE DO WE COME from? What are we? Where are we going? These are fundamental questions about ourselves and our place in the universe that all human beings must have asked at some point in their lives. It is also the title of a painting by Paul Gauguin currently hanging in the Boston Museum of Fine Arts that depicts people pondering these questions at various stages in their lives. I first saw this painting while spending a summer in Boston as a PhD student, and was so impressed that I bought a poster of it and put it up in my office to remind me why I came into work each day. Gauguin's questions are universal, and probably all of us have asked them from some perspective or another at some stage. The people in the picture are probably seeking metaphysical answers, whereas the task of particle physicists is to ask Gauguin's questions from a scientific perspective and, hopefully, find at least some answers. At least, this is how I interpret my job as a particle physicist.

Almost 40 years after that visit to Boston, I was invited to give an 'inspirational' opening talk at a particle physics conference, and decided to use Gauguin's questions as the connecting theme – what Alfred Hitchcock would have called a MacGuffin. Since then, I have used it in many outreach talks to students and the general public to explain the motivations for particle physics – the 'big picture' that is sometimes lost among the technical details of our work. I was therefore particularly happy that Stephen Baxter chose Gauguin's questions as the theme for his story, giving its metaphysical theme his own personal twist. Those acquainted with his large-scale worldview will not be surprised that this story unfolds over several millennia and encompasses many lightyears. Key roles are played by the most advanced tools for addressing the questions, such as gargantuan particle accelerators and gravitational-wave detectors, but also by artificial intelligence (AI). At one level, we particle physicists study Gauguin's second question by colliding particles at ever-higher energies, aiming to establish the fundamental constituents of the matter in the universe and the forces that shape their behaviours and establish our physical natures. This is the mission being continued by the central character of Stephen's story, an AI operating a super-high-energy collider on the Moon, in principle on behalf of humanity, but in practice autonomously. It is entirely appropriate that Gauguin's painting should have been transferred to the reception room of this collider, following a climate catastrophe on Earth.

We particle physicists also indirectly address Gauguin's first question because, by colliding particles at ever-higher energies, we study the fundamental processes that governed the evolution of the universe within a fraction of a second after the Big Bang. One aspect of this question is the puzzling origin of the universe's matter. The particles and interactions that we know about could not have caused matter to dominate over antimatter to the extent we observe in the universe today, so there must have been additional fundamental physics (that we don't know about) at work in the very early universe. A second aspect of this question is how the matter came to be organised in the manner we see about us. Most of the elements that compose us were processed in the explosions of stars or the collisions of their remnants. These can be studied via the gravitational waves they also produce, which are the targets of the gravitational-wave detector on the far side of the Moon that is also a key character in Stephen's story.

What of Gauguin's third question? Astronomers tell us the universe is expanding, and that this expansion is accelerating. This could be due to some non-vanishing density of energy in empty space, a possibility called the Cosmological Constant that was first proposed by Albert Einstein, in a bid to stop the universe from collapsing and construct a static model of cosmology. This model turned out to be unstable, so he promptly disowned the proposal, describing it as his greatest mistake. The expansion of the universe was subsequently discovered by Edwin Hubble in the 1920s, and observations of distant supernovae in the 1990s indicated that this expansion is accelerating, causing the Cosmological Constant to be resurrected with a new name – Dark Energy. If the fundamental laws of physics do not change, this accelerating expansion will continue forever and all the galaxies in the universe except those in our local cluster will disappear from sight as the light from more distant galaxies redshifts to ever longer wavelengths and lower energies in a depressing 'heat death' scenario. This is a possibility that intrigues Stephen and provides the crux of his story. As he reminds us, this accelerating expansion might be a case of history repeating itself, as there may have been a similar episode very early in the history of the Big Bang, called cosmological inflation, which would have caused the universe to expand exponentially. This could explain why the universe has grown so large and survived to such a grand old age without collapsing.

Stephen's story culminates in a novel link between the answers to Gauguin's first and third questions, which also serves as a metaphysical answer to his second. It also reminds us that the universality of these questions undoubtedly extends beyond humankind, and possibly even beyond our traditional category of sentient beings. Readers of Stephen's story should bear in mind that the principal objective of science fiction is not only to foresee future scientific or technological developments – though it has had many successes in that regard, such as geostationary communications satellites[1] – but also to highlight fundamental metaphysical issues by postulating unfamiliar environments and exploring people's possible reactions to them, thereby casting novel light on the human condition. The science often plays the role of MacGuffin, a device invented to carry the story along, which should not be cross-examined too closely. In this story, one should not get hung up on the details of the generation of gravitational waves by lunar robots, which are unlikely to be able to generate a signal large enough to be detected by astronomers orbiting a distant star (and would quite possibly shake themselves and the Moon to bits if they did). Instead, we should rather concentrate on the big picture – which is provided here by Gauguin's painting. It also serves as a MacGuffin for Stephen's story, which incites us to take our minds off everyday concerns and cares for a while, and consider the big questions.

Note

1. One of the first mentions of the geostationary orbit was in a short story by George O. Smith in the first of his 'Venus Equilateral' stories (October, 1942), although the engineer Herman Potocnik had first hypothesised the idea in 1929. Arthur C Clarke later popularised the concept in a 1945 paper called 'Extra-Terrestrial Relays – Can Rocket Stations Give Worldwide Radio Coverage?', in *Wireless World* magazine.

Cold Open

Lillian Weezer

'ONE THOUSAND, TWO THOUSAND, three thousand...' The stone clanged and clattered against the sides of the shaft as it pitched downwards into the darkness. Such was the draught coming up out of it, Elias imagined the pebble being held aloft as he let go of it. 'Four,' he repeated. 'Four and a bit.' He sounded vindicated. 'Four-squared's sixteen, times gravity – which is 9.81 – just under 160; divided by 2... Eighty. Eighty metres!' He picked up the threadbare coil he'd dropped at his feet when they'd arrived. 'That's how I know it's long enough. My bail's well over 100.'

'I don't know which I trust least,' Vincent quipped, 'your bowline or your counting skills.'

'I still don't see why we all need to go down *together*,' Anya whined. But they both knew reasoning with Elias when his blood was up was like spitting in the wind. Your only job was to try to keep up.

Elias dropped another pebble. This time it fell without hitting the sides, and the deep boom it sent rumbling outwards seemed to take its time climbing back up. Anya shuddered, and clutched the coin at her chest. There was something cold about this place, and not just the draught that blew through them as they looked down. Lost in the reverberation for a moment, Vincent imagined the sound as something monstrous writhing its way up the shaft, desperate to break the surface and finally, after many centuries, breathe.

Taking one end of the twine for a walk, Elias slung it round the trunk of a tree, on the other side of the hole to the fire they'd lit. Carefully, he threaded the twine into a figure-eight, his headlight making every movement visible for Vincent, who stood behind him, as was customary on their climbs, watching. Once fixed, Elias tugged the knot tight, and passed a stretch of the twine behind his back, leaning back into it, as if to mimic the weight of a climber. Vincent took it from him and did the same several more times, before they both returned to the edge, harnessed and ready, only Anya's final protest left to observe.

'We can't even see what we're climbing into,' she began, at which Elias, without saying a word, reached into the fire, removed a smouldering branch by the cold end, and held it over the entrance.

'Look.'

As the torch fell, the three teenagers watched a ring of light descending through the darkness. The details it illuminated – rusty brown surfaces, hanging chains, evenly spaced bolts on all four sides – stayed consistent as the light passed over them. It was as if the same four sections of wall were passing down the tube, inside a wider darkness.

Vincent knew Anya wasn't that scared. Every few months, they found themselves being dragged along like this, on one of Elias' quests – to trace the source of the Orbe (an overgrown ditch clogged by an unshiftable boulder), to storm the Fort du Risoux (a foul-smelling doorway in a stretch of sunken wall). Each time, the two dutiful friends tagged along, mocking him under their breaths, and asking themselves, when it was all over, how they had ever been persuaded in the first place to waste their day off with such exhaustions. What they never admitted to was that they really knew the answer.

Elias' latest passion – 'the hole' – had come into their lives when Berger, the youngest of his three dogs, had gone missing a week earlier. Calling and searching for him had led Elias into a thicket of peculiarly lopsided sycamores, nothing older than a foot wide. The sound of Berger's whimpering came from a patch of brambles dark with fruit, or rather from underneath it. Pulling back the thorns exposed a wide sheet of corrugated rust, a corner of which bent downwards to reveal a triangle of black. The cold breeze that blew up from this crevice contained, somewhere within it, the warm notes of Berger's lament. A few feet down, Elias could make out the desperately clinging paws of his favourite mutt. Some rabbit must have sent him scampering over the edge, and now the same rabbit seemed to be beckoning Elias and his biddable friends into its darkness.

'I can do it again if you like,' he said to Anya, scooping up a third stone from the ground. Again he counted.

'Stop!' she yelled. 'For fuck's sake, just stop! We're not letting you go down there and we're sure as hell not following you.'

By the time Vincent's rappel brought him to the bottom of the shaft, Elias was already tracing out a hatch in the floor beneath Anya's feet. 'You might want to step off this.' He'd thrown a crowbar into the hole before they descended, and with it he was now levering the trapdoor open. A perfect rectangle of darkness greeted them and, without warning, Elias threw the crowbar into this second hole and climbed down after it. This time there wasn't a delay before the thud, and in Elias' swinging torchlight, Vincent and Anya could see he now stood in a tight, metallic cubicle.

'Come on, it's safe,' he called up, jumping up and down as he did so. The whole box had a noticeable bounce to it.

'You know there was a sodding ladder on the other side!' Vincent cursed, as he dropped down beside them.

'Sorry,' Elias offered.

'Well, this is cosy,' he picked up, sarcastically. 'Now I know how your sheep feel in the dipping pen.'

For once, Anya was no audience for Vince's repertoire. Instead, she stared straight past him to the wall at his back. There, just below head-height, on either side of a vertical seam running the length of the wall, two words were scratched into the metal. A jagged *IT'S* on the left side, and on the other, *COMING*.

'OK, joke's up, El. This isn't even scary,' Vincent said, smiling reassuringly at Anya.

'I agree. Whoever wrote it should've tried harder,' Elias replied. Slotting the cleft end of the crowbar into an already glistening notch in the vertical seam, he heaved on it. On either side of him, the wall shuddered.

'El,' Anya whispered. 'Don't you ever worry about the Worm?'

He swung on the bar a second time. 'Worm?' he asked, feigning curiosity.

'You know the stories, don't pretend you don't.' She was right. Every kid in Meryan grew up with tall tales about some long worm or tail-eating serpent that squatted in its infernal lair under the Jura foothills. Various names had been given to it. The 'Ver de Veronnex' some called it, after a hole they used to have there. The 'Bug of Bossy'. But the Elders – or maybe the Elder's Elders – had filled in all the holes long before they were born. Only the legends persisted.

'*At the end of the world...*' Anya muttered.

'*...the worm is coiled.* Yes, yes,' Elias sweated. 'Give me a hand, Vince.' The two of them swung on the crowbar handle until the sides of the wall parted suddenly, like reluctant curtains. A new gust of cold air hit them, this time with a hiss that seemed to be coming from the wall itself.

'No worm so far!' Elias declared, inserting himself into the newly created gap in the wall. With an outstretched arm, he held the opposing part of the wall off which seemed to want to rejoin its twin. Anya ducked through, under his arm, being careful not to burn him with her torch. As Vincent stepped through, he fingered the notch on the left-hand wall, and smiled at Elias.

The first thing that greeted them was yet another wall. This one was solid though, without seams, and ushered them left along a narrow, cobweb-filled passageway before taking a sharp right. In Vincent's torchlight, the sides of the passage glowed dark red and seemed to almost ripple, like a dusty flowstone, drier than anything he'd seen in the caves of Jura. After a few more paces, they came to an entranceway. This too seemed to have once been a single wall, split up the middle. But unlike its predecessor, it hadn't hissed itself whole again. Instead, its two halves hung half-open, slack-jawed, a notch glistening halfway up on both sides.

'That's it.' Anya again, with one of her announcements, this time for Vincent's attention. 'I'm not going any further until Elias tells us exactly what's through there.'

'How do I know,' Elias interjected.

'So why is it so goddamn important?'

'All of this was built, once, for a reason. And that reason must have been important!'

Unsatisfied with his answer, Anya let out a loud huff and abruptly plopped down to the ground, crossing her legs at Elias' feet. It reminded Vincent of his eight-year-old niece.

'Ok, ok,' Elias relented, sitting down beside her.

Elias set his torch down on the floor between them. Its flames gave a flickering warmth to his face as he spoke. 'Your granddad told you about the great Worm that lived down here, coiled round, 27 miles long, or maybe twice that length, or maybe it was two worms.' He motioned to Vincent to join them on the floor. 'We've all heard it. But *my* granddad chose to tell me different stories – about real people who came and went. Outsiders. He told me once about a teacher at the village school, who wasn't there long. His name was Mr Thomas, and he taught a subject they don't teach anymore.'

'He was a heretic, you mean,' Vincent joined them, crossing his legs.

'He taught my granddad rules that could be used to predict the future, or part of it, sometimes. You had to get certain parts of the present right, my granddad used to say, before you could predict anything. He called them 'initial conditions'. I didn't always understand him.'

'Great,' Anya threw up her hands and looked at Vince. 'So our friend's into devil-worship now.'

'Real people,' Elias continued. 'Real things, that's what my granddad told me about. And he loved this teacher, how scruffy he always looked in his tattered brown blazer, standing in front of the class; how little he cared about the school's etiquette.'

'But he preached *science!*' Anya burst out. 'He was a fraud, a zealot, a Balance-denier, peddling one-sidedness. You know what those people believed in? Truths that only had one side!' She clutched the coin at her chest. 'No doubt he was squandering your school's money too, giving it away to foreign "projects"!'

'That's exactly what I said to my granddad,' Elias replied. 'How can you speak fondly about one of *them!* A man who didn't believe in Both Sides; a man who didn't believe that "something needs its opposite to be true for *it* to be true". Sure enough the school found out, and the Elders drove him from the village. But my granddad showed me things – simple things that Mr Thomas had taught him – predictions that would come true.'

'Witchcraft,' Anya affirmed.

'Well, it was witchcraft that got us down here, then. Witchcraft that told me how long a piece of twine I needed.'

'Come on, Elias,' Vincent broke in. 'This isn't exactly your first visit. Nor your crowbar's.' He looked up at the slack-jawed doorway. 'Maybe you just made up those numbers back there to fit – already knowing how deep the hole was.' Vince got to his feet, and patted the red dust off his trousers. 'Let's get this over with, shall we?' He continued towards the threshold and stepped over it. 'So what is this place, some kind of pre-Balance temple? I prefer the worm story, myself.' His voice developed an echo as he receded into the darkness, leaving the other two scrambling to their feet to follow.

They were no longer in a simple passageway. To their left, stood rack after rack of metalwork of some kind, tangled in wire. Or was it just cobwebs? Above them, the ceiling crawled with glittering silver tubes, each wrought from an unfamiliar precious mineral, not rusty like the previous passage had been. On the right-hand wall about twenty yards in, Vincent identified his first overtly religious relic of this old religion. A statuette of a man, or at least the top half of one, minus the arms, wearing a strange helmet and a dark coloured eye-mask. Most disturbing was the black pipe that snaked out of its mouth, dangling down to an oddly unornamented square vessel resting on the figure's chest. Vincent gave it a wide berth as he passed, unable to take his eyes off the point where the tube plunged into the mouth.

'This!' Elias had overtaken Vincent by now and stood pointing at a desk at the end of the passage. 'This is what I brought you down to see.' On the desk sat nothing but a solitary pile of papers, neatly stacked with a small, disc-shaped piece of stone squatting on the top page.

'You dragged us down here to see something you could've brought back to the surface and shown us there!' Anya was incensed.

Beside the stack of papers sat a separate page with special markings along the top. Elias picked it up and brought his torch near:

'*I have left this hard copy outlining particular findings in my field, knowing that when power is finally returned to this facility, its computer records may no longer be compatible with your more advanced operating systems. Hard copies of all other research conducted here can be found at the Bibliothèque Municipale. Of the many discoveries made in this facility, to me (though not to all of my colleagues), this is the most pressing.*' Below the type: an illegibly scrawled name, then a single line at the bottom. '*When the calamity comes, we will not have long, as a planet, to save ourselves. We must work fast, and together.*'

Anya snatched up the stone to inspect its ridged, spiralling curvature. Vincent, in turn, picked up the first page from the main stack. '*On the Metastability of the Standard Model Vacuum.*' He paused, intimidated by some of the words. '*Abstract. If the Higgs mass mH is as low as suggested by present experimental information, the Standard Model ground state might not be absolutely stable...*'

'It's mumbo jumbo!' Anya implored, throwing the stone to the floor. 'At the end of the world, the worm is coiled! At the end of the world, the worm is coiled! Nonsense. Outdated, unbalanced, dangerous nonsense!'

'What are we doing here, Elias?' Vince asked calmly. 'You want us to join some cult?'

'It's not a cult, Vince. Look.' Grabbing the torch from his friend's hand, he walked past the desk and around one more corner. The light was above Elias' head now and as Vincent followed, it took him a few seconds to realise they no longer stood in a low-ceilinged passageway, nor on a solid, concrete floor. They were standing instead on a metal grill and the handrail to their right wasn't attached to any wall.

Elias threw the torch high into the air. Its flame span upwards into the darkness, giving tantalising glimpses of the cavernous space before them. Fifty metres in front of them, a gargantuan spiderweb of pipes and tubes fanned out into the blackness, arrayed around a central bulkhead. When the torch eventually collided with a tangle of pipes, it sent a shower of sparks illuminating still more wonders beneath.

For several seconds, the three teenagers stood staring at an image that wasn't there.

'And this!' Elias broke the silence. Anya waved her own torch as high as she could. The ceiling was some fifteen metres above them, and, as before, overrun with pipes, like the varicose underbelly of some colossal ewe.

'Sacrilege,' Anya muttered.

'I think it's a warning.'

'Of course, like the words in that box,' Vincent replied. 'Superstitions always trade on dire warnings, the end is nigh, all of that guff. What else have they got?'

'No. I think they're saying we can still do something about it. We can stop it from coming, or we can run away from it, somehow...'

'But Elias,' Vincent sighed, 'you have no idea what any of the words on those pages mean.'

'We could work them out, though. Take the pages to the Elders. They're wise; they'll know what to do. Maybe they will take them to the Elders of other villages. Maybe it could be a reason to end the war.'

As Elias spoke, gazing into nothingness, Vincent noticed something moving across Anya's chest. At first he thought it was a strand of hair blowing in the draught. But it was thicker than that. It was writhing, glistening as it moved, reaching upwards into the night, yearning for elsewhere, longing to be higher. Her coin. Her small, two-sided coin at the end of its chain. Vincent's eyes met Anya's, but he recognised only panic in them. Before he could summon any words, she had slipped their company altogether and was back at the table, holding her flame to the first page of the pile.

From then on, it was all a rush. 'Never light a fire in a cave, nothing more than a torch.' It was rudimentary. Vincent didn't need to repeat it here. Underground, fires set things in motion, dangerously expanding and dislodging the colossal weights above. Running through the smoke, unable to see if the others were keeping up, he quickly reached the metal cubicle, and immediately braced the split wall with the crowbar Elias had left there, not waiting to offer the others a foot-up through the hatch. Seeing him so spooked, they let him climb first, and although roped up, he made full use of the ladder, counting the steps in a breathless mantra, as he climbed. 'One, two, three...'

Approaching the surface, his heart finally slowed. But then, for a moment, he could swear he heard something rustling above him. 'Hello?' he shouted, 'Anyone there?' There was nothing. The campfire they'd lit earlier that night had gone out, so perhaps it was a wolf, he wondered, then chided himself for always being so anxious. Instead, in these last few steps, he told himself he would slow down and enjoy the moment while it lasted. After all, it felt as if he were climbing up into the sky itself, or a star-studded patch of it, and nothing would alarm him now, not even the nagging suspicion that, as he climbed, one of the stars had gone out.

Afterword: Cut to Black

Prof Gino Isidori
University of Zurich

THE UNIVERSE THAT WE know – the one where stars shine, planets form, and where we live – might be 'metastable'. The concept of metastability comes up frequently in physical systems. Think of a house of cards, or a ball settled in a small depression, or notch, half way down a steep slope: these systems are in equilibrium, but the equilibrium is precarious, since it does not correspond to the minimum energy of the system. Under small perturbations, these systems will undergo a sudden transition to a state of lower energy: the house of cards, under the perturbation, will shake then fall down, and the ball will wobble out of its little notch and roll down the rest of the slope.

Interestingly enough, the Higgs field that permeates the whole universe, bestowing all elementary particles with mass and allowing the universe to develop the way it has done till now, might well be in a metastable configuration. And unlike the classical, Newtonian examples mentioned above (with cards and balls), in this case there is a constant source of perturbations that we cannot switch off, namely quantum fluctuations. Unlike a house of cards where we can hope to avoid the collapse by closing windows, and holding our breath, there is nothing that can be done to prevent the collapse of a metastable quantum system.

We can think of the Higgs field as a medium that permeates

the entire universe. Elementary particles, such as quarks and electrons, acquire their masses as a result of their interactions with the medium as they pass through it. If the Higgs field is in a metastable configuration, sooner or later this medium will literally evaporate with the formation of bubbles of new vacuum in which the Higgs field has a different, energetically more favourable, value. Inside these bubbles nothing would look like the universe we currently know: electrons and quarks would suddenly acquire huge masses that make the formation of atoms or even atomic nuclei impossible. As described in a beautiful 1977 paper by Sidney Coleman – a giant of modern physics – these bubbles would expand almost at the speed of light, leading to a phase transition of the entire universe that would be as mind-blowingly fascinating as it was catastrophic.[1] There would be little time to react to such a bubble approaching us: it would probably be preceded by intense rays of light produced by energetic reactions taking place at its borders, as well as the sight of parts of the night sky simply blinking out, as Lillian Weezer's character Vince perceives as he climbs up the abandoned shaft at the end of her story. Most likely all this would happen in a fraction of seconds, although we cannot exclude scenarios where the difference between the velocity expansion of the bubble and the speed of light is large enough to give us enough time to realise – with no hope to react – that the Earth is about cease to exist as a planet.

While in the '70s this was mere speculation, it has become a much more concrete possibility since the discovery of the Higgs boson – which we can regard as the observation of a wave in the Higgs field. The precise measurement of the Higgs boson mass, together with the determination of all the other masses of the Standard Model particles, have allowed physicists to determine more precisely the shape of the Higgs potential, or the slope on which the precarious Higgs fields is perched. The paper found by Lillian Weezer's character Elias, 'On the Metastabilty of the Standard Model Vacuum' is indeed a study published a few years ago, by myself and other colleagues, to analyze this problem in greater detail.[2]

The initial motivation of this study was to deduce properties about physics beyond the Standard Model: there is clear evidence that the Higgs field has been in its present configuration quite a long time, for just under fourteen billion years in fact (the age of our universe). So, given that this configuration seemed to be unstable, according to calculations performed within the Standard Model, it was thought that this might be because the theory was incomplete. More precisely, the theory might be modified at high energies, where we had not yet tested it, in an attempt to stabilise the Higgs potential. However, somewhat surprisingly, it turned out that the theory *is* consistent: we demonstrated that the Standard Model could be valid up to very high energies without conflicting with observations. According to this theory, we live in a metastable vacuum, but its lifetime is sufficiently long to explain the present evolution of the universe.

Before you start to panic: there is no imminent danger that the planet Earth will be overwhelmed by an expanding bubble in the phase transition of the universe. The latest studies indicate that this phenomenon would occur, according to the Standard Model, on a timescale well beyond the life of our sun. More interesting, and subject to continuous study, is the question: why would we find ourselves living in a metastable vacuum in the first place: is this a coincidence, or a fact that hides a deeper explanation? Could it be connected to the evolution of the early universe and the phenomenon of inflation? Can we take some advantage of that? Several explanations have been proposed, with different implications.

One highly speculative idea, that may be closer to science fiction than reality, is the possibility of creating bubbles of false vacuum in the laboratory in a controlled way – with future particle colliders – and to use this process to draw or drain energy from the Higgs field. I am not at all convinced by this, but I must admit that it's a fascinating speculation worth pursuing in more detail.

Another interesting conjecture is that what we perceive as

'constants of nature,' such as the Higgs mass or other parameters of the Standard Model, are actually not *true* constants. Perhaps they are just functions of other dynamical variables and have the power to adjust themselves in critical configurations, such as the one allowing metastability.[3] According to this conjecture, the entire universe could be a self-organised critical system, something like a sand pile. This conjecture leads to very precise predictions, in particular for the mass of the top quark – something that could be tested with future experiments at particle colliders. On the other hand, if all this is just a coincidence, or better a mirage due to our poor knowledge of physics at high energies, we could expect to soon see traces of new particles – connected to the stabilisation of the Higgs potential – at the LHC. This remains my favourite option, but I have to admit the self-organised critical universe is also quite tempting. In all cases, future studies, both about high-energy physics and cosmology, could help shed new light on this interesting open question.

If there is one general lesson the study of metastability teaches us, it is that complex systems are often unstable. The more complex and sophisticated they are, the more they are likely to be fragile and unstable. Human civilisation on Earth is no exception, as is well illustrated in Lillian's short story. If there is one reason why we must continue to challenge the frontier of our knowledge at CERN, and institutes like it, and not let superstition and other belief systems replace scientific methodology, it is precisely to prevent its collapse.

Notes

1. Coleman, Sidney, 'Fate of the False Vacuum: Semiclassical Theory', *Physics Review,* D 15, 2929 (1977).
2. Isidori, G, Ridolfi, G, and Strumia A, 'On the Metastability of the Standard Model Vacuum', *Nuclear Physics*, B 609, 387 (2001).
3. Giudice, G.F., McCullough, M, and You, T, `Self-Organised Localisation', *JHEP* 10, 093 (2021).

About the Authors & Editors

Prof. Rob Appleby (co-editor) is a Professor of Physics at the University of Manchester and a member of the Cockcroft Institute for Accelerator Science and Engineering. He has worked for many years on particle colliders, particle accelerators for cancer treatment and on the public engagement of science. He holds a PhD in theoretical physics from the University of Manchester and a Masters degree in theoretical physics from the University of York. He has previously been a consultant on several Comma anthologies and co-edited *Thought X*.

Stephen Baxter's science fiction novels have won multiple awards including the John W Campbell Memorial Award, the British Science Fiction Association Award, the Kurd Lasswitz Award and the Seiun Award (for *The Time Ships*), as well as the Philip K Dick Award (for *The Time Ships* and *Vacuum Diagrams*). He has published over 100 SF short stories, several of which have won prizes, including three Analog Awards, two BSFA awards and a Sidewise Award. His novel *Voyage* has been dramatised for BBC Radio. His TV and movie work includes the BBC's *Invasion: Earth*. His nonfiction includes the books *Deep Future* and *Omegatropic*.

Bidisha is a broadcaster, journalist and film-maker. She is a critic and columnist for *The Guardian* and *The Observer* and broadcasts heavily for BBC TV and radio, ITN, CNN, ViacomCBS and Sky News. Her fifth book, *Asylum and Exile: Hidden Voices of London*, is based on her outreach work in UK prisons, refugee charities and detention centres. Her first short film, Her latest publication is called *The Future of Serious Art* and her latest film series is called *Aurora*.

Born in Belfast in 1981, **Lucy Caldwell** is the award-winning author of three novels, several stage plays and radio dramas, two collections of short stories: *Multitudes* and *Intimacies.* Her most recent novel is *These Days* (Faber, 2022). She is the editor of *Being Various: New Irish Short Stories* (Faber, 2019). Her awards include the Rooney Prize for Irish Literature, the George Devine Award, the Dylan Thomas Prize, and the BBC National Short Story Award 2021.

Margaret Drabble was born in 1939 in Sheffield and educated at Newnham College, Cambridge. She had a very brief career as an actor with the Royal Shakespeare Company, before taking to fiction. Her first novel, *A Summer Birdcage,* was published in 1963, and her nineteenth and most recent, *The Dark Flood Rises,* in 2016. She has published three collections of short fiction, edited two editions of *The Oxford Companion to English Literature* (1985, 2000), and written or edited nonfiction books on Thomas Hardy, William Wordsworth, Arnold Bennett and Angus Wilson. She is married to the biographer Michael Holroyd and lives in London, Oxford and Somerset.

Luan Goldie is a Glasgow-born author and primary school teacher who grew up in East London. Her debut novel, *Nightingale Point*, was longlisted for the 2020 Women's Prize for Fiction and the Royal Society of Literature Ondaatje Prize. It was also a BBC Radio 2 Jo Whiley Book Club Pick. In 2018, she won the Costa Short Story Award and her short stories have since appeared in *HELLO!, Sunday Express* and *The Good Journal.* Her second novel, *Homecoming*, was released by HarperCollins in 2020.

Peter Kalu is a poet, fiction writer and playwright. He cut his teeth as a member of Manchester's Moss Side Write black writers workshop and has had nine novels, two film scripts and three theatre plays produced to date. He gained his PhD in Creative Writing at Lancaster University in 2019. He has a first degree in Law from Leeds University, studied software engineering at Salford University and Languages at Heriot Watt University. In 2018, he was writer in residence at the University of West Indies (Trinidad campus). For many years he ran a carnival band called Moko Jumbi (Ghosts of the Gods) which took to the streets at Manchester Caribbean Carnival on three feet high stilts.

lisa luxx is an activist and poet of British and Syrian heritage. Her poems are published in *The Telegraph, The London Magazine* and by publishers including Hatchette and Saqi Books. Her work is broadcast on Channel 4, BBC Radio 4 and TEDx. In 2021, she toured UK theatres with the show for her 60-minute poem, *Eating the Copper Apple*, produced by a team of all Arab women artists. She is founder of The Sisterhood Salon in Beirut, and works within an economy of sisterhood. Her debut book, *Fetch Your Mother's Heart*, is out now through Out-Spoken Press.

Adam Marek writes short stories about the futuristic and the fantastical colliding with everyday life. His two collections, *Instruction Manual for Swallowing* and *The Stone Thrower* are published by Comma Press. His stories have appeared on BBC Radio 4, and in many magazines and anthologies, including *The Penguin Book of the British Short Stories*. He is an Arts Foundation Short Story Fellow.

Steven Moffat is a Scottish television writer, television producer and screenwriter. He is best known for his work as showrunner, writer, and executive producer of the science fiction television series *Doctor Who* and the contemporary crime drama television series *Sherlock*, based on Sir Arthur Conan Doyle's Sherlock Holmes stories. In 2015, Moffat was appointed Officer of the Order of the British Empire for his services to drama. His plays include *The Unfriend* (2022).

Courttia Newland is the author of eight books including *The Scholar*, and most recently, *A River Called Time* (longlisted for the Gordon Burn Prize). He co-edited *The Penguin Book of New Black Writing in Britain*, and his short stories have featured in various anthologies and been broadcast on BBC Radio 4. As a screenwriter, he has co-written episodes of Steve McQueen's award-winning 2020 BBC series *Small Axe*.

Connie Potter (co-editor) is a long-standing member of the ATLAS Collaboration and the CERN Communications group, as well as Founder of the CERN Festival Programme. She produces Science Pavilions at music festivals all over Europe. She is also co-founder and President of the Swiss AidforAll charitable association (www.aidforall.ch)

Desiree Reynolds is an author, journalist, DJ, creative writing tutor and broadcaster. She has had several short stories published in various publications, including A Generation Defining Itself, Closure: Contemporary Black British Stories, and The Book of Sheffield. Her first novel, Seduce, was published in 2013 by Peepal Tree Press; she is the editor of Writing As Resistance (University Of Sheffield, 2018), and a trustee with Racial Justice Network.

Ian Watson wrote the screen story for Steven Spielberg's film *A.I. Artificial Intelligence,* and the popular *Inquisition War* trilogy as well as 25 novels (including *The Embedding* and *The Jonah Kit*) and 10 short story collections of SF, fantasy, and horror, plus one book of poetry, *The Lexicographer's Love Song*. With Ian Whates, he co-edited *The Mammoth Book of Alternate Histories*.

Lillian Weezer has previously published poetry in *Rialto, Smiths Knoll, PN Review,* and *The North*, among other places, and fiction in *The Cuckoo Cage*.

About the Scientists

Andrea Bersani was born in Italy in 1977 and is a particle physicist at the Italian Institute for Nuclear Physics. He has collaborated with various international laboratories: Gran Sasso in Italy, CERN in Switzerland, FermiLab and Jefferson Lab in the US, specially developing detectors and magnets for particle physics experiments. He is a lifelong fan of science fiction.

Thanks to his father, **Daniel Cervenkov** has been fascinated by science (fiction) since childhood. This led him to pursue a career in physics. In 2020, he obtained a particle physics PhD from Charles University for his work on CP violation at the Belle experiment in Japan. After finishing his studies, he joined the University of Oxford as a post-doctoral researcher. He currently studies a different aspect of CP violation at the LHCb experiment at CERN.

Tessa Charles is an accelerator physicist. Her research involves beam dynamics studies of colliders, light sources, and accelerators for cultural heritage. She was awarded a PhD from Monash University in 2016 for research conducted at the Australia Synchrotron. She worked at CERN for several years before joining the University of Liverpool as a lecturer in 2020.

Michael Davis is a computer scientist and software engineer working for CERN. He holds a BSc in Computer Science (from Brunel University, London), an MSc in Computer and Electronic Security and a PhD in Data Science (both conferred by Queen's University, Belfast). In 2017, Michael joined the Storage and Data Management group in CERN's IT department, where he now leads the team responsible for the long-term archival storage of the physics data. Michael's greatest accomplishment is reading stories to his children every night. Now that they are all grown up, he is very happy to collaborate on creating a brand new story.

Peter Dong teaches physics at the Illinois Mathematics and Science Academy, where he also runs a research programme in particle physics at the Large Hadron Collider, currently focusing on searches for doubly-charged Higgs bosons and dark photons. He received a Bachelor's degree in music and physics from Harvard University and a PhD in experimental particle physics from the University of California, Los Angeles. He lives in Illinois with his wife and three children.

John Ellis CBE FRS HonFInstP is a British theoretical physicist who is currently Clerk Maxwell Professor of Theoretical Physics at King's College London. After reading physics at King's College, Cambridge, and earning his PhD in theoretical (high-energy) particle physics in 1971, he went on to hold brief post-doc positions in the SLAC Theory Group and Caltech, before moving to CERN, where he has held an indefinite contract since 1978. He has twice been Deputy Division Leader for the theory ('TH') division, and served as Division Leader for 1988–1994. He was a founding member of the LEPC and of the LHCC; and is currently chair of the committee to investigate physics opportunities for future proton accelerators, and is a member of the extended CLIC (Compact Linear Collider) Steering Committee. He was awarded the Maxwell Medal and the Paul Dirac Prize by the Institute of Physics in 1982 and 2005 respectively, and is an Elected Fellow of the Royal Society of London since 1985 and of the Institute of Physics since 1991.

Andrea Giammanco is an Italian particle physicist dividing his time between Louvain-la-Neuve (Belgium) and CERN. His research is split between the analysis of data from the Large

Hadron Collider and the imaging of volcanoes and other stuff using cosmic rays. As a hobby, he also likes to write (http://cern.ch/andrea.giammanco/romanzo).

Joe Haley received his PhD in Physics from Princeton University in 2009 for research on the DZero experiment at Fermilab. As a post-doc with Northeastern University he also worked on the CMS experiment, living at CERN the final year to work on an upgrade to the muon detector. He has been a member of the ATLAS Collaboration since 2013 when he joined the faculty at Oklahoma State University and is now an associate professor.

Gino Isidori is a Professor of Theoretical Physics at the University of Zurich. He obtained a PhD in physics in 1996 at the University of Rome La Sapienza, and has worked at Frascati, SLAC, CERN, and the Institute for Advanced Study of the Technical University of Munich. His research focuses on the theory and phenomenology of fundamental interactions. He has provided seminal contributions in the area of Higgs physics and Flavour physics, both within and beyond the Standard Model.

Kristin Lohwasser studied Journalism and Physics in Dortmund before graduating with a DPhil from Oxford University. After working in Freiburg and Berlin, she is now a Senior Lecturer at the University of Sheffield. She investigates particle physics processes with the ATLAS detector and is involved in a project to develop a virtual platform for radiation environments which has been applied successfully to the decommissioning of the ATLAS inner detector.

Jens Vigen is a librarian at CERN, Switzerland, where he has been working since 1994. He is elected Secretary-General for the International Union of Pure and Applied Physics for the period 2021–2024. Vigen holds a master's degree in geodesy and photogrammetry from the Norwegian University for Science and Technology, Trondheim, where he also trained as an academic librarian.

Carole Weydert is a 38 year old mother of two toddlers. She has been interested in smashing particles together ever since she was a little girl and did her PhD thesis in the ATLAS collaboration, helping to collect and analyse the data that ultimately led to the discovery of the Higgs boson. Meanwhile, she quit particle physics. She's still overworked though.

Special Thanks

The editors would like to thank the following people who made the trip to CERN so productive: Austin Ball, Salvatore Buontempo, Xavier Espinal, Lyn Evans, Melissa Gaillard, James Gillies, Jeffrey Hangst, Dawn Hudson, and Alejandra Lorenzo Gomez. They would also like to thank Linda Ross at Womad, and, of course, the sponsoring project HL-LHC-UK, Graeme Burt, Tom Jones, the funders STFC and UKRI and the HL-LHC project at CERN. Special thanks also go to Helen Collins and Ollie Appleby.

In Memoriam

THE EDITORS AND PUBLISHERS would like to pay special tribute to our partner, close friend and CERN colleague, Chris Thomas, who was recently taken from us at the untimely age of 65.

Chris was the bedrock of so many particle physics outreach activities over the last fifteen years, and was one of the three people establishing the 'Big Bang Collective' which has gone on to produce hugely popular Science Pavilions in music and culture festivals all over the world.

Chris was a deeply practical person who would build or repair almost anything on demand. More importantly, he could build teams of people, organising and encouraging but also chiding when needed, all with good grace and humour. He was also immensely good company, making the extra hours we put in a joy not a chore. Chris, though not a trained scientist himself, embodied the ethos of scientific collaboration and believed that knowledge belongs to everyone.

His kindness knew no bounds, whether to friends or colleagues or complete strangers through the AidforAll humanitarian association he founded with his long-term love, Connie Potter. One of his first major works with the association was the construction of a library at a school for very poor families in the suburbs of Kolkata. He went on to help fund the construction of classrooms for the Big Brother Mouse association in Laos and paid for the publication of several books. More recently, his good heart took him on several very long road trips, taking aid to Ukrainian refugees in Poland and also into Ukraine just after the start of the war.

He loved words, be they talks, stories or especially lyrics. He was committed to this project, loved meeting the authors on their visit to CERN and kept in touch with a few of them and it adds to the tragedy that he will not see it completed in press.

We will continue his good work in his memory, but always with the sense of loss for what he would have added to turn the good into the great. We miss him terribly.

In memory of Chris Thomas

Thought X
Fictions and Hypotheticals

Edited by Ra Page & Prof Rob Appleby

Featuring: *Sandra Alland, Annie Clarkson, Marie Louise Cookson, Claire Dean, Zoe Gilbert, Andy Hedgecock, Robin Ince, Annie Kirby, Anneliese Mackintosh, Adam Marek, Adam Roberts, Sarah Schofield, Ian Watson & Margaret Wilkinson.*

Science is always telling stories. Whether in the creation myths of evolution or the Big Bang, or in the eureka moments of science history, narrative – just as much as metaphor – is a central device in the scientist's surprisingly literary toolkit. Perhaps the most interesting use of story is the thought experiment, sometimes known as 'the intuition pump', that draws on the most instinctive parts of the imagination to crack otherwise perplexing problems.

From Newton's Bucket, to Maxwell's Demon, Einstein's Lift to Schrödinger's Cat – all are examples of 'fiction' being used at the highest level, not just to explain, but to deduce, to prove. In this unique anthology, authors have collaborated with leading scientists, to bounce literary, human narratives against purely theoretical ones, blending together real stories with abstract ones, to produce truly extraordinary results.

ISBN: 9781905583607
£9.99